PENGUIN BOOKS

THE TELLING OF LIES

Timothy Findley was born in Toronto and now lives in the country nearby. His novel, *The Wars*, was a winner of the Governor General's Award and established him as one of Canada's leading writers. He is also the author of *Famous Last Words*, a best-selling novel of gripping international intrigue, as well as *The Last of the Crazy People*, *Not Wanted on the Voyage*, *The Butterfly Plague* and *The Telling of Lies*, which won an Edgar Award. His two story collections, *Dinner Along the Amazon* and *Stones*, were published to immediate critical acclaim, *Stones* winning the Trillium Book Award. His most recent work is the novel, *The Piano Man's Daughter*. Findley was made an Officer of the Order of Canada in 1986.

THE TELLING OF LIES

A MYSTERY

TIMOTHY FINDLEY

Penguin Books

PENGUIN BOOKS

Published by the Penguin Group

Penguin Books Canada Ltd, 10 Alcorn Avenue, Toronto,
Ontario, Canada M4V 3B2

Penguin Books Ltd, 27 Wrights Lane, London W8 5TZ, England

Penguin Books USA Inc., 375 Hudson Street, New York,
New York 10014, U.S.A.

Penguin Books Australia Ltd, Ringwood, Victoria, Australia

Penguin Books (NZ) Ltd, 182-190 Wairau Road, Auckland 10, New Zealand

Penguin Books Ltd, Registered Offices: Harmondsworth,
Middlesex, England

First published in Viking by Penguin Books Canada Limited, 1986
Published in Penguin Books, 1987
Published in this edition, 1996

3 5 7 9 10 8 6 4 2

*Although one or two events depicted in this novel are based on actual happenings,
all the characters here are fictitious and any resemblance to actual persons living
or dead is purely coincidental.*

Manufactured in Canada

Canadian Cataloguing in Publication Data

Findley, Timothy, 1930-
The telling of lies

ISBN 0-14-024115-9 (Trade format)

I. Title
PS8511.I38T44   C813'.54   C86-094365-8
PR9199.3.F56T44

Lyrics from "Heart Like a Wheel" reprinted by permission of Anna
McGarrigle, Garden Court Music, copyright © 1970.

To: The Atlantic House Hotel
and all who sailed in her

The telling of lies is a sort of sleight of hand that displays our deepest feelings about life.

John Cheever, *in an interview.*

The one thing an author is not allowed is to look at the tragic background of life and the constitution of human nature for evil...*with surprise,* for surprise denotes that he is newly come from a conviction that it was otherwise.

Thornton Wilder, *in his Journals.*

THE TELLING OF LIES

A MYSTERY

1: I write this on the first day of the last summer I — or anyone — will spend at the Aurora Sands Hotel. Ellen and Quincy Welles have decided they can no longer bear the burden of the past and have opted for the present. (I cannot say *the future*.) They have sold the ASH for "an offer they could not refuse." I am told this by Arabella Barrie, who says the offer was several million dollars. All our efforts to have the Hotel declared an historic landmark have failed — at the cost, no doubt, of a mere few thousands thrown to the local Assemblyman responsible for zoning by-laws. And so our white clapboard haven will be razed next fall and in its place will rise the very symbol of these times — a condominium complex. Gracious living — with all the conveniences of party rooms, guard dogs and valet parking — has won the day.

2: On the 16th of August, about a month from now, I will have — if I live — my sixtieth birthday. What a pity all my summers have not been spent on the beach out there across the lawns, beyond this window at which I sit. (Back, as always, in Room 33.) I was brought here first in the summer of 1926 — one year after I was born — and, barring the years of my imprisonment, I have returned incessantly ever since. But still — and forever — I lack five seasons here. They can never be regained.

Nothing I can think to say or write reflects my sense of loss. I feel not only dispossessed but impotent. Incompetent. On the one hand cheated of reasonable expectations, I also sense a failure in me to do some duty. Though what that duty might be I cannot tell. Something I wanted to save has been destroyed behind my back.

Besides the sorrow, I feel a kind of rage. That a handful of strangers will now take this sanctuary away from the untold hundreds of us who have come here forever is somehow incomprehensible. To think that I shall never look upon this view again — of lawns and dunes and sand and waves — of the ocean stretching south, unbroken all the way to Brazil. I find it inconceivable. They might as well have barred the way to the whole state of Maine, as close the Aurora Sands Hotel. Not to return is one thing; not to be allowed to return is quite another.

3: Some people do the queerest things. They give the oddest gifts. A case in point is this very book in which I write. Lily did it. Lily Porter. Came up onto the porch from the lawn this evening and handed it to me all done up in Lily Porter paper; tied with Lily Porter ribbon; knotted with Lily Porter bows. Pink and white and baby blue: the colours of a pastel patriot. "What," I said; "is this?"

"Don't you have a birthday soon?" she asked.

"No," I said. "Not till the 16th of August."

"Oh," said Lily — completely unperturbed. "Not for three weeks..."

"Four," I said. "Today's July the 18th."

"I never could count, Vanessa," she said, and I believed her. Lily Porter — devastating in all her teeth and nails. In all her diamond rings.

"The 15th of August is Assumption Day," she said. And I thought: *one Blessed Virgin deserves another.* But I knew she hadn't meant that; couldn't have meant that. Lily is too naïve to say one thing and mean another. It was only idle chatter, rattling off the dates of the religious calendar, saying: *aren't I smart to remember Assumption Day is the day before your birthday?* That's all it meant.

"Aren't you going to open it?" she said.

"No," I said. "I'll wait."

"Oh," said Lily, "No, Nessa; please don't wait." Smiling her chewed-off smile; all that *Kermes* she nibbles; one tube a day, I swear. (What a name to give a lipstick. Only a man can have done it. Kermes is a dye that comes from dead female insects who were pregnant.) "Open it now," she said. "I want you to..."

Lily is still a child. Of fifty-five. All she wants is to give and get pleasure; to witness pleasure, the way she always has. And so I opened her package — just to please her — praying the contents wouldn't embarrass me. The porch was filling up with guests who were drifting out of the *Ashbar* — pre-dinner drinkers, most of whom have known us all their lives and most of whom would hoot if Lily had given me (as Lily might) a book on how to make plastic flowers or *A Pensioner's Guide to Downtown Miami*. But, lo and behold, she had given me this. And with it, an exquisite card depicting a six-fold Japanese screen — the paintings of which show ladies of the court.

4: I cannot describe my surprise. It was such a thoughtful gift: logical and tasteful; everything, in fact, of which I have always believed that Lily Porter was incapable. What, after fifty years of knowing her, can have slipped past my sentries unobserved, unchallenged into her character? Everyone has always known that Lily has a heart of gold; but we have also known it's a chocolate heart and the gold is only a wrapper made of foil. Show is Lily's forte — and her downfall. She wears that chocolate heart on her sleeve and it melts all over her gown.

The sentimental have so little taste and yet, I'm sitting here in my room tonight, writing on pages set between covers, fine and elegant as any I've ever seen. Leather: *Bound in Great Britain by William Clowes Limited, Beccles and London*. In unadorned maroon. And the paper just off-white so it doesn't glare.

What can have happened here?

I was intrigued enough to ask.

"Why have you done this?"

I was smiling with pleasure; running the flat of my hand across the leather and looking inside: *To Vanessa Van Horne — for her last birthday ever at the Aurora Sands Hotel — from Lily Porter.*

"Well," she said; "seeing that we won't be coming back, I thought perhaps there might be something you'd like to write..." (Lily's sentences drift away in little dots — the way her gaze is always drifting off — her focus faltering.) "Your photographs," she said. "You're always taking photographs, Vanessa, and I thought — there might be something you'd like to write..."

"Instead?" I said.

"Oh, no!" she said. "To go with."

"And this," I asked her — holding up the Japanese greeting card in its cellophane wrapper; "why have you given me this?"

Lily just laughed and said; "oh, Nessa! Don't be ridiculous..."

I could tell she did not know how to articulate her reasons. She had hoped I would do that for her simply by accepting the gifts, unquestioning.

"No," I said. "I want to know."

"Well," she said; "it's *Japanese.*"

"I know it's Japanese," I said. "But why have you given it to me?"

"You like things Japanese," she said, adding — embarrassed; "in spite of...everything."

"Yes," I said. "I do." In spite of everything... (My little dots — not hers.) I looked at my feet; I felt I must apologize.

Her gift was taking on the attributes of reason.

Lily waved her hand above the ladies on the card and explained that she hadn't removed the cellophane for fear of marking the surface. "It shows them with their gardens and their flowers," she said; "and I thought it was very you..."

I noticed then her eyes were beginning to fill with tears.

"It's very kind of you," I said. But I said it rather coldly, I'm afraid. I didn't want her to cry — and I thought if I told her what I really felt, she'd weep all over me.

"The card was so lovely," she said. "I couldn't resist. It was part of a set of twelve — and I bought all the rest for myself." She smiled so broadly when she told me this, her tears were completely forgotten. "It was such a wonderful shop," she said. "I came away with bag-loads!"

Yes. *With bag-loads* describes the Lily I know.

5: So here I sit with Lily's book beneath my pen and Lily's card across the room — unfolded and sitting on the dressing-table.

After dinner, I wandered into the library alone and looked at the photographs there on the walls — some of them mine, but most of them not. The display, in fact, is quite unnerving. Served up in uniform frames and beautifully mounted, the pictures date from as early as 1854 and as late as those I took last summer.

I often go to stare at all the faces there — the very old and the very young. I'm there in all my stages — and, before me, all my people; Mother's family all the way back to when the Hotel first opened. But this evening, I went on purpose just to look at me and Lily.

Lily was Lily Cotton then, and she first appears when I was nine or ten and she was five. At first, we did not have much to do with one another, partly because of her age and mine — but mostly because of her mother. And mine.

Maisie Cotton was not acceptable and not accepted at the Aurora Sands back then. She came to be, but only after much persistence. The pictures — circa 1935 — give evidence of her determination, showing her crowding into the background of other people's family tableaux — or hanging off towards one side, her smile as wide and her gestures as broad as some dreadful comedienne; much white powder, many wide hats and far too many bows adorn her image. Lily — petulant, unsure and unsteady on her little fat legs, at first, is there in those pictures entirely by force. And always overdressed and over-plump. She was not quite fat — but the next best thing; she was round. But she was lovely, even then.

My mother, Rose Adella, was as formidable as her name. She could not abide surprise. If only someone had told her it might one day come to this — her expression says — that common folk should be allowed to mingle where she paced the beach, afraid of the sun. If only someone had warned her, she might at least have prepared a proper distance she could keep from the Maisies and the Lilys of this world; but the warning had not come — and there was Maisie Cotton standing right beside her, holding out her hand with something in it from the sea, as if to offer it.

Well.

The years passed. And over time, as the difference in our ages mattered less and as Maisie's persistence wore us all down, Lily began to turn up over and over in the photographs with me. With me and Meg — and even with me and Meg and Mercedes.

The four of us — girls together — all of slightly different ages — Meg and Mercedes the eldest. And all of different backgrounds.

Mercedes Mannheim, even to this day, has never given up her name in spite of all her marriages. And though I have still to see her this summer, I cannot believe she has changed an iota. Beautiful in a cool, patrician way — aloof, with her toes not quite upon the earth — she was always the most assured of us — the most demanding and the most resourceful. She came to us down the beach from another country — or so it always seemed. Her father was still alive, before the War, and his summer home on Larson's Neck was the centre of the world. Mister Hoover came to visit him there — and Mister Hearst and Mister Ford. Mercedes would drop their names like bricks on our toes. "I've just escaped from Mister Vanderbilt," she'd say. And mean it.

And Meg — before the world fell in.

The four of us yesterday — children — yes; but also, each of us showing the woman who would be. And now, since Meg arrives tonight or tomorrow, the four of us today, with all that has happened to us in between that other time and this, together yet again. For the very last time.

What do we really know of one another — even after all these years, I wonder. More, I suspect, than any one of us has said of who we are and what we've done. Lily, for instance, reading the private me I didn't know she knew. The me behind the me, who seldom speaks and hardly ever shows herself and never tells the story of her life; the me who was in prison all those years. But it is to that me — the silent, imprisoned me, that Lily has given this book. Not to the me she nods to across the Hotel dining-room; whose picture has appeared in *Landscape* and *Time* and *Architectural Digest*; the me who designs gardens and wins prizes; the me who was once consulted by Ludi Mies and Frank Lloyd Wright. Certainly not the me who walks on these beaches, staring at people through her binoculars, taking photographs and making enemies. That's the me she curries favour with — and fears. But she gave this book — that card — to the other me; the absolutely private me I didn't realize she knew — whose solitude must surely have seemed, for all these years, so self-engrossed, self-satisfied and unnatural because it has been so disciplined. Why — of all people — did Lily Porter want to give that woman a gift? If a friend had given me this book, if one of my students had given it to me, or Meg — or even Mercedes — then I might have understood.

But, Lily Porter?

6: I will dedicate this book to Colonel Norimitsu — who, with one hand, killed my father and with the other made of my father's grave a garden. Death before life. So very Japanese.

7: It is night, now; one day after Lily's gift; three days after the advent of the new moon. There seems to be much darkness — more than seems fitting. Every star that one can imagine is up there — out beyond the screens. The curtains are blowing. I think my window has the only burning light on the whole south wall of the Hotel. I cannot tell what time it is — and I don't intend to look. If my watch read three o'clock, then duty to detail would drive me to bed: the detail of failing, imperilled health, the pills, the regimen, the warnings. But not tonight. I can't.

I have so much to write — so suddenly — and cannot yet believe so much has happened that must be written only one day after the gift of all this paper. There's a coincidence for you; dreadful. But then, I don't believe in coincidence. It must be a sign — if only a sign of my will to co-operate with fate. I always accept what I've been given — and make of it what I can.

Right now, a fly is caught in the drain of my sink and the sound of his buzzing is endless; forlorn and helpless. Sad. The voice, perhaps, of this dying Hotel. If I write, I can shut it out — or might.

And so; I begin.

8: A Friday in July. The solstice is well behind us, though we still endure a heat wave. Ninety-eight degrees for two whole weeks and not a breath of wind. Every night the doors stand open all along the halls and as I walk back to my room, the sound of electric fans is like a lullaby. I can hear Elsie Northcott trying to hum along and give the thing a tune. Impossible. Every open door is stoppered with a tennis shoe, an unread book, a vase of flowers.

At night, the halls of the Aurora Sands Hotel are filled with signatures: Maurice Penderton never fails to stop his door with baskets filled with foreign magazines — *I speak a dozen languages, you know* ... The Hopes use emptied, elegant boxes from Cartier's, laden with rocks, and Laura Ashley shopping bags with pebbles inside; and there are children's doors with Teddy Bears as stoppers — elephants and smiling dragons — their guardians, no doubt, against the dark.

My guardian is chains. God help me, but I cannot give them up. I have them installed wherever I reside. Whether to keep this prisoner in or to keep the other prisoners out, I'll never know. I do not care to know. I only know I need my chain and always prop my door with something soft: a cast-off sweater rolled into a ball. Perhaps I have a fear of potential weapons, left invitingly — *come in and kill me; here is a shoe — a brick —*

a bottle. Or perhaps it's just the sense — (I prefer this version) — of implicit anonymity in old blue buts of shapeless wool, of which I have a plenitude.

9: I once shared Room 33 with Mother. Now, this summer, I sleep here alone. As always and ever, I have Elsie Northcott on one side, humming through the walls. My other neighbour, David Brodie, drinks. At night, he's never still. He marches barefoot round his room and mutters — swears and whispers shouted threats. He's full of diatribes, although I never hear the words. Most nights — convinced he's plagued with light — David Brodie comes out into the hall between my room and his and tries to unscrew the bulbs in the fixture there. He never seems to learn he isn't tall enough to reach them — and always has to return to his room and drag back a wooden chair, upon which he stands. Using a wash-cloth so as not to burn his fingers, he turns the bulbs until they go out. Moments later, the student watchman comes on his hourly rounds and — being over six feet tall — he simply reaches up and screws them back in place. He does this four or five times a night, till David Brodie tires and goes — at last — to sleep.

The watchman's name is Bert. He never complains and he never reports what David Brodie does. He makes his nightly rounds, sees everything and never says a word. Bert is nineteen years old; a college student, (Yale), and he's reading — I've noted — Henry James. So far, this summer, he's gone through *The Portrait of a Lady, The Princess Casamassima, Washington Square, The Golden Bowl* and *The Wings of the Dove* — and it's only mid-July. I asked him if, there being so many more, he intended to read them all. And he said; ''I've read them all before, Miss Van Horne. This time, I'm reading them just for pleasure.'' I had no reply for this, not having known there could be pleasure in Henry James.

10: Calder Maddox's room is right above my own. It's number 59.

It seems the older you get in this hotel, the higher up they put you. Perhaps they want to assure the guests that — if they should die in residence — heaven is waiting four storeys closer than hell. Last time his age was mentioned, Calder Maddox was "approaching ninety."

Who, I wonder, does not know the name of Calder Maddox?

For years, he's shared the beach with us, the dining-room, the porches, lounges, lobbies of the ASH. Ever since the war, I guess. I have no memory of him back in the 1930s. Calder once claimed, without batting an eye, he "owned half the world and rented the other half." The word most often used for what he did — for the means by which he garnered half the world — was *pharmaceuticals*. Though I think, somehow, that hardly covers it. We know the summer man. The world knows the other, who feeds them pills; who gave them *Maddonix* to put them to sleep and *Maddonite* to wake them up. And *Maddoxin* to calm them in between.

Though given as close to ninety, his age has never been known. He's always looked a hundred or more, though, of course, this look was mostly acquired — and maintained — by illness. "Allergies, afflictions, conditions," he said last year in *Newsweek*. "I've never had a disease — not one — in the whole of my life." This may be true. But a man without *diseases* is not a man without complaints. His heart was bad (a *condition*). His teeth were soft; his skin was plagued with boils; the whites of his eyes and his fingernails were yellow (these were his *afflictions*). And — finally — his innards "blew him up or bled" if he fed from any one of forty-eight things he kept on a list and these — what else could they be? — were Calder's *allergies*. It was because of these — his *ailments* — that he chose a career in pharmaceuticals. Not that he wasn't qualified. The piece in *Newsweek* said he went through Harvard and M.I.T. like a dose of salts, picking up scholarships and prizes left, right and centre. On his letterhead, behind his name, are two solid rows of Doctorates and Honours — some of them military — some of them foreign — all of them impressive and most of them intimidating. (What is a PHm?)

Calder Maddox thought about death — his own — from the time (it is said) he was three years old and ate the first of his forty-eight proscribed foods. No one remembers what it was, but whatever it was, it caused a violent reaction. Thus, in the latter half of his life — that half in which he made half the world his own — he was able to commandeer whatever medical attention he wanted whenever and no matter where he went. Up here in Maine, there was never much to worry about. In terms of stand-by doctors and pre-booked operating theatres, Calder has always had the whole of Boston's medical profession — only just a hundred miles south of here — waiting on call to monitor his latest ache and soothe his latest rash. Everything in order. For Calder Maddox, all the paper work and all the mental anguish — all the legal details of wills and codicils and patents — all the emotions and all the necessary orders had long ago been dealt with. Nothing remained but death itself: the process.

And today he died — on the beach at the Aurora Sands Hotel.

The room above me now is empty. And that is why I cannot sleep.

11: All lives come to an end, but few — as Calder's did — with all their mysteries intact. He might have been, in terms of what we really knew of him, any old body lying on the beach; nothing but the name-tag of his face to tell us who he was. His fame — the stories of his wives and mistresses — the rumours of his far-flung influence — the revolutionary tranquillizer bearing his name: *Maddoxin* — the sinister things we heard, from time to time, about his work in progress; these were the things we knew, but not much else. The enormity of his wealth, perhaps — which no one has ever claimed to calculate. The well-known fact of his enemies, who came in legion to his door and were ignored. Too powerful to sue — too cold to care; there was nothing, it seemed, that could move or harm this man. And yet — today he died.

12: Lily Porter knew his daily routine by rote. Perhaps, in all, a dozen people did: his various secretaries — his strange chauffeur — his cook. Also the boy who brought his breakfast here at the ASH. Of all the Hotel's staff, it was only this boy — whose name is Joel Watts — who ever saw the man in the context of his private wretchedness, bound to his chair, his bed, his bathroom and his breakfast tray. Perhaps, to know the routine was to know the man; though what *to know* might mean, in Calder's case, is to ask a great deal more of words than words might want to give. Calder himself gave only the facts; he would tell the *whens* and the *wheres* of his life, but never the *whys*. You had to guess at these and, eight times out of ten, you might be right. Easy enough, for instance, to guess he'd gone into pharmaceuticals to seek the cures for all his ailments. But failure to grasp the *whys* of Calder's life had nothing to do with a person's lack of imagination. It only had to do with certain things that common people do not know. Can never know. And by *common people*, all I mean is those of us who are devoid of any genius for evil.

13: There were mysteries about this man that defied all enquiry. The larger mysteries concerned his endless capacity for chemical invention — his wealth — his "empire." Somewhere in Wyoming — or any other northern state you care to name — it is said that what appears to be a small-scale oil refinery is actually one of Calder Maddox's hundreds of chemical plants. Though what is made in these plants has never been declared, the rumours range from Agent Orange to Byblow B. And other products not yet named.

On a smaller scale, the mysteries concerned the way he smiled; a certain way he had of casting aspersions out of the blue — of making deprecating remarks when you least expected them; smiling — always smiling. His choice of enemies — his need for enemies — could be remarkably sinister. "You!" he would say — when his gaze had fallen even, perhaps, on a perfect stranger; "come over here." And then he would proceed by means of insinuation, castigation and tone of voice to destroy his victim.

The bodies could be numerous. In any given day, he might demolish three people. It all depended on his mood. But you couldn't read the mood — not like a formula. You couldn't foretell its coming over him. It simply came. And the victims might be waitresses, passing youths or some old friend who'd done nothing more than enter Calder's sights in the Hotel lobby. Even a child might fall beneath his axe.

And it was an axe he carried — somehow concealed in the folds of his tight little smile. The thing was, he never did this — never attacked someone — unless he had a mistress on his arm; a mistress or that dark chauffeur (who disappeared today, as soon as Calder was dead) or maybe, back in the past, a wife. Someone near to him had to witness the killing. Someone had to be intimidated by it; embarrassed by it and somehow broken by it. The mistress on his arm — most often in my experience — was Lily Porter.

14. Calder never came after me with his axe. I write this only to confirm — for my sake only — that nothing I'm writing here has personal overtones. Nothing brought me any closer to Calder Maddox than the fact we shared the same Hotel from year to year and the fact that — yes — I made him the subject of what can only be called unflattering photographs. But he posed for these. And willingly.

Calder was always trying to find the lens of my camera —

and whenever he succeeded, I hardly needed to throw unkindly thoughts in his direction. All I needed to do was — *snap* — and there he was: himself. Whatever unflattering aspects this produced could not be said to be of my doing. They were all there in him. He didn't know how to grace his own presence. He had no skill when it came to grace. And that is all I can say about that, except to add that Calder was not a physically ugly man. It was just, I think, that he made as much an enemy of my objective lens as he did of any other innocent who crossed his path.

He needed enemies the way the rest of us need friends, and he needed obstacles the way the rest of us need paths. I don't know why. I never will know why. It doesn't interest me.

15: *No one is totally monstrous: not even monsters.* Colonel Norimitsu said that to me when I was just eighteen. Two of his men had just been forced to kill themselves because they had tried to rape a woman in our compound. We had to watch them die. Their punishment was meant for all of us; for guards and prisoners alike. It was not until much later that I came to understand that the Colonel's reference to monsters was meant to reflect on him and not his men.

16: The day that Calder Maddox died began with fog, in spite of the fact the sky was bright and cloudless. All night long the stars had shone. Calder had watched them from his windows.

He liked the stars, and still, however ancient he was, he was quite convinced it was possible to count them. Amused, I made the mistake of expressing my amusement to Lily.

"Balderdash!" I said.

Lily rose above it. She treated my scepticism sweetly.

"You don't understand," she said. "Not everyone can count the stars. But Calder can. I've seen him..." blinking — smiling — nodding — "Calder has been counting stars since he was four years old..."

Calder himself, while making his various claims, could be insufferable — but Lily's wistful defence of him was touching. He was her evangelist. She was his true believer.

Calder Maddox slept so lightly that anything — even the light-footed watchman going his rounds — could wake him. "It isn't easy," Calder said to me, once; "to have the ears of a bat."

Nonetheless, according to Lily, he fell asleep last night — in his chair by the window — some time after the watchman had passed at three o'clock. I can verify the essence of this, because I heard the three o'clock watch myself and — shortly thereafter — Lily Porter clicking out of Calder's room. (She never fails to sound a door.) I was also aware of her coming down the stairs and passing along the third floor hall. Lily's room is below mine on the second floor and three sets of windows over.

By five o'clock — pre-dawn — when I myself was awake again, I noted all the stars had gone but one. The morning star.

17: The morning star is poignant; always in peril and brightest just before it dies. It should have been called *Cordelia* or *Camille*. Yet it seemed completely unassailable yesterday morning — Friday — riding out above the unseen ocean, red as a beacon above the fog. I cannot quite believe that Calder, who believed in "signs," can have failed to have some qualm about the day to come when he saw this burning star. But he did, by all appearances, fail to grasp it entirely. Nothing that followed pointed to a man with anything but utter confidence and welcome expectations. "I counted all the stars, last night," he said to Joel, when the boy brought his breakfast tray. "I counted every one!" he announced, as he left the elevator later in the morning, making his way across the lobby and through the doors and over the porch and down the steps. "I counted more than all the Ptolemys and all the Galileos put together!" Fifteen times he must have said it; fifteen different ways. "I counted all the stars! Beat that!"

Since no one could — it's clear that Calder Maddox went to his death the champion.

18: As a photographer, I have always been intrigued by fog. Consequently, I was up and dressed and down on the beach by six o'clock.

Some days are camera days and other days are not. It has to do with the sort of light being offered. All days provide light; some days present it. Fog-lit days are presenters. The aureoles of fog-lit birds and rocks and flotsam — the aura of the sand itself — is quite the most magical in all my experience — and I've learned that if I can be there and ready when the sun comes up, my chances of catching definitive images are doubled.

I must admit, too, that yesterday morning I could not have stayed in bed if ropes had tied me there. Meg and Michael Riches had arrived in the night and the prospect of seeing them — plus a sense of physical well-being I had not enjoyed in weeks — drove me up and out and down to the sand. I carried both my cameras — the Pentax, the Nikon — round my neck and the full range of lenses for the Nikon in my camera bag. I also had my file cards and pencils and all the usual

paraphernalia for a day of picture-taking. My immediate
thoughts were on the images of loons I'd heard as I was dressing. Nothing prepared me for what I found in their place.

19: About Nigel Forestead, I shall try to be brief. The thing
is, he belongs here — precisely here — in the tale of Calder's
death and its consequences. The day cannot unfold without
the help of Nigel's figure moving through the fog.

Poor, dreadful Nigel. I cannot imagine a more unlikeable
young man.

The facts I'm about to reveal are second-hand. But I came
by them honestly. I got them all from Nigel's wife: the pale,
malevolent Maryanne.

I rarely speak to anyone, but many people speak to me. I'm
not a volunteer, when it comes to words. I have suspicions,
however, that something in my "elected silence" attracts the
attention of gabblers and gossips. They suspect that, on the
one hand, I am lonely — longing for their company — and, on
the other hand, that silence — in anyone — implies a kind of
universal wisdom. In other words, these people seek me out
in order to fill my "lonely" days with verbal versions of the
National Enquirer, thinking: *this will cheer Vanessa up!* Also, in
order to disencumber themselves of personal problems for
which they have no answers, supposing that: *since Vanessa Van
Horne does nothing else but think, she must have all the answers.*
Ha!

At any rate, because of her misplaced faith in my great
wisdom, Maryanne Forestead plonked herself on the sand
beside my chair about a week ago. She then proceeded, as she
said herself, to *dump on me.* "Pardon me while I dump all over
you," she said. And what she *dumped* was more or less what
follows, though her language was less precise than mine, being overburdened with many *"kind ofs"* and *"sort ofs"* and
"you know what I means?"

Maryanne Forestead thrives on disaster. Whatever horrors do not exist — she dreams up. A day without mental anguish is simply not worth living through. *You know what I mean?*

Herewith, my version of her tale of woe as it affected me yesterday morning on the beach.

20: Shortly after seven o'clock, Nigel Forestead had just begun his morning run and was now approaching Halfway House.

Halfway House sits midway along the crescent of sand that stretches between the ASH and Larson's Neck, to the south. The distance, if you measure it the way a runner does, is just under two miles. This is from the tip of Sutter's Rock, at our end, to the Pine Point Inn, which perches high on the Neck, its silhouette dominating even the silhouette of *Ramsgate*, the Mannheim "cottage." The distance is not two miles, however, if you draw a line across the bay from point to point. That is more like a mile. Neither is Halfway House *half-way*. It is, rather, about a third of the way along the beach — but having the appearance of a landmark, it was given long ago the name by which we know it.

The house itself is a large Edwardian cottage, built before the First World War and long since abandoned by its original owners. For over twenty years it has been a rented convenience, and every summer, troops of new strangers take up residence. Some of these troops have children; some do not. Some are sedate and pull all the shades and never speak to passers-by. Others are gregarious, rude and rowdy, leaving their beer cans and magazines sitting on the steps and their children's toys all over the sand. They wave and shout "How are ya!" when you pass. Some are reflective, sitting high on the porches — staring — or making notes in little pads (like me). Rumour has it folk like these are famous writers or Soviet spies. Sometimes, rumour has it, they are both — writing their romantic novels, coding their reports to Moscow filled with the numbers of tankers passing along the Atlantic horizon heading south to Boston. It is my conviction, however, these people are either counting birds or making shopping lists.

Some of the occupants, however, are mysteries of quite another kind: disturbing presences whose comings and go-ings are plainly intended to provoke response and speculation. It is one of these — a woman apparently alone — who has taken up residence there this year, arriving shortly before the weekend of July the Fourth. It is she who is providing Nigel Forestead with his crisis, Maryanne Forestead with her *angst* and me with a mixture of amusement and dismay.

Every morning for at least a week and a half — according to Maryanne — as Nigel makes his run from Sutter's Rock to the Pine Point Inn, this woman of indeterminate age (though I call her a "girl") has risen from the waters in front of Halfway House — half naked. Easing her ample breasts (I believe that is Maryanne's phrase) slowly back inside her halter top, she has taken to smiling provocatively at Nigel, while crossing his path in order to mount the steps and disappear beyond his reach. She has never spoken once. And she does this, accor-ding to Maryanne, only so that Nigel will be enticed.

Maryanne herself has witnessed the scene on more than one occasion, shivering down in the dunes with her binoculars. Naturally, she recognized at once what the girl was up to. But Nigel did not so immediately comprehend. He is like that. Thick.

An absolutely rigid young man who works in some capacity for the Canadian Government, Nigel Forestead has sublimated all of life that cannot be accounted for in *Robert's Rules* and has taken up residence inside a permanent body cast of moral rectitude. Nothing Nigel does in public is done before he smooths his hair and pops a mint and clicks his heels. As a concrete image of this, I offer the following picture, taken during last summer's fifteenth false alarm for fire.

All the bells go off at six o'clock in the morning. This is par for the course. The rest of us are merely bored, we have heard the bells so often, but we rouse ourselves and take at least the minimal precaution of gazing into the yards to see if anyone there is looking up and shouting "fire!" Since no one is ever doing this, we usually hasten back to our beds. However, on this particular morning, someone *is* there: Nigel. Not shouting *fire!* — but standing all alone in the very centre of the lawn and calling up to Maryanne. "Hasten," he cries in his plaintive, nasal voice; "before you burn." Not *hurry up!* or *run!* — but *hasten*. He says it testily rather than with concern, and then he turns and stands in profile for all of us to see.

He is wearing a perfect pair of black leather slippers, a pure silk, polka-dot robe and blue pyjamas. I swear the robe and pyjamas have been pressed. Furthermore — and this is the sum of all his parts — Nigel is carrying, *chained to his wrist*, a leather briefcase.

The thing is, Nigel has never appeared with his briefcase before. The only thing chained to his wrist, till now, has been his ego. Consequently, the best conclusion I can come to is: Nigel's Ottawa rule book doesn't tell him to chain the brief-case to his wrist "unless the Hotel is on fire." By all means, Nigel — leave it behind when you go to the beach, and please — for heaven's sake — don't even think about it when you've left it lying on your bed for all the world to see and your door wide open the whole night long, while you play Scrabble down in the lobby. But if the Hotel should catch on fire, take chains and bind the briefcase to your person!

That is the essential Nigel Forestead: the official Nigel Forestead. But the Nigel Forestead who runs the morning beach is another man entirely. That man — forced under every other circumstance to crouch in the cell of his own imagination — is let out once a day — according to Maryanne — just like a dog, and allowed to have his way until the run is over. Thus it is that, when he runs, Nigel wears the ugliest bathing suit I have ever seen — a knee-length, shapeless black affair with yellow stripes. *Bee-legs*, we call him; but Nigel seems perversely proud of it — much as if some Olivia had begged him to go "cross gartered" over the sand.

I have written that Nigel Forestead took some time to comprehend the scheming of the girl from Halfway House. I get this from Maryanne, whose witness I must trust — though I take it with a grain of salt. Maryanne, after all, has a vested interest here. Nevertheless, I now have witness of my own and can vouch that, once his comprehension bloomed, he became a fanatic. The girl herself never said a word; but for Nigel, her naked silence might as well have been the *Kama Sutra*.

Day by day — according to Maryanne — as the morning runs were turning into Marathons, Nigel watched and waited for the girl's appearance: *Aphrodite rising from the sea*. And every day, she rose and every day she smiled and every day she tucked her ample breasts inside her halter top — one and then the other — saying nothing.

But the truth — (the sad truth, I suppose) — is that Nigel has lived so long inside of *Robert's Rules*, his imagination has died in there of suffocation. He could not — as a consequence — conjure up what he and this girl might actually end up doing together. Something sexual — but what?

All he wanted was to have that *something* happen.

Anything. Otherwise, he would have to stop his running. The sight of the girl had become too distracting to bear and Maryanne was already complaining to him that he was *drifting away into the arms of...* (here, she was careful) *some other woman*. Which, of course, she knew he was — since she herself had been drifting into her dune in order to follow him.

And now, on this particular morning — yesterday — in the

fog, I can only suppose Nigel was determined to force some kind of confrontation; to match his Aphrodite's magnetism with some magnetism of his own.

It is here — precisely — that I come blundering into the picture, wandering along the beach, completely forgetting that Nigel is there — completely forgetting, in fact, where I am myself and only aware of the pair of loons I am tracking by their sound — their callings — out on the water, lost in the fog. I want to capture their image more than I can say, and in order to get it, I have already tucked up my skirts and removed my canvas shoes, which are strung around my neck, together with my cameras.

I am wading through the ebbing tide when...

God!

I can only speculate.

Approaching their usual rendezvous, Nigel has slowed his pace in order to catch the slightest indication of where the girl might be. All along the beach — (as I surmise) — he must have been dreaming of Aphrodite rising from the water — not with her usual gesture of tucking one and then the other of her breasts inside her halter top, but coming towards him out of the fog completely naked.

Surely that is what he was thinking.

What else could he have been thinking?

My ankles are getting cold. I decide to leave the water and warm myself before I pursue the loons any further. And so I blunder onto the beach — in that very place where, every previous morning, the mystery girl has risen from her wave. And there is Nigel Forestead — waiting for Aphrodite — rubbing himself in ways I have never imagined — and not a bathing suit in sight.

21: I was so completely startled, the truth is I barely saw him. So startled, too, that — already numb about the ankles — I was just unsteady enough to lurch towards one side — which meant I had to clutch my cameras, in order, should I fall, to hold them above the water.

Certainly, if I had time to know who he was, Nigel Forestead, too, had time to know who I was. And the consequence of this — in spite of all its humour, in spite of all its sadness — is sure to end in disaster.

The thing is: he thinks I took his picture. And I did not.

22: I went back slowly. I went back alone. I knew that Nigel would not follow me — could not follow me without his bee-leg suit and would not out of fear and confusion. It would take him a very long time to reassemble the man from *Robert's Rules*.

But it took less time than I might have imagined for me to recover. I wasn't all those years in prison for nothing, I guess — though I must say here that anything connected with sex that happened there had nothing at all to do with display. The Japanese soldiers went so often in their loincloths to their baths beyond the fence — their nakedness lost its sexual connotation. All we ever knew of sex was attack — and counter-attack. And ritual suicide.

I knew I had fully recovered when I realized I was angrier at Nigel for having made me lose my chance at the loons than I was over what he'd done. I had wanted the loons so badly, their being the rarest of the rare to photograph, because they are so shy of human beings.

The sun had risen long before this, but I don't think I'd taken it in until I started walking back towards the ASH. If the morning star had merely been red, then I can't describe the colour of the sun. To begin with, its light was entirely diffused because of the fog, and besides this diffusion, it had to rise above the obscuring shape of Surrey Island, lying north and east. But its light was everywhere, shining in every particle of moisture, and I walked — illuminated even from the gleaming sand — inside a Turner painting. Orange, I guess. Burnt orange.

I had thought I would go straight back to the landing by the bath houses — sit down and dry my feet, put on my shoes and go up to breakfast; go up to Meg and Michael, who must, by now, have arrived. I was cold. I shivered. I remember that vividly; that I shivered. And then I thought: *I'd best do up my cardigan*; and stopped to do this.

Looking down to find the buttons, I caught the first vague intimation of a shadow. A shape. It was difficult to tell. I do know this: it was on my right-hand side; the water side. And large.

I thought: *that's strange. If that's a lobster boat, it's awfully big.*

And so I turned. And saw it.

23: Where was I standing? Exactly?

I must have been closer to the boardwalk; closer to the row of bath houses raised above me than I'd thought — because I was vaguely aware of voices. I couldn't move.

I think I already knew what it was.

But I still couldn't move.

I was already facing it — shoes in hand — and I began to hear the actual words the voices were saying, though I know for certain I didn't turn to hear them.

"Is that you Roger . . . ?" A woman.

"Yes. It is." The beach boy: Roger Fuller.

"I left a pair of sandals here last night," the woman said. "You find them, by any chance?"

By this time, I had begun to shift — though I did hear Roger saying; "yes" and the woman (I think it was Myra Audley) chattering on about how "grateful" she was and how she would "never be able to find another pair that fit like that in a million years.'' But I was running across the sand by then; almost back the water's edge.

24: I think then I must have called out; "quickly! Come!" or some such words. I still hadn't turned away — I still hadn't turned around — I know I was calling over my shoulder — and I also know I was taking pictures and thanking Saint Teresa I had put a battery into the Nikon just that morning. I know, too, I heard people running — slapping their bare feet over the sand and I could hear them breathing. I could also hear the panic in their voices — because they must have thought I was drowning.

"Come!" I cried. "Come quickly!"

"Hurry! Hurry!" someone said. "It's Miss Van Horne…"

And then I heard; "Nessa? Nessa?"

It was Meg.

She told me later that, in spite of Michael, she'd had to come down to say *hello* to the sea. We all did that, our first day there; but Marguerite Riches did it in her nightgown — and without her robe.

"What is it, Ness?" she said. "Are you all right?"

"Yes," I said. "But look out there."

It was then that all the lobster boats — hidden out in the fog — began to fill the air with the sound of their horns and the gulls and the crows flew up over the roofs of the ASH like creatures rising from the grave and all the guests began to pour down over the steps and along the path towards the beach. Some were still in their dressing-gowns and some were barely dressed; some still carried towels and those who had been eating breakfast carried their napkins and their bowls of cereal, glasses of orange juice or bits of toast and all of them were silent — even the children — as they stumbled onto the boardwalk.

Here, they stopped and made a crowd of perhaps a hundred people — while others, who were trapped by age or nakedness in their rooms, threw up their windows and peered out over the lawns towards the sea.

"What is it? What?" said all the voices together — singing it *sotto voce* like a choir. "What is it? What?" they whispered.

At first, there wasn't any way for them to tell; no more than I had found a way to tell; believe. It seemed that what we all beheld was either someone's nightmare — or a joke: a hoax.

But it wasn't any of these. It was real. I knew that, of course, already. I had looked too long for it to be a dream.

The gigantic shape of what appeared to be an island was moving through the fog in our direction.

It was an iceberg.

25: What is it? What? This instinct to raise the camera in the face of wonder — to stare through a viewfinder into the face of calamity? How do the fingers know how to find the *f-stop* in the dark — and how do they know how to make the right adjustments — speed and light and distance — even compensating for the fog? What? What is it? All this picking up of pencils and pens and cameras, brushes and tubes of paint and broken bits of charcoal, all to record bewilderment.

The only images I've ever created in all of my professional life — consciously and with a vengeance — have been the studied shapes of gardens. Nothing, by will, but images of order and peace. And in my photographs? What *is*. But never accidents; never the overturning of reality. Not anarchy.

And now this; just as the prison rose around me out of the garden of my parents' lives — an iceberg rises out of the trusted sea before my eyes. Meaningless and awesome — but only meaningless because of its absurd and incomprehensible presence where it should not — cannot possibly be. It might as well have risen in my bath.

Even as I write these words — it sits out there in the dark. It will not go away by dint of wishing or of blinking or of waking up and saying: *I have only dreamed an iceberg*. There it is. I can feel its emanations through the screens — cool at the centre of this heat wave. And its weight is like a magnet — pulling the Hotel down across the lawns and out to sea. Yes; it is terrifying — just as the prison was, because it will not go away, in spite of reason.

I seem, however, to be the only one to react to it this way. Everyone else is thunderstruck by what they call a miracle. Not even Doctor Menzies — a scientist, after all — knows what to make of it. The shape of its huge, white mass presents an eerie likeness to the Capitol Building in Washington, D.C. and this prompted Arthur Wilson to remark that "if only our location had been somewhat south of here, we might have looked out and said: *there goes Washington, crossing the Delaware...*"

Some half-dozen laughed. And stopped.

It wasn't, after all, a laughing matter. To begin with, the iceberg's size was truly immense — larger by far than any Capitol Building. None of us had ever seen its like before, though some had much experience of both the sea and icebergs. One who stood there with us was Sybil Metsley. Sybil had been on board the *Titanic* in 1912. And Sybil said: "it's even bigger than ours."

After she had spoken, we all fell quiet again. Sybil's quavering voice had reminded us of what it must have meant to be on board the *Titanic* — and for three whole minutes, the entire congregation stood as if in silent prayer on the sand.

A breeze rose. The fog began to lift in earnest.

The iceberg grew in size.

I tried to take more pictures, but my cameras fell against my chest like leaden weights. I cannot properly describe what happened next. The sand — having been exposed by the retreating tide — was cold and hard. But just at that moment, the tide began to turn. It turns — as anyone will know — with a single wave — and the turning wave that morning had the force of an explosion.

Bang!

Just once. Like that. A bomb beneath our feet.

26: We drifted away by ones and twos and families — entirely baffled by what we had seen — reluctant to leave the beach. If we turned our backs on it, the iceberg might evaporate.

I came up with Meg.

We walked like children through the dew — both of us barefoot, eschewing the tar and cinder path — me in my cardigan and dampened skirt; Meg in her flannelette nightgown with its buttoned collar and its pale blue flowers. Around us, the birds had fallen silent — some in the trees and some on the grass. They scuttled, crablike, on their awkward feet as we approached. But they would not fly.

The smell of food from the kitchens drew us forward — familiar and safe and simple: scrambled eggs and coffee; toast. And the smell of marmalade and flowers. No one hurried. No one ran. Even parents lacking their children refrained from calling out. They went back slowly to collect them, glad perhaps to have an excuse to stare once more at the thing in the bay from which we had all somehow escaped.

It felt like that: escape; recovery; rescue. The long, eccentric column of people in assorted states of dress making its progress towards the absolute safety of the porches reminded me of the day we were released from prison; Bandung, 1945. Though of course not so desperate, the sense of confusion — the sense of bewilderment was just the same; the violation of reality. Today, an iceberg out in the bay — on that other day, an open gate.

27: Meg and I strolled up the lawn. The air was already hot and humid, damp with intimations of debilities yet to come: the failure of energies, the inability to stay completely dry. By the time the day had fully risen, we would all be felled, one way or another, by its relentless heat. But for now, it was good just to walk towards the familiar façade of the ASH, with Marguerite Riches once more beside me as she had been summer after summer all our lives.

In front of us, Doctor Menzies was attempting to explain the presence of the iceberg to Major-General and Mrs Welch. Mrs Welch — all shoes and tailored precision, including her tailored hair — kept nodding and saying: "yes; yes; yes," as if she understood every word of Doctor Menzies's treatise. And the General — dense and bad tempered, from Winnipeg — told Doctor Menzies the only thing to do was "blow the bugger out of the water." An iceberg, after all, was not unlike an alien warship. The word to bear in mind was "menace." (Meg shook with silent laughter and gripped my arm.) But Doctor Menzies reminded Major-General Welch "this iceberg is one of yours." And surely, it seemed a little strange the General, being a Canadian, should advocate the destruction of one of his own.

"An iceberg flies no flag!" the General insisted. "It could be anyone's. Could be a Greenlander — even a Russki!" Doctor Menzies hid a quiet cough behind his hand. Mrs Welch said: "yes; yes; yes — a Russian berg." I could see the blood begin to rise above the General's collar as he pressed his point with ever increasing vehemence. "These Russki bergs come down the Murmansk Run — just the way our sailor boys used to do, before you Yanks were even in the war. Lives lost; incalculable losses," he boomed. "No one to help us. The Murmansk Run…"

Here, Doctor Menzies cut him off decisively with science; "no iceberg in the world could possibly come that way, because of the prevailing currents." At which the General bristled, brushing away his wife's insistent, soothing hand. "If our brave boys could manage it, an iceberg can! Prevailing currents be damned! The ice-cap is melting! Don't you scientists know that? Prevailing currents are all a thing of the past!"

Meg pulled me back at this moment, afraid we would burst out laughing.

"Wait," she said. "It's too embarrassing."

"Why?" I asked her. "You think it's only you Canadians who claim the ice-cap is melting?"

"No," said Meg. "It's *'blow the bugger up!'* What with? A howitzer?"

"Not the way I've heard it. The way I heard it, they bomb them."

"Bomb them?"

"Yes."

Meg looked at me slyly; not believing. But I was serious. I'd seen them doing it on *60 Minutes*.

"Where?" said Meg. "All those icebergs in the Coral Sea?"

She had wanted me to laugh at that. And I almost did. But, looking over my shoulder, reaffirming my witness of what was in the bay, I didn't. Neither — when Meg, too, looked again — did she.

28: After breakfast, I went to visit Meg and Michael in their rooms.

Ever since Michael Riches had been confined to a wheelchair — now about five years — they'd had to take the only guest-rooms on the bottom floor. These were situated off to one end — the northeast corner — in the apartments occupied once by a founding family. This family's name had been Penderton and so the rooms are in what we call the Penderton Wing. They consist of a living-room, sun porch, bedroom and bathroom — plus a tiny kitchen where Meg can make their breakfast. Lunch and dinner — depending on Michael's condition — they mostly eat with the rest of us in the dining-room.

Michael Riches is old before his time; old and childlike. This is a tragedy. Once, he was one of Canada's top ambassadors — posted to Prague and Moscow and Vienna. His expertise had been in Soviet relations — a brilliant, conciliatory diplomat. He saw his country's relations through the most difficult years of East-West confrontation following the Second World War — in the years when the Iron Curtain dropped — and later, at Prague, when the Russians entered that city in 1968. In those days, Michael was valued as much by us as by his own. Our Government's hard line made getting people out of Czechoslovakia almost impossible — whereas the Canadians, largely due to Michael's efforts, managed to extricate a vast contingent of scientists, intellectuals and political refugees. Now, in his custom wheelchair, Michael Riches is a shell; a broken old man with pure white hair and the manner of a five-year-old.

Questions provide few answers. Meg has simply not been forthcoming — not to me and not to anyone. She guards him jealously and wheels him proudly — defiantly — through what remains of his life, in much the same manner, being Meg, she would wheel a retarded, crippled child. If such a child had been hers, she would have denied it nothing, on the one hand, and would have presented such a child — denying nothing — for all the world to see, on the other.

There is something almost indecently virtuous, now, about the way she presents him to us; Michael. Virtuous — provocative — angry.

There is also something akin — within this presentation — to the way I have seen some veterans of war put on display. It is shaming — an embarrassment. One wishes fervently it

would not be done. A man's wounds — a person's scars — are
private. Not for show. And Michael is scarred; he is wounded;
a spectacle of tremors, loss of control and of childlike
dependency. Yet Meg parades him over the porches and along
the walks as if he had no pride.

Still, it is not my affair. It is not my business. I have never
spoken of it to anyone — least of all to Meg. I have winced, it
is true — and doubtless she has caught me wincing — but not
a word has passed between us on this subject. Her love for him
is vehement. Whatever reason she has for forcing the rest of us
to confront her husband's infirmities — and him to endure
those confrontations — it is hers and hers alone.

This morning, when I went in first, he was back in the
bedroom where Meg was making him ready for the day.

I heard the toilet flush. I heard Meg's voice. "We have a
visitor." I heard the sound of her heaving him into the chair.
I heard — I swear — the sound of her kissing the top of his
head. (She did this so often, bending down from behind him
and pressing her lips against his skull. He had been so
beautiful, once.)

I called out; "only me. Nessa..."

"There," said Meg — to Michael; "our very best friend."

This lifted me greatly, for I considered her to be my own
best friend and Michael revered and loved enough to be no
cause for jealousy. I want no part of Meg that is his; no part of
him that is hers. It is a friendship — not a love affair.

I've never had a love affair — of which I'm aware.

They came in — one being — a living chair with bones
beneath its skirts. Michael's head, as ever, was down — his
chin upon his chest — his hands, arthritic, liver-spotted, wax-
en, clutching the edge of the blanket over his legs. I could see
his booted toes — and the cuffs of his dark grey flannels. He
wore a shirt, a tie and jacket — tweed — impeccable. Meg, the
other part of this being on wheels, stood up behind and her

fingers, gripping the handles, were white, I judged, with a rare attack of nervousness. This, after all, was the first of Michael I had seen since a year ago.

He has not improved an iota from our last encounter. Much the opposite. I have to remind myself he is barely seventy — and might be Calder's age — or more.

Meg stopped the chair in sunlight.

I stood in shadow.

"Here's Vanessa, Michael," she said. "She's come to say hello."

I did not budge.

"Hello," I said.

Meg reached over the back of the chair and lent her fingers to Michael's chin. She raised his head.

"Hello," I said again.

"Hello," said Meg — his only voice.

"Do come," she said, for herself — and nodded me forward.

How could I do this? Kiss him and not weep?

The face I saw, as I stepped into the light and knelt before him, was a pale, stroke-ridden mask. Its muted lips clung tight to one another. Its eyes stared out from pits of darkness, their expression filled with the panic of not being able to speak.

I closed my eyes and kissed him on the cheek.

I was about to rise, when I felt his fingers scrabbling over the blanket — broken birds — to find my own.

"...o," he said; "...a."

Hello, Vanessa.

29: Meg and I sat on their tiny, screened-in porch. Michael was still in the living-room listening to a radio.

"Well," I said. "What happens next?"

Meg looked over the lawn towards the sea — towards the

iceberg. "Death," she said. "Here, I hope. I want him to die here."

I took this in as best I could and then, regrettably, I said; "do the Welleses know this?"

Meg said; "people have died here before. They've coped."

"These Welleses are very young," I reminded her. "Not like their parents. They've only run the hotel for five years."

"The same five years of Michael's illness. They aren't blind. They know he's going to die."

"All right," I said. "But is it fair to him?"

Meg didn't answer this. Instead, she said; "where would you prefer to die, Vanessa?"

I nodded. "Yes. You're right."

And she was. There can be no better place for dying.

Then Meg laughed and said; "I almost didn't get him here."

I asked her why — supposing there had been some problem at the border. Coming from Montreal, the Riches always enter the U.S. at Champlain, one of the more innocuous crossings.

"No," she said. "They're used to us there. It had nothing to do with that. It was right up here at Sutter's Hill."

"Oh? What happened? Your car break down?"

"No. No. Nothing like that." She lit a du Maurier — lifting it carefully out of its red, foreign box — smoking it, as always, with pleasure.

"What, then?"

"You don't know?"

I shook my head. I was getting testy. I dislike childish guessing games.

"I wondered," said Meg. "They didn't seem to know about it at the Desk, either." She took a deep puff and exhaled. "There were swarms of Police," she said — and squinted through the smoke. "State Police — a dozen cars. They were setting up a road-block."

"Really? I wonder what for. Had there been an accident?"

"Nothing visible. No. It was something else — though I don't know what. Something along the lines of security, I'd say. They stopped us and asked me questions; some of them impertinent, I thought."

I smiled. When were the Police not impertinent? "How?" I asked.

"They wanted to know where I was born; where Michael was born and if we had ever been here before..."

"A census," I joked.

"No," she said. "Not a census. Not a joke. They had a list of names..."

I sat forward. "Oh?"

"Oh, indeed. They had a list of names and, apparently, we were on it."

"Really?"

"Yes. Really. The State Police. Then they asked me the nature of Michael's illness. I wasn't inclined to tell them. The bloody cheek! But when they looked at their list and said; 'it doesn't say here he's ill' — I absolutely hit the ceiling. Blew my stack! I got out our passports and that did it! *Pass*, they said. The buggers. *Pass*, they said. You'd think we'd come into Russia."

I blinked.

Pass, they said.

Pass?

As if it was a border. At Sutter's Hill.

Meg was looking at me. She smiled — and patted the back of my hand.

"It's good to see you," she said.

30: The library here at the ASH is almost always deserted. It sits between the lobby and a section of the dining-room reserved for large families. Glass doors lead in either direction — the doors standing open to the lobby, but closed to the dining-room. Windows look southward onto a part of the porch we call *The Bulge*, because it does just that — it suddenly balloons out of all proportion above the lawns.

Ferns and begonias fill the old wicker planters set out between the cushioned library chairs. The colours here are green and cool. An awning shades the windows — preventing the sunlight from fading the backs of the books on their shelves and the photographs hanging on the walls. It has always been a favourite room of mine — quiet, unpopulated, provocative.

I went there after my visit with Meg and Michael in much the same way I used to go and sit — because I had to — in the visitors' lounge at Slattery's when Mother was dying. Michael, helpless in his wheelchair, was too reminiscent of Mother in that high, impossible bed in which she died. Every time I left her room I couldn't breathe — and, after seeing Michael, I couldn't breathe again and I had to sit down somewhere alone.

It was there in the visitors' lounge at Slattery's Private Hospital I felt the first symptoms of a heart attack coming on. It came a few days later, while I slept, apparently. The big one didn't come for another month — and thank God, not until

after Mother's death. But I knew that morning at Slattery's I
was in trouble. Something gave way inside me; something
turned over — fell. Whatever it was, I knew it was not just a
momentary blockage of the intestine — not just another
spasm of the phrenic nerve. It was the signal of something
final; definitive; mortal. And after seeing Michael, it happened again — as I crossed the lawn to the steps. Or rather, it
started to happen again.

I prevented it by thinking of my pills. I told myself I'd taken
one and that — if only my heart would be patient — and if
only my legs would co-operate — I'd get us all to a chair where
we could pause and breathe again.

It worked.

I've never questioned that ability to subdivide my person,
so to speak, into separate units — isolating one and concen-
trating on another. This, at Bandung prison, was how we dealt
with hunger, illness, loneliness and pain of every other kind.
That I can lie to my heart and keep it pumping by telling it
I've taken a pill I have not taken is a direct result of my training there. And by such lies, I may yet survive another attack.

31: Perhaps it was not incidental that I chose the library in
which to recover. Honor — who was setting the tables for
lunch — saw me through the dining-room doors and brought
me a cup of tea. The dear girl could tell I was poorly off —
though nothing was said. She's waited on me now for two full
years and this — her third — will of course be her last. She
understands my reticence — just as I understand her sombre
dedication to purity. Honor has what now must be considered
out-of-date, old-fashioned standards. These make her life
amongst her contemporaries difficult, to say the least — and,
more than once, she has come to the dining-room red-eyed
from weeping. Still — she wins her battles, and I admire that.
Immensely. The more so, because she wins them alone. And

that I understand in ways I can never tell her — and never tell anyone.

And so, she went back in behind the glass doors and set more tables while I, with my cup of tea, sat very still and gazed around me at the photographs.

One in particular held my attention for quite some time.

It shows me with Meg and Michael after the War, in 1946. We are all very young and thin and beautiful. Yes; even I am beautiful.

Michael wears his summer uniform. He was a Captain in the Canadian Army — but had been attached to British Intelligence all through the War. I suppose he was then about twenty-seven or eight and Meg was twenty-six or seven. I know that I was twenty-one that summer and Mother was bringing me out that fall. I had what passed for an elegant wardrobe that year; elegant for such a dark, depressive time. So much of 1946 was cold and it always seemed to be about to rain.

The marks of our late starvation and deprivation were still upon us — and Mother revelled in the dreadful styles because she said the padded shoulders gave us the look of having flesh — and the long, full lines of the skirts were useful for hiding our shapeless legs. Both my bathing suits that year had skirts — and Mother insisted I wear a robe as much as possible. She behaved as if it had been she and not the Japanese who had starved me; she was ashamed of how I looked.

But the bones in my face were good and the sparseness there of flesh was useful.

In the picture, I look pensive; tense and tentative — quite unlike myself. I remember only that, aside from Meg and Michael, I rather distrusted everyone here that summer. When, I kept thinking, will they reveal their true character and stop pretending they had suffered through the War? I was an awful prig, I guess. But it made me want to strike Mrs

Godbold, for instance, when I heard her complaining that her piece of steak had been overcooked. I should have known better and paid no attention.

Michael was still a mystery to me. That was the summer we met — and I could not take in the fact that he and Meg were married. Even Mercedes hadn't married in 1946. And Meg seemed so much younger than any other married lady I knew. This shows so vividly there, in that photograph. She's standing just behind Michael — resting her chin on his shoulder — and both her hands are in his jacket pockets. The look on her face is one of indescribable contentment; happiness; youth. She actually wears a bow in her hair.

Michael looks sheepish; not quite embarrassed, but somewhat uncertain what he should do to preserve the dignity of his uniform, given this woman who was defiling it with her greedy arms and fingers. He's smiling, though. What else could he do?

I stand beside them — demonstrating perfectly the bridesmaid complex of the lost best friend. Not that I'd been Meg's bridesmaid, except in the honorary sense. Their marriage had taken place in London in 1944 — while I was still behind the wire in Java. But I was the lost best friend — the best friend who was lost in her ignorance of how to behave towards this wonderful man who had come between us.

I'm wearing a hat with a wide, straw brim — and its ribbons are hanging down across my almost painfully obvious collarbones. I squint. I do not know — apparently — how to address the camera's lens with confidence. And so — instead — I retreat and hang my hands in knots at my sides and seem to want to leave.

Of all the pictures taken in our youth, it is the only one that shows us, in any sense, at odds with one another's mood. I'm glad it's there on the wall. It reminds me of the dangers of deprivation. Not the obvious dangers to health and hope and happiness — but simply the dangers of separation for too long from what we know and trust.

32: Leaving the library, having finished my tea and having actually taken a pill and received the benefits of both — I caught, from the corner of my eye, a much more recent photograph. Last year's photograph, in fact, of me with Mother and Arabella Barrie, Ivy Johnson and Jane Denton — the latter all my mother's contemporaries. "Do come and stand with us," Mother had said.

I hate it. In fact, I might just ask Quinn Welles if it couldn't be removed. Not because of pride. But because I cringe to see myself so completely in the company of Arabella, Ivy and Jane. Surely the word *dragon* must have been coined for Arabella Barrie. She has breathed her fire on me all my life.

Oh, well.

I did not linger to focus on this photograph. Still, I could not help but see it in juxtaposition with the other I had been watching. For here, with Mother and her friends, I am shown so clearly as I am today — my hair quite white, my features displayed in all their fineness, my figure unadorned, my posture as I have striven so hard to keep it — upright, squared and firm; and my expression as I wish it always to be. It tells no secrets and it makes no statement other than: *here I am.*

I admit — and not without satisfaction — I was smiling as I left the library and entered the lobby. The person in the second photograph had definitely survived the person in the first. And yet, the person in the first had not had to die in order to guarantee that survival. Both are still with me; intact.

33: Calder's death did not occur till later in the afternoon. The day that had begun with fog had become, by three o'clock, a day of blinding sunlight and almost morbid heat.

Not wanting any lunch, I repaired to the beach, where only the diehard swimmers and tanners had stuck out the noonday sun.

Like a dog that has lost its people — the iceberg appeared to be reluctant to leave us. In spite of Major-General Welch, we had not done anything violent to drive it away. Consequently, it sat not quite a mile offshore, directly in front of the Aurora Sands Hotel, waiting — in the dog analogy — for someone to come and collect it. As itself — in its role as *iceberg* — its Arctic chilliness and chiselled stillness gave it the eerie appearance of an anchored *prop*; perhaps from a propaganda film about Canadian/American relations — *your* ice sculpture — *our* Capitol building.

Unfortunately, word of its presence had spread as far as Portland and the local press had already been dispatched to photograph it and ask questions about its initial appearance. They also wanted to take my photograph, and I told them: *thank you; no.* I hid my cameras in my canvas carryall as soon as I saw the familiar yellow-haired girl and the red-haired man coming off the end of the boardwalk.

Because, from time to time — in spite of all our efforts — the presence of the Hotel's celebrity roster slips out from under our control; these same two marauders have been here before. Consequently, I know them both by sight — the girl being tall and tired and super-blasé and the man a five-foot midget with mile-wide credulity. (Someone spread the rumour, once, that "sacks of gold ingots were washing ashore" and the red-haired midget came down from Portland to photograph the evidence!) The iceberg, therefore, must have seemed, to him, to be divine retribution on all the non-believers of this world. When he first saw the iceberg, he strutted so belligerently you might have supposed it was his own creation. "Well!" he kept saying; "now ain't that something!" With his arms, for heaven's sake, *akimbo.* I think his name is Biddolph.

The girl's name is Faye Reynolds. Though she took a negative view of things, she was at least a change. To her, the iceberg was "okay enough, if you like that kind of thing." It was "neat" and "cool" — but "really just another manifestation of the times we live in." More of Nature's hyperbole. Faye has seen too many beached and bloated whales, interviewed too many survivors of freak storms; filed too many stories on the victims of AIDS and legionnaire's disease and acid rain. She has the kind of mouth and eyes I remember seeing when the War was over — a kind of settled hardness; taking the next blow before it fell.

My heart went out to Faye the first few times we met — but I finally pulled it back, because she borrows other people's troubles and neglects her own. I discovered she has two children whom she never sees. "My mum takes care of them. I'm too busy." One day, I'm certain she'll write about their troubles and wonder where they came from.

I gave her a quick and cursory interview and asked her not to print my name. I said; "just call me a guest at the Hotel." She also asked if her paper could use my early-morning photographs of the iceberg looming out of the fog and I said (God forgive me); "what photographs?" And she said; "come on, now, Miss Van Horne — I did a whole interview with you last summer about your picture-taking. And six dozen people have told me already you shot a warehouseful of film this morning." But I maintained my ignorance of any such pictures, and finally, she went away to talk to someone else.

Before she went, however, I thought to ask her about Meg's road-block. Had there been an accident the night before? Or were they looking for a criminal? "No," she said. "It's just an emergency exercise. They do that all the time, these days — pretend the bomb has fallen and stuff like that."

And stuff like that. Neat, I suppose, and *cool*.

In the meantime, the red-haired Biddolph had been taking

his own warehouseful of midget-eye-views of the iceberg and — at last — by one o'clock or so, they were gone — in order to make the deadline for their afternoon edition.

There were others who came to stare, but most of them were in boats and aeroplanes, and because the berg was lying at a distance from the shore, we were not too troubled by their presence. The sailboats, in fact, made quite a pleasant picture, caught against the ice-blue visitor's shape.

34: In the meantime, I had wandered further off, and by two o'clock, I was sitting on my favourite bit of sand — a high, rounded dune that hasn't changed its shape all season, in spite of the winds and rains that occurred before the heat wave. I wanted desperately to be alone in order to digest the sorrowful spectacle of what I had seen that morning — and the sad-bitter things that Meg had said. I felt I could not yet bear the weight of what she carried — and had carried now for so long. Even the thought of the weight was daunting.

Michael's illness had been such a long time manifesting itself — beginning as long ago as ten years, perhaps. He became exhausted; went for treatment — finally, into a clinic. They called it that appalling euphemism for nine hundred versions of despair — *a breakdown*. And then — in the last five years, he began the series of strokes, paralyses and loss of memory that left him as he is today.

If only they weren't so much in love. If only Meg were not so committed to her devotion. Devotion kills. Who knows better than I? Love is not good to those who love with all their being. Meg's grief for Michael has played such havoc with her spirit. Gay and charming as always, her smiles and her laughter have taken on the shape and sound of performance. *Play up! play up! and play the game!* I could kill the man who wrote that. And only a man *would* write it.

Enough of that.

Sitting on the sand, I was also recalling — I confess — a little of what had happened before the iceberg — earlier in the fog: the sight of Nigel Forestead standing naked on the shore — me as his Aphrodite. Another "performance." Nigel Forestead stars as *Canadian Diplomat of the Year!*

It didn't bear thinking about — except for amusement's sake — but it did cue in another thought — and a crucial one. This was the thought of my cameras in my canvas carryall and the rolls of film I had started that morning.

I've never cared to leave a camera loaded with unused film. The quality deteriorates. The film dries out; becomes brittle; the colour fades and the details of your pictures lose their sharpness.

I had taken more pictures of the iceberg with the Nikon than with the Pentax. Perhaps I had ten frames left in one; eighteen or twenty in the other. And, just as I was wondering what I might use as subject matter for the remaining frames, I was given the perfect image.

35: Looking to my left along the beach in the direction of the ASH, I could see the congregation of guests seated in its deck-chairs beneath the Hotel's blue-and-white umbrellas. Coming down to join them — having had his lunch and all his medicines and then his nap — was Calder Maddox. And his retinue.

Roger Fuller, the beach boy, was leading the way, with Calder's deck-chair held like a shield and Calder's folded beach umbrella like a jousting lance. Next came Calder himself, supporting — or supported by — Lily Porter, and Lily Porter all got up in something long and flowing and carrying her beach towel over her arm and trying to wave at everyone as she and Calder stumbled through the sand towards the chosen place, where Roger was already setting out the chairs and setting up the umbrella. Behind them all,

Calder's dark, mysterious chauffeur — dressed in full uniform — muscled his way in his slippery leather boots between the clusters of people, balancing a large, white metal cooler — doubtless filled with food and ice and wine, which he plonked beneath the shade of his master's umbrella as if he had delivered a shipment of crystal he was determined — for purely sadistic reasons — to smash.

It was all so precisely like something in a European movie — Fellini, Visconti — that I thought I'd better record it for posterity. The colour — everything blue and green and yellow — was ravishing and Lily, admittedly, was beautiful in all her flowing skirts and sleeves.

I shaded my eyes against the glare from the sand and pulled down the brim of my cotton hat and got out the Nikon. Filters would be useful — and the telephoto lens to squeeze the distance.

I got busy. I was grateful my dune of sand was far enough away from everyone that I could remain more or less unobtrusive. Every lift of the camera to my eye would not be witnessed and the sound of the clicking would not be heard.

The place where Calder and Lily sat was the bit of beach directly in front of the long white row of bath houses, just below the boardwalk. It was absolutely packed. This bit of beach has always been considered the choicest location for chairs and umbrellas. We have always called it *The Cockpit* and ten to a dozen families — always the same — have taken up their daily stations there since I was a child: the Barries, the Johnsons, the Dentons, et cetera; the Woods, the Baumanns, the Mackeys and — yes — the Van Hornes. I sat there in *The Cockpit* every summer before and every summer after the War; hovering always beside my mother till she died this winter. Now, I'm free of it all and all its obligations and limitations; its entanglements and memories.

The families of *The Cockpit* are, for the most part, matriarchies — and the present matriarchs are of my mother's generation. Arabella Barrie, Ivy Johnson and Jane Denton still maintain the hold on our *petit monde* that was given them by their mothers-in-law — a group — indeed a race of women whose tenure began before the First World War. Old Mrs Metsley, for instance — whose husband and son went down with the *Titanic* and whose daughter Sybil is now advancing into her eighties — was the doyenne of my childhood. Every evening, all these women hold their court in the dominant corner of the Hotel lobby. They have sat there as long as human memory can conjure. One Mrs Barrie simply replaces another — and another Mrs Johnson and another Mrs Denton, *ad infinitum*.

The word *court* may be misleading. I do not speak of Dowager Queens and Ladies-in-Waiting; I speak of Judges. It is a court like that. Supreme. And because they sit propped up with whalebone corsets and because, when they lean towards one another in order to hear and tell, they lean unbending — and because they rattle their knitting needles like bones — and because their expressions never change but merely show, by tilting this way and that, the positive and the negative aspects of a single visage cut in stone — and because they all have hair of Druid blue — we call their court *Stonehenge*. Dread things are decided and condoned — or so we have always imagined — whenever they lean together, all towards the centre of Arabella Barrie and we see them nod in unison. But they have a pact — and what is decided — what is condoned is never told.

My mother, before her marriage, was a Woods and so I have a cousin, Petra, whose mother — my Aunt Lydia — sits in *The Cockpit*, still. The only time I venture there now is to sit — very briefly — with her. Petra never visits. But my camera often visits *The Cockpit*. The subject is irresistible.

36: As I write this, now, another day has come and gone.
And, another night. The results of my picture-taking sit
before me — and what I have written on their envelopes is this:

TAKEN BY V.V.H. THE DAY THAT
CALDER MADDOX WAS MURDERED.

37: There is something wonderfully touching about these
photographs. They show a rare and poignant unity of focus —
by which I mean the focus of the subjects, not of the camera.
In some, this unity of focus is almost theatrical; as if a Director
had been standing out of sight and saying; ''I want you all to
concentrate on me.'' So that every eye and the angle of every
head is bent on a single view. It is only obvious when the pictures of *The Cockpit* are shuffled with those of the iceberg,
precisely what it is they are staring at.

I shot the remaining frames on the Pentax and the Nikon
and one whole film with the telephoto lens on the Nikon;
forty-seven pictures in all. What I shot with the Pentax is not
in league with the rest. The sense of isolation is not the same.
In the Nikon sequences, the people in *The Cockpit* are like the
survivors of a shipwreck — huddled, almost; crowded
together on their raft of towels and mats — some of them
perched high up on deck-chairs, others lying down and some
reclining, arched against their backrests. Some are standing
— a few are kneeling; but all are staring out from under their
shaded eyes towards the iceberg.

I could not have planned the outcome of this shoot if I had

contrived it, and even as I took the photographs, it was in my mind to offer them for publication. The colours are muted by distance and haze and the figures might have been drawn by Géricault; but still I am proudest of my decision to use the telephoto lens, because — in pushing them away, in pushing them together — it has left them isolated — seemingly abandoned in an acid sea of sand.

In all but one of the photographs, Calder Maddox has already been deserted by Roger Fuller — the beach boy — and by the dark chauffeur. In the single photograph in which these two appear, they are walking away together — Roger in the lead and the chauffeur looking over his shoulder, as if perhaps Calder had spoken to him: made some final demand, more final than either the chauffeur or Calder can have imagined.

Calder himself, in all the photographs, has taken on a mummified look. He is either swathed or about to be swathed in towels. He wears, besides the towels, a yellow bathrobe, a white cotton hat and what we used to call bathing shoes: light canvas shoes with rubber soles. The towels are to cover his legs and his arms — and any other part of him exposed when he removes the yellow robe. Calder's need for the towels is obvious. His skin is so sensitive, it peels away at the drop of a hat. His hands, his ankles and his face are covered with a bilious ochre sun-cream — very likely a sun-cream devised in his own pharmaceutical laboratories — made especially to cater to his special needs. It comes in a yellow tube — the very same yellow, I'm prompted to say, as Calder's robe. Yellow must be his favourite colour.

Lily Porter is in most of the pictures with Calder. She leaves them twice; once to go and wash her hands in the sea and once to greet Meg Riches. Otherwise, Lily is Calder's constant companion; standing beside him, sitting beside him — rising, from time to time, in order to converse with someone who has wandered by. In some of the photographs, Lily Porter is applying the sun-cream to Calder's feet and hands and face —

a certain sign of her devotion. She is also shown sitting back on her heels admiring her work; as if she were an artist. I find these pictures amusing because, in them, Lily Porter is most herself: a daubing, delighted child.

There are pictures in this sequence of some of the women who make up *Stonehenge*; of Arabella Barrie, the Hotel's present doyenne, with most of her numerous daughters-in-law — and of Natty Baumann and her dog, Boots — of Eileen Ross and Lydia Woods, who is cousin Petra's mother, widow of my Uncle Benjamin. Cousin Petra is problematical and married to Lawrence Pawley — a doctor. Lawrence himself appears in the pictures. Petra does not. There are shots that show Nigel Forestead sidling up to Major-General Welch. Maryanne Forestead does not appear. She must, in spite of her dim-wittedness, know better than to butter up Pelham Welch and has stayed in her place outside *The Cockpit*.

There are seven in the Nikon sequence showing Meg. I saw her bringing Michael onto the boardwalk in his chair. But I did not shoot this, because I cannot bear the prospect of catching them, awkward and vulnerable, in crisis. I did, however, take one of them together — after Meg had braked the chair in the shade of the bath-house roof. She had come down onto the sand by then and stood below him. It was charming. She placed her hands on his knees and looked up into his face and Michael — his head tilted down towards her — reached with great effort to cover her fingers with his own. Afterwards, she went away from him and stood with *The Cockpit* before her — and having looked around at all the people — ninety percent of whom would be known to her — she then moved off behind the sea of umbrellas.

In another sequence, Meg is greeting Lily, who has run up from Calder's side to say *hello*. They stand in one of these photographs with Lily's back to the camera, obscuring most of Meg. In others they are obviously going through the motions of Meg's polite refusal to "come and say hello to Calder." Lily then retreats and Meg is left standing alone, looking bereft and indecisive.

After this, I went on shooting *The Cockpit* and Meg is again lost from view until the sequence nears its end. She is in the last two frames I took of the group as a whole — without her robe — without her carryall — and towelling her hair as if she must have been in swimming.

In the final pictures — taken entirely by chance and only because I had those few remaining frames inside the Pentax and wanted just to get rid of them — Calder and Lily Porter, Natty Baumann, her dog and Major-General Welch are the only figures remaining in *The Cockpit*. Nigel and Maryanne Forestead can be seen vacating the beach in one of these photos and Roger Fuller is raking the seaweed in another. Then, they are all gone. The lot of them. All that is, but Calder Maddox — and he is dead.

38: I did not know he was dead, of course. It is simply that, in that moment when Calder was left there alone, I ran out of film and also, I guess, momentum. I got up, then, and gathered all my things together and prepared to leave the beach. I took a last and lingering look at the iceberg — thinking: *I almost hope it doesn't drift away, because . . .*

I remember that thought distinctly; I remember the word *because*, because it was the very word that got cut off by Lily's cry.

39: *We have all heard Lily Porter's cry, over time. If you live, people die. And, when they die, then death demands a voice. It need not be that death is unexpected. I gave that cry myself, when my mother died — having waited fifteen weeks in the absolute certainty that her death was due in the next five minutes. The air at*

*Bandung had carried such a cry each day. And I am certain, now,
that what it announces is not the fact of someone's death — but our
horror of the void that death creates.*

40: Running in sand is never easy — unless you happen to be
running down below the tide-mark where the sand is hard.
But I had been up on my dune, where the sand is pliant and
hot. Reaching Lily was a nightmare run, my camera bag
thumping against my back, my carryall banging against my
leg and threatening to spill its contents. Thank heavens I was
wearing shorts; thank heavens I'd put my shoes on; thank
heavens I didn't stop to think about my heart.

It was now past five o' clock and the beach was all but
deserted. The majority goes up at five to run its bath and open
its gin. The only people left, besides myself and Lily, were
Roger Fuller, Lawrence Pawley and Natty Baumann. Roger
Fuller, having begun his retrieval of the day's scattered beach
trappings, was at present staggering under the weight of
twelve folded deck-chairs, using his extended arms as racks.
Now, as he turned to Lily's cry, there was the horrendous
sound of twelve metallic frames cascading onto the sand.

Lawrence — attempting a dozen push-ups on the boardwalk — floundered on his face and couldn't stand up until
he'd rolled over. Far off down the beach, Natty Baumann in
a purple dress was walking Boots-the-dog. Natty, too, had
heard Lily's cry and was trying to run; but her arthritic legs
could only manage to "hurry." Boots, who is very old and
very small, could do no better. Consequently, Lawrence and
Roger got to Calder before me — but I got first to Lily.

41: *"I thought he was only asleep,"* she kept saying. *"I thought
he was only asleep . . . "* Her voice kept rising with every word
— and every word was like a staccato shout.

She was kneeling on the sand beside him and I was trying to

pull her away. Plainly, she was hysterical; totally out of control. I couldn't find her body inside her robes — too many layers of silk and cotton — and my hands kept missing her. Lawrence said; "hit her" — but I didn't dare.

Lawrence Pawley — as I've said — is married to my cousin Petra. He's a doctor and I've known him since 1946. I guess he was two, then; maybe three. This puts him in his early forties, now, but you'd never know it. He looks to be in his fifties; tall and alarmingly thin. He has the largest hands and the largest feet I have ever seen; the largest elbows and the largest knees. Also the largest Adam's apple. His thinness is truly painful to see. He has the look of a man consumed by disease — though I suspect the disease is ambition. His mouth is drawn tight; his eyes repel all sympathy. On the surface he is a gentleman. His tension produces a hoarse, quiet voice and a restrained repertoire of gestures. I have always assumed that these — the pitch and modesty of his presence — have much to do with a wilful effort to conform. We have never been close — though we walk sometimes together on the beach. In his marriage to my cousin, my sympathies lie all with him.

Now, however, I saw the other side of Lawrence: the brisk, authoritarian, professional side — and it was a shock. Without a second's hesitation, he leaned out over Calder's body and struck Lily hard across the face with the flat of his hand.

She hit him back.

"He was asleep!" she yelled. Her voice broke. "He was only sleeping!"

And then she fell back into my lap and wept.

"I wouldn't have left him," she said. "You know I wouldn't have left him, Nessa, if I'd thought he wasn't just asleep..."

"It's all right, Lily," I said. "It's all right. No one is blaming you..."

"I am," she said. *"I am..."*

I looked at Lawrence. He was pulling all the towels away from Calder's body, trying to unknot the sash of the yellow robe. Calder must have pulled it closed and tied it, because the last time I had looked at him, the robe was open and his chest and stomach were plastered with the same white towels that also covered his legs and arms. There was a dreadful smell — acidic — and I assumed it must have come from Calder's medicine bag — his constant companion. Something, I supposed, had spilled inside it — or perhaps, over time, the bag had simply taken on the stink of all the medication it carried.

Lawrence, at last, succeeded in untying the sash and he pulled the robe aside. Calder had been propped — in sleep — against his backrest and now — with Roger's help — Lawrence lowered him all the way to the sand. I heard, as this was done, a distinct and quite alarming sigh. Lily must have heard it, too, because she stiffened in my lap and put her hand — a fist — against her mouth. The body, now exposed, was blue — which, under the ochre smears of the sun-cream, gave it a greenish cast.

This is when Natty Baumann finally reached us.

"He's green," she said.

"Mrs Baumann," said Lawrence; "do you think you could get your dog away from here?"

"Well," said Natty — who has a habit of making everything the subject of a debate. "If you really think I should."

"Yes," said Lawrence. "I really think you should."

"I could pick Boots up," said Natty, who obviously didn't want to leave until she'd had her fill of Calder's death.

"Take him away, Mrs Baumann. I insist." Lawrence was getting angry; restraint and modesty were jumping ship.

"Oh," said Natty. "In that case — come along, Bootsy. Doctor Pawley has told us to march!"

She began to move towards the boardwalk — but the dog

did not go with her. Boots, I should add, is just a cairn terrier — a bit of fluff — but large in spirit.

"He thinks you want to play," said Natty, smiling affectionately. "It's really quite understandable. You're all kneeling down, you see. You'll have to stand up."

Lawrence's temper failed him completely. He muttered a curse I didn't hear — stood up and turned away. So did Roger. But Lily would not, and I'm afraid I began to panic. The dog — (who really did want to play) — had turned away from Calder and had its nose at Lily's knees. Its tail was wagging slowly to and fro and I could see its all too merry little eyes as it placed its paws on Lily's legs. I knew it was going to bark.

"Call him, Natty," I said. "*Call* him!"

"Boots! Here, Boots!"

Boots barked.

Lily picked him up and threw him into the sand.

If she hadn't been weakened by shock, and sitting down when she did it, Natty's dog would surely have broken its neck and been killed. As it was, it gave a howl of pain and ran up onto the boardwalk. Natty burst into tears and — wailing — followed him, with much theatrical exaggeration of her arthritic condition.

The only good thing about this incident was that it drove Lily Porter onto her feet and I was able to pull her away as Roger and Lawrence returned to the body.

42: I didn't want Lily to see what I had seen — that Calder's face was green and that his mouth and eyes were open. I was hoping tears and hysteria might have prevented her already from seeing him too clearly. She tried again and again to pull away from me in order to go back to him, but I kept her walking — twisting the sleeves of her robe around my wrists like handcuffs and urging her up the sand towards the Hotel.

It was only then that I noticed the silent knot of people

standing on the boardwalk. A dozen — including the ubiquitous Nigel Forestead.

He — and he only — came down onto the sand. The others — anonymous — stood close together and were mute. Nigel began to move towards the crouching figures of Roger and Lawrence, where they hung above the body. "What's going on?" he called. Officiously, of course. Surely his ancestors must have been among those who fled our Revolution. I believe in Canada they call these deserters *Loyalists* — Tories who rule by right of natural selection. Mere enquiries are beneath them. To ask is to demand.

I am proud of the fact that none of us answered him. A glance would have told him exactly what was going on — but Nigel was above such things as drawing his own conclusions. Consequently, he was forced to wander democratically all the way to the body. What surprised me was that he didn't turn a hair or falter for a second when he looked directly down at Calder's face. It seemed, on the contrary, to bolster his diplomatic immunity.

It was then that Lawrence produced a master stroke. He decided to take advantage of Nigel's pre-emptive nature and asked him to bear an important message up to the Hotel. Would he be "good enough" to call an ambulance?

Nigel Forestead beamed with self-importance. "Of course," he said. "At once." And turned on his heel.

Lily and I had paused to witness this and had just begun to walk in our circle again, when Lawrence's voice rang out — addressing itself to Nigel.

"You must also call the Police," he said.

Nigel gave a kind of salute. "Yes, yes," he said. "I'd thought of that." And turned, yet again, to trot up onto the boardwalk.

But Lily stopped him.

"Wait!" she said. "Just wait one God-damned minute!"

She pulled away from me — ripping her knotted sleeves and burning my wrists. She was frantic.

"WHAT DO YOU MEAN HE MUST CALL THE POLICE?" she yelled at Lawrence. "WHAT DO YOU MEAN POLICE?"

I have virtually never seen her in such a state in all the years I've known her. She had become a virago; kindred to her mother's class, but a mile from everything Maisie had worked so hard to erase — the coarseness — the fish-wife voice — the blood-reddened face — the total loss of control.

"WHAT DO YOU MEAN *POLICE*?" she screamed again.

"I'm sorry, Mrs Porter," said Lawrence; "but there's no way around it. When a person dies in a public place, the Police must be informed."

"But this," said Lily; *"this* is not a public place! *Our beach* is not a *public place!"*

"The public have access to it, Mrs Porter. All I'm doing is obeying the law. As I must. I'm a doctor."

"You cannot call the Police," said Lily, something of the lady slowly returning to her tone and choice of words. "I will not allow you to call the Police . . . "

"I already have, Mrs Porter." Lawrence waved his hand at Nigel and Nigel departed — rapidly — up the walk and across the lawns to the Hotel — pushing, not incidentally, one or two people out of his way as he went.

It was done — and no turning back. The Police were as good as on their way.

43: Meg appeared.

I don't know where she came from, though I suppose she must have come off the boardwalk, out of the crowd. The crowd had grown, by now. Twenty-five or thirty people stood with folded arms and stared at us.

Meg came over to me and Lily.

"Rumour has it," she said; "that something has happened to Calder Maddox..."

"He's dead," I said.

Meg lost something of her posture for a moment. Her shoulders fell. "Oh," she said. "Well." Then she straightened her back and turned to Lily. "I'm sorry, Lil," she said. "Truly sorry."

Lily did not reply.

Meg looked over at the body on the sand. I saw her clench her hands. I thought of Michael and all that Meg was going through and wondered how she could bear this other death so closely preceding the death she was anticipating.

But I also knew how strong she was.

The clenching finally stopped and her hands hung down at her sides, relaxed. Her lips moved — without making words. And then — not looking at Lily — she spoke to her. "Believe me," she said, "I know how you feel. And you know I do. But Calder, after all, was... ninety, Lil. He was nearly ninety years old. He did have his life. The whole of it." Then she turned and smiled at Lily — sadly. "We can't all say that," she said.

Lily stared at her. Medusa.

"I'll remember to say that the day *you* die," she said.

Finally, the ambulance came.

It screamed across the lawn and into the yard behind the bath houses. I could see the pulse of its flashers — red and orange — and the whirling of its turret — round and round and round, flinging off bits of coloured light like drops of water.

Two men in white came running across the sand. They carried a stretcher with them and a tank of oxygen. Apparently Nigel had failed to tell them the rather crucial fact that Calder was already dead.

44: The ambulance driver and his assistant were adamant. They would not touch the body until the Police had come.

"But I'm a doctor," Lawrence told them. "I'm a doctor and I want him put on that stretcher."

"Is this where you found him?" said the driver.

"Yes."

"Right here?"

"Yes."

"Then this is where he's gotta stay. Until the Police come."

"I tell you — I'm a doctor. I'm a doctor and I want him put on that stretcher. *Now.* And if you don't put him on it now, I will lodge a very serious complaint against you. Is that understood?"

"Yessir."

They lifted Calder and put him on the stretcher.

"Thank you," said Lawrence.

"Thank you," said Lily. Softly.

Lawrence lit a cigarette and broke the match in half. I knew he was trying not to smoke. But I sympathized. A saint would have smoked in Lawrence's place. I could see he was more than angry. He was also troubled. It was obvious from the way his fingers moved around the cigarette — pinching it and rolling it — using it as a single worry bead.

He must have been able to feel that I was watching him, because he turned and looked at me. I held his gaze. He took a deep breath and looked away. I was electrified. His eyes had been full of fear.

45: I was about to speak to Lawrence when the ambulance driver cut me off.

"You people know this man?" he asked.

"Indeed, we do," I said. "He was a guest at this hotel. His name was Calder Maddox."

"Don't tell them that!" said Lily. "Don't tell them his

name." Her voice had begun to rise again.

Lawrence looked at her — but his expression had changed. Now it was one of — what?

No longer fear — but suspicion.

Lily turned away.

"Any relatives?" said the ambulance driver.

"Yes," said Meg. "He has a wife."

"She here? She been informed?" the ambulance driver wanted to know.

Lily said — across her shoulder; "she lives in Boston. But we don't know where..."

"Maybe they'll know at the Desk," said the ambulance driver.

"No. They won't," said Lily decisively. Turning.

"Oh?" The ambulance driver seemed amused. "They divorced, or something?"

"Or something," I said. "I really don't think that's any of your business."

Nigel now reappeared.

"Everything in order?" he asked.

We stared at him. Order?

"The Police have not arrived," said Lawrence.

"They certainly should have," said Nigel. "I spoke to them at length."

I dare say.

Nigel had changed from his bee-leg trunks and was wearing, now, a pure white suit, a cream silk tie and a pair of yellow shoes. He had obviously showered and taken some time with his toilette. Every single hair was set in its very own place. And sprayed. I could smell the spray ten yards away. He wandered over to Lawrence — with a handkerchief in his hand — and I heard him saying — over Lawrence's shoulder; "where did you get with the cause of all this?"

"He had a stroke," said Lawrence.

"Ah, yes," said Nigel. "Do you think I could have a cigarette? I'm afraid I forgot to slip mine into my pocket just now. I was rather hurried."

Lawrence did not reply. Instead, he handed his Viceroys over his shoulder. And then — very slowly — his packet of wooden matches.

I was still caught up in what Lawrence had said.

A stroke.

He'd said it — yes — but I could tell absolutely he did not believe it.

46: The Police had still not arrived when an hour and a half had passed. And this, in spite of the fact that Nigel was re-dispatched to phone them. When he returned this time, he was justifiably mystified. "They left right after I called the first time," he said.

It did not — and could not — make any sense. The ambulance had arrived within twenty minutes. Maybe even fifteen.

"Never mind," said Meg. "Here they come, now."

And come they did.

Three police cars — sirens blaring and klaxons whooping — were speeding towards us along the beach. They were coming from Larson's Neck — and heaven help anyone who got in their way.

The tide was coming in and one of the police cars was racing through the shallow surf and sending up a flume of water on either side as it careered past the others. I really did think, for a moment, we should all be run down. When it finally braked, it fish-tailed for another hundred feet and slid towards us sideways — its doors already opening and policemen already spilling out of it — running.

Lawrence is never one to avoid the obvious.

"Where the hell have you been?" he said.

But the policeman who answered was already angry.
"Where have we been? We've been all over hell's half-acre trying to find *you*," he said.

A man of higher rank came up behind him and pushed him
aside. "I'm looking for someone called Forester," he said.

Everyone but Nigel knew he meant Forestead.

Not that it mattered. Nigel — in his diplomat's capacity —
would have stepped forward, whether he had been named or
not.

"Are you the one who phoned?" the policeman asked.

"Yes," said Nigel.

"Step over there."

"Yes," said Nigel. "Of course." In the presence of the
Police, he became what he truly was: the perfect and absolute
yes-man.

47: When Lawrence asked them again why they had been so
long in coming, their answer was: *we went to the wrong hotel* . . .

When Lawrence wanted to know how that could possibly
have happened, their answer was: *we didn't know whose body
we were looking for* . . .

When Lawrence opened his mouth to speak again, he was
told to: *shut up*.

This was shocking. No one knew where to look.

Lawrence, to his credit, did not pursue the matter there and
then. His main concern was to get Calder's body off the
beach, so he filed his complaint in the back of his mind and lit
another cigarette: *displacement activity*. I did feel sorry for him.
Beginning with Lily's hysteria and Natty Baumann's dog, the
whole event of Calder's death had been a trial for Lawrence.
Now, he was being abused and insulted by the Police.

His appearance did not help him. In the course of our long
and tedious wait — tedious in spite of all its tensions —
Lawrence had begun to shiver. He was wearing nothing else

but bathing trunks, a misshapen T-shirt and running shoes.
Now the sun was going down and it was chilly by the water.
Perhaps, too, the iceberg added to the cold. Since nothing else
was immediately available — and since we had not dared leave
the beach during our endless wait for the Police — I had offered Lawrence my cardigan. So it was that the person who
confronted the authorities with all the *impertinent* pertinent
questions was all too easy to dismiss as some eccentric beach
inhabitant; the sort of transient you say *shut up* to all the time.
If you happen to be a policeman.

Overall, the behaviour of the Police was mystifying, to say
the least. Beginning with their melodramatic entrance — their
attitude seemed more appropriate to the U.S. Marines than
policemen. Instead of feeling relieved when they finally
arrived, I felt distinctly disoriented — as if, somehow, I was
waiting with all these others — Lawrence, Roger, Lily, Meg —
to confess a crime. I had no notion, then, of course, that a
crime had taken place. But I was given the impression it was
a *crime* the Police had come to investigate. Yet nothing should
have given that impression. A man had died. That's all. Of a
stroke. On the beach.

It went through my mind that perhaps the Police were
bored and needed some excitement. It also went through my
mind — once they'd begun to ask their questions — perhaps
they were incipient storm-troopers.

*Who are you? What are you doing here? Stand over there! Come
over here!*

Those exclamation points are not one whit out of place.
And, while I fully recognize the rhetoric of words like *storm-
trooper*, I make no apology for them. We, after all, were
citizens, standing on a beach in the State of Maine. America.
Once, long ago, I stood in the company of other citizens —
civilians who had just been captured by the Japanese
equivalent of *storm-troopers* — and we had been spoken to in

exactly the same way. Believe me, I recognize a tone of voice when I hear it.

I heard them saying things to Lawrence I could not believe.

How do you know when he died? He could have been lying there dead all day, was one of them.

How do we know you're a qualified doctor when you haven't any identification? (This to a man in bathing trunks and somebody else's cardigan.) That was another.

They were not any kinder to Lily.

What was your relationship to this man? was the second thing they asked her. The first thing they'd asked was her name-address-and-marital status.

Wonderful, isn't it. They had her pegged for a whore in two sentences.

48: I was fascinated by Nigel's relations with the Police. Once they had established he was the mysterious "Forester" — the Police seemed to consider him not only as their equal, but in some way their man-on-the-spot; their agent in our midst. Nigel exudes — for those who are prone to being exuded upon — a sense of being in the know; a candidate for every inner circle in town. He uses phrases such as *quite true* and *I think not* and has a way of placing his hands together — finger ends to finger ends — and smiling enigmatically when he says these things. He's also mastered the visual equivalent of the phrase "if you only *knew!*"

People on the fringe of status tend to fall for Nigel's tricks. Only a fool would underestimate his effectiveness, no matter how off-putting that effectiveness might be. The trouble, this evening on the beach, was that Nigel had taken on — had been accorded — the rank of official expert. I was given the impression his readings and opinions of those of us involved in the *Calder Affair* were being accepted by the Police as gospel — no questions asked.

It was hard for me to understand why this should be, until I turned my mind to the telephone calls that Nigel had placed. Something he'd said to the Police had definitely left them with the impression that Nigel Forestead had what a policeman might think of as inside information.

But — inside of what?

49: Their questions of me were not the sort of questions I would have asked myself. For instance, I would have wanted to know something more of Calder's background. *Had he been ill? Was there a heart condition? Had I spoken to him today — and, if so, when? Had he mentioned not feeling well to anyone?* And: *since Doctor Pawley has told us he died of a stroke — was there a history of strokes?* Et cetera.

But not at all.

"How did you become aware that he was dead?"

Lily's cry.

"Was Mrs Porter the only person near the body when you heard her call for help?"

It was not a "call for help." It was a *cry.* A sound; a noise.

"But was she there alone?"

Indeed.

"How long did it take you to reach Mrs Porter?"

Et cetera.

During the whole of the questioning, I was never once addressed by name, in spite of the fact that I gave it to them and they wrote it down, together with my New York address and my marital status.

"I have never married," I said.

"I see," the policeman said; "you're a spinster."

When I saw him writing that down, I stopped him.

"Young man," I said; "what I said to you was: *I have never married*. I did not say anything about my profession."

He looked dumbfounded — which did not surprise me.

"A spinster," I said; "is a person who spins. For money."

50: We had almost reached the end of twilight and the questioning continued. The sky was a brilliant amalgam of green and orange and the evening star had made its appearance.

The police cars — as police cars will — had been talking non-stop, though no one amongst the Police was paying any attention. I could hear — between the bursts of static — anonymous and distant voices announcing various traffic accidents and runaway children. I also heard something about a *secretary arriving by helicopter* — and the figure *2035*.

By then, they had come to Meg.

I suspect the Police do not know how to cope, under any circumstance, with people like Meg. Charm is lost on them — humour is lost on them — honesty is lost on them. The fact is, not only are charm and humour and honesty beyond their comprehension they are also, it seems, the stimuli for instant antagonism.

I heard her saying to them; "I'm afraid I really can't tell you anything. You see, I was one of the very last to arrive — and I believe you'd already been called before I knew that Mister Maddox was dead."

The interrogator, a Captain, did not care for Meg's answers. He had found her arm-in-arm with the rest of us on his arrival — and he intended to treat her just as he had treated Lily, Lawrence and me, which is to say — belligerently.

"What was your relationship to Calder Maddox?"

None.

"There must be some connection. You seem very buddy-buddy with all these others."

Buddy-buddy?

"You were found, on our arrival at the scene, in the closest company with..." he consulted his list; "Mrs. Porter, Doctor Pawley and the woman Van Horne..."

(*The woman Van Horne???*)

Meg told them she had never heard of *the woman Van Horne* — and I wanted to cheer. She told them, however, that Vanessa Van Horne was her closest friend. The questions, after that, became downright hostile.

Knowing what Meg had already endured from the State Police the previous night, I could not allow them to bully her any longer. I crossed the sand and stood between them.

"Since nothing you have asked Mrs Riches would give you the slightest notion of this, I feel I must tell you she has only just arrived from Montreal — Canada — and she is, therefore a guest in our country. Her husband is also extremely ill. Your behaviour here is outrageous, Captain, and she does not need this!"

His answer was astonishing.

"If she didn't need this, lady — then she shouldn't have come down here."

51: Up until this moment, not one of the Police had paid the slightest attention to Calder's body. It had lain beneath its sheet on its stretcher with only the two men in white to watch over it. For their part, the two men in white seemed to be enjoying themselves. They were seated on the sand and they were smoking cigarettes, just as if they had come down onto the beach to watch the tide come in.

52: It was at this point the other doctor arrived.

"I was driving by and I saw the cars on the beach," he said. "I thought perhaps there might have been a drowning."

He was small — immaculate — precise.

The Captain seemed delighted to see him.

"My name is Chilcott," the doctor said.

He was wearing a gabardine topcoat and carrying a hat. Sweeping the topcoat back in order to produce his identification, he revealed he was also wearing evening dress.

"Good of you to come, Doctor Chilcott," the Captain said.

I looked at Lawrence Pawley. His face was blank.

The Captain was explaining the situation to the newcomer. I distinctly heard him saying that a body *had been found* on the beach.

I wanted to scream. *Found?*

The Captain now took Doctor Chilcott over towards the stretcher. The ambulance driver and his medic got up off the sand and threw down their cigarettes.

I asked Lawrence if he'd ever seen Doctor Chilcott before.

"How do I know?" he said. He was testy, but I could hardly blame him.

He was staring along the beach towards Larson's Neck where the lights of the Pine Point Inn were wavering beyond the lights of Halfway House. The sun had now fully set and its colours had left the sky. An aeroplane, I could hear, was approaching from quite far away.

Lawrence lit yet another cigarette.

"Aren't you going to go and consult with him?" I asked. "With Doctor Chilcott?" I felt that Lawrence was being professionally maligned and I'd hoped he was going to insist on being present when Chilcott made his examination. But he seemed not to care.

No. I have written that badly. *He seemed not to care* is not quite right. He cared — but his professional status was not what he was thinking about. He was struggling with something else — an idea — a thought.

I followed his gaze and looked along the beach beyond the parked police cars at the Pine Point Inn. It was so like our own Hotel in some ways — so absolutely unlike it in others. It was not as old, to begin with. The ASH had been built in the 1850s — the Pine Point not until 1910. Its architecture was more self-consciously picturesque than ours, though nothing downright vulgar had been done with it. Whereas the ASH was sided with clapboard, the Pine Point Inn was sided with shakes. We were white — and it was blue. Its roofs were covered with tiles from Spain — rust red — and ours with green asbestos tiles from upstate New York. It was staffed, as we were, with college students — but ours wore simple white dresses and plain white jackets. At Pine Point, the bellboys and busboys all wore red and the waitresses had uniforms with aprons. It had valet parking — we had not. It had an orchestra — a dance floor and two bars. We had a bar. The rest of our drinking was done in our rooms and in the dining-room. Otherwise, it must be said that both hotels were of the "grand" variety — that both had enviable clientele and both were perfect examples of the very best that Maine had to offer.

It must also be said that those of us whose families have patronized the ASH since time began would not be caught dead in the Pine Point Inn. Except, from time to time, on a Saturday night — as dancers.

The aeroplane was getting closer; small and loud and irritating. Lawrence, however, did not appear to hear it. He was staring, still, along the beach.

"Aren't you freezing?" I asked.

He didn't appear to hear that, either.

Meg came over and stood beside us.

"Do you think they'll ever take the body away?" she said.

I said; "it really is unconscionable."

For a moment the three of us were silent — hearing the voices but not the words of Doctor Chilcott and the Captain behind us as they studied Calder's corpse. The whole scene was lit with the glare of headlamps, swept with intermittent blips of red.

"Did you know," Meg said; "that if you look too long at flashing lights, you'll have a seizure?"

"No," I said. "I've never heard that."

Out of his reverie, Lawrence said; "only if you're epileptic."

"Oh," said Meg.

"Are you epileptic?" Lawrence asked.

"No," said Meg. "But the person who told me that is. Was. I think. Had problems like that."

She did not elaborate.

Lily came.

She was like a ghost in all her sleeves and skirts. Her voice had died and she could barely whisper.

"It isn't fair," she told us. "They won't let me listen. And they're treating Calder as if he was *anybody*. It isn't fair..."

Meg looked at Lawrence. "Shouldn't you go over there and speak to them?"

"My sentiments, entirely," I said.

But Lawrence said; "no. They'll call me if they want me. However..." he added; "I doubt they'll want me."

He looked along the beach again, shutting out the police car lights by raising his hand at arm's length.

"What *are* you looking at?" I asked.

"Just the beach," he said. "The line of the beach."

I put my own hand out to cut off the lights and looked as well. The beach made its great, wide arabesque of double curves and the dark mass of trees stood up behind the dunes. It was a sight I knew by heart. I could have "seen" it with my eyes closed.

That aeroplane was making a dreadful racket, now — blinking and winking hovering above the Pine Point Inn. In fact, I thought it must be in trouble. It seemed to be stalled.

"It's a helicopter," said Lawrence. "It's going to land on the beach."

At this point, some of the Police began to return to their cars. Not all of them, but most. For the first time, I realized one of the cars was not the same as the other two; it was from the private police force up on the Neck — a service the citizens of Larson's paid for themselves. The other two were State Police cars. The local policeman now got into his cruiser, slammed the door, turned on his siren and took off down the beach. In passing us and leaving us, he hadn't said a word.

I turned away. The combination of helicopter rotors and sirens was quite unbearable.

The ambulance crew was about to remove Calder's body. But before they did, they lifted it off the stretcher and held it almost over their heads. I wondered what on earth they could be doing.

One of Calder's arms slid down towards the ground and pointed at the place where he had died. Lily stepped forward as if to help, but Meg pulled her back. Doctor Chilcott lifted Calder's wayward arm and folded it, together with the other, over his chest. The attendants now slid the body into something like a laundry bag — and drew the strings. After that, they laid it down again on the stretcher.

Lily said; "oh."

Doctor Chilcott shook the Police Captain's hand and — placing his Homburg squarely on his head — he followed the stretcher up to the boardwalk. I felt so badly for Lily. And worse for Meg. It was true, after all; she didn't need this. One death is quite enough at a time.

53: More than forty years ago, I stood in the glare of other lights in another place and watched as another body — this one lying in the rain — was hovered over — poked and prodded and dispensed with. Searchlights, then, and wire — not mere policemen — had kept the rest of us at bay.

"What was he doing there?" someone said.

"He was trying to see his wife."

"And they shot him? For that?"

"Yes. For that..."

The monsoon rains made steam in the boiling air.

"Well — he must have known the chance he was taking..."

"Yes. But who could believe that such a thing would actually happen?"

They rolled the body over. Prodded it with toes and bayonets. Dead. Absolutely. His face, I remember, was tilted into the light — his arms thrown up above his head — his ankles crossed — like someone who, lying out in the sun, had fallen asleep; who — any minute, now — would wake and laugh because it was raining and his clothes were getting wet...

And someone — one of us, not one of them; an internee, not a Japanese — had said; "Well — if he didn't want to be shot — he shouldn't have been out there."

"Please. Be quiet," another voice said. "We have his daughter with us..."

We have his daughter with us. The daughter was me. And that was how my father died. Between the Women's Compound and the Men's. At Bandung. Java. 1943. My prison.

The echo of that scene — and the scene that had just been enacted on the beach below the Aurora Sands Hotel became entwined in my mind as I walked away with Meg and Lily and Lawrence that night. I almost expected — looking up — to discover the visible perimeters of some new compound stretched around us as we crossed the lawns. How grateful I was that nothing was there.

How grateful. And how wrong.

54: A final word about the body on the beach.

Calder's eyes — wide open — were staring at the iceberg.

"Help," he seemed to be saying. *"Help me."*

But icebergs are hard things. Killers; deaf and dumb. And cold.

Calder Maddox would have understood all that.

From what I know.

55: Make of it what I may, time has its own schedule and goes its own way. I no longer keep pace. I fall behind — and have lost all touch with the sequence of these affairs. What began as an effort to write my daily lot became, as events began to multiply, a physical and mental impossibility. I fear too greatly the consequence of pushing myself beyond the limits. I make no apology for that. When my chest begins to bind and my arms begin to ache, I have to stand up and count away the apprehension — dismiss it by numbers, so to speak; advise myself that I am not going to die.

(One day, I shall no doubt drop in the midst of saying that. When, I wonder? Where? Can a person drop at her own feet?)

I will attempt to keep pace — and order — as things unfold; but, already, I am two days behind the incidents I next describe.

56: The lobby of the ASH is filled with wicker furniture. The seaward doors give onto a screened-in porch. A fireplace dominates one wall. Long, narrow tables carry such things as magazines, ashtrays, lamps and large displays of wildflowers arranged in pitchers and Chinese bowls. The pitchers are those that remain from before the advent of indoor plumbing — and the Chinese bowls, most of which are porcelain — but two of which are brass — came back with a member of Quinn Welles's family, who long ago was a missionary to Beijing. I myself am responsible for some of the floral arrangements.

The colour scheme in the lobby, while not overtly maritime, is still predominantly blue and white. Accents of orange and yellow have been mixed with other shades of blue — paler, darker than the blue that dominates the walls. The cushions on the chairs — the pillows on the sofas — are plump and malleable; none of that foam rubber nonsense; nothing like a brick in the small of your back. The lamps are tall and plentiful; plain shapes with pleated shades. The pine floors have grass mats. The dispensation of the chairs and sofas and tables is quite deliberate. Though not appallingly formal. There is only one setting that is sacrosanct. Woe betide the fool who thinks she can tamper with that corner where *Stonehenge* sits. Because of its long tradition, the creature comforts of every chair and settee and every cushion and pillow in that corner are off-limits to any who are not accredited members of that august court.

The real Stonehenge — the one on England's Salisbury Plain — is thought to be a neolithic structure, possibly from the early Bronze Age. A date has been affixed — as I discover in one of the books in the ASH library; 1680 B.C. Now, it is a wondrous ruin — but when it was first erected, there were "two concentric circles of upright stones" (I quote). These enclosed two rows of smaller stones — and a central block of cold blue marble, known as the *Altar Stone*.

Our blue marble block is Arabella Barrie.

57: It was in the lobby that Meg and Lily and Lawrence and I were to find ourselves the centre of everyone's attention following our ordeal on the beach. Because it was already dark outside as we entered, the lobby seemed to be a blaze of light; a mass of people.

Not one person spoke for fully thirty seconds.

Lawrence was still clothed in his hideous bathing trunks,

T-shirt, running shoes and my cardigan. Lily still wore her flowing robes and she and Meg were carrying armfuls of Calder memorabilia — his binoculars, his towels, the books he'd pretended to read; his rubber shoes and his smelly medicine bag. I was overloaded with my camera bag and carryall and Calder's canvas backrest, which Lily had been determined to save as "the last bit of comfort he had known..."

We were not exactly prepossessing.

"Good evening, Vanessa."

This was Arabella Barrie.

She was sitting behind me with her companions. I turned.

"Good evening," I said.

Still, no one else spoke.

Arabella's needlework was in her lap. Her scissors were poised in the open position. A yellow thread had just been knotted and waited in Arabella's fingers — cringing, no doubt — as I was.

This woman had been my mother's closest friend. My mother, until last summer, had been her lieutenant here — second-in-command of *The Henge*. Much had been made of the likeness of their names: Rose Adella — Arabella. Her place, now occupied by Ivy Johnson, was on the cushion next to Arabella, the *Altar Stone* — centre stage. I had often — much too often — stood, as a little girl, before this woman — waiting to be looked at; listened to; dismissed. Sometimes, I had to recite the events of my day — just to have it proved, for my mother's sake, I could articulate such things as luncheon menus and what some woman had been wearing on the beach.

Now, where Mother used to sit, Ivy Johnson was winding wool into a ball. The skein was held by Jane Denton. The wool was peach — the colour of flesh. Ivy was knitting a sweater for a pregnant grandchild and half the sweater was displayed beside her — armless, as if it had been designed for someone malformed. Neither she nor Jane gave any appearance of listening to what Arabella and I were saying, except — from time to time — to give a tiny nod.

The rest of *Stonehenge* — Natty Baumann, Eileen Ross and Lydia Woods (my aunt) — were glued quite openly to every word.

"It's late," said Arabella. "You've missed your dinner."

"Yes," I said. "We were detained."

"The Police detained you?"

"Yes."

I was quaking. Why was I still afraid of this woman?

"It was a stroke?" Arabella pulled at the knot between her fingers. "A stroke he died of?"

"Yes. A stroke, Arabella."

"The Police have confirmed it then?"

Her eyes made the briefest detour in Lawrence Pawley's direction.

I did not know how to answer this, since the Police had neither confirmed nor denied what Lawrence had stated. All they had acknowledged was that a body had been found on the beach.

And so, I lied.

"Yes," I said. "The Police have confirmed it."

Arabella pulled the yellow knot into place against her canvas and cut the thread.

I noticed, then, a very slight commotion behind me. Arabella looked up — glanced beyond the camera bag slung from my shoulder — and gave a little cough.

I turned.

Over by the Front Desk — his back towards the lobby at large — was Doctor Chilcott, still in his gabardine coat. He was just in the process of taking his leave of Quinn and Ellen

Welles and I heard, quite distinctly, the words: "thank you for your kind co-operation."

I immediately wondered why on earth Doctor Chilcott was still in our midst. Because he was in evening dress, I had assumed he was on his way to a party. He had almost said as much. *I was driving by,* he'd told us; *and I saw the cars on the beach.*

Inadvertently, I looked at Lawrence.

Once again, he looked perturbed.

Arabella said; "there goes a very formal little man."

"Yes," I said. "He was on the beach."

"Like *that?*" she asked — amused.

"Like that," I said.

When I looked again, Doctor Chilcott had gone and — shortly thereafter — I heard a motorcar leaving the portico.

Arabella was threading a new colour. Green.

"His face," she said — holding her needle up in front of one eye — "is more than vaguely familiar. Wouldn't you agree, Vanessa? Was he a friend of Calder's?"

"Not that I'm aware of. No," I said. I told her his name. "Chilcott. Yes."

This seemed, somehow, conclusive — as if the name had registered for her precisely as she had thought it would.

"I've never seen him before," I said.

"Yes, you have." Said with that dreadful authority of hers.

Arabella cut the green thread and prepared to go on with her work. I was waiting for her explanation.

Instead, she gave a look at Lawrence.

"You'd best get that one back to his wife," she said — to me, as if I had prevented his going, somehow. "Maybe she can give you all some dinner."

This was the end of the audience. Arabella looked at her canvas — lifted it and struck it a blow from underneath with the needle.

I didn't want any dinner, just then.

But Lawrence insisted. Petra would give us an omelette. They were staying in Rossiter Cottage — one of three such cottages rented by the ASH — each one named for a founding family. (The other two are Barrie and Denton.)

Lily and Meg had gone away in the course of my talk with Arabella. Lily had a dreadful headache. Meg, I presumed, was fairly desperate to return to Michael. She had left him in the charge of Baby Frazier, who qualified by dint of having seen her own late husband through a massive stroke.

And so I went over and ate a cheese omelette, which Petra threw together with all the grace of a farmer feeding his pigs. Really — that girl! She was angry because we'd interrupted the reading of her book. I wish, at least, it had been a cookbook; but no — it was one of her interminable network of novels. The classics.

58: My father's posting had been to Surabaja. He had gone, at first alone, in April 1940. Mother joined him there in the autumn of 1940 — once she had settled me at Miss Hales's Academy. I myself was not allowed to join them until the following autumn; October 1941.

The dates, as I write them here, have aureoles about them. Anyone who lived through that time will recognize their significance. It is always so difficult after events to see back all the way to the innocence preceding them. The War in Europe, though dreadful, was sufficiently remote to be more like something in a film than a part of everyday reality. We saw things in newsreels — appalling, to be sure — but only barely real. When Hitler entered Paris, for instance, in June 1940 — it all looked so staged it seemed like a scene from a Hollywood spectacular. He stood above Napoleon's tomb and his presence there was so patently ridiculous the audience watching him laughed. Charlie Chaplin might have played the scene better. And so, when Father and Mother went away to Java — far away as anyone could be from Europe — the thought of the War spreading there was quite beyond all imagining.

Now, looking back and knowing what I know — and knowing what we all know — I cannot help but wonder why we went there. My father went because he was in the oil business. He was young, then — or relatively so — and eager for adventure and the allure of foreign places. Above all, the East was like a wonder got entirely from books. We all read Mister Maugham — even I read Mister Maugham, as a schoolgirl — and loved the prospect of wearing all that white and of having a dozen Chinese servants. If you were in the upper classes, there was nothing he described, outside of the sordid details of people's actual lives, that was not within the purview of what you could anticipate if you journeyed into that region. The staterooms on the upper decks of the ships that took you there — your place at the Captain's table — and the great, exotic hotels he described; they were all awaiting you — all a part of your natural expectations. The East was a place of absolute privilege, its horrors hidden far away beyond the shutters and the screens that censored everything but the smells of joss sticks and incense rising from temple courtyards.

I had all this for two brief months — and then the shutters opened and the screens were torn aside and the full, appalling picture was revealed.

The Japanese War began on Monday, the 7th of December, and it seemed to have begun a great way off. "They will not come; they cannot come," we said. It was all you heard. *They will not come; they cannot.*

And they did.

We stood in the lobby of our hotel with our suitcases packed and sitting on the tiles beside us. My father was not with us. He was organizing the destruction of storage tanks out beyond the harbour. The air was filled that night with the smell of burning oil — and the sky was lit with a light I shall never forget; the flames were yellow, orange and blue and they fed a great mass of oily clouds that lowered above the docks.

A Dutch Captain — his uniform black, as if he had bathed in crude oil — came into the lobby with two young soldiers. When the Captain removed his cap, his pale hair looked incongruous and comic, set above his darkened face — and he was as oily in his words as he was in his appearance. He kept apologizing for "the inconvenience of the destruction of the city." He was so very, very sorry to tell us we would have to surrender ourselves to the Japanese — as if this, too, was a mere inconvenience — an embarrassment of discomfort. He looked around at all our luggage and he said; "I fear you will not be able to carry so much. But if you leave the excess in your rooms, I promise you it will be taken care of by the authorities."

Of course, we never saw our excess baggage again. The world of our excesses was done for.

Mother said: "and what might a person retain, then, Captain?"

"One small suitcase, madam."

"And what is to be done with us?" my mother said.

The Captain replaced his cap on his head, effectively hiding the blond authority of his hair. And he said; "you will be interned. Until we return."

After which, he departed.

Until we return. Of course, we never saw that young Dutch Captain again. Nor any of his kind — until August of 1945.

We stood there waiting all night long — without electricity to light our vigil. But none was needed. The fires — which I thought of then as my father's fires — were ample to the task. Someone threw open all the shutters, and the white we wore turned yellow and rose and tangerine — bizarre Technicolor costumes, in the reflection of our burning city.

All of us were women in that hotel lobby.

The younger children had been sequestered in the dining-room with their Chinese amahs.

I remember very clearly, though I cannot remember what her name was — or even if she was known to me — that, just as we heard the Japanese arriving in the courtyard, one of the women opened her pocket-book and took out a bottle of eau de cologne. She opened it and pressed it to her fingertips — dabbing it behind her ears and at her throat. She smiled at me, this woman, as she re-capped the bottle and replaced it in her pocket-book.

''Ready?'' she said.

And smiled.

That was how it began — our imprisonment. In a hotel lobby — filled with women: smelling of fire and cologne.

59: I cannot sleep. It is 2:00 A.M. Since 1:00 I have sat in my window, my lights off, staring out at the sky. The moon is now a six-day moon and her image, reflected in the bay, is very pale. The sea is barely moving at all.

I should probably have stayed here, wrapped in the dark until I slept, but — at last — I've had to give it up and turn on my lamp and pick up this book. My eyes won't close. I cannot rid them of Calder's face as he lay there dead — and I see it juxtaposed against the shape of my iceberg, floating out at the end of Surrey Island. Every forty seconds, the Cape Davis Light gives its double wink and the iceberg flashes on and off. It is all surreal: the iceberg; Calder's death; the moon; Cape Davis Light; the iceberg...

Poor Lily Porter.

That night — the Friday Calder was killed — she thought her headache was going to kill her. But Meg found something in Calder's medicine bag that eased it a little and calmed her down. I brought back some pears and cheese from Lawrence and Petra and I was amazed to find Meg still with Lily. ''Baby can cope with Mike just fine,'' she said. Perhaps she was glad to be away from him for a while. She ate; Lily wouldn't. We sat, the three of us together in Lily's room, holding one another's hands — drinking Scotch and munching pears. Just like three girls at college, waiting for some dreadful crisis to pass. If only our crises now could be as simple as they were back then: an essay failed, an invitation that hadn't materialized; a dress we loved but couldn't afford to buy... Lily kept saying; ''I killed him. I killed him.'' Finally, she slept and Meg and I departed, propping Lily's door with a satin slipper — slipping, each towards a separate stairway, with waves and sighs — marching resolutely into another sleepless night like this one — swearing we could hardly keep our eyes from closing.

Then — as now — I sat in this window, watching as another hapless insomniac went wandering the beach. I could see — beyond the dunes — a light that was passing back and forth and back and forth, as if in time to music. Some weekends, the student help take their beer and hot dogs down to the beach and build a bonfire. Other times, they just go down and drink their beer and swim. Often, you can hear them laughing. But not that night. Not Friday.

Whoever this was was agitated. Angry, even.

The light went back and forth and back and forth and...

Then, it went out.

I wondered who it was.

Maybe it was Calder's ghost — gone looking for another place to count the stars.

If only he could rest. If only all of us could rest. Tomorrow — we will have to live it all again: his death — when all the front pages of all the papers will tell the world: *the inventor of all our drugs is dead.*

The thought of it makes me tired.

And the moon is gone from the sky. And I am going to bed.

60: I rose the next morning and went at my usual hour to breakfast. I found long ago through trial and error that the youngest of the children have finished their eggs and toast by eight o'clock and are eager to vacate the dining-room. They come out as I go in. This is what I call a fair exchange: they are not required to endure the dreadful silence of the old and we are not required to endure the dreadful clamour of the young.

Saturday morning, however, there was very little noise of any kind and the children remained some time in their seats. Their parents must have subdued them, one supposes, by means of bribes. I noted — at the table next to mine — that little Terry *Fidget*, the Williams boy, had been coerced with crayons into total silence. He was drawing, under his mother's tutelage, several versions on several pieces of paper of the iceberg beyond the windows. Most of his icebergs were floating castles — huge, flat-bottomed Capitols; some of which even sported the Stars and Stripes. Just as I was seating myself, I heard Jane Williams saying to him; "these are lovely, Terry. Very pretty, dear. But something's missing. Don't you remember Daddy telling you last night how much of the iceberg hangs below the water? Look; like this." And she took a lime-green crayon and put the appropriate keel of ice in its place. I could only suppose her choice of colour had to do with keeping the menacing part of the berg as "pretty," in her own words, as the "lovely" part above.

I sat and flashed my paper open. *The Boston Globe.* (*The New York Times* does not arrive at the ASH until nine.) *That's odd*; I thought, as I took my first glance. *No mention here of Calder's death.*

Not on page one. And not — as I soon discovered — on any page.

Nothing of Calder Maddox there at all; in spite of all his Boston connections — his Harvard degrees, his work at M.I.T. — his Brookline Laboratories. Nothing.

I set the *Globe* aside and paused to eat my Kadota figs before I opened my *Portland Packet*. Surely it would have something to say since the ASH was in its purview.

But no. Not a thing. Just a grossly out-of-focus half-page photo of the iceberg and the story — ("reprinted from yesterday's late edition") — of how it had first been spotted by "one of the Hotel's guests." Of Calder Maddox — not one word.

I lingered over my breakfast — savouring, as I always do, my poached eggs and toast, my bacon and my marmalade. The chef at the ASH is quite superb and the morning's eggs are always tender and the bacon *al dente*: perfection. Unlike my usual self — at least since the heart attack — I had three cups of coffee, caught up entirely in watching the parade of Saturday people making their various ways to their various tables: the families, the couples, the trios and quartets of friends, the single women like myself — of whom there are many — and the single men, of whom there are so few.

We singles — widows, mostly — have tables ranged along the northwest wall. The tables are in single file (no pun intended), each beside a window and all the windows looking out across the parking lot towards *The Dorm*, where the help live. Amongst ourselves, the guests have always called these tables *The Train*. This, because all of us who sit there face in one direction, looking over one another's shoulders — much like passengers aboard the *Twentieth Century*. But it came to my ears before I sat there myself, that the student waitresses' name for our train of ancients is *Death Row*.

The morning after Calder's death — it seemed appropriate.

I waited for Meg and Michael to appear. Weekdays, she made their breakfast herself: Saturdays and Sundays they splurged. I knew that Lily was playing the Queen and would not come down, no matter what day it was. But the Riches were late. In fact, they barely made it into the dining-room before the doors were closed at nine o'clock. I could hear the wheels of Michael's chair. They needed oil. Perhaps the damp sea air was hard on them.

Their table — with only one chair — was on the far side of the dining-room, facing the sea. I thought, at least, that Meg would wave or smile. But as soon as Michael was parked, she put her nose inside *The New York Times* and thumbed methodically through the pages.

She's looking to see if Calder's mentioned; I thought. She scanned the whole first section — then the second and then the first again. Then she set the whole paper aside and spoke to Michael. The red-headed waitress came and filled their coffee cups. Meg lifted Michael's cup to his lips and looked out the window. She did not look across the room at me; not once. It made me feel odd.

61: When I returned to my room, I found the door was ajar. I thought nothing of it; perhaps the chambermaid was still inside. In fact, as I came along the hall and saw the stream of sunlight spilling through the crack, my mind was on the gossip I might enjoy with the maid, a charming child with auburn hair whose name is Francine — or Frankie. What, I would like to have known, were the other chambermaids and waitresses saying about the death of Calder Maddox? What —

for instance — if anything, had Calder Maddox meant to their generation? Were all his tranquillizers and anaesthetics considered miracles or merely the routine stuff of twentieth-century life? To my generation, they had — of course — been miracles. We — after all — had grown up without the benefits of penicillin, sulpha drugs or any kind of antibiotic.

But Frankie was not in my room. And had not been, yet, for all I could tell. The bed was still unmade; the water carafe had not been filled; my nightie hung on the back of the cupboard door...

A chill; a shiver ran up my neck and I felt the little hairs on the backs of my hands stand up.

I had not left my cupboard open. I *knew* I had not left my cupboard open. I knew it, because I had wanted to see myself full length in the mirror and the mirror is on the open side of the door. But this particular cupboard door will not stay shut unless you put on the hook. It has no latch, and without the hook in place, it gives in to gravity and swings wide open.

I had put on the hook. I knew that.

I looked inside.

All my shopping — shoe boxes, dress boxes, sweater boxes — had been tampered with. Not thrown about, or left in disarray — but very definitely opened, inspected and left out of order.

My evening bag and my brown leather pocket-book — both empty — were standing open. I knew that nothing had been stolen from them. Nothing had been inside. But, like the boxes, they had both been opened, inspected and put back out of order.

I turned to face the rest of the room with some trepidation.

What of my valued things? My cameras, my books? (I keep my pearls and Mother's rings in the office safe.)

All there.

But the cameras had been opened.

I thanked my lucky stars I had removed the film.

I also thanked my lucky stars that, since I intended to have the film developed at the Maine Mall later that morning, I had already put it — all four rolls — in my canvas carryall and taken the carryall down to breakfast.

But if my films had been the object of this search, then who had done the searching?

I would not be able to answer that until I had looked at the developed pictures myself. Only then could I determine what it might be that someone else must be so desperate to see. Or not to see.

62: I have already given a basic description of these photographs — but, as things turned out, I would have to be satisfied with the cursory glance I had taken when the pictures were handed over to me at the *One-Hour Photo Service* kiosk in the Maine Mall. Before I got home to the safety of the ASH, other events had taken precedence.

One of these events had to do with my driving back from the Mall. I had been past the infamous Sutter's Hill road-block twice — seen it with my own eyes — and even nodded at the State Police. Whatever "exercise" they were engaged in was certainly a well-kept secret. For all I could tell, they were simply parked there beside their blinking red lights and yellow saw-horses, smoking cigarettes.

Ever since my heart attacks, I'm leery of driving my car — afraid another attack will occur while I'm behind the wheel. My special fear is of hitting someone else. I shouldn't drive. I know it. But I do. I tend, however, to drive at speeds that only hearses get away with. I mean, I drive at thirty miles an hour. Or less.

There is a place along the Pine Point Road, as you approach the lane that leads to the ASH, where the view of the road going on ahead to Larson's Neck is very clear. The view is brief — but absolute. And, in the instant when this clarity was at its maximum, I saw another car approaching.

Not that catching sight of another car is news in itself. But catching sight of this car was.

It was travelling slower than I was—and that, in itself, is remarkable. Its driver—a shadow at first—a mere silhouette—turned out to be none other than Lawrence Pawley. It was his motorcar that gave him away; a dilapidated ten-year-old Buick—which makes me cringe with shame because it belongs to a member of my family.

Lawrence—the world's worst driver—was watching, not the road, but the trees that line the road: the pines, the spruce, the maples and the beech which constitute the woods of Maine. They make a charming study—but hardly one to conduct from a moving vehicle.

At last, our mutual approach made mutual acknowledgement a dire necessity. Otherwise, we would have crashed. Lawrence's fascination with the trees and mine with him had pushed us both beyond all awareness of our predicament. However, Elsie Northcott—arriving at the foot of the hotel lane with every intention of pulling her Rabbit straight out onto the road—at that moment jammed her horn. Otherwise, there might have been a three-car pile-up.

My Volvo and Elsie's Rabbit survived. But Lawrence's Buick rammed straight into a fence post.

Elsie—doubtless because she had averted a major accident—was blissfully unaware that a minor accident had occurred and she pulled out onto the Pine Point Road and sped away to Sutter's Hill—waving to me gaily as she went.

I pulled well off the road—parked and got out to see what might be done to help poor Lawrence.

He was slumped against the wheel, his forehead resting on his arms.

"Are you all right?" I said.

He looked up. "Yes."

But he wasn't all right. Not that he was physically hurt. He was just so deeply lost in thought, he seemed not even to be aware the accident had happened.

"What *is* wrong with you?" I said. "You were driving like someone in a coma."

Lawrence didn't answer. Instead, he slowly got out of his car and—stooping—walked around to see what damage had been done. Not a great deal. A fender had been crushed and was pushed back in towards a wheel.

He lit a cigarette.

"Do you trust me, Vanessa?"

I had to think about that. I said; "what makes you ask?"

"I mean," he said; "as you stand here looking at my fender—would you trust me to drive your car?"

"Absolutely not," I told him.

He banged his fist on the hood of the Buick and gave a heavy sigh—making me feel I had refused to save his life—or at least, his sanity.

"All right," I said—with some caution; "why do you want to drive my car?"

"I want to show you something." He looked at me, much as to say: *the world depends on this, Vanessa. You can't say no.*

How, I do not know, but I also understood that what I would be shown had something to do with Calder's death.

I turned away. I had my own crisis regarding that death. I wanted—and needed—a chance to look at my photographs in peace; I wanted to be alone; to take a few deep breaths and tell myself I was going to be all right. But what I said was; "yes."

63: The first thing Lawrence did was get his golf clubs out of his own car and put them in my back seat.

"Don't ask," he said. "I'll tell you why in a moment."

We both got in and I told him that if he was going to smoke, he had to open all the windows. When this was done, he folded himself behind the wheel and turned the key.

"Where are we going?" I asked.

"The Pine Point Inn," he said.

We drove there at thirty-five miles an hour. I suppose he felt he owed me some consideration.

Once there—and Lawrence had still not said a word about why we had come, or what it was he had wanted me to see—we turned at the bottom of the drive and sat, with the motor idling, while Lawrence smoked and I made a fan of the photographs in their envelopes and tried to keep the smoke from choking me. We sat there for two minutes on his instruction. Then he spoke.

"I don't want to tell you anything yet," he said. "I want you just to look around and tell me what you see. Anything that strikes you as odd."

I stopped fanning and stared.

"To begin with," I said; "I can see two limousines, a Mercedes-Benz and a BMW; all drawn up to the portico. I'd have to call that unusual, I guess. The limousines, I mean."

"Good."

"There are also two police cars."

"Good."

"And there are several..." (I counted.) "There are five rather humourless men in five very similar suits—and all of them are congregated on the steps of the hotel."

"Very good. Excellent. Now, we can go."

"Go?"

"Yes. Back down the road towards the ASH."

He threw the car into gear and put us in motion.

"I've already done this three times this morning," Lawrence told me. "That's why I brought the golf clubs. In case I got stopped. I wanted to have some good excuse for being here."

The Pine Point Golf Club was on our left; the woods on our right and—beyond the woods—the sea. With the windows open, the surf could just be heard.

"I want you to keep your eye on the right-hand side of the road," Lawrence told me; "the whole way back to the foot of our drive. That's very important; the *whole* way back—no blinking."

As Lawrence drove, I did as he asked—though I must admit I blinked once or twice.

When we finally arrived where his Buick had struck the fence post, Lawrence stopped the car and said; "all right; tell me what you saw."

"Trees," I said.

"Trees, yes. And what else?"

"Hilliard's Greenhouse and Nursery. The D.A.R. Retirement Home and... Nothing else. Trees."

"Trees, trees and more trees? Is that it?"

"Yes."

"Good," he said. "Now; can you remember what Doctor Chilcott said when he arrived last evening?"

"Something, I think, about seeing the police cars down on the beach..."

I went no further.

Lawrence was smiling.

He must have perceived the truth of it dawning on my face: no one could possibly have seen those cars on that beach if they were "driving by." They could not have seen the *beach*. Not anything. But trees.

"Oh," I said. "Yes," I said. "I see."

"Exactly," said Lawrence. "Doctor Chilcott lied through his teeth."

64: Lawrence said there was more.

I told him I didn't think I could take any more. "It's eleven o'clock," I said. "I don't feel well—and I want to go and lie down."

He said; "all right. You can come and lie down at Rossiter. Petra can pamper you; we'll send the children out to ride their bikes—and I can fill you in on the rest of what I've discovered."

"I have to go to my room," I said. "It's imperative." I was thinking of my pills. My photographs.

"All right. Go to your room. Do whatever you mean by imperative and come straight over to the cottage."

I wanted none of this; I wanted peace—not Petra—children—chaos—and more intrigue. I must have heaved a sigh—disconsolate.

"I insist." Lawrence said and gave his *doctor-smile*. "If you don't," he said; "it may well prove injurious to your health."

I gave up.

Lawrence drove the Volvo to the ASH and said that, while I was in my room, he would go back down to the end of the lane and retrieve the Buick. I made him promise to park the Volvo under the trees. I didn't want it sitting out in the sun. He promised. I should have known better, of course, than to trust him. When I had occasion to use the car next day, I found it full of flies—its windows still rolled down—and sitting squarely as far away from the trees as it could get. There was also a tiny scrape along one side, where he'd hit the post on his way into the lot. Thank heaven Lawrence is not a surgeon. The malpractice suits against him would be legion.

65: When I arrived at my room—having commandeered the elevator in order to circumvent the attack of angina I felt so certain was imminent—I discovered Frankie hard at work in the sunlight, stripping my bed.

"Morning, Miss Van Horne," she said.

"Good morning, Frankie."

I marched straight over to the table in the window where I write this book and snatched up a bottle of pills. What I hadn't dared tell Lawrence was that—much as I might complain about his appalling lack of ability to concentrate — my own ability to concentrate was showing signs of rebellion. I had forgotten—of all things—to take any medication with me that morning.

By now, I was truly in a panic and tried to swallow one of the pills without the usual glass of water. Consequently, I choked.

Frankie dropped the pillows on the floor and raced to the sink. Filling the glass—she asked if I wanted her to clap me on the back. *No!*

I thrust my hands out, and spilling much of the water on the floor, I threw the glass against my lips so hard I almost broke my teeth.

"You sure know how to scare a person, Miss Van Horne," said Frankie. Even her freckles had paled.

"All I can say," I said between breaths; "is I'm certainly glad you were late making up my room this morning. Otherwise, you wouldn't have been here with that glass of water when I needed you. Thank you." I handed the glass back over. She filled it again and put it into my hand. Then she went back to her pillows.

"Not me you should thank, Miss Van Horne," she said. "Thank the gentlemen who came and asked all the questions. That's what delayed me."

Her back was to me. She had one pillow under her chin and was shaking out a clean white pillowcase.

"Oh?" I said. I was busy extracting my pocket-book from the carryall and putting the bottle of pills inside amongst the key chains, lipsticks, wads of Kleenex and my change purse. "What gentlemen who came and asked all the questions? Not more reporters about the iceberg, I trust."

"No, ma'am." Her back was still to me, and the pillow thudding down into the case. "Not about the iceberg. Just about…"

The telephone rang.

It was Lawrence — though I could hardly believe it,

thinking he must still be off at the foot of the drive.

"Why aren't you here?" he said.

"I'm on my way," I told him.

I hung up, looking askance at Frankie. She had finished covering the second pillow and was plumping them both in place at the head of the bed.

"Those gentlemen," I said. "You were saying?"

"Oh..." Her attempt at nonchalance was ridiculous. She became no longer my freckled Frankie but a swan-necked *Francine*; innocent—limp wristed—evasive. "That was nothing. Just a few questions about the Hotel."

I was preparing to vacate the room. I knew, by her manner, she was lying. I tried to laugh it off. "I hope you didn't tell them anything you shouldn't," I said.

She looked up—actually alarmed.

"Oh, *no*," she insisted. "Nothing I shouldn't. They told me Mr and Mrs Welles had given them permission."

"Ah, well. They were more than likely Health Department Inspectors. Or, perhaps, the Fire Marshals."

I got no response to this. She simply went about her business—pulling the coverlet tight at the foot of the bed.

"I have to hurry, Miss Van Horne," she said.

And so did I.

66: Under the portico, I paused and looked past the crowded tennis courts towards Rossiter Cottage. Lawrence was already standing out on the stoop awaiting me—a glass of beer in hand. Crowding through the door behind him, passing around to the shaded side of the cottage, his sullen children—Hogarth and Denise—picked up their dull blue bikes and rode away towards the Pine Point Road without so much as a wave or a word of goodbye.

I started across the compound, skirting the courts, avoiding contact — eye or otherwise — with those who were playing there. I wanted no other conversation than the one I was about to have with Lawrence—the one I had objected to; the one that promised *more*.

I could see my cousin Petra—seated on the south porch of Rossiter—leaning back in her chair—her fingers dabbling in her hair—intensely reading, as always. Her hair, it seemed, was shorter every summer so there was less and less to dabble with. Because the porch she sat on is heavily screened and shaded, I could not tell exactly what she wore. But I knew that whatever it was—its colour would be military: khaki, blue or green. There was never any variation beyond that chosen range. Her shirts, her skirts, her jackets and her jeans were issued exclusively—so it seemed—by the Pentagon.

The joke in this apparel lies in the fact that, whatever the Pentagon might be up to, Petra is always on the other side. She only wears army surplus, I guess, to prove there *is* another side—in uniform.

67: Lawrence greeted me almost pleasantly.

"Welcome," he said. "You don't come over here enough."

I reminded him I'd been there only the previous evening, eating an omelette and stealing pears and cheese.

"That," he said; "was an emergency. Emergencies don't count."

He ushered me into the cool interior, letting the screen door slam behind him. I noticed, as I went, the Buick with its dented fender, sitting under the trees. It looks so utterly unlike a doctor's car that only its licence plates give it away—with their MD code. The Buick itself is covered with dust and scrapes and scratches. Its bumpers are rusting and its tires are ancient. Whatever Lawrence and Petra do with their wealth—which, knowing the size of Petra's inheritance from Uncle Benjamin—and knowing, also, the lucrative practice Lawrence has in Stamford, Connecticut — I can hardly

believe the way they live—the way they dress themselves and
their children. The meagreness of their respect for even the
least of wealth's accoutrements—a decent car—a decent
wardrobe—a sense of decorum—alarms and confuses me.

Lawrence made room for me to sit on the book-strewn sofa
and offered me a beer.

"Thank you, no," I said.

"Oh, yes," he said. "Of course. Some grapefruit juice."

When this had been produced and both of us were seated
and more or less comfortable—Lawrence launched at once into the *more* he had promised.

His method of exploring this was very much in the Holmesian mode of question and answer. But, in spite of Lawrence's
profession, it was I who was cast as Watson.

First, he asked me to consider the fact that Doctor Chilcott
had not—as he claimed—been able to deduce the crisis of
Calder's death on the beach by means of having "seen" the
police cars there. How, then, *had* he become aware of what
was happening?

I shrugged. I could not even begin to guess.

Lawrence said; "go back to how the Police arrived."

"They were late," I said.

"Not only late, but late by over an hour and a half."

"Indeed."

I waited.

"Why do you think they were late?"

"They said it was because they had gone to the wrong hotel.
They said—I don't remember the very words—but it was
something like: *we didn't know who we were looking for.*"

Lawrence corrected me; "no," he said. "What they really
said was: *we didn't know* whose body *we were looking for.*"

He was right. I remember that.

"Now," said Lawrence; "what I'm going to say next is
very, very important."

I interrupted him.

"Are you sure we want to go into this?" I said. "I certainly don't want to hear it. This morning we had an accident. Also, this morning, someone searched my room. Enough is enough. We've all just been through a death."

"But it wasn't just a death, Vanessa; it was a murder."

There.

The word had been said.

I was at a loss. I couldn't even drink my grapefruit juice. I did, however, stand up.

Lawrence continued. "Let me take you back to what the Police said."

The room was growing increasingly stuffy with the smoke from his cigarettes. I walked to the door that led to the screened-in porch and leaned against the jamb. I closed my eyes. I could smell the sea. I could smell—I swear—the iceberg. I also heard the slow, deliberate turning of a page. Petra.

Lawrence—behind me—quoted the Captain of Police. "*We went to the wrong hotel* was the first thing he said; and *we didn't know whose body we were looking for* was the second thing he said. Now, Vanessa; put the word *because* between those two statements."

I hesitated—already rebelling against what I sensed was coming.

"Say it, Vanessa. Please. If you say it—you'll hear it. Otherwise, you won't."

"All right." I sighed like a petulant child being made to recite a poem for Arabella Barrie and Co. My back was still to Lawrence. I had a more immediate audience in Petra. "*We went to the wrong hotel* because *we didn't know whose body we were looking for.*"

Yes. It was a single statement. There could be no avoiding it. I returned very slowly to the sofa.

"Now," said Lawrence—who seemed in a rather unfortunate way to be relishing his role as Sherlock Holmes, sending up reams of Holmesian tobacco smoke and narrowing his eyes; "tell me how it was the Police were summoned."

"Nigel Forestead phoned them," I said. "At your instigation."

"Forget at whose instigation. Concentrate on Nigel."

I blinked.

"Nigel," said Lawrence. "*Nigel* made the phone call. And so?"

"Don't say *and so* like that," I snapped. "I'm not a detective, Lawrence. I am not equipped. Just tell me the answers. Tell me."

"No. I want the answers to come from you. Don't you see how important that is?"

"No."

"Look," he said. "If I can elicit the answers from you — and the answers you give are the ones I've already given myself— then we'll *know* this isn't crazy; what I'm suggesting. So try. Try to answer. Please."

"I forget the question."

"The question is: if Nigel Forestead telephoned the Police and—afterward—they went to the wrong hotel . . . specifically because they did not know whose body they were looking for—then what does that suggest to you?"

"That Nigel Forestead cannot be trusted to pass on a message."

Petra said that. She came in off the porch—spoke—and went on into the kitchen.

I looked at Lawrence. "She's right, you know."

"Ignore bloody Petra, Vanessa. Give me an answer."

I swallowed my shock at his vehemence and said; "it suggests . . . that they might have expected to find a body at some other . . . They expected that if there *was* a body—they would find it at the Pine Point Inn."

"Precisely," said Lawrence. "Yes. Absolutely."

"But why?"

"Think about Nigel."

"Must I?"

(If only Lawrence would laugh.)

"Yes. Who is he? What is he? How might he tell the Police what had happened?"

"He's a self-important, minor official in the Canadian diplomatic corps."

Petra came in—sat down—and added; "a pompous ass."

Lawrence still ignored her. "Before he allowed the Police to see him, Nigel changed his clothes," he said. "He presented himself in white. He gave the impression of so much importance, they actually took him aside and..."

"...treated him as if he was entirely worthy of their confidence," I finished.

We sat with the image of Nigel Forestead making his entrance onto the beach in the character of *Mister Forester.*

"What did he tell them on the phone, Vanessa? This is where I get lost," said Lawrence.

I was silent.

Petra said; "if they went to the wrong hotel—then he must have forgotten to tell them where he was calling from."

"Forgotten?" This time, Lawrence was neither impatient with her presence nor unforgiving of her words.

"Well, if he's a self-important pompous ass," said Petra; "isn't there every likelihood he might assume they would know where he was calling from?"

"Some—but it's slim," I said.

"Go on," said Lawrence. "We can come back to that. Get to the part about not knowing whose body they were looking for. The thing is—if Calder Maddox had died—would Nigel Forestead—*diplomat extraordinaire*—be apt to say so?"

"No," I said. "Of that I am absolutely certain. His rule book would demand that he not discuss the victim's identity over the telephone. Especially when the victim is a national..."

Petra suddenly laughed. I looked at her sharply.

"...figure," I finished.

Petra shrugged. "I thought you were going to say *national treasure*."

I went back to painting my picture of Nigel, jammed in the humid hot-box of the telephone booth. I described him watching Judy, the girl on the Desk, to make certain she wasn't listening in to his conversation. Here, after all, was the man who left his family behind to save his briefcase; the man to whom protocol and self-preservation were everything. Such a man would surely feel compelled to withhold the name of the victim—but he would have to—being Nigel—underscore the importance of the victim. The importance of the victim was all that lent importance to his call, and thus to him.

"Good!" said Lawrence. "Now—let me go one more step. If what Nigel said to the Police was something like: *I insist you come because we have a very important person here who has died. On the beach*. And you combine that with the statement: *we went to the wrong hotel*, what do you get?"

"Exactly what we did get," I said. "An hour-and-a-half's delay."

Petra kicked her shoes off and spoke as one who knows what others can only guess. "They went to the Pine Point Inn," she said; "because there really is someone there whose death—if it occurred—would warrant three police cars and the presence of the Police Chief. All without a sound..."

We looked at her.

"Well," she said; "it's true. I didn't hear any sirens up here. Not when they went to the Pine Point Inn."

Lawrence was silent. So was I.

Only Petra could continue. "And when they discovered their mistake—they came on down the beach of the Aurora Sands Hotel—all sirens blaring."

"Go on," said Lawrence—very quietly.

"What do you mean go on?" Petra asked. "I've told you what happened."

"No, you haven't," said Lawrence. "You haven't explained why it took them an hour and a half to get here."

"I can't answer that," said Petra. "It's somebody else's turn."

"Well," said Lawrence; "I guess it must have something to do with whoever the other important person is. Up there at Pine Point."

"What about Doctor Chilcott?" I wanted to know. "Where does he fit in?"

Petra had no problem with that. "When word got back that our very important victim was Calder Maddox," she said; "then a very important doctor was dispatched post-haste to discover what had happened to him."

Very important doctor? Chilcott? I didn't understand.

"But, of course," said Lawrence.

I still didn't understand.

"His practice, Vanessa, is in Bethesda, Maryland." said Petra. "Didn't you know that?"

I felt cold. Then hot. I flushed.

Arabella Barrie had been right. I simply hadn't twigged when she'd told me I knew him. Concentration—memory again.

I "know" Doctor Chilcott the way most people do, from having watched him day in, day out, three years ago, during the weeks that followed the President's by-pass operation. Every night, for almost a month, Doctor Chilcott had appeared on the six-o'clock news.

Perhaps it had been the gabardine coat, the evening dress

and the Homburg that had fooled me on the beach. But they shouldn't have. Looking back, I even see that I have written—after watching him bending over Calder's body: *he was small—immaculate—precise*. The same three qualities that had so impressed the nation when he held our President's life in his hands three years ago.

I dare not consider who else might be down at the other end of the beach. I don't want to know.

68: All that remained of our conversation was conducted by three different people than the trio who had begun it. We sensed now that we knew something. It was the difference between suspecting you have a cancer and discovering you have.

"Calder's death isn't even mentioned in the papers," I said. "There isn't a single word. Not anywhere."

"I know," said Lawrence. "It was after I saw the papers I thought I'd better check the road."

"You knew all along he was lying, didn't you. Doctor Chilcott, I mean. It bothered you, even last night. I could tell."

"It was knowing who he was that bothered me," said Lawrence. "Knowing who he was and wondering why he'd lied. A man in his position doesn't need to lie."

Petra coughed and raised an eyebrow.

Lawrence looked away and stood up.

A horde of images was flooding out amongst us; of gestures and of groupings on the beach that had merely been bothersome when they first occurred. On the beach, the Police and Doctor Chilcott had been rude; authoritarian—almost brutish. Now, those gestures and those groupings were reforming and making sinister images with which we could barely cope.

"What are we going to do?" I finally said. "What can we do about it?"

Lawrence shrugged—unwilling to answer.

But Petra said; "nothing. It's none of your bloody business. If they want to bump each other off—so much the better."

69: For someone with a heart condition, the taking of a pill can be exhilarating—then tiring. There's a wonderful sense, at first, of having been saved; of having survived; of having your life pumped back into your veins. It depends which pill you've taken, of course. I have several to choose from.

No. Not to choose from. They choose themselves according to the crisis. The pill I had taken earlier, up in my room, was potent. My others were less so—alleviators—tamers of varying degrees for the varying degrees of what we have been taught to call *anxiety*. I dislike that word, when given in the context of prescriptions, pills and palliatives. My own preferred word is *apprehension*.

Petra was neither right nor wrong when she said that Calder's death and Chilcott's involvement in it were none of our business. Whatever the moral question—whatever the ethical question—it had to be our business because it had foisted itself upon us. Petra might as well have said the iceberg was none of our business. But the fact is—the iceberg is out there — throwing its shadow over our beach. And Calder's death is the same. It is *there*. And so is Chilcott; *there*.

Now, I even remember his first name: Thaddeus. A few hours before, I hadn't been able to place his face. I wish it had stayed that way — but it hadn't.

And now I wanted a pill to curb — if not to wipe away completely — the mess we had stumbled on. I wanted the mess to go away — or, at least, to assume proportions with which I could deal. If only what was happening would clarify; clear up its fuzzy edges; come completely into focus.

Though I know there is no comparison in terms of impact — the feeling I was beginning to have was reminiscent of Java,

1942. The sweep of those larger events — which no one could truly believe were happening — was drawing closer; forcing a daily dose of reality down our throats. Back then, we sat in our houses and hotels listening to radios and scoffing. The leaps of the invading Japanese armies so took our breath away, we decided they could not be real. Hong Kong had fallen? The Malay Peninsula? The island of Singapore? All "impregnable" — all now subdued — defeated — in enemy hands? *Impossible*. Surely, we said, they won't come here. They *can't* come here!

It wasn't only that we were fools and blind; our blindness and our foolishness were willful. What was the drug we took back then, I wonder.

I can only think it was those prescriptive words on which we fed each day: it cannot happen to me; it cannot happen to us; it cannot happen here.

And when it did, we claimed we were not responsible — which, I guess, is sort of the same as saying: *it was none of our business*.

On March 9th, 1942, the Dutch East Indies fell. Within a week, my father, my mother — and all European and American nationals — were interned.

No. This is not the same. But the blindness is. And its willfulness.

70: I took the sound of bicycles out in the yard beside the cottage as my cue to leave. The children had arrived.

I looked across at Petra — even as I rose—to see what sort of reaction her returning children aroused. Her divorce from them was legendary within our family; not unlike the divorce between her mother and herself. Aunt Lydia simply isn't "in" to Petra. Neither is Petra "in" to Hogarth and Denise.

She puts things in front of them — calls it food and tells them to eat. She dresses them, as said, in drab. She even needs from time to time, it seems, to be reminded of who they are. Much more often, she needs to be reminded of where they are — though the where might be as close as the very next room. It is not — (I don't know how to describe this) — a lack of love or a lack of concern; it is simply a lack of awareness. I think that Petra isn't quite with us in this world. She drifts beyond us, somewhere.

Though I'm really her cousin, Petra has always regarded me as her aunt. There's a twenty-year difference in our ages and I suppose — in her eyes — that makes me a candidate for smelling salts and lace caps. The difference in our ages is due to the fact that Petra's mother was my Uncle Benjamin's second wife.

More important, I think, is her way of creating distance between us; the habit — unique in my experience — of casting the people around her as background characters in whatever book she happens to be reading. This means that few of us get to impress our actual selves upon her. Instead, we dance along the edges of her text, slipping into and sliding out of focus.

The whole of last summer, for instance, the entire population of the ASH was trapped with Petra inside *Remembrance Of Things Past*, while she worked her way through every word of its complexities. This marked the longest period of time I have ever been cast in a work of fiction. The shortest period was when she was four or five in the early fifties and reading *Peter Rabbit*. Not that anyone is assigned a specific role in these fantasies; it is just that the world of Petra's books is extended—fully fleshed—beyond the pages while she reads. Consequently, for the duration of *Peter Rabbit* the adult world around her was cast among the leafy heads of lettuce and of cabbage. Props in a pop-up garden.

In fairness, it must be said a person can find herself deeply involved, whether wanting to be or not, in certain aspects of Petra's reading. During her Proustian period she caught us all up in the Dreyfus case. We were divided into camps of Dreyfusards and anti-Dreyfusards, and for about two weeks, the sense of *fin de siècle* became a little too real and more than a little provocative. It caused a number of highly emotional exchanges and at least one schism that is permanent; Arabella, a Dreyfusard, has not yet broken the silence she established last August between herself and Myra Audley. Myra was very definitely an anti-Dreyfusard and believes to this day that Esterhazy's death—in fact quite peaceful—was the result of a Zionist plot. Since Esterhazy has been dead for over sixty years and Dreyfus—the man he ruined—dead for over fifty, I dare not think where this places the political currency of my fellow guests.

Presently—and most unfortunately—I notice that Petra is reading *Death In Venice*. This is almost too alarmingly appropriate. And, I suppose, amusing. Now we shall all be cast as Thomas Mann's vacationers, circa 1913, sitting out an otherwise perfect summer on the Lido, watching for signs of the plague... Need I say more?

The very name of that story's hero—Aschenbach—sends a shiver down my back, considering the name we have given our Hotel. And since I have read that little novel more than once myself, I dread the hour when Petra turns its final pages and finds the image there of Gustave von Aschenbach, dead on the beach in his chair.

I wonder if—when that page is turned—she will still be saying: *it's none of your bloody business.*

I fear it may be so.

I took my leave full of apprehension. Anxiety had nothing to do with it.

71: That I had failed to grasp that my would-be thief of the early morning was Nigel Forestead astonishes me. It goes to prove, however, that events of importance to some have no importance at all to others. Nigel must indeed have presumed I had taken his picture Friday in the fog—the day Calder died. And of course, I had not. How he must have agonized, not being able to imagine this! He truly seems to believe the motto of the world is: NIGEL AT THE CENTRE.

My discovery of his guilt came about by accident.

Having returned from Rossiter Cottage, I was sitting by this table in the window. I opened my packets of photos. I wanted to see what evidence they might provide to bear out Lawrence's theory of Calder's having been murdered.

The first thing I looked for was strangers. But the only stranger I found was the iceberg.

I set all the iceberg photos aside.

Nothing; nothing; nothing. Then I came to Calder's march to the beach with all his people—his entourage. One of these photographs stopped me cold.

Calder's entourage was dispersing; Lily was fiddling with her chair; Roger Fuller, the beach boy, and the dark chauffeur were walking away.

Roger Fuller and the dark chauffeur...

Where was the dark chauffeur?

Since Calder's death, I suddenly realized, he had not been mentioned by anyone. Nor, to my knowledge, had he been seen.

Not that anyone had looked. The fact was, everyone had *over*looked the chauffeur. We had all forgotten him. Entirely.

I rose and turned, and leaving the bulk of the photographs sitting on the table, I walked to my telephone. I carried only the single picture of the dark chauffeur and Roger Fuller marching away from Calder and Lily—the chauffeur looking back, as if his name had been called.

I picked up the receiver and waited for the switchboard to answer. When the girl came on—this time Cathy, not Judy—I asked for Doctor Pawley in Rossiter Cottage.

"Yes, Miss Van Horne."

I stood there tapping my foot.

The phone at the other end was ringing. Finally, Petra answered—out of breath.

"Hello?"

And I said; "it's Vanessa. Is Lawrence there?"

"What do you want?"

Taken aback, I simply said; "I want to *talk to him*, Petra!"

Truly, the young and surly are incomprehensible.

I hung on—staring at the chauffeur, who—in turn—was staring back at Calder Maddox. My heart began to race—in spite of all my pills. This man had disappeared, and his employer was dead. Surely there had to be a connection.

Lawrence was too long coming to the phone, and before he arrived—someone else had arrived. At my door.

My telephone, being by the bed, puts me out of sight to anyone coming in from the hall. When the door stands open, it creates a kind of three-sided box.

Now, the door swung wide and I was obscured.

Nonetheless, I had a good view of who was entering.

Nigel Forestead. Canadian *diplomat extraordinaire.*

There could be no doubt about his intentions. He made a bee-line for the table in the window.

I held my breath and watched him. *Dear sick heart—hold on.*

I felt as if the telephone had become my lifeline.

Nigel picked up the photos. I had removed them all from their packets—ninety-six prints. He started to shuffle through them.

At that very moment, Lawrence Pawley came on the line and said; "hello?"—very loud—and very out of breath.

I froze—and pressed the receiver close to my ear in order to muffle the sound of his voice.

"Vanessa? Is that you? Petra said you wanted to speak to me..."

Of course, I couldn't say a word. Nor could I hang up. I couldn't even put my finger down on the button to break the line. Either one of these actions would have caused an instant and audible *click*. So—I stood there, praying that Lawrence would have the good sense to hang up himself.

But he didn't. Maybe because of his doctor's instincts. At the end of an open line—a person might be dying.

"Nessa? Vanessa...?"

Nigel, all this while, was leafing through the pictures—looking for that damning, non-existent photo of his naked self.

I then heard footsteps out in the hall.

"What the hell are you doing in there?" said a welcome voice. It was Meg.

Nigel shuddered—and the pictures fluttered out of his hands. Some fell down on the floor beneath the table. Others fell beside him, under the bed.

He turned—and I must admit, his performance of "calm" was rather good; the dismissive wave of the hand; the "pleasant" unpleasant smile; the ready excuse.

"It's really quite all right, Mrs Riches," he said. "Miss Van Horne informed me I might want to see these..."

"These?" Meg asked. "What?" She was standing right in the arch of the doorway, so I couldn't see her. The back of the door stood squarely between us.

"These...photographs," said Nigel. "Of the iceberg."

"Ah, yes. The iceberg." There was the briefest pause. "Did Miss Van Horne also give you permission to enter her room?"

"Of course," said Nigel. "Surely you don't think I'd come in here without permission."

"Yes, I do," said Meg—and I almost laughed out loud. "On the other hand, Nigel, if you say she gave it to you, there's not much I can do about it, is there."

"No, ma'am." Smiling. And, oh—the smile. Uriah Heep could have taken lessons.

"Still—I'd feel happier," said Meg; "if you could forego the photographs until Miss Van Horne comes back. You wouldn't mind that, would you?"

"No, ma'am."

(Clearly, he did mind.)

"Why not just leave them, then, and we'll close the door. I'm sure you'll get more out of the photographs by having Miss Van Horne explain exactly what it was she wanted you to see."

Nigel made no answer to this. He simply gathered up the pictures—including those on the floor—tapped them back inside their envelopes and headed out of the room.

I almost died as he crossed the floor towards the door, because I could think of absolutely nothing to say if he saw me.

But he didn't see me—and I survived. He moved out into the hall and pulled the door—unboxing me—behind him. I heard him say goodbye to Meg and go his way. I also heard Meg going along the corridor and down the stairs. It didn't even occur to me to wonder why she had come up here when her rooms are on the ground floor.

I sat—at last—on my bed and spoke into the telephone.

"Lawrence," I said; "I've just had a visitor."

And I told him everything.

72: The final words above are not quite true. I did not say anything about the non-existent photograph that had started Nigel's search. I couldn't bring myself to do that. I never speak of sex. I never have and I—(never say *never*, Vanessa)—doubt that I ever shall.

When Lawrence had heard me out, he suggested I keep the

photographs with me. "They'll fit in your carryall, won't they?"

"Of course they will. They're only snapshots, Lawrence."
(I did not say merely snapshots. I have more pride than that.)

"Well—tote them for a while," he said. "It can't do any harm and it will keep certain people's grubby fingers off them. What about you, have you looked at them?"

"I was doing that when I called you."

"And...?"

"There's someone in the photos we've forgotten. And I'm almost afraid to mention him."

"Yes...?"

"He's missing, Lawrence. Someone I'd completely forgotten till I saw him again in the pictures. And—since Friday—he's disappeared."

"Stop beating around the bush, Vanessa. Tell me who it is."

"Calder's chauffeur."

There was a pause. "Good Lord. You're right."

"I don't even know his name. Do you?"

"No I don't."

"The Desk would know. Judy and Cathy."

"Yes. But I don't want to ask the Desk."

"Why not?" I asked.

"I just don't want to, that's all. There's too much at stake. We're only speculating, here; and if we start throwing out red herrings—all hell could break loose."

I waited for a moment, thinking: *when he says we're only speculating, is he saying he isn't sure it was murder?*

Then I said; "Lily Porter would know the chauffeur's name. I could ask Lily. Surely, she must wonder herself where he's gone."

"No," Lawrence said. "Don't ask Lily Porter."

I waited, thinking he must be going to qualify that—but he didn't.

"Why," I said; "can't I ask Lily Porter?"

"Because," he replied. "We don't want to tip her off."

"Tip her off?" I was incredulous.

"Yes," he said. "After all, Lily Porter is a suspect."

I see.

73: Lily is a suspect.

Yes. She is.

Lawrence is a suspect. So am I. Roger Fuller is a suspect. Natty Baumann is a suspect. Boots, the dog, is a suspect, for all that. Anyone left on the beach that evening—keeping company with Calder's corpse—is a suspect. Nigel. Meg. And Doctor Thaddeus Chilcott.

That's where I'd put my money. Squarely on Chilcott; though how or why I cannot even begin to think. Calder was already dead when he got here; so we are told. So, I believe, I witnessed. But...

Still—that's not the point. The point is—once you have a murder, someone must have done it.

Lily?

What do I know of Lily Porter—barring the fact I've known her all her life? She's five years younger than me. I know that. Her husband, Franklin, died. I know that. (In jail; I know that, too.) In 1968 or 1969—I don't know which. But I do know Lily made a splendid widow. In all her finery and feathers. Cheapening over the years. When she was a child and still Lily Cotton—still Maisie Cotton's "little girl" and "baby doll"—she dressed in pink. *Was dressed* is more like it—and only fair. After all, Lily didn't choose those foul pink things; her mother, Maisie, did. (I wonder if Bert the Watchman has yet to encounter *What Maisie Knew?*) We all knew what Maisie knew: *nothing*. Poor Lily Cotton. Her father died and her mother was an imbecile.

All of Lily's men have died, now I come to think of it—and none of them at peace. Her father died beneath the wheels of a trolley car, I think. Her brother, Eustace Cotton, died in the War. Her husband died in jail and Calder Maddox died on a beach in Maine.

And not one word of it has reached the press.

Something is very wrong. It has to be.

Lily Porter is a suspect.

That cannot be right.

Lily is a gentlewoman down to her toes. Her eyes grow tears and her fingers shake if the tide so much as washes up a butterfly. She is kind at heart and wonderfully thoughtful. Stupid, maybe—but thoughtful, nonetheless. Her taste embraces forms of madness from Moral Rearmament to worshipping at Disney World. Her choice of men is equivalent to that of a gun moll—Franklin, Calder—both of them gangsters in their way. And I have the vaguest memory of yet another man who got her to invest in a bogus chain of Homes for the Elderly. But I don't recall his name. On the other hand, she maintains a strict, though appallingly sentimental, sense of morality.

As for the joy she takes in giving pleasure—surely her mother accounts for that. *To please is to survive.* That is what Maisie knew—and pretty well all she knew. And she passed it on to Lily; infused her with it—pink and pearly and passive. Sad; because all it has brought her is tragedy.

Lily gave me this book. Purely, out of the goodness of her heart. And yet—I've already begun to castigate her—deride her—suspect her, here on these pages. She handed them over to me with such innocence. "Here," she said; "I thought you might want to write things down; the way you take your photographs." And that's what I've done.

74: Always now it is night-time as I write. The air is still and moist and I perspire. The window screens are covered with moths and mosquitoes wanting in and flies wanting out. The iceberg gleams in its place and the moon—a paring, nothing more, can barely compete. Out on the lawns, the sound of crickets, frogs and tree-toads and far away—or so it seems—the muted whispers of the waves. The curtains hang as limp and limpid as mosquito netting. Someone coughs from another window down the line. Probably no one sleeps, the heat is so oppressive.

I reach for a Kleenex and wipe my palms and blot this page where perspiration has marred the letters. All at once—just now—a day bird sang, alarmed in its sleep. The jungle might as well surround this place. The birds there sing all night.

I imagine everyone sitting as I do, wide awake and waiting. All of us in one place—each of us apart—all our voices silent—all our thoughts alike: *will it rain? A man has died. There's an iceberg. I'm afraid.*

I sat like this that night with Mother and Moira; the three of us holding hands on my cot. We wore our cotton dresses—shoes made of straw—and Mother wore a hat. Our bags were packed. One bag each—with all the diminished things we still could call our own: some underclothes—a blouse—a skirt—shorts. A spoon. A forbidden page from some forbidden book.

Mother held a rosary—also forbidden—and, from time to time, she withdrew her hand from mine and counted over the beads. I heard the occasional *blessed art thou amongst women*, even though I tried to keep her from telling the beads aloud. She claimed she couldn't help it. Habit. The Virgin expected to hear you.

Moira Livesay was just a girl. As I was—legally and nominally. On the other hand, I never thought in terms of being a girl or being a woman. All I knew was that, once—for a while—I had been a child and now I was an adult.

But Moira, in the truest sense, was still a girl—and pregnant. Everyone hated her for that—her pregnancy. The rest of us couldn't get pregnant if we'd tried ten thousand ways. All that stops in a prison like Bandung. Your periods cease, in time; the ebb and flow is gone. Most of us rejoiced in that—for purely practical reasons. Not to have to contend in the midst of starvation—deprivation—horror—made at least one aspect of our lives a little easier. But Moira's periods had only begun in the fall of 1944. That's how young she was. And she entered Bandung in the spring of 1945, already pregnant.

April. And Moira.

The father, it all too quickly became apparent, was a Japanese. Moira's mother rushed to tell us that. She wanted us to know exactly why they were there.

"This child seduced him. She was in love with him," Mrs Livesay informed us.

Moira said nothing. If Mrs Livesay had only been silent—then none of us could possibly have known; the pregnancy had barely begun—and showed not a whit.

It turned out that Moira's parents had been collaborators up in Singapore. Or rather, that Mister Livesay had been a collaborator—and Mrs Livesay had gone along for the ride, and taken poor Moira with her.

I always thought—and I still maintain—that Moira Livesay did not love the father of her child. She wouldn't speak, the first three months in the Camp—and only, thereafter, monosyllabically to me. Her mother disowned her—and refused to sleep in the same barrack. Consequently, Moira ended up in my barrack, sleeping on the floor beside my cot. She refused to share the mattress with me—jerking away whenever I tried to persuade her at least to rest at my feet. I did, however, persuade her—after weeks of protest—to share my mosquito netting, torn and tattered as it was.

She was such a pretty child; with honey hair and soft blue eyes as pale as flowers. I loved her—I think.

Don't lie, Vanessa. Yes. You loved her. As a parent loves a child. She became, in the end, entirely your own.

She did.

She was rejected and reviled by many. Not by all—but many. Far too many—given the fact that we were a congregation of women entirely and Moira, after all, was our sister. Still. A congregation of women is human as any other congregation—and it is all too human not to forgive. I know this very well, myself—since I have not forgiven many; and stake no money on the chance I will.

75: That night that was like this—the night at Bandung when the three of us sat on my cot—my mother and Moira and me—we waited, wide awake, through all the dark and all the dawn and even the first two hours of daylight.

It was unbearable—the tension there; the sense of apprehension. Late—late in August it was; of 1945.

The War, in fact, had been over fourteen days and nights before we heard of its conclusion. The Colonel stood before us in the rain one afternoon and spoke with a terrible simplicity—telling us a bomb had fallen on his city, Nagasaki. And he said: *the bomb has fallen down on all of us and it is over, now.* The War. Forever.

We thought this meant we were free to go. But he told us: *no.* We were to wait. *And in the morning . . .* he said. And did not finish. He saluted us. He turned around—and went away. And we never saw him again. The Lord and master of all our days and nights since June of 1942.

And we sat—that night that was so like this—and thought about the bomb that had fallen down on all of us and no one understood what he'd meant by saying that—and so we gave it up and simply waited for the morning and our freedom. Mother and me and Moira.

I had been delegated—left, is more like it—to shepherd Moira through the gate. Mrs Livesay was off in her own daft world of mixed betrayals—ready to throw herself on the mercy of whoever first appeared at the edge of the jungle where the road to the rest of the world emerged.

But no one came. And we did not go out. And Colonel Norimitsu and all his men had disappeared. And Moira's hand in mine was like a thing of ice—and frozen to my flesh.

Why is it Lily reminds me of Moira? And why, I wonder, am I suddenly afraid for her?

76: Here is a scribble—nothing more; the story of my life in passport terms. I tell it here—I place it here, because it gives me concrete evidence of what I know in the face of what I do not know.

I am Vanessa Teresa Van Horne. I was born in New York City, 16th August, 1925. Only child of Nicholas James Van Horne III and Rose Adella Woods—deceased. My father died at Bandung Prison, Java in February of 1943 and my mother at Slattery's Private Hospital, Borough of Manhattan, N.Y.C. in January 1985.

Occupation: Landscape Architect.

Attended Miss Hales's Academy, Philadelphia and Smith College, Northampton, Massachussetts—one semester only.

Imprisoned, March 1942 to August 1945 on the island of Java, Dutch East Indies—now Indonesia; three months internment at Surabaja—thirty-nine months at Bandung.

Anything else?

Well—yes. I was born in the year of the Ox, the children of whom—so one of my Japanese books informs me: *say very little and are patient.* It says we will *achieve success* through our *innate ability to inspire the confidence of others.* But it also says we are *bigoted, eccentric* and *do not trust our parents.* We have *patience, reticence,* and *perspicacity* all on our side. Also: we are *quick-tempered, easily provoked* and—I rather like this—it says that: *others should avoid an Ox-person when she is angered because she is rash when confronted.*

So there is my concrete evidence.

And I wonder what I have ever done—to date—that might have been rash.

Perhaps that is still to come.

77: Something has now begun to happen that is more unnerving, perhaps, than anything else so far concerning Calder's death. It is more unnerving because it is neither supposition nor speculation—but absolutely factual. This has to do with an issue that—if only I had not been so distracted—I would have recognized the minute I heard of it. Now—alas—the scope of Calder's death has broadened. It draws more people into its mystery.

I have already written—and quite unwittingly—the first episode concerning this turn of events. I mean my conversation with Frankie, in which she blurted out the fact she had been questioned by "some gentlemen."

Well; the gentlemen have returned. And here is why.

78: I go back to Calder Maddox and his daily routine. Again, I rely on Lily Porter for much of the detail.

Morning: Once the sun had risen, Calder himself would have risen and drunk from his thermos of herbal tea. His breakfast tray would then have arrived outside his door and the shy, too-frightened boy who brought it would have knocked so faintly even Calder, with his bat-like hearing, might have failed to hear him. Then, with the tray on the table before him, he would ask the boy to pour the coffee and peel the orange. All of this happened every morning.

Next: the ritual of helping Calder on with his gloves. He had to wear these gloves in order to hold and read the morning papers. Something in the newsprint could make him flare with a rash for which—if it took—he would have to be hospitalized. The gloves—he had a dozen pairs—were kept together with other sartorial eccentricities—white cotton socks, white cotton stockings and white cotton pantyhose—everything white in the top two drawers of his bureau.

Mavis Davis, the Hotel housekeeper—whose name is all too real—had long ago been charged with keeping the supply of Calder's "whites" in spotless condition. She nearly went mad with counting them. Once, he accused her of stealing them; *all*. Calder never made his accusations by halves. One missing glove was tantamount to twenty-four. Of course, there isn't even the remotest chance that Mavis Davis would steal his gloves—or anything. The thought alone is absurd.

After the boy had left him, Calder would have read his papers—*The New York Times, The Boston Globe, The Wall Street Journal, The Washington Post*—drunk his decaffeinated coffee—removed his gloves and eaten his orange. He would then have drawn his bath, laid out his clothes and shaved and bathed and dressed for the beach. This way, he began each day; and thus he began his last.

Though Mavis Davis, I have no doubt, has been questioned

too, the important person in what I have just related is the
boy—Joel Watts.

I know Joel fairly well. Shy as he is, he makes a delightful
companion and we sometimes walk the beach together, slowly
picking our way to Larson's and back in one of Joel's rare
bursts of talkative energy. He winds up, silent for a week, and
then unreels the whole of everything he has to say in a non-
stop, breathless display of words. I knew him first last season,
when he brought my mother's breakfast tray and became
intrigued with my cameras. He is one of the nicest lads I have
met in many a year of good and decent lads who serve in this
Hotel. It pleases me that he returns the favour of my trust and
liking — and it was only because of these, I am certain, that he
came to me on the sand today with the tale that follows.

79: Two men — he did not call them *gentlemen* as Frankie had
— approached Joel Watts behind the Hotel last evening. Joel,
whose shift was over, was walking between the kitchens and
The Dorm. (*The Dorm* is that large, white building which we
see from our tables in *The Train.* Our summer help — all
students — live there. In my mother's youth, *The Dorm* was a
stable for the horses.)

Both the men in question put themselves forward in a very
easy manner — pleasant, gossipy about the weather, full of
questions about the district — the perfect *perfect strangers.*
Joel, at first, was leery; shy, as I have indicated, by nature —
reticent always about the approach of men in pairs. They offered him a cigarette. He doesn't smoke. They asked if he
roomed alone in *The Dorm.* He told them: *no.* They asked —
in that case — if there was somewhere private they could talk?
Joel said: *about what?* And they said: *Calder Maddox.*

"Calder Maddox is dead," said Joel.

"We know that," said the men. "It's about the way he
died," they said.

"I don't know anything about the way he died," said Joel. "He had a heart attack; that's all I know. A heart attack on the beach. A heart attack or a stroke; they haven't said — I haven't heard which one it was. I think it was a heart attack."

"It was a stroke," said one of the men. "And that's what we want to talk to you about..."

Then the other one said: "you *are* Joel Watts?"

When Joel had confessed his name, he asked the men who they might be.

"Maybe, if you co-operate, we'll tell you," said one man, smiling. "The thing is," said the other man; "we need your help."

Joel didn't care for this. He didn't care for being cornered out in the yard, with everyone else inside. At dinner-time, the yard is dead. The only people Joel could see were inside, eating — or sitting on the porches, drinking. All his own friends were either serving in the dining-room or playing their records up in *The Dorm*.

"What kind of help?" he asked.

"The kind of help that pays," said one of the men. "The kind of money that could put you through college," the other said. And smiled again.

Joel was in a panic, now. Two men — perfect strangers — were offering him money; the kind of money that "puts you through college" — and that kind of money runs to the thousands. What could it possibly be they wanted him to do, for which they were willing to pay him thousands of dollars? Two things occurred to him — and here I must be forthright, as Joel was forthright with me. The two things were: sex and drugs. The thought of either appalled and terrified him. To begin with, sexual matters, as Joel so wonderfully said; "are not a matter for discussion with strangers, Miss Van Horne." I had to hide my smile. Somehow, his earnestness conjured the image of much discussion of sexual matters *not* with strangers. As for the other possibility — drugs — Joel, like all of us, was keenly aware that only a month ago, a million dollars' worth of drugs had been seized, together with the fishing boat whose crew was attempting to land the drugs on a beach just south of Freeport. Freeport is only forty miles up the coast from here and the news had seemed to be almost local. All four people aboard the boat had been arrested and surely, Joel had reasoned, they would go to jail for a hundred years.

"Perhaps," he said — addressing the pair before him; "I should call the Police." And he turned, as if to walk away — because he thought he was free to walk away.

He wasn't.

"Maybe," said one of the men; "you don't need to call the Police."

Still walking, Joel said, over his shoulder; "oh, yes. I think I should . . . "

By this time, both the men had followed him and one of them, now, got round in front of him and blocked his way.

"Oh, please," said Joel. "I haven't done anything — and I don't know what you want."

"We want your help," said the man in front of him. "We *are* the Police." And he flashed his badge in Joel's face.

It should be said that Joel Watts is anything but blind. His vision is quite exemplary. And quick. It comes, he claims — this quickness — from playing video games. The badge that was flashed in his face was not; "very definitely not a policeman's badge, Miss Van Horne." He couldn't tell what it was precisely; his "video-eyes" were not *that* quick — but he knew a policeman's badge is kept in a black leather wallet. This badge — the one he was shown — was kept in a pale blue wallet; possibly leather.

It was not, however, the badge alone that persuaded Joel to walk down the drive towards the road with the men. It was having seen, as the man before him reached for his badge, a shoulder holster — worn in a fashion he could only judge — (from movies and television) — was the accepted fashion for men whose violence was officially sanctioned. At this point, he hardly cared who did the sanctioning. Also; the handle of the revolver had a crest or an emblem stamped on it. Something in a circle.

The driveway leading to and from the Aurora Sands Hotel is long and charming, twisting and turning four or five times as it passes beneath our stand of pines and maples. At the Hotel end, it widens into a sizable parking lot — fenced like a paddock and grassy, too, like a field in which you might expect to find horses rather than motorcars. Down at the other end, it comes out onto the Pine Point Road by the sign where Lawrence had ruined his fender. The prospect of the drive itself is usually peaceful — calming; the sort of place you go to gather your thoughts or to walk off a heavy meal.

Joel was losing the edge of his fear and gaining the edge of his curiosity. Here was a scene like a scene in the movies. Maybe that was all it was. A kind of game. Certainly, it bore no resemblance to anything he'd ever encountered before.

They went along the drive beneath the trees — the two men — the boy — looking, perhaps, for all the world like brothers; two older brothers, suited and fresh from the city, come to visit their younger brother, blue-jeaned and T-shirted, working his way through college at the great Hotel.

Working his way through college.

It was now they came back to it; the money and what they wanted.

Of course, they had not intended to offer Joel Watts a sum that was anything like the thousands he'd feared. But they spoke of hundreds.

The subject — as already stated — was Calder Maddox and his death.

"We understand you took his breakfast to him every morning."

"Yes. He always had the same. And he liked to have his orange peeled."

"He tip you?" one of them asked.

"Well — yes — he did," said Joel. "I took the tray up every morning, even the days I wasn't on breakfast duty. Mister Maddox had a thing about his routine. He couldn't stand to have it changed or for anyone to get it wrong. If I ever got it wrong, he'd yell at me."

"You like him?"

"Well..."

"You did and you didn' t."

"Yeah. He could be mean sometimes — but mostly he was okay, I guess. I kinda felt sorry for him; all those allergies and everything; his age. He didn't seem to have many friends — but, then, he didn't seem to want too many friends."

"You noticed?" said one man; smiling.

"A person couldn't help but notice," said Joel. "But he did have some friends; Mrs Porter was one of them. She was always in his room, or with him on the beach. They ate together sometimes, too."

"What do you mean she was always in his room?"

"Sometimes. Not like the whole day or anything — but a lot. She was there a lot."

"You ever get the feeling she spent the night with him, Joel?"

They were quite far down the drive at this point. The man who had asked this question stopped and sat on the fence. He lit a cigarette and Joel thought: *whenever they light a cigarette, they're getting serious.* He also wondered — much to his credit — what he might be doing to Lily Porter's reputation if he told too much. But — the fact was, he said; "no. I never saw her there all night. Never in his bed, if that's what you mean, when I took the breakfast in."

(Joel didn't know this, of course, but Lily Porter most always left Calder's bed by two or three in the morning; never, never later than four. I'd heard her often enough — clicking doors and tip-toeing down the halls, sighing — with all her little dots in tow...)

"Tell about last Friday, Joel," said the man on the fence.

"I don't know what you want to know," said Joel.

"You took the old man his breakfast — and then what?" said the other man — who was standing, hands in his pockets, right in the middle of the drive and staring back at the Hotel. The Hotel could not have been visible; maybe a window or two; a chimney-pot; a part of the roof beyond the tops of the trees.

"I poured the coffee, peeled his orange and got out his white gloves."

"Yeah... And then?"

"Don't you want to know about the white gloves?" Joel had thought the white gloves would fascinate these men.

"We know about the white gloves," one of them said. "What then?"

"I handed him the papers."

"Uh-hunh..."

Joel could hear a car, way off down the road to Sutter's Hill, coming through the salt marsh.

The man who was sitting on the fence spoke next.

"You sure he was alive, then?"

"When?"

"Friday morning. Breakfast time."

"He had to be. I..."

"What makes you say he had to be?"

"Well — he was," said Joel. "He died that day, but he died much later. Down on the beach."

The man who stood in the middle of the drive said something then that Joel couldn't understand. It was; "we've been told different. We've been told he died up there in the room.''

''I'm sorry,'' said Joel. ''But whoever told you that is wrong. He died on the beach.''

The man on the fence stood up and threw his cigarette down on the road and stepped on it. Joel could hear the car approaching and part of his mind — the boy part — wondered what make it was; the sound of it was deep and heavy — maybe a diesel sound — perhaps a Mercedes. But the man who had risen from the fence was talking and his voice got in the way of the car.

''What we're saying,'' he said; ''is that maybe you're wrong and maybe we're right. And, maybe, if you want to get it right, you'll listen to what we have to say. You understand me?''

The other man coughed and took his hands from his pockets and folded his arms across his chest. Joel was now between the two of them again; one on one side, one on the other.

''Listen to me, Joel, and listen very carefully. Okay?'' This was the man who'd had the cigarette; the man who did most of the talking.

''Yes,'' said Joel. ''Okay.'' Inside, he was quaking. He wanted desperately to get away.

''What happened, we figure, is that Mister Maddox passed away some time the night before. You see? The night before or — maybe — very early in the morning. Friday. Maybe just a half an hour or so before you got there with the breakfast tray. Could this make sense?''

''How can it make sense?'' said Joel. ''It didn't happen that way.''

''But we say it did.''

There was a long drawn pause while the two men stared at Joel and Joel stared back at one and then the other, trying —

but unable — to understand why it might be that these people — who hadn't even been there — were insisting something that hadn't happened *had*. Happened.

The motorcar was now much closer — almost down at the foot of the drive. Joel heard its engine shift and slow its pace, as if it would surely turn in towards the ASH. And he thought: *thank goodness — if someone comes, I can make a break for it.*

But they didn't come.

They waited; by the gate.

"What happened then?" I asked him.

"Well," he told me; "they offered me six hundred dollars. Cash."

"What did you say?"

"Six hundred dollars!" he shouted at them. "Why would you offer me six hundred dollars?"

"You haven't been paying attention, have you Joel. And that's a pity," said the man whose arms were folded. He took out his badge again and played with it, shifting it back and forth in his hands. And Joel thought: *he's playing the badge as if it was a gun. He's threatening me.* And, of course, the more the man threw the badge from hand to hand, the wider his elbows shoved against the air and the wider his jacket opened, exposing the real weapon there; the snub-nosed Magnum.

Joel did not know what to say, except that he could not say Calder Maddox had been dead when he'd delivered Friday's breakfast tray. How could he say that? To begin with; "twenty million people had seen him dead on the beach, Miss Van Horne."

"How about we make it eight instead of six," the other man said at this point. "How about we make it eight hundred dollars, Joel? Could you say it, then; that Calder Maddox died in his bed? And you found him there?"

"Why?" said Joel. "Why do you want me to say that?"

One man looked at the other.

Perhaps there was a cue-word, here; a signal; something Joel could not decipher or did not perceive. But, all at once, as if by mutual agreement, both men turned to him and smiled. Just as if, indeed, they had done nothing more than play a game with him and now the game was over.

"All right," said one; "we've found out what we wanted to know." This seemed conclusive.

"Too bad," the other said. "It really is too bad you couldn't bring yourself to accept our offer. Eight hundred dollars down the drain. That could have gone a long way towards paying for your tuition. We'd hoped you'd understand."

Joel was now completely lost. The two men seemed to be saying he'd told them something — something vital that maybe he shouldn't have told them. And on the other hand they seemed to be saying he had failed to grasp the opportunity of their visit and the full extent of the meaning behind their offer.

The two men left him, after that. They went on down the line to Pine Point Road, adjusting their jackets and running their fingers through their hair, making themselves presentable. It was only then that Joel understood the purpose of the car that had come to the bottom of the drive but had not passed. It had been waiting there — with its motor running — standing by to take the two men away when they had finished whatever they had come to do.

Before he turned and made his own way back to the safety of *The Dorm*, Joel paused just long enough to hear which way the car drove off.

It drove towards Larson's Neck and the Pine Point Inn.

80: I've always been good at standing alone and — ever since Bandung — I've made a point of carrying my weight alone. I spent my childhood alone at Miss Hales's Academy. I spent my fifteenth summer here alone (with Uncle Benjamin) while Mother went off to join Father in Java. I made that journey alone — from San Francisco to Honolulu, Manila, Surabaja. I've been alone forever — so it seems.

The night they killed my father, I watched his blood being washed away by the rain. In my mind, the rain became his blood. Pools of it stood next morning in the Compound. I was surrounded by it — standing on an island. I was traumatized — but I remember standing there and thinking: *I dare not get down and walk.* It would have meant wading through my father's blood.

My island was just a hummock; a bit of earth that covered a bit of bulging root — the root, I think, of a tapang tree that grew beyond the fence. (The trees that grew along the fence had all been cut down for fear we would climb to freedom. But the roots of a tapang tree are vast. The tree itself was yards away.) I stood there all that morning, afraid to move. I wore — I can still feel it clinging to me — a pale, cotton dress with buttons down to the waist. The dress was old and torn and mended. My hair was plastered to my skull and some of it fell like knotted string across my face and blinded me. I wept. I wept for hours without a sound. I know I wept, because my tears were hotter than the rain. I also urinated, standing there, and the warmth of my urine wrapped itself in streams around my legs. I didn't care.

My mother — Rose Adella — leaned, all through the latter part of this ordeal, with the arms of other women about her — seated in the open corner of the wide veranda that stretched across the front of the barrack where we lived. Her flat, oval face was quite expressionless and all her unbearable beauty was left to its own devices; every trace of animation had been swept away forever. *If only my father had not been killed before her eyes.* They died — her eyes — as surely then as he did. And they stared at me as any eyes might stare at a stranger standing — crazy — in the rain.

All the other women, silent — almost comatose under their steaming canopy of tin — stood in that corner with her — watching me, too, as if I was a figure in their dreams. Some leaned back against the posts, with folded arms and half-closed eyes. Others, pressing against each other with their shoulders, bent with their arms drooping down across the railing, trailing their empty hands as women who lean from boats do, in the streaming air. And the rain that fell between us made — and still makes — a beaded curtain through which I saw, and will always see, my mother fading into the distance — borne away as on a ship. She didn't even wave goodbye. She simply stared at me and left me — abandoned.

I looked at her and told myself I was an orphan, now. I decided, then and there, that — no matter how long my mother lived — she would never be my mother again. She was now her husband's widow, and though I do not think I could have known this then, I knew something like it; that I would never allow myself to be defined as someone's widow or as someone's mother but only — forever — as my *self*.

I stood less helpless, after that. I pulled my hair away from my face and made a plait of it — no need to wet my fingers — and hung the plait inside the back of my dress. I thought: *I must stand up straight and I must step down off this place and walk across to the barrack just as if I had come to pay a visit.* I turned and looked beyond the fence where my father's body had lain all night and I blinked, I guess, a kind of prayer. I wanted always — always — to remember what it looked like there. *When we are gone,* I thought; *this place — this prison — will fill with trees and vines and I will never, never be able to find this place again.* And I was thinking that — thinking: *never again* — when I saw the Colonel standing on his own veranda — watching me.

No tin roof for Colonel Norimitsu. His roof was wooden — laden with moss, and silent. I wondered if he knew it was my father he had killed.

I took off my shoes. This gesture, at least, I knew the Colonel would understand. And then I got down in the mud and I walked, from rusty pool to rusty pool, all the way through my father's blood to the steps below my mother's stare. Looking back, I saw Colonel Norimitsu wince. He knew. My vigil in the rain had meaning after all.

81: The order of events — with all its obvious importance — depends on witnesses; on testimony. I testify according to my witness. Whatever happens next to me creates my personal sense of order. Whatever happens next to someone else will, necessarily, create a different sense of order and, therefore, a different sequence of events.

This, in part, was the meaning of Joel's encounter with his interrogators out in the lane. They wanted to impose a sequence of events that didn't jibe with his experience; his witness. Their motive was sinister; yes. But it need not have been. I, too, have rearranged the order of events — according to my ability to grasp their meaning.

Memory is like that. It buffets you with stories out of sequence. It harries you with the past and it blinds you to the present. It seems to take all its cues at random — failing to deliver what you want to know, while it offers up data that seems to have no bearing on the moment.

Of course — I know better.

Memory is also a shield. A form of self-protection. There are things we do not want to know. Only now am I beginning to grasp what I have not wanted — all these years — to know about Bandung. And only now am I beginning to understand what I do not want to know about Calder's death.

I did not want to know that anyone could die the way my father died — before my eyes. And now, I do not want to know that anyone can kill the way I fear they have — before my eyes.

To be a witness is to be accountable.

And I do not want to know that.

82: I was beginning now to be afraid of the accumulation of menace; of ransacked rooms and men with guns and questions; of badges of authority — though whose authority, no one would say — and of doctors who ministered to presidents and silenced the news of murders. I was afraid to be alone; equally afraid of the crowded beach as I was of empty rooms. I was afraid of what I was thinking and I wanted desperately not to think it — that Lily might have something to do with Calder's death. I wanted to share my apprehension with someone I loved and trusted absolutely. And so — I went in search of Meg.

83: I rang the buzzer for the elevator.

The elevator at the ASH is one of those tiny old-fashioned affairs we used to have to suffer in Park Avenue apartment buildings; lots of brass for the doorman to polish and two rattling sets of accordion gates — one for staff and one for residents; a front-door gate and a back-door gate and a little brass stool for the operator to sit on. At the ASH, the operator is always the boy on duty in the front hall. It was John, this time, who came up to get me.

"Hello, John," I said — as I stepped on board. "I'm going down to see Mrs Riches, please."

John pulled the gate closed and dropped us to the lobby — a journey long enough for him to say; "it's not much fun when you get your own iceberg, is it, Miss V.H.?"

"How do you mean, not much fun?"

"The people it brings. They're arriving by the busload, now."

"I hope you don't mean that literally."

"Well — one busload, anyway. Over fifty screaming kiddies — all wanting chips and Pepsi! I'm glad I'm not Roger Fuller, Miss V.H. You couldn't pay me to be in charge of that beach when *they* get loose on it!"

We arrived.

John pulled the gate open.

"I'm surprised the Hotel let them in," I said.

"Special dispensation," said John — and he smiled. "You can't really blame them. It isn't every day a kid in Maine gets to see an iceberg sitting on his doorstep. Specially one that's stabilized."

"Stabilized?"

"That's the word. I got it from *The Packet*. That article they did. There's a scientific explanation. Something to do with the iceberg's weight and the off-shore currents and the fact we've had no rain and the fact it's July and the fact we're in Maine and a dozen other scientific facts. They call it a *stabilized renegade* . . ."

Someone on the third floor was ringing the bell for the elevator. John gave a wave and closed the gate and slowly rose

from sight. I could hear him singing as he ascended — using
the tune of *The Streets of Laredo*:

> *"I'm just a poor iceberg,*
> *A stabilized iceberg,*
> *A renegade, stabilized iceberg am I....!"*

He sang it rather well.

84: It was now about 11:45 and the lobby was slowly beginning to fill with people from the beach who were coming up
for lunch. Older people, mostly; my own generation.

I asked if anyone had seen Meg and Michael.

"Yes," said Maurice Penderton — overly protected from
the lobby's dim light with a pair of immense dark glasses. "I
saw her running down the path across the lawn just now. I
called out *bienvenue, Marguerite!* — but I think she didn't hear
me."

"Running?" I said. "And where is Michael?"

"Michael," said Maurice — removing his glasses and
blinking at me; owl's eyes above a pencil-thin mouth.
"Michael is parked out there on the walk."

"Thank you," I said.

"À votre service, ma chère Nessa!" said Maurice as I banged
my way onto the screened-in porch and onto *The Bulge*.

I could see Michael's chair — and Michael in it — part way
down the walk. I thought: *that's funny — she's left him stranded
in the middle of nowhere and not a lick of shade.*

I started towards him — calling his name and telling him I
was coming to save him.

Suddenly, the chair gave a kind of shake — as if perhaps its
occupant had shifted his weight — and it started to roll away
before my eyes — just too distant for me to reach it.

The chair — with Michael in it — took off down the walk
and across the lawns with truly alarming speed. It was headed

for the bath houses — and all it could do was collide with them.

"Stop him!" I cried. "Stop Michael Riches!"

Everyone came running — chasing after him; one-armed Peter Moore and Baby Frazier — girls and boys and kitchen help — Natty Baumann and Boots, the dog — even Elsie Northcott, carrying her noon martini.

"Stop Michael Riches before he gets to the boardwalk! Help! Help! Help!" they all cried.

In a crazy way, it was almost a joyous scene, with everybody racing over the grass in pursuit of a renegade wheelchair. Wonderful and giving rise to helpless laughter.

Roger Fuller saved him.

The beach boy, carting seaweed in a barrow, lurched to one side and threw himself directly in the wheelchair's path — crouching like a football player — tackling the wheels.

The whole world was out of breath. And smiling. And the whole world included Michael, who — when I reached him and lifted his chin so I could look into his face — was merry as a Santa Claus with eyes as bright and full of life as they used to be when he was well.

We put him in the shade and Maurice went to buy him a ginger-ale.

"I'm going to get Meg," I said to Michael. "We'll make her pay for this!" And I laughed.

But I didn't feel like laughing. Something had gone very wrong. That Meg should abandon Michael and run away — for whatever reason — was daft and out of character as anything she could have done.

85: The bath-house yard was blinding hot and the sun, it now being noon, was doing its best to kill us all. I threw on my hat and put on dark glasses, fumbling them out of the carryall as I hurried down the boardwalk. No more running for me.

I could already hear the busload of children on the sand as I approached the beach. John had not exaggerated their energies, though he'd somewhat overdone their numbers. Still, a busload-of-children is a busload-of-children, whether there are twenty of them or two hundred. The noise was deafening.

Their counsellors were doing their best to control the children's exuberance — but faced with an iceberg, their work was daunting, to say the least.

I stood at the lip of the boardwalk, scanning the beach for Meg. The sinister effect of Calder's death had been dispelled — if only by the presence of the children. Even the umbrellas looked brighter.

I clambered down and went across the sand. I had seen Meg's back beyond the horde.

But, when I got within hailing distance of her, I stopped in my tracks and didn't utter a word.

I was shocked by what I saw. So shocked, I almost turned away.

Meg was fighting with a child.

Not arguing; not a mere contretemps, as Maurice would have said; but fighting. Physically.

I had to approach. I had to.

The child — a boy — was weeping. Meg was yelling at him: *let go! Let go!* and tugging at something in his hands. The racket they made could hardly be heard above the excited cries of the other children and — indeed — when I called her name, Meg did not hear me.

"Meg!"

The boy, however, saw me. And the look on his face, of relief that someone had apparently come to rescue him from this mad woman, was so wide and so plain that Meg, on catching sight of it, turned all at once to see the cause.

I cannot describe her face. It was unknown to me and it took whole seconds for it to rearrange itself into anything even remotely resembling the face I loved.

I didn't know what to say.

"Is there anything I can do?"

"No."

This answer — for Meg — was appallingly curt.

"All right," I said. "I just wanted to be sure."

I looked at the boy.

Meg had turned sideways — facing away from both of us. I mouthed the words: *are you okay?* at the boy — and, wiping his cheeks, he nodded: *yes.*

"You scoot, then," I said — as pleasantly as possible.

And scoot he did. He raced away across the sand to rejoin his friends.

In the meantime, just as I had been about to speak to the boy, I had noticed that Meg — in turning away from us — had put something into the pocket of her shorts and that her hand now remained there.

"I assume he had stolen something. Is that it?" I asked.

"Yes." Almost as curt as the *no* had been.

"Do you want to . . . ?"

"No." There was a beat here — and then; "thank you."

"Do you want to go back up to the Hotel or . . . what?"

"The Hotel."

We began to walk.

"Someone tried to rob me, too, the other morning," I said — in the hope that I could lighten the atmosphere.

"I know," she said. "That bastard Nigel."

"Oh," I said, ignoring her vehemence. "Well . . . you know, then."

Of course, I already knew she had been there; but I hadn't been prepared to tell her I was there, too. And her vehemence had also thrown me. Not that Meg doesn't cuss. We both cuss, time to time. But not like that; it was the way she had said it.

"Mine was photographs," I said. "What was yours?" I saw her stiffen. "You don't have to tell me, of course. I'm just . . . nattering on, I guess. You scared me, Meg. I'm sorry — but you did. I was afraid you were going to strike that child."

"I did strike him."

"Oh."

"He'd stolen . . . something of Michael's. I couldn't bear it. Grubby little hands on something I . . . I hate theft! I cannot bear it!"

"Yes," I said. "I agree with you. Theft is hateful."

We got to the boardwalk.

"Are you all right, now?"

"Maybe. Let's go and have a drink."

She started up the walk — not even seeing Michael parked in the shade with Baby Frazier helping him to drink his ginger-ale.

I said; "do you realize Michael's right there? His chair escaped."

Meg gave an almost cursory look at her husband and Baby Frazier.

"Baby's with him," she said.

Now, I was totally disoriented. It seemed that Meg was about to abandon her husband and go on walking.

"Why don't we take him back up, together?" I said. I didn't dare risk her leaving him there. The thought was too alarming — presenting, as it did, an image of Meg too callous for me to comprehend. I couldn't have dealt with that.

So — in order to assuage my fears — forgetting altogether what Michael might have felt if Meg had left him there — we took turns pushing the chair until we got it all the way to the steps below their rooms. Baby followed after us — carrying the ginger-ale.

86: Quinn Welles had thoughtfully installed a ramp outside the Pendleton apartment the first year Michael had to use the chair. Now, Meg pushed while Baby went ahead and opened doors. I stood helplessly aside — afraid to participate more than I already had.

I sat in the cool of the sitting-room, listening to Meg in the back, cajoling Michael into using the toilet.

Baby came and stood by the door and smoked a cigarette from one of the packets of du Mauriers lying on the coffee-table. Baby was like that; she lifted little things like cigarettes and drinks and rides to Boston, where she lived. Baby's money was all tied up in impossible trust funds. She had a million — but her father's stipulations had been cruelly over-protective. He hadn't wanted her to waste his hard-earned cash on her ne'er-do-well husband. This, of course, had been before the advent of Bradley Frazier's stroke — though it must be admitted that, before that dreadful event, he had been something of a playboy. Baby's father had died — but the stipulations of his will had been engraved in stone. Nothing could be done through Bradley's suffering to free the money — and so — in a relative way — they'd had to "make do" as best they could. It wasn't easy. Baby insisted — as Meg had done with Michael — that institutions were out of the question. She had cared for him at home over six long years, during which Bradley was immobilized and bedridden.

Now — he'd been dead for what seemed a very long time — and Baby was at loose ends. She hung about the fringes of various marriages, making herself useful — now a surrogate aunt — and now a surrogate nurse. With Meg and Michael, she played the latter role. A person cannot begrudge her the odd cigarette or glass of Scotch — or even a trip to Boston, now and then.

We hardly ever speak, Baby and I. There seems to be little

to say. But that morning, lounging in the doorway between one room and another, Baby said; "I think Meg's changed, don't you?"

I was taken aback.

"How?" I said.

"Colder. Less loving."

"Don't be ridiculous, Baby. Do you mean less loving of Michael?"

"Everyone. She's brushed me off a couple of times. Then she uses me. It isn't like her."

She blinked at her fingernails and took a drag on her cigarette.

"You heard her laugh this summer — yet?" she asked.

"Once," I said. "Yes. Once or twice."

"It isn't like Meg not to laugh."

"Well — I should have thought you — of all people — would understand this, Baby. It's been five years. The pressure of Michael's condition must be unbearable."

"I don't mean that. I mean — she's different. Coarser."

"Coarser?" I said. This was an astonishing epithet. One thing Meg could never be was coarse.

"All right," said Baby. "I've used the wrong word. But something's different about her. Basically different. I'm not sure I like her any more."

"Well," I said. "I *love* her. And I love her just the way she is — whatever changes may be taking place. Really, Baby. You astound me."

I tried to laugh. It had to be funny.

Baby was quite unmoved. Her expression didn't even flicker. Then she said; "you two have been thick as thieves ever since you were kids, haven't you."

"Not thick as thieves," I said. "But friends, yes. Always."

"Some people say you're the only friend she's got."

I felt oddly faint. What on earth could Baby mean?

"Whoever told you a thing like that?" I asked her.

"It's around," she said. "People notice these things. Aside from asking me to come in and mind him every once in a while, you're the only person she speaks to. Haven't you noticed that?"

"No. I haven't."

That was honest. I hadn't noticed. It seemed to me that Meg was Meg.

Or had been — until I found her fighting with that child on the beach.

"Have it your own way," said Baby.

"I will," I said.

"I'm only remarking..." Baby finished. "That's all. Just remarking."

Meg came back then — with Michael.

She fixed the chair in place by the window and turned to Baby.

"Vanessa and I are going for a drink," she said. "We'll be in the bar."

Then she went to the door — and was through it before I'd had a chance to even get to my feet.

Baby looked at me.

"See what I mean?" she said.

I saw. But I didn't say so.

Instead, I leaned over Michael's head and kissed his hair and said; "we won't be long."

87: I felt betrayed that Meg would not tell me what it was the boy had stolen. After all, I had gone in search of her just so I could unburden myself of my own deepest fears. I know that even the best of friends have rights to privacy that no one should invade. But still, I felt betrayed.

In prison, there is no such thing as a private possession — even in the deepest reaches of the deepest pocket. Nothing of

your body — none of its functions — none of its desires —
none of its idiosyncracies, failures or strengths is sacrosanct.
Or can be. All your life is lived in the open. Your mind is the
only pocket that stands half a chance of repelling invaders.
And far too often, it fails. The reason is obvious; in prison,
each and every secret — even modesty — even meditation are
threats. Think of Moira Livesay. *What is she hiding? Why
won't she show us? What is she thinking? Why won't she tell?*
Anything not identified — anything unnamed can put a
person in dreadful jeopardy. We failed a woman once — by
letting her sicken and die — because she would not tell us
the name of her affliction. She suffered terribly. We tried to
help — but kept on asking all the wrong questions. We
thought she was obtuse, at first, and then we thought she
was deliberately taunting us by refusing to answer. In the end
— but not until she was dead — we discovered it was
something congenital that shamed her. She could not bear to
tell us. We might have guessed — but we had forgotten even to
think of her pride.

Pace. Pace.

88: Still, I could not bear the silence Meg was keeping.

"A drink, you said," I said.

"Yes," she said. "A great, tall, double Bloody Mary — and
a bowl of Planter's peanuts. Look at me, Ness. I'm soaking
wet. I must have lost a pound of salt!"

She stopped midway across the grass between the Pendleton
ramp and the steps up onto the porch. She threw her arms out
wide so I could see how much she'd changed. But she hadn't
changed. She looked as vibrant and strong as ever.

At last, she laughed. "The nerve of that child! Attacking an
old, defenceless woman!"

I had to join in the laughter, thinking: *if only Baby hears this!*
Meg was as healthy as all the proverbial horses put together.

She always had been. Big-boned and tall to begin with, she gloried in her size and had never tried to disguise it. In the summer of 1938, when she was still Marguerite Mackey, she won all the hearts of all the boys and all the men at the Aurora Sands Hotel by making her entrance onto the beach one day in an Olympic bathing suit of matchless design. She strode non-stop into the furthest waves at low tide, drawing every eye and every male in her wake.

She was just eighteen that summer — the summer of my thirteenth year — and to me she was the paragon of everything a woman ought to be. Above all else — she was herself. She cared not a hoot how many heads she turned. (But she knew she turned them!) She walked without a care, inside that glorious body, and has never lost that sense of carelessness. Her hair and skin were the flawless emblems of perfect health. In any other woman, they might have driven you mad with jealousy. But nothing in Meg's character and nothing in her actions ever prompted feelings of envy or malevolence. The only flaw I do recall — and, yes, I recall it vividly — was the galling sense of certainty she had about her destiny. She would cure the world of many ills before she was through with it! Oh — what she would do with her genius!

Her natural flair for science was immense. Already, it had won her several offers of scholarships from Harvard and Yale and Cambridge and Tübingen. (She studied that year at Yale and then went on to Tübingen. As a consequence, she was in Germany when war broke out. The War, for her — because she is Canadian — began in September 1939. But that's another story.)

Meg always had and still maintains an innate theatrical sense of how to move and how to hold herself. I don't mean flamboyant. Quite the opposite. Her figure, in a crowd, stands out because of its stillness. But the stillness contains — from time to time, a sense of imminent explosions. Something is always being withheld. Yesterday, I would have said it was something remarkable. Merely remarkable. Today — tonight, as I write — I want to say: *something unsafe*. Her outburst on the beach — especially in view of all the hurt and rage she's managed to withhold so well through Michael's decline — was wholly unexpected and wholly unlike her. Baby, in that sense, was absolutely right.

Meg was always immensely strong. She might have been a swimmer, if she'd wanted to follow her body's lead. Swimming was the only sport I ever saw her engage in — but it failed to attract her sense of competition; she never wanted to win in terms of time. Only in terms of distance. *Further — not faster* might have been her motto. Recently, her physical strength has been augmented, rather than depleted, through taking care of Michael. Lifting him into and out of his chair, pushing him everywhere they've gone for five cruel years. Meg's shoulders and arms, her wrists and hands exude alarming evidence of this — of the terrible strength she has gained. Also of the tenderness with which that strength has been dispensed. Michael is like a shrivelled, starving child; almost an animal — now that the end is in sight; tragically malformed — all bone and membrane; white-haired and luminous. The strength and the tenderness required to lift and alleviate this creature's dreadful pain is what — above all else — gives Meg her eerie, contradictory aura of intense tranquillity.

So now, we climbed the steps.

We turned to our right at the top and made for the *Ashbar*'s screen door. When we opened it, I almost didn't — almost couldn't go in.

Doctor Chilcott was sitting there with Arabella Barrie. And Lucy Greene.

89: I had been leading such a private existence with Doctor Chilcott's spectre hovering over these pages that it did not occur to me that Meg would not recoil from his presence as I did. For me, it was entirely natural to turn away from the sight of him and I couldn't understand why Meg just kept on walking into the bar. Fifteen seconds later, having come to my senses, I followed her.

If only there had been a crowd. If only everyone had chosen that moment to come and celebrate the iceberg — dozens of people pouring into the *Ashbar* — strangers, especially; bodies to get amongst. But, no. Three of the dozen tables were empty and Meg made straight for the one that was nearest Thaddeus Chilcott, Lucy Greene and Arabella.

Luckily, I found my voice before she sat down.

"Let's sit over here," I said — and sat in a chair that was near the porch. "If there's even a hint of breeze we'll catch it through the window."

Meg came reluctantly and joined me; she preferred to be nearer the bar.

"We'll have to sign the bill," she said. "I didn't bring my purse."

The barman's name is Robin. In Maine, you have to be over twenty-one to serve liquor — so Robin was not a student. A soft-spoken lad of twenty-five or so, he's made a great hit with the women. Especially the older women. Meg tried to catch his attention, but couldn't. She did, however, catch the attention of Arabella and her guests.

Arabella nodded at us.

It being Arabella — we had to nod back.

She leaned across the table to her guests and spoke — it was all too obvious — of our presence.

I prayed especially that Doctor Chilcott wouldn't turn. I wished profoundly I had never discovered his identity. I didn't want to know why he was here. I didn't want to know why Arabella had called him down from the other hotel or what it was she had to say to him. She never fails to go for the jugular; the linchpin; the keystone — and, knowing that, the sight of her seated in deep conversation with this odious man

was unnerving, to say the least. He, after all, was the only one
— so far — who showed himself to be at the centre of whatever
mystery lay in Calder's death. His presence on our beach in
the wake of that event could not be construed as anything less
than sinister. And his presence now, in the *Ashbar*, was no less
sinister, given his table companions. Lucy Greene — aside
from being a woman I detest — has much importance up on
the Neck. Her husband — Daniel — is currently pushing for
— and looks as if he will gain — an important Cabinet post in
President Warner's administration. Lucy's ambitions are immense. She fancies herself a social arbiter. Her money — got
from Canadian mines — has financed Daniel's rise to the top.
On the Neck they call her *Lucy Greeneback*. Mercedes Mannheim is her sworn enemy and their social rivalry is legendary.
I have been aware of Lucy now for almost forty regrettable
years.

"Who is that man?" said Meg.

"Which man?"

(*As if I could get away with that!*)

"The man with Lucy and Arabella."

"You saw him on the beach the other evening."

Thank heaven, Robin was finally coming in our direction,
ready to take our order.

Meg said to me; "oh, yes. The one who calls himself a
doctor."

"That's right."

Meg could not care less about Doctor Chilcott's credentials. The fact he had saved our President's life means little
or nothing to her. Unless — in her amused way — she hates
him for it. Meg had never made any bones about how she
feels when it comes to our Republican wonder man. President Warner and all he stands for are anathema to her.
And for that reason, she feels the same way about Lucy and
Daniel Greene. It particularly galls her that Lucy is a fellow
Canadian.

Robin was now at our table, wiping it off with his cloth and setting down coasters and a bowl of peanuts.

"Mrs Riches wants a double Bloody Mary," I said; "and I'll have a double Virgin."

Meg threw back her head and roared with laughter.

"Rose Adella *must* be dead, when you can order a double Virgin and not even blink, Ness!"

I could have killed her. Not because of what she had said — but because she had laughed so loud.

Now, Thaddeus Chilcott could not help but turn in our direction. Arabella — beyond him — sat up even straighter than her corselet demanded. *The very idea that a woman should laugh out loud! In the bar! At noon! Judge Mackey, Meg's father, would have died!*

General Welch came through the door at that moment and broke the tension. I saw Arabella's eyes shoot over in his direction — away from us — and the tilt of Doctor Chilcott's head was altered accordingly.

Pelham Welch is a most impressive figure of a man. The same might be said of Agnes, his wife, whose moustache is plainly visible at a dozen yards. She has never, in all the years I've watched her, endeavoured to remove it or disguise it. Instead, she has turned it to good effect by adopting pseudo-military dress and a military walk. She wears her sensible, military shoes in every season, and I have a deep suspicion she accepts salutes behind the Major-General's back.

Arabella obviously thought it would be a good idea to introduce the Welches to Doctor Chilcott — *more distinguished Canadians*, she would say — smiling at Lucy Greene — and she was in the very act of raising her hand in their direction when I saw Doctor Chilcott freeze her impulse with an almost shocking curtness. He shot his own hand out across the table and literally forbade her to speak. It was that kind of gesture; an unmistakable *don't*.

Arabella fell back into the arms of her chair with a graceful attempt at a shrug of indifference. Pelham and Agnes Welch passed by — on parade — but unsaluted.

The episode had been informative.

While eager enough to hear whatever it was that Arabella Barrie had to say to him — and willing enough to pay the price of sitting in a relatively public place to do so — Doctor Chilcott was not the least bit eager and not at all willing to have his public face and all too public name be used as currency. If he must — he would sit there together with her and Lucy Greene. But he would not allow Arabella to say so. Lucy, for her part, shrugged the Welches off — as she did the rest of the world that was not in her stratosphere. Perhaps the image of Lucy Greene can be frozen here by saying that — up in Maine, in the unpretentious bar of a fine old family hotel — she had chosen to wear a hat. And gloves. At noon.

90: My intention in finding Meg had been to lift the burden of what I had been discovering — and all its consequences to date. But there was no possibility of going into that in the *Ashbar.* Certainly not in the presence of Thaddeus Chilcott. After all — Chilcott's involvement was part of what Lawrence and I had uncovered. Nor could I bring myself to speak of these matters in Arabella's presence.

I admit my fear of Arabella Barrie has mostly to do with her power as the central figure of *Stonehenge*. This, of course, goes back to my fear of *Stonehenge* as a child. Part of it, however, remains Arabella's lifelong connection with my mother. One does not exist — for me — without the other, even though one of them is dead.

Rose Adella and Arabella are joined — it seems — forever in the manner of Siamese twins. That one of them is in her grave bears not a jot of weight on the matter. My mother's seemingly empty plate of a face remains a haunting spectre. But now its overriding character is one of deep suspicion. It rides on Arabella's shoulder — ghostly cheek by living jowl — hissing from the corner of its mouth into Arabella's ear: *beware! Beware!* I could no more have spoken of Calder's "murder" in that ghostly presence than I could of my father's "murder" while my mother lived.

Ever since my father's death, my mother's opinion of that event had been that he had died in her arms, the victim of an unnamed plague. It was as if she had never seen him lying in the rain. When reminded he had died specifically because he could not reach her arms, my mother denied it vehemently. She looked upon all who tried to tell her the truth as if they had been infected with the same disease she imagined had killed her husband. But whether my father had died of bullets or bacilli, my mother preserved her own secret truth about his death and she kept this hidden in the darkest corner of her heart. For all that remained of her life, she harboured the fear that — because my father had loved her — she had been the cause of his death. And she feared that I believed this, too. Love was the disease.

It was my mother's tragedy — and mine, I guess — that nothing I might have said or done could persuade her from that belief. All the evidence I might have offered to soothe her was forbidden before it reached my lips.

91: Based on the notion that mothers — even surrogate mothers — have a right to keep an eternal eye on their children, Arabella took her role as watcher far too seriously. This woman could watch a person to death. So there she sat — perhaps the surrogate mother of us all — preventing words on every side; her own — and mine and most of Doctor Chilcott's. Lucy Greene had chosen to be silent, anyway.

Still, if I was afraid of Arabella, Meg was not.

"Do you think, when we've had this drink, we should go and see how Lily is?" she asked — quite loud. "Poor Lil — she's had the devil of a time — locking herself in her room like that — not coming down to meals — even refusing to answer the phone. I think it's time we insist on seeing her."

Doctor Chilcott must have heard Meg's words. He turned in his chair and looked directly at us. I — in the way people have of staring disaster in the face — could not turn away. Luckily, the Doctor himself had turned away and was speaking again to Arabella before I discovered — to my horror — that, of all the possible expressions I might have mustered, the one that had risen to my features was a smile. Thank the Good Lord — he didn't see it.

But Meg did.

"You like that little man?" she said. "That bogus doctor with Arabella and Lucy?"

"Quite the opposite," I replied — making sure I was facing the window before I spoke. "But I wish you wouldn't call him bogus, Meg. The fact is, he's rather well known, down here in the States."

"That funny little man?"

"That's right. That funny little man, it so happens, was responsible for saving President Warner's life."

She looked at him.

"The famous by-pass operation?"

"That's right."

"That funny little man!" she roared.

"Meg — please."

She sat away from the table and leaned well back in her Captain's chair.

"All doctors," she said; "are bogus." She failed, however, to raise her voice this time. "The lot of them."

"I think we should go and see Lily," I said. "I think that's a very good idea."

"Not until we've finished our drinks," said Meg. "I'm going to have another one — and I urge you to do the same." She moved back up towards the front of her chair. She fetched her lighter and a scarlet pack of du Mauriers out of her pocket.

The lighter was one I had never seen in her possession; an elegant butane affair with ivory sides and a silver top.

"Is that what you lost on the beach?" I said — the sort of question you ask without thinking.

"Lost?"

Her colour drained.

She looked at the lighter just as if it had set her hand on fire.

"That boy," I said. "Is that what he stole?"

"No," she said. "No."

"Oh well — I guess it's none of my business, anyway," I said.

"That's right."

She had lit her cigarette by now, and was putting the lighter away. I noticed she almost put it back in the right-hand pocket from which she had extracted it; the very same pocket into which she had thrust whatever it was the boy *had* stolen; and then — mid-way — she changed her mind and slipped the lighter into her left-hand pocket. On the table top, she toyed with the box of du Mauriers.

"Pretentious, isn't it," she said; "the way they package things."

I did not reply. She was entirely unpretentious herself. Her "packaging" was total simplicity. Today, she was wearing a khaki skirt and one of Michael's shirts. She had always liked men's shirts — and wore them well. This one was white and open at the collar.

"Why don't you show me the photographs? I'm dying to see them." She waved at Robin. "You want another Virgin, Ness?"

I shook my head and lifted up my carryall and sat it on the

empty chair beside me. I started fishing out the pictures.

The *Ashbar* was now full — all twelve tables and all the stools.

I pulled out the four thick envelopes of pictures and put them on the table.

"Some of them are icebergs," I said. "I'm rather proud of those. And some of them are..."

"Calder dying," Meg finished.

"That's a pretty gruesome thing to say," I said. I was taken aback.

"Gruesome, but true. Isn't it?"

If only she knew *how* gruesome.

Robin brought Meg's second double Bloody Mary and took her empty glass away.

"You never stop with your pictures, do you Miss Van Horne," he said, looking down at the envelopes. "Are those of the Hotel?"

Before I could answer, Meg said; "no; they're of yesterday's events on the beach."

"The iceberg?"

"Some..."

"Yes," said Robin, guessing; "that really was too bad — about Mister Maddox."

"Indeed," I said. Non-committal.

Meg was now spreading the photographs out on the table top and gazing at them critically. The smoke from her cigarette rose up around her. Robin departed to service another group and Meg began to push the pictures about — creating sequential order.

"Fascinating," she said. "These really are very good, Vanessa. The light is wonderful."

I noticed she had set the icebergs entirely aside and was making a little pile of them, one on top of the other — not like the others — all set out in series and rows.

"Don't set your drink on them, please," I said. "Tomato juice is bad enough — but alcohol is death to photographs."

I could feel myself tightening. I didn't like what she was doing. I didn't want my pictures on display in the *Ashbar*. I didn't want them anywhere on display; not these. Especially not in the presence of Thaddeus Chilcott.

"Couldn't you look at them some other time?" I asked.

Meg's eyebrows lifted in mock amazement.

"Well!" she said. "Me you don't trust! But Nigel Forestead gets the go-ahead!"

I didn't know how to reply to that. I was caught completely off guard. I could not pretend to have given Nigel permission to see my pictures — certainly not to peruse them in my bedroom. Neither could I pretend I hadn't. If I did that, Meg would immediately twig to the fact that I must have been there and overheard their conversation. What might she think of me, then — and what might she think of the photographs? Surely, she would have guessed at their importance — though she might not guess at the source of that importance.

But I was saved.

John, the singing elevator boy, came banging into the *Ashbar*; crossed to our table and handed me a note. "I've been asked to give you this, Miss V.H.," he said. Then he smiled and added; "I see you found Mrs Riches."

"Yes," I said. "Thank you, John."

John, still humming his iceberg song, went away. I opened the note; just a piece of paper, folded. I was acutely aware of the Barrie-Greene-Chilcott table; its eyes, its ears, and its stethoscope.

The note itself was banal.

Meet me on The Bulge; I read. *This is urgent. Lawrence.*

Meg paid no attention. She was too engrossed with the photographs. I edged my chair back slowly and gave a look across my shoulder.

There — beyond the screens — was Lawrence, waiting on
The Bulge. His back was to me.

"Excuse me," I said. "I'll be right back."

"Good," said Meg, still perusing the pictures. "When you
get back, we can go see Lil."

Leaving, I think I went unnoticed. Arabella was watching
Thaddeus Chilcott and he was watching Meg. If only I hadn't
given her the photographs.

92: On the porch, Lawrence said; "I saw our doctor friend,
so I couldn't come in. You're taking an awful chance, you
know, sitting in the same room."

As if I needed telling.

He guided me towards the row of rocking chairs lined up in
front of the family dining-room windows — the windows filled with geraniums. Red geraniums; yellow rocking chairs. I
had taken their picture many times.

"I'm sorry, but I had to get you out of there," Lawrence
said. "Something's happened. Two things have happened. I
found something and saw someone."

His hands were shaking.

I started to sit down.

"No," he said. "Don't sit down. You have to come and
verify something."

"Verify something — what?"

"Look," said Lawrence. "Please don't faint and please
don't speak and don't think I'm crazy."

I wasn't given the opportunity.

"I have found Calder Maddox's body."

I started to slump. Almost to fall over.

"What?" I said.

"It's still here on the premises."

Oh, I thought; *worse and worse.*

"And," Lawrence said. "There's someone in the lobby
you've got to see."

I waited — reluctant but obedient.

"Calder's chauffeur has come back, Vanessa. And he's brought someone with him."

I knew at once who the "someone" was. "Calder's wife?"

"Yes."

"Oh, my."

"She's in the lobby," he said; "and she's asking for..."

I did it again.

"She's asking for Lily Porter."

Lawrence nodded. "The wife has come to see the mistress."

Damn.

I sat down.

This time, Lawrence could not and did not stop me.

I looked back into the bar. I saw Meg sitting with my photographs. I was torn. I wanted to get her out of there — but I didn't know how. Almost anything I said in Doctor Chilcott's presence would tip him off. So I had to leave her there — and the pictures, too. And pray.

93: Did I want to protect Mrs Maddox from Lily Porter — or Lily Porter from Mrs Maddox? Sitting there in the safety of my rocking chair, I thought it hardly mattered. Lawrence had said that Calder's body was still on the premises. If anyone needed protecting in that moment, surely it was me. For a minute, my reason was paralyzed.

The visions conjured by what I'd heard were totally bizarre. *Mysterious Blonde Attacks Miami Socialite Over Body of Estranged Husband!* And, conversely: *Miami Socialite Attacks Mysterious Blonde Over Body of Octogenarian Lover!* I don't know how or why I had decided Mrs Maddox must be a blonde — but a state of mind that produces scenarios filled with *Octogenarian Lovers!* and *Socialites Programmed for Attack!* can hardly be held responsible for the triteness of its imagery.

What Lawrence said next was rather surprising.

"Have you taken a pill?" he asked.

"Yes," I said; "and I can't take any more. Pills, I mean." I looked at him and tried to smile. "Do I really look that bad?" I said.

"Pale," he said. "Yes."

Too much was happening. That was all. I was still inside the bar with Meg — but my body was out on *The Bulge* with Lawrence. I couldn't grasp what was really happening.

"I can't imagine what we're going to do," I said. "I can't imagine any of this. Are you sure we're right, Lawrence? I mean — we could be wrong. It might be more interesting, you know, if we *were* wrong. Wouldn't it?"

"I don't know what you mean by wrong," he said.

"Well — " I gestured over my shoulder into the body of the Hotel; "that woman in there; the one you think is Mrs Maddox — maybe she's just arrived to identify the corpse. Maybe she's just . . ."

"The chauffeur brought her, Vanessa."

"Well, that's all right. Isn't he *her* chauffeur? All in the family — that sort of thing."

"Think what you're saying," said Lawrence.

"I don't want to think what I'm saying. I don't want any of this."

"You told me over the telephone you have a photograph of Calder's chauffeur."

"That's right."

"Where and when was it taken?"

"Yesterday, on the beach." I subsided. "Of course you're right," I said. "When the chauffeur left — Calder Maddox was still alive."

"So?"

"So *what?*"

"So, what does that suggest? What is your deduction?"

I stood up.

"I've said this before — and I'll say it again. I will not play detective, Lawrence. I *will* not, any longer. I hate it."

Major-General and Mrs Welch strode by.

" 'F'noon, Doctor! 'F'noon, Vanessa!"

" 'F'noon," I whispered.

Lawrence could hardly suppress his laughter.

"Don't you laugh at me," I said. "I mean it."

Lawrence waited for the Welches to clear the porch before he spoke.

"All right, Vanessa; I was only laughing at you and *'F'noon.* Tell me your deduction."

"Simple," I said. "The photograph shows the chauffeur looking over his shoulder in Calder's direction. Obviously, he's taking instructions — and now — " I glanced towards the lobby over my shoulder; " — it seems quite clear the instructions had to do with the chauffeur's going to Mrs Maddox's hideaway in Boston, collecting her and bringing her back with him this morning. In his absence, Calder Maddox died. Consequently — due to the fact that no one here knew where the chauffeur was — or how to get in touch with Mrs Maddox — they arrived here ignorant of what had happened. All of which — duly taken into consideration — explains why none of the papers has carried a single word about his death. They have waited until the next of kin were informed."

I walked across to the edge of *The Bulge*, turned and leaned against the railing, folded my arms and blinked at Lawrence.

"There," I said. "Is that what you wanted?"

"Good. But you made a mistake."

I waited.

"You said that Calder had died," he said.

"He did die."

Lawrence shook his head. *"Murdered,"* he said; "remains the word of the day.

I turned away from him and stared across the lawns.

Murdered — yes — in this lovely place, was all I could think. *Murdered in this safe, congenial Hotel, where all our memories are memories of loved and loving people drifting over the lawns towards those dunes, towards that sea, in an endless parade of blue and white. So — all our memories are wrong. The violence has been here always.* And I thought; *we are the genteel Mafia — playing our family games of power while claiming we are perfect citizens; good Americans; exemplary. We only have the good of the nation at heart and...*

"You play a mean detective," Lawrence said.

"I know," I said. "And that's why I don't want to go on playing."

We waited in silence while Lawrence lit what must have been his fiftieth cigarette of the day.

Finally, I said; "tell me what you mean about Calder's body still being on the premises. Explain."

"I can't," he said.

"I beg your pardon?" I looked at him, bewildered and astonished.

"Here comes Chilcott," he said. "I'll tell you in a minute."

I turned — unthinking — just in time to see the Doctor walking with Lucy Greene — but Lawrence pulled me around again to face the lawns. He didn't want the others to see us.

When we heard the door to the screened-in porch slap hard against its jamb, and then the door to the lobby, Lawrence took my arm and hurried me in that direction.

"Don't say anything," he cautioned me. "Just fade into the woodwork. Get as good a view as you can."

"A good view of what?" I asked.

"Of what Doctor Chilcott does when he sees Mrs Maddox.

And of what Mrs Maddox does when she sees Doctor Chilcott.''

94: There she was; the mysterious, third and final wife of Calder Maddox.

She was seated on the far side of the lobby, where the arches narrow, confining the view of the lower hall and Front Desk. To her left, though out of sight around the corner, was the driveway entrance to the Hotel. To Mrs Maddox's right, the hallway led through a series of other arches towards the dining-room. Spread out behind her was the lobby proper, with its charming colours, wicker furniture and all its Chinese vases filled with that day's flowers.

It was the flowers — a mixture of Queen Anne's Lace and ox-eye daisies, purple loosestrife and burnt orange lilies — that offered Lawrence and me a perfect screen for our vantage point. We did precisely what all such people do in dreadful, unimaginative films; we pretended to look at magazines — *New Yorker*s and *Newsweek*s — while we stared, in fact, at our prey.

Our prey was a distinguished-looking woman, wearing a soft green suit of woven Italian silk and a pierrot hat with a veil that barely came to the tip of her nose. The hat, the veil and her Spanish leather pocket-book were all the colour of smoke. Her shoes, I assumed would be the same. I could not see her legs and feet, out of sight on the far side of her chair. The angle at which she sat gave us an excellent view of her profile. Only once, when she turned — her face tilted upward — to see some man who was passing, did we see her whole countenance. The smile she gave this man — though he paid no attention — was warm, expectant and friendly and showed Mrs Maddox to be the absolute antithesis of my hyperthyroid killer in a brass-blonde wig.

Her age was also something of a shock. I would put her at

forty-five; over half her husband's age — but neither young nor old. I had expected a woman of one extreme or the other — not a woman of middle age. Not that it would be hard to imagine Calder wanting to marry this woman — and not just because she was a "beauty." She was also a woman of taste and poise; reasonably intelligent, on sight and — judging by the way she held herself and stared the world in the face — she was also healthy, vigorous and unafraid.

Why on earth would a woman so self-possessed and self-reliant ever have wanted to marry Calder Maddox? In everything I could see; in the way she sat and the way she presented herself; in the liveliness with which she stirred from time to time — there was not a trace of anything a person could connect with the dire and dreadful master chemist. Nothing.

I looked — or tried to look — around the lobby to see if there was any sight of Doctor Chilcott or Lucy Greene. None. And none of Lily Porter, on whom this woman had come to call — so Lawrence had said. Nor could I find the elusive chauffeur, who seemed to spend so much of his time as a piece of living sleight of hand.

The thing was, Mrs Maddox was so obviously waiting for someone she fully expected to appear, it was hard to tell which of the four absentees it might turn out to be: Lily, the chauffeur, Lucy Greene or Chilcott. If, indeed — for whatever reason — it turned out not to be any of these, then I could think of nothing that would make her sit so self-possessed — so still — so certain she was not alone.

The dining-room door was open and most of those who took a noonday meal were already inside. The sound of their cutlery and china could be heard — and the soft, cool buzz of their noonday talk; never the same as the swarming sound of dinner talk or the mild *harrumphs* of morning. (I write, of course, of all meals minus children.)

The smells from the dining-room were of melon salads and lobster bisque; of home-made rolls and tomato aspic; chicken *à la russe* and watercress soup; chilled pears with ginger; strawberry sherbet; iced tea; coffee; French cigarettes. I realized only then that I was starving.

To distract myself, I said; "what makes you think Doctor Chilcott and Mrs Maddox know each other, Lawrence?"

"Instinct."

"Wonderful!" I muttered. "And you a doctor! I guess I can wait to have you diagnose my next disease."

"I haven't done too badly with my instincts up to now," said Lawrence. "In my field, I'm considered the best there is...in Stamford, Connecticut."

I smiled — and looked at him to share the smile.

He was glaring at the empty hall beyond the lobby.

It was true; the thing he'd said about his reputation. As a geriatrician, his theories and practices were widely known; certainly known within the purview of doctors who have treated me in New York's finest clinics and private hospitals.

"There he is," said Lawrence — almost aloud.

Thaddeus Chilcott, now without Lucy Greene.

He was coming out of the elevator — which meant he must have been visiting with someone.

Who else, besides Arabella, did Chilcott know at the Aurora Sands Hotel — this man who pretended to be a stranger here — to have wandered in from the road because he saw some lights on the beach? Who else?

I looked at Lawrence — totally mystified. But he refused to take his eyes from Doctor Chilcott's progress through the lobby.

Chilcott paid no heed to us behind our magazines and loosestrife. He neither hurried his pace, nor slowed it. He walked as a man will walk who knows precisely where he is going — and has the absolute faith he will arrive.

Here, now, came the test.

Between Doctor Chilcott and Mrs Maddox there was space for a journey of twenty — maybe thirty — steps. No one — nothing — obstructed their view of one another. She looked up and he — though he made no effort to look in any specific direction, neither at nor away from where she sat — could not have failed to see her unless he was blind.

Yet, neither one of them batted an eye.

Surely a person will twitch if there is even a flicker of recognition. But Mrs Maddox stared right past him — forgetting, or perhaps foregoing the friendly smile she had flashed at others passing through.

As for Chilcott, he only gave a hoisted hand and a terse *my thanks* to Cathy at the Desk — and was gone.

I looked at Lawrence. Silent.

He was perturbed.

They should have spoken: should, at least, have nodded or bowed or waved at one another. Something. They could not *be strangers.*

All this passed through his eyes and through the way he slumped the bones of his shoulders in towards the bones of his chest.

"I don't believe it," he said. "I do not believe it."

"Well," I said; "I'm sorry. I know it would have helped if there'd been a smile or something. Just to give us some connection." But then I said; "that woman there; of course, she could be anyone, Lawrence. Whose word are we taking she *is* Mrs Maddox?"

"His," said Lawrence. And he nodded towards the hall. "Watch this."

There — just coming round the corner from the front entrance — was the dark, dishevelled chauffeur.

My goodness, he was a handsome lad; but sinister.

He was sweating, now, and not his usual, elegant self. He

had his jacket on — but all unbuttoned and somewhat dusty. His boots were dusty, too.

"He's ready, ma' am," I heard him say.

And so it was true. The connection could not be denied. The woman was more than presumably Mrs Calder Maddox. The chauffeur's presence had named her.

Now, she rose from her neatly cornered place and said in the soft, over-cultured tones that only Charleston, North Carolina could possibly have bred and borne; "the 'romas from that dinin' room have driven me nehly to distraction! I just thank heaven you found your way back to save my poor sanity!"

Well!

I hadn't heard anyone cut the language like that since the last time I watched Aunt Pitty-Pat in *Gone With the Wind*.

As she disappeared from view with the dark, unnamed chauffeur preceding her, I heard her fluting, further off; "you have to be just as surely famished as I."

Then I looked at Lawrence and burst out laughing.

"Katherine Anne Porter lives," I said.

Lawrence — who never reads a book — did not understand me. Petra would have got it in a flash.

No sooner had Mrs Maddox vanished, than Lawrence was rounding the table and throwing down his magazine in order to follow her.

"But we dasn't follow her," I said — trying to catch him up. "She'll see us!"

"No she won't," he said. "She doesn't even know we exist."

And he raced ahead of me — his jagged bones in a turmoil, visible beneath his shirt and slacks — and his running shoes slapping against the floor like wetted rags.

As the woman Maddox went down the steps and approached her waiting motorcar, I hung back behind the screen door, unwilling to join Lawrence's graceless intrusion into her departure. But I heard her loud and clear as she raised her surprising voice to say; "not dead — just absent! Isn't that a tonic, Kyle — to know that? Not dead. Not. But just *away* . . ."

Kyle — who finally had a name — held open the door of Calder's Silver Cloud and Mrs Maddox climbed inside. I have never seen a more flawless entrance into a motorcar. The Queen could do no better. I almost expected Mrs Maddox to wave from the leather interior.

Kyle closed the door and went around the front of the Silver Cloud to the driver's side.

That is when I saw it happen.

Lawrence was standing on the steps beneath the portico — managing to lounge like any man who might have wandered out by chance into the too-bright light of the early afternoon. For one half-second, he played his role too well — and began to rub his eyes, as if to clear away the blaze of sunlight. And in that moment — I cannot tell how alarmed I was to see it — Mrs Maddox stared at Lawrence with such a look of hatred and contempt that I knew — (it was absolutely inescapable) — that all through our vigil in the lobby, she had known we were there; known why we were there and what it was we knew. And if Kyle himself didn't know it — then I'm a fool. Because he was looking, too.

At me.

Then it was that I knew what had happened.

All that while we had been in the lobby — *she* had fooled *us* — waving the magic wand of her wonderful pose, her Italian clothes, her exquisite gestures — playing through our guessing game — *you wonder, wonder — don't you, who I am.* And all that while we had been in the lobby — tracking Mrs Maddox — Doctor Chilcott had been upstairs. Went up and came down — stepped right out of the elevator with me and

Lawrence watching — me even thinking: *I wonder who it is he knows up there...?*

Not thinking once — not even when I made my quip about Katherine Anne — of our very own Porter.

Lily.

95: My fingers have pushed against the screens of this Hotel for such a long time I can conjure, anywhere I go, the feel of them. Soft. Not like the screens I've pushed against elsewhere — harsh and brassy with strands of metal sticking up to lance that delicate skin beneath your nails — which never seems to heal. The screens of the Aurora Sands Hotel — and it may well be the screens of Maine or all New England — are more like pliable cloth and if you press against them hard, your fingers leave an imprint. That's what I remember of that moment; the moment I thought that Lily Porter might be in danger. My fingers were pressed against the wide screen door — and I could smell the dust that rose from the drive as the Silver Cloud was driven away; the smell of dust, exhaust and lobelia.

The lobelia was trailing down, in all its various shades of blue, from all the planters on the porch — and all the shades of blue were true to Lily Porter. And I don't why, but I felt — again, as when I'd thought of Moira Livesay — afraid for her. Perhaps it only had to do with the dust — or the fact of my fingers pressed against the screen. It may just have been the sight of Mrs Maddox, caught behind her bullet-proof glass, being spun away in her Silver Cloud. Or a gown that Lily wore, with trailing sleeves of various shades of blue.

I cannot tell, except by definition, what a premonition is. I have never had a premonition. I have only ever experienced foreboding.

"Lawrence?"

Lawrence, not listening, stepped down onto the drive and shaded his eyes.

"Lawrence?"

But he didn't want to hear me; he was watching the Silver Cloud as it disappeared around the loop of the shaded parking paddock — past the white and shadow-painted walls of Barrie Cottage — on down the drive to the Pine Point Road.

"Lawrence — *please!*"

I pushed out through the door.

"Be quiet!" he said. "Be quiet, Vanessa!"

I subsided — went down the steps to join him and stared away in the same direction — having to squint against the bright, white light.

I guessed he was listening to the receding sound of the Rolls.

I wondered if he had seen the faces inside, in that final moment before they departed. I wondered if he'd seen what I had seen — their earnest awareness and their hatred of us.

The sound of the great, impeccable motor faded away — but not completely. We could hear it vanishing, reappearing, vanishing, reappearing as it made its way around the loops in the drive — and the moment when it paused at the lip of the road, where we had paused and had our accident.

"Lawrence," I said — but I whispered it.

"Wait!" he said. "Wait..."

He took a few steps forward to place himself beyond the baffle of the portico.

I followed him.

And waited.

Then we heard it.

A second motorcar, gunning its engine.

Lawrence held up one of his hands — and one of its fingers — extended.

I held my breath.

And then, the sound of two engines shifting — being shifted into drive and of two cars turning — (Lawrence's fingers all shot up and stiffened — waiting) — Sutter's Hill, right — or Pine Point, left?

Left.

Lawrence's back subsided and his whole arm fell to his side. He turned to me and beamed.

"Well," he said; "Now we know what Kyle-the-Chauffeur meant when he said; 'he's ready, ma'am.' "

"Doctor Chilcott," I said.

Lawrence nodded. "He meant that the good Doctor would be waiting for them down at the foot of the drive."

"It was all a performance — for our benefit."

"And not only do they play their parts superbly well, they also have impeccable timing. Two bits, Vanessa — Kyle was waiting around that corner — might have been waiting the whole damn time we were there — just to take his entrance cue from Chilcott's exit."

"I don't know why it pleases you so," I said.

"It doesn't please me a whit, not a whit, Vanessa. It simply lends a sense of order to it all. It means that none of this is a helter-skelter... scramble-scramble... *what happens next?*... operation. It means that all of it — *all* of it — has been meticulously planned."

I folded my arms at him, as if to keep his enthusiasm from touching me.

"Now may I speak?"

"Yes, yes. Go ahead."

Still, he was only half listening — turning half away and lighting, yet again, another maddening cigarette — and this only doubly maddening because he had to find a new packet in his pocket and undo all the cellophane, and then, he had to look for his matches.

"Go ahead. Go ahead," he said.

"Has it occurred to you that, in the last half-hour or so, you yourself were the one who said Mrs Maddox had asked specifically for Lily Porter?''

Lawrence looked at me as if — in mentioning Lily — I might have mentioned a stranger.

"Lily Porter," I said; "was the reason given for this woman's visit. The reason, at least, that you gave me."

"Yes," he said. "I heard Mrs Maddox say that."

He finally extracted and finally lit his cigarette.

"Well — come on, Lawrence! Whatever came of that? Did Lily ever appear? Did she? Did Mrs Maddox ever go up to see her? Did she? No, Lawrence. Lily Porter did not appear and Mrs Belle-For-A-Day Calder Maddox never disappeared! But I'll tell you who did disappear. Doctor Chilcott. Yes?"

"Well?"

"What do you mean *well?*" I was very angry — angry and already retreating up the steps towards the Hotel entrance. "Where's Lily, Lawrence? That's what I'm saying. Where is Lily Porter?"

Lawrence came after me and actually took my wrist in his hand in order to prevent me from turning back.

"Vanessa; I do not know — and I do not care where Lily Porter is. Not now." I began to pull away from him. "Not *now*, Vanessa."

I stared at him — thinking I was with a crazy man. How could he say he didn't care where Lily Porter was? How could he say that? What if she had been harmed?

He could see this in my expression and he let go of my wrist.

"I want you to come with me," he said — a little too evenly. "You have to."

"It's lunch-time," I said. "I'm hungry. And I have a date with Meg."

I knew better than to mention Lily again. He really had hurt my wrist. I wanted to get away from him. I wanted him to calm down; come to his senses.

No such luck.

He looked at his dreadful shoes and stuck both hands in his pockets as if to reassure me that no more violence would occur.

"All I want you to do," he said; "is walk with me over to *The Dorm*. That's all you have to do, Vanessa. And then..."

I stiffened.

"In one breath you tell me all I have to do is walk with you to *The Dorm*. In the next breath, you start to tell me something else I have to do. No, Lawrence. *No*."

"But — it's Calder's body," he said. "I have to have a witness."

On the word *witness*, the screen door opened in my face. I stepped aside just in time to let Lucy Greene emerge from the depths of the Hotel and descend the steps. Arabella followed her — striding with her out towards the parking lot.

I said; "hello," to Lucy.

And Lucy said; "oh — hello," to me.

But it was just as if I had been a stranger. And Arabella didn't say a word.

After they were well and truly gone, I looked back through the screen door into the lobby. Cool, it was in there. And out here, boiling.

"Please," said Lawrence, pressing his case at once. "You don't understand."

Quite true. I did not understand.

I stood stony still. "Say more. Convince me."

"We can't let them get away with this, Vanessa."

I waited. "Away with what?"

"Do you remember," he said — staring off towards Rossiter Cottage, where Petra had just come through the door onto the porch with a beer in one hand and *Death in Venice* in the other; "the disappearance of Jimmy Hoffa?"

"Of course I do," I said. "He was murdered."

"Was he?"

"Yes. He was murdered and — they..."

"Yes?"

"Jimmy Hoffa was murdered, Lawrence. Everyone knows that. Murdered and disposed of."

"Murdered and disposed of..."

"Yes." I swatted a fly.

Petra sat down behind her comfortable screens and faced the sea. I watched her sigh — contented — open her book and begin to drink her beer. I wondered why Lawrence — since he insisted on playing Sherlock Holmes — hadn't chosen her as his Doctor Watson. Maybe she read too much and would best him.

"How do you know he was murdered?"

"Who?"

"Hoffa."

"Because he *was*." I said. "It's common knowledge."

"Common knowledge maybe — but no one has ever seen the body, Vanessa."

"All right, Lawrence. What are you driving at?"

"I think they may have done it again. I think they may have done it again, and now, they're preparing to dispose of another body. Calder's body. Except..."

I waited.

"I don't think they've figured out how to do that. Yet. And so — it's lying over there in *The Dorm*."

I took a deep breath, squinted and looked away towards the sea and thought about what might happen if I did not pay attention to what was being said. I raised my hand and shaded my eyes against the double glare of the iceberg.

Iceberg.

The iceberg of which Little Teddy *Fidget*'s mother had said; "there's more..." Or words to that effect. "There's more — you haven't put it all in." And she'd put it in, herself: lime-green...

I suddenly saw Mrs Maddox — small and green and perfect in her Italian suit of woven silk — seated in our lobby; smiling at the strangers in our lobby: the lobby of our — of *my* Hotel — through which, only yesterday, her husband had passed on his way to death.

"All right," I said. "All right, Lawrence. If I will cater to your mad whim — and walk across to *The Dorm* and view these suspect remains — will you — immediately after I have seen them — cater to my mad whim and come with me to Lily Porter's room?"

"Of course, I will," he said. "Of course, I will."

I stepped down onto the drive.

I took his arm.

"Don't you think we ought to wave at Petra? She's watching us, you know."

"I know she's watching us," he said. "I told her to."

Ah. So he had enlisted her.

Perhaps as Mrs Hudson.

96: In the early afternoon, *The Dorm* is either deserted or sparsely inhabited by resting members of the staff. Most of the off-duty students go down to the beach at that time of day and do their sleeping there while soaking up the sun. I could, however, hear a distant radio as we approached the old building, but nothing else that gave any sense of occupants.

The thing I have not indicated before about *The Dorm* is

that — besides its function as a sleeping quarters — it also
serves as a laundromat, which gives off the very pleasant —
to me, at any rate — aromas of soapy water and bleach and
spanking clean sheets. Since prison, all indications of
cleanliness — from the sound of running baths to the smell
of laundry — have been among the greatest pleasures of my
life.

The yards out front are shaded by immense old chestnut
trees — and I cannot think of a single occasion, when entering
their purview, that I have not recalled the lines: *Under the
spreading chestnut tree/ the village smithy stands.* The sense of
the past is very telling in their presence.

Lawrence wanted total nonchalance. And, to that end, he
was carrying on what appeared to be an animated conversation. In fact, it was nothing of the sort. He was telling me —
sotto voce — how it was that he had come upon Calder's body
— but disguising his narrative with many inappropriate
gestures and grimaces; smiles and laughter.

"You may — or you may not recall that, when you phoned
me this morning about the photograph, it took some time for
me to answer?"

"Yes. And you were breathless."

"That's right. Petra and I were organizing our laundry."

"Organizing your laundry puts you out of breath? It
doesn't me."

"Well — maybe you don't have to lug it up and down the
stairs, Vanessa. Anyway — that's what we were doing. And it
was Petra's turn to do it. Bring it over here, I mean — and sit
with the machines. She never minds — she has her books to
read and she loves the sound of water. I think it acts as a tranquillizer. Well; she was sitting here reading, when she suddenly felt a chill."

"A chill — in this weather?"

"Her reaction precisely. She thought there must be
something freaky — so she got up to look."

"Freaky?"

"Odd — you know — unusual. Maybe a sudden storm or something. So she stepped out here and there was an ice truck..."

We had reached the door of the laundromat — but we paused before we went in.

"An ice truck?" I said. I had not seen or heard of ice trucks for years.

"They still have them out in the National Parks and the like," said Lawrence. "And, I guess, that's where this ice truck must have come from. One of the parks up the coast from here. Anyway — Petra being Petra, she didn't want to engage the fellow in conversation — so she came back inside and started to read her book again."

"Engage what fellow in conversation?"

"The iceman."

"Ah."

"The long and the short of it is, that — after a lot of crashing and bashing and cursing — the fellow appeared at the laundromat door — not this one, that one." He pointed to the back door. "And he said to Petra, who was here all alone: *can you sign for this?* Well — naturally, Petra said: *no. I can't. I didn't order it. Go to the Hotel office.*"

Here, Lawrence paused — put on the iceman's burly character — and then said; *"I haven't the time to do that, Lady. I'm in a hurry.* So Petra signed it. She signed it, thinking maybe it was the kids who'd ordered the ice for a party — or just to cool off *The Dorm*. But when she glanced at the invoice, she thought: *my God, that's a lot of ice for a bunch of kids to buy!* The bill was for over two hundred dollars!"

"Good grief."

We had now reached the back door and were stepping through into the lane that runs behind *The Dorm*, where most of the students park their broken-down cars and bikes and motorcycles.

"Petra was curious — needless to say — and she came out into the lane, right here..." said Lawrence.

We were now retracing her steps.

"...and she saw where the earth was obviously wet; right there." Norman pointed.

I looked.

The ground was perfectly dry, now. The heat had made short shrift of any moisture there might have been. But the door through which the iceman had delivered his goods was plainly visible. It was a stable door — of the kind the grooms would have used when coming and going to the horse stalls. Sometimes they call it a Dutch door; cut in half on the horizontal, so you can let in the air and keep out the dogs. Both halves were closed at present.

There was also a padlock.

"Don't be dismayed about the padlock," said Lawrence. "I'm good at this; it's my doctor's training."

He then produced some sort of lethal-looking instrument and proceeded to pick the lock, which gave to his expertise within fifteen seconds.

I wondered what else there might be about doctors I didn't know.

We then went inside — not only into the dark — but into a cavernous space; chilled and damp and hollow.

Lawrence closed the door and switched on the light — a single, unmasked bulb that hung from a wire that dangled down from the ceiling. For a mere second, I swore I could see my breath. But it was only dust.

We were standing in the central aisle between the box stalls — the box stalls all in a dilapidated state and their bars all rusted. The air was permeated with the smell of horses dead so long my mother would have remembered them from her childhood. It is a smell I dearly love, myself — and my first reaction, standing there, was one of immense pleasure and overpowering sadness. Gone — so many wondrous beasts. A dozen box stalls — a granary — a tack room.

"Come here," said Lawrence.

He was standing by one of the furthest box stalls — having pulled its iron gate wide open. The rust was damp and it had rubbed off on his fingers.

As I joined him, he said; "I'm sorry — this isn't decent, what I'm about to do."

He went inside the stall and told me I needn't follow him, yet.

Inside the stall there was a good deal of old, scuffled straw, a few decaying cardboard boxes and several burlap bags that had been strewn about with what I could see at first glance was a phony, deliberate sense of chaos.

Up against the far wall, there was a packing crate of immense size — almost as big as a piano crate. It, too, had been strewn with phony-looking debris; too many newspapers, too much binder twine.

I held my breath and tried to calm myself. I wanted to know what was there. But I didn't want to see it. I've seen enough of that; of people dead, their corpses abandoned.

Neither of us spoke. I realized part of my job was to listen for intruders. So I did that — and tried not to get any rust on my clothes as I watched Lawrence working.

He pulled aside all the carefully created mess from the top of the packing case and then he crouched down in order to apply his weight to opening its lid.

When this was done, he leaned the opened lid against the wall and stood away so I could see what had been revealed.

A very modern, and — in fact — brand new Maytag freezer. Beige.

Now Lawrence did speak — but only briefly.

"I'm afraid you will have to step forward," he said. "I'm sorry."

He lifted the lid of the freezer — and I took — I should say — precisely five steps forward from the box stall gate. I required no more distance than that to see what must be seen — to verify what must be verified.

Packed in finely crushed ice, lay the undoubted remains of Calder Maddox. They were still encased in the body bag into which the ambulance drivers had tipped them on the beach — but Lawrence had loosed the draw-string to reveal the face.

Excepting the necessary change in their colour — Calder's features were almost exactly as I had seen them last, when Doctor Chilcott had lifted the wayward arm and folded it across the chest.

I looked away and returned to my gate.

All right: I thought. *It's true. Calder Maddox died of having enemies. Maybe enemies in high places. Just like Jimmy Hoffa.*

I could hear Lawrence pulling down the lid and scattering the bogus debris.

I could feel the cold of the ice — and I shivered, hating it in spite of weeks of unbearable heat. This ice was just as alarming and just as sinister as the iceberg out beyond the Aurora Sands Hotel in the Bay.

I may not know exactly why: I thought — *and I may not know exactly how it was done; not detail by detail. But I do know this; whatever the reasons — whatever the means — Calder's enemies — his killers — have put us all in jeopardy. And now, any one of us can end up dead like this — grotesquely dead in a packing crate.*

Just before Lawrence closed the gate, I took one final look, and said to him; "what does it mean, that our President's physician is involved in this? Because he is involved. To the hilt."

Lawrence said; "oddly enough, it's only Chilcott who holds my interest in all of this. To be perfectly frank, I didn't give two hoots when that old man died." He nodded at the box and closed the gate. "Everyone's better off without him."

I thought it was strange that Lawrence — being a doctor — should feel that way about Calder Maddox, given all the medicines Calder had put at his disposal. But I didn't say that; I don't know why. Perhaps it was a kind of cowardice; I didn't want Lawrence to think I had approved of Calder — when I hadn't. I had disliked him intensely — mostly because he was a bully — though bully seems a weak and inappropriate word for someone as ruthless as Calder had been. I guess what I really didn't want to admit was that I hated Calder Maddox. Even now, as I write that down, I want to cross it out.

"*We* aren't better off without him," I said. "It's only because he's dead that we're in all this trouble." I looked around at the box stalls, with their remorseless reminders of prisons — bars and gates and the feeling of entrapment. Not ten minutes before, I had been saddened by the wonders of what they conjured of the past. Now, because of the packing crate in their midst, my view of them had changed irrevocably.

That everything is relative can now be numbered amongst the trite and true realities that Calder's death is forcing upon me.

We stood there beneath the ghastly light of the naked bulb — and I knew how my neighbour, David Brodie, must feel when, every night, he is driven into the hallway to dispense with all white, merciless light. It prompts every ounce of paranoia into the open.

"There's no one we can tell," I said. "We can't get help from anyone. The Police are part of it — the Government appears to be part of it — Calder's own wife appears to be part of it. We can't get help from anyone," I repeated. I think my voice was rising.

Lawrence said; "we don't need help. Not yet."

And I said; "how can you say that? What if they come after *us* — these people — whoever they are? What happens then?"

I had a sudden image of Nigel Forestead rummaging in my belongings — turning my pocket-books inside out — rifling my cupboard. And I thought of the Secret Service Agents who had come to question Joel about Calder and Frankie about me.

"They're onto me already, you know," I said. "These people, whoever they are." I told him about the *gentlemen* who'd come with all their questions. "What can they think I have to do with this?" I said. "With Calder's death?"

Lawrence brushed his hair back off his forehead. "They don't think you did it, if that's what you mean," he said.

"Well what, then?"

He looked at me then with what I now realize must be the expression he uses when he has to give a patient the very worst news; a kind of final smile. And he said; "I guess they think you know who did."

"But I don't. You know I don't."

"I know you don't; yes. But they don't know it."

I pulled my collar up around my neck.

I spoke towards my shoes.

"Do you know," I said; "who did it?"

He shifted — ungainly as always — from one foot to the other. He put his hands deep down inside his pockets. "Yes," he said. "I think I do."

"Well?"

"I think it was Chilcott."

I looked at his face. In the brazen light, his expression was cold as the ice in Calder's crazy, cryogenic capsule.

"I don't know how he did it," he said. "Not yet. But — I'm going to find out — and I'm going to crucify him."

I waited a long time before I spoke.

"Why do you hate him? Chilcott, I mean."

Lawrence removed one hand from his pocket and toyed with the string that hung down, tied to the chain that pulled the light switch.

"All hate can't be explained in a sentence, Vanessa," he said. Then he added; "there's a dead man back there lying in an ice chest. He and the man I think may have killed him used one another to gain ascendancy over a very important aspect of medical practice here in this country. One made drugs — the other pushed them. He pushed them in conjunction with his magic by-pass operations. Ordinary doctors, trying to save ordinary lives under ordinary circumstances got caught in the middle. I mean they got caught by being pushed aside."

"I'm sorry," I said. "I didn't realize Chilcott had harmed you."

"Not personally," Lawrence said. "He didn't come into my clinic and say: *get out!* He said it to my patients. Once he'd done that, he didn't have to say it to me. There's nothing like a walking, talking, breathing, smiling President to prove your point. That's what you call credentials with a capital C."

"All you sound is jealous," I said. I had to say it, because it seemed to be the truth.

"No. I'm not jealous. Only bitter. It's made my work too hard to bear, sometimes. I have lots of walking, talking, breathing, smiling patients of my own, Vanessa. They just don't happen to go by the name of Owen Warner, President of the United States."

"What's the difference? They're all alive. Including the President."

"So we are told, yes. So we are told."

"What in heaven's name do you mean by that?"

"I mean my survival rate is greater than Chilcott's. Because it's not augmented with drugs."

"Oh." I felt blank. "You mean the President is going to die."

"Yes. But — frankly, my dear . . ." he wrapped the string around his finger. "I don't give a damn."

He smiled.

I wish he hadn't smiled. It made him one with all the others. Just another petty seeker of revenge.

"Do you think we could leave? I said. "I need to leave here. Right now."

Lawrence turned off the light.

We left in the dark.

97: Now it was Lawrence's turn to cater to *my* whim.

Lily.

The first thing we did was something I have never done before. Walking down the lane behind *The Dorm* — we went around the end of that building and entered the Hotel through the Service Entrance. We did this without consulting one another. I cannot say what Lawrence's reason was; I only know my own was shame.

I was ashamed of what I had seen; ashamed of what Lawrence had said; ashamed of what it implied. And, yes, it is true — I was also afraid.

Given my prison background, I knew that most of what is frightening and much of what is evil happens by the light of day. No need for darkness. Caesar, after all, had been murdered in the presence of a hundred people and more — some time between high noon and five o'clock. Right in these waters off the coast of Maine, the most terrifying sharks are the ones we see in the radiance of fear. The real ones — darkened below us — do no harm until they rise towards the light. If only, I began to wish, it would get dark.

So we climbed up past the garbage pails and the piles of discarded cardboard boxes onto the kitchen stoop and through the screen door with its banging flies and fifty years of accumulated grease, until we stood in the stairwell, beyond which the sounds of pots and pans being washed were almost deafening. Also the sound of someone singing.

Some say a heart is just like a wheel,
When you bend it — you can't mend it.
And my love for you is like a sinking ship
And my heart is on that ship out in mid-ocean.

I led and Lawrence followed — and by the time we had reached the landing on the second floor, I was already quite out of breath. I paused, my hand on the fire-door, waiting for my pulse to settle.

Lawrence said; "you want me to go through first?"

I shook my head. If something had happened to Lily Porter, I had to be the first to know what it was.

I pulled on the door and went through.

Lily's room is up towards the front of the Hotel. I dreaded passing all those doors along the corridor — and the inescapable probability that someone — it hardly mattered who — would be in the hallway. I didn't want to see anyone and I didn't want anyone to see me or Lawrence. I will make no attempt to explain this feeling — it was simply there inside me. *Hide.*

We got — for whatever reason — lucky. Perhaps it had to do with the hour of the day. It was not yet three. Whoever slept in the afternoon was sleeping — and the rest were on the beach or playing tennis.

At the ASH, most people return year after year to the same rooms — often to the same rooms we had as children. My room — Number 33 — was one of these. I used to sleep in there with my parents — and, after Mother and I returned alone from the War, I shared it with her. Now, even though single, I still have a large airy room with a charming bath and other amenities usually afforded only to couples.

Lily's room is on the second floor and all but the last before the stairs that lead down into the lobby. It has always had the rather strange number, 2-A. There is no room 2. The

explanation for this lies so far off in the past that no one living
has ever been able to track it down.

Lily first shared this room with her mother — and when
Lily married and Maisie Cotton died — then Mr and Mrs
Porter took up residence in Room 2-A.

Lily's husband — Franklin — died, as I have already written, in 1968 or '69. None of the other guests, including
myself, ever really cared for Franklin Porter. He was vain and
cruel and was long suspected of illegal practices before he was
finally charged and convicted in 1965. He died in his prison;
of cancer. He had been a corporation lawyer, whose
embezzlements had paid off handsomely.

Lily must be given full marks for bravery. She returned to
the ASH the summer of Franklin's conviction and the only
concession she made to her shame was the pair of dark glasses
worn, rain or shine, the whole of that season. She was not yet
forty, then. Her innocence of everything Franklin had done
to incur his downfall was absolute. Her blindness to his faults
was total and foolish and devoted as her blindness was to
Calder Maddox. Some women seem to suffer from terminal
myopia when it comes to men. They take no part in the choos-
ing. They are chosen. Lily was always being chosen by the
same man. She would wait for him to arrive — and because
her bags were always packed and ready, he would carry them
away into his life — and she would follow. Now we were to
discover Lily had followed, yet again.

98: The door of Room 2-A — while not ajar — had not
clicked shut; an open invitation to push it wide.

I don't know what I expected to find. I had hoped against
hope it would only be Lily — possibly asleep. When Meg and
I had seen her last, she was coming out of shock and heading
deep into mourning. She had complained of a headache —
over and over: *my head hurts — oh, it hurts*; she had said.

But with the aid of drink and pills, she had finally gone

to sleep. The last I saw of her was of her pinched and painted face against the pillow — and her hands in fists on the edge of the sheet, holding it there against her chin, as if in modesty.

Now — as I pushed the door wide open — I saw the room was empty. No Lily — no luggage. Only the room, so undeniably hers, with all its Lily Porter trappings in place — its long silk scarves — its wide-brimmed summer hats and its delicate mohair afghans — its rows of shoes and boxes filled with tissue paper and its note stuck into the corner of the mirror and held in place with a Lily Porter hat-pin.

Gone — I read. And: *Back whenever. Lily.*

Not in Lily's handwriting. All I have to do is look in the front of this book to see the note is not in Lily's hand. Her airy arabesques have all been squared, in the note; and all her formal language twisted.

Back whenever . . . indeed!

Lily Porter would never have written that in ten million years. It would take that long to tell her what it means.

I checked the drawers. A portion of her clothes was missing. The wardrobe told the same tale. Some, but not all were gone.

"Look in the bathroom," Lawrence said. "See if her toothbrush is there."

No. No toothbrush. Nor any other necessary thing that I could see.

"Wait here," I said. "I'm going downstairs to the Desk. Maybe someone saw her leaving."

I started across the room — but halfway over the scatter rug, I stepped on something small and hard.

A button. Black and square.

I held it up.

"It looks like a uniform button," said Lawrence. "The kind I used to have when I was a Cadet."

"Were you ever a chauffeur?" I asked.

In my mind, I could see the buttons — most of them undone — on the front of Kyle's jacket.

Lawrence didn't speak.

I squeezed the button tight in my hand and tried not to lose the image of Kyle in the lobby when he came to fetch Mrs Maddox.

"It would explain why he was sweating," I said.

"What would?" said Lawrence.

"If Kyle had been up here getting Lily packed and out of the Hotel."

"Getting Lily packed and out of the...?"

I wasn't even listening. I was crossing all the way to the door and going out into the hall.

"Lawrence," I said; "come here."

He joined me.

"Look," I said. And pointed.

A mere six feet away, the stairs led down to the very screen door where I had been standing when it first occurred to me that something terrible might have happened to Lily. From where I stood at present, I could even smell the lobelia.

I looked at Lawrence.

"I don't care," I said; "whatever else we do, we must find Lily Porter."

99: I could not imagine — did not dare to imagine — what her disappearance might mean. Kidnap, of course, was first on the list of possibilities; kidnap, collusion or death. If Lily

Porter had been kidnapped, it was perfectly clear who must have done it — Kyle. He was strong enough to have taken Lily by force. He had, after all, returned to the lobby looking dishevelled and definitely perspiring. But why she might have been taken, I could not tell.

Collusion was harder to believe. If Lily had agreed to go with Kyle and Chilcott and Mrs Maddox, she must also, then, have agreed — at some other stage of the game — to Calder's murder. This I could not credit. It was quite impossible. It simply wasn't in her. Lawrence agreed with that.

As for death, I feared this possibility most but could not make it real.

Lawrence and I went back into her room and closed the door. Whatever clues might trick us into an answer must be somewhere in there.

Lawrence lit a cigarette. The curtains billowed — New Hampshire sheers. Being Lily's sheers, they billowed in slow motion. They are like no others — Lily's curtains — weighted with shells and velvet ribbons — the shells suspended at the end of silver threads.

Her whole room is like no other. Most of its colours are muted; rose and grey and violet; Victorian shades of brown and green. Scents I can barely identify, of gardens kept in bell-jars and petals pressed in books, perfume her drawers and cupboards. The room is filled with visual shouts and whispers — with all the familiar incongruities of Lily's person; the serious photographs of all her men — all dead — and of laughing women I have never met and whom she never names; with tasteful hand-painted scarves from the Metropolitan Museum of Art and dreadful caps — flamingo pink — with *Miami Vice* written across the brim in electric blue. On the dresser there is a yellow plastic duck that advertises: LEMON DUCK! THE WINE WITH A DIFFERENCE. It sits beside a pair of crystal and silver art nouveau perfume bottles signed by Tiffany himself; (I looked).

How, in the midst of such consistent inconsistency, could a person possibly hope to discover clues? Clues, after all, stand out against whatever background is known and recognizable and shout "I shouldn't be here!" What — in Lily Porter's room — could ever hope to say that? Let alone shout it.

Finally, Lawrence said; "all we have is the note. And I agree with you — Lily would never use a phrase like *back whenever*. Somebody else wrote this." He went into the bathroom, threw his cigarette into the toilet and flushed it away. When he came back into the room, I said; "she's been kidnapped. I'm absolutely certain of it."

"Yes," he agreed. "I'm afraid so."

"And taken to Pine Point."

"Yes."

"What on earth are we going to do?" I asked.

"Go and get her," he said.

100: Coming down out of Lily's room and moving through the lobby, I overheard Lena Rumplemeyer talking to someone on the telephone. Lena Rumplemeyer is over eighty — but not yet ninety. She smokes cheroots and wears a wig that makes her look like a Gibson Girl. She smiles so rarely people think there must be something wrong when she does. For all her great age and tenure at the ASH, Lena is not a member of *Stonehenge*. She doesn't wish to be. She disapproves of *claques*.

When I asked her, once, if she didn't mean *cliques*, she fixed me with her beady stare and said; "I mean clacks. It's all their teeth — clackity-clacking in the corner. No thanks!"

This afternoon, she was talking, as I passed the booth, to someone I presumed was in Australia.

"Stop shouting!" Lena shouted. "I'm not deaf, Caroline. Will you come or won't you?"

There was a pause, during which she held the receiver away from her ear. Even I could hear the voice at the other end.

"What time?" it shouted.

"Eight o'clock!" Lena shouted back at the receiver. "Dancing starts at nine! I like to get there at eight so I get a decent table! Also gives you time to knock a few back before the music starts!"

By this time, I had reached the far side of the lobby and was about to exit onto the porch. The last thing I heard from Lena was an absolute roar.

"Stop shilly-shallying, Caroline! You dancing tonight or not...?"

And Caroline's *yes!* from the Outback.

Dancing.

Every Saturday night, there is dancing at the Pine Point Inn and, every Saturday night all summer long, Lena Rumplemeyer and a handful of others go up and dance till dawn. The Clintons, the Davies and the Dentons always go. Younger people, too — but only couples. It isn't proper to go alone and no one ever has — from the ASH. When Lena Rumplemeyer leaves the Hotel on Saturday nights, the Boys go with her.

The Boys are our resident bachelors — Ivan Mills and Peter Moore. They met here in 1944, when both were in the OSS and the Hotel served as a training centre. Peter Moore has only one arm (his left) and is currently *emeritus* at the Harvard

School of Economics. Ivan — though younger, in fact, than Peter — seems to be the elder of the two; he stands very straight and speaks from a great height; six-feet-five, taller than Lawrence. Ivan brays when he laughs and seems unable to close his eyes. His field is Nineteenth Century European History — but he never talks about that. He goes on for hours, I'm afraid, about the news. He seems obsessed with it — though he also seems to misinterpret it all. He gets all the names wrong. But we love him just the same — because he has weathered Peter's tragic proclivity for drink and has got him through a life-long battle with manic-depression. They've had a most creative relationship and we dread the day when one of them dies. What Lena will do without them cannot be imagined.

I have been so seldom to the Pine Point Inn, I cannot recall the last time I danced there. Years ago, I'm certain. But Lena's conversation had proved an inspiration. Since we had to find some way to extract Lily without unduly drawing attention to ourselves — what better way could there be than to masquerade as dancers? I would telephone Lawrence and issue the invitation.

First, I made my way to the *Ashbar*, thinking Meg might still be there. I wanted to retrieve my photographs.

It came as something of a shock to discover it was almost half-past four in the afternoon. I had left Meg sitting there over three hours ago.

Robin did not know where she was, but he reached down under the bar and brought up a large manilla envelope. Sealed.

"Mrs Riches asked me to give you this," he said.

"Thank you," I said. "I'd like a Bloody Mary."

I went to the table where Meg and I had been sitting before lunch. Her lunch, not mine. I still hadn't eaten.

Robin looked over the counter and said; "did you say *Bloody Mary*, Miss Van Horne?"

"I did," I said. "And you say nothing."

"No, ma'am. Not a word."

Fifteen minutes later, I called him back to my table.

"Robin," I said, "did anyone other than Mrs Riches happen to look at these photographs?"

"Not that I saw, Miss Van Horne."

I had just discovered, on looking them over, that all the pictures of Meg were missing.

"Only thing I remember," said Robin; "is that Mister Forestead went and got the envelope for her from the Front Desk. Otherwise, Mrs Riches sat there alone. She left about an hour and a half ago."

"Thank you, Robin," I said. "I'll have another Bloody Mary."

The bar was empty. I sat there alone. I felt as if I had found another body in another box.

101: I've come to my private dune and I'm sitting here slightly drunk — but safe. Everyone can see me — no one can watch me. I'm too far away for that; for being watched. I find it fascinating. Ever since Calder's death, no one has dared to look along the beach with binoculars. They train them only on the iceberg. I suspect the meeting of eyes — even when met through lenses — is too off-putting. Indeed — there's a very great lack of staring, all at once. Amusing.

The iceberg is a gift; it gives us all something legitimate to focus on. I dare say that's what everyone wants; anything to focus on but the thought of Calder lying there dead. I think it must be that we all see ourselves reflected in his corpse.

I was staring at the iceberg myself, just now. The sun, descending, has pushed all the jagged shadows back across its frozen shape — which makes it look a little less like Washington, D.C. — a little more like a mountain. Everest, I suppose. It lacks for nothing, now, but a few adventurous, miniature mountain climbers: little Sir Edmunds — tiny Tenzings — with threads for ropes and pins for picks. Because it's there.

102: I'm feeling more than slightly mortal; sad.

Everyone I love and everyone I trust appears to be in trouble.

This place has become, in its way, a little like Bandung. We try to go about the daily business of being alive as if there were nothing wrong; as if it were normal to have a person lying dead on the beach. Calder's death has become a wire around this beach — a fence around our behaviour. The road-blocks out by the highway don't help, either. Not that anyone mentions them — not that, among the general populace, there's any awareness of how serious the situation is. Too many children are running, for that, and laughing. Too many adults are standing about in bathing suits talking about the stock market — and telling each other anecdotes about their babies and other new acquisitions. Life goes on at every level, above and below the stress line. I look at some of the faces around me and I think: *if only you knew.* And then I think: *I'm glad you don't.*

I sat for half an hour just now — knees up, chin on my forearms — watching the horizon, squinty-eyed and sweating; mesmerized. The smells, the sounds, the heat on my back as the sun began to sink; I could just as well be twelve; the way I feel, as fifty-nine. I want to resist the thought that being alive is over; that things are coming to an end.

That, in itself, is a prison thought. The eternal longing to be somewhere else in another time. Also — the constant sense of wonder that one was ever unaware of pain and the longing especially for the particular form of innocence: life without pain — life without awareness.

All this ambivalence — all this wanting to know and not to know — to be and not to be accountable; I watched Colonel Norimitsu go through the very same thing.

An acquaintance of my mother's was dying. I cannot say she was a friend. My mother had not been out there long enough to garner friends before the War threw all of us together behind the wire. Most of the women she knew were Europeans — Dutch or British, plus one or two Australians. Americans were difficult to come by. Women especially. Most of the men involved with my father's business had come without their wives — or hadn't wives to begin with. A lot of them were very young.

American oil interests hadn't been able to penetrate the Dutch East Indies market — and Father, in fact, had been offered his job originally because of his Dutch-sounding name. He'd been hired by a consortium who needed his particular talents. He went to Surabaja "on loan" from my Grandfather Woods; sent — in fact — by that astute and acquisitive man, with specific instructions to "infiltrate the oil fields on our behalf." The War in Europe had already begun — and Grandfather Woods saw very clearly that Dutch and British interests — particularly the Dutch — were ripe for picking. My father never did get to accomplish my grandfather's wishes — but he did ingratiate himself. He was making impressive inroads into Javanese colonial society, with my mother's help — when December of 1941 intervened and brought it all to an end.

I have to say that my father's popularity was justified. He was adored by everyone and I think that part of my mother's problem, after his death, had to do with what had once been her rather charming bewilderment that "someone as *ravissant* as James Van Horne" had come into her life and wanted to stay there. All through their marriage, she kept expecting him to leave. As for me — I saw them both as beautiful and exceptional, until he died. It was only then that I encountered Mother as she really was: a reflection stranded in an abandoned mirror.

The woman who was dying — my mother's acquaintance — was one of those figures who crop up from time to time in other people's lives, bringing both magic and mystery with them; unexplained and inexplicable. They seem, these people, not to have anchors. Or — more accurately — not to have a need for anchors. Mercedes Mannheim is one of this breed. The Mercedes I know lives her summer life on Larson's Neck and only touches my existence there — and, very rarely, flying through a dinner party we might both attend in New York or Washington. The Mercedes that someone else might know would be met in the airport at Caracas — or share a sleeping-car on the Trans-Siberian Railroad. That is what this other woman was like. Her name was Dorothy Busch.

She had come down to Surabaja from Singapore and to Singapore from Shanghai. Before Shanghai, she had made several films in Hollywood. She had got to Hollywood from Nome, Alaska. You learn very quickly not to ask how or why such leaps are made by the people who live these lives. They are simply *made* — and I doubt very much that they themselves know how or why.

In 1944, the winter she lay dying in Bandung's makeshift infirmary, Dorothy Busch would have been about forty-five years old. Her hair was blonde and straight and — before our internment — I recall a woman of extraordinary beauty with a throaty laugh and a way of tipping that straight blonde hair as it fell towards one eye. She seemed, forever, to be winking at you. Her beauty was not extraordinary in the way of Garbo's or Dietrich's. It was extraordinary because it was made of elements not connected, in the conventional sense, to beauty. Dorothy's beauty was in her sense of presentation. She took your breath away by coming round a corner, dressed (I remember, once) in a pale beige cotton suit — almost the colour of her hair — and her sharp blue, witty eyes snapped up all the best people in the room in seconds. A dozen people might flock to her — and she would seem to be alone with each and every one of them.

I had quickly fallen under her spell. I loved the way she told the bits and pieces of the story of her life as if it were the most normal thing in the world to harpoon whales and smoke in the opium dens of China and tell Charlie Chaplin you didn't want to marry him. And now she was all too obviously dying. The disease that had struck her was a form of cerebral malaria that affected the victim with appalling headaches, fevers and long, alarming hours of unconsciousness. It was among the hybrid diseases that had begun to appear in the latter years of our imprisonment — and therefore its treatment was impossible to predict. None of the pitiful range of medicines we had gave any relief at all.

It is hard to say what drove my mother to send me to the fence with all that remained of her personal jewellery. We had all watched other people die — some of them close to us, though the closeness had only come in the prison. Mother had remained unmoved — especially since Father's death.

I dislike the word *unmoved*. It is like the word *hate*. They do not always tell — as words — precisely what is meant. I do not mean that Mother was cold or cruel when it came to other people's sorrows and pain — and certainly nothing of the kind

when anyone died. *Unmoved*, in prison terms, means
something else; and perhaps it means something it cannot
mean anywhere but in a prison. It meant, in Mother's case —
and in the case of countless others, myself included — that
feeling was masked. It was not withheld. Even *masked* sounds
cold. It was not.

At any rate, Mother's feeling for Dorothy Busch — her
connection to Dorothy being as tenuous as that she might
have had for a neighbour in an apartment down the hall
at home — was greater than any feeling she had shown
for any other prisoner. Her witness of Dorothy's suffering
pushed my mother beyond the limits of the harsh control she
had exercised up until then over her emotions. She came
to me in the dark one night and knelt beside my cot beyond
the netting.

"Wake up," she said. "You must go on an errand right
away."

I see her very clearly, even now, beyond that netting in my
mind — her round, lovely face glistening with sweat — and
her eyes, as hard as marbles, washed with tears.

She gave me her wedding ring — which up until then, she
had sworn she would never abandon. She had kept it braided
into her hair — discreetly hidden. All our jewellery had been
confiscated — except whatever pieces we had managed to
secrete during our first hours in the prison at Surabaja. Over
time, each piece had been donated to our survival — as illness,
malnutrition and other problems had called for goods that
could only be got at the fence.

But we — my mother and I — had never gone to the fence
ourselves. That job — so appallingly risky under the eyes of
Colonel Norimitsu's guards — had always been delegated to
sister prisoners whose backgrounds had been less protected
than ours. Mother's personal qualms regarding the fence had
all to do with "breaking the law." Though she might have

broken as many laws as anyone else — in the moral sense — she had never broken a civil law. The very thought of doing so made her quake. My own qualms were much less complicated. I was a coward — and I freely admit it. The bullets that had killed my father had been too real for me to put aside, but I am perfectly aware a great many other forms of terror can be put aside, if only because they remain unreal until they have been witnessed. The women who used the fence most often were mothers with very young children, and certain of the nurses, who were qualified to judge the merits of whatever medicines might turn up in the market-place beyond the wire. Mothers went there for food. Any food.

It should be said that two black markets existed at Bandung. The one I am describing — where the commerce took place at the fence between prisoners on the inside and "merchants" on the outside — was the deadly market-place. The other — held on a more or less routine basis — was more like a "town market," where goods — including goods that had been purchased through the fence — were exchanged between prisoners. This black market was held almost every morning behind the latrines. The latrines were the one sure place that everyone was certain to come in contact with everyone else. They were also the place least likely to attract any protracted observation from our guards. The horrors of those latrines — the stench, the exposure to disease, the visual purgatory — the presence of snakes, spiders, insects of every kind and, above all, of the giant maggots moving through the effluent — were enough to keep away anyone who was not desperate. How we endured them, I cannot now imagine. The market there was daily — but the brevity of the trading was remarkable.

Mother said; "take this ring and go to the fence right now. There's a trader there with pure quinine. Also with aspirin. Get every one you can. We need them for Dorothy."

The expression on her face — and everything I knew of her confirmed reticence regarding the fence as a place we went ourselves — put an end to any argument before it began. I got up at once and pulled on a dark cotton dress I had been hoarding for the day of our liberation — hoarding it not for its colour but its relatively impeccable condition — and I took the ring and left my mother still kneeling by my cot.

There wasn't any moon that night and the sky showed only its stars. The rains had been with us for over a month and only the night sky was cloudless. The laneways between the barracks were simply rivers of mud. I went in my bare feet, counting the corners of the other barracks as I made my way to the fence.

The portion of the fence where the market was held was the portion that faced the jungle. Those who came to us there had reached us by routes we could not imagine — our never having been beyond the fence in any direction other than the one that faced north, where the open savannah separated our compounds from the rain forest and the road to Bandung and Jakarta.

At first, I thought I had come the wrong way. I could find no other people. But it quickly became apparent I was not alone.

Someone hissed at me from under the barrack nearest to where I stood. I had put Mother's ring on my finger — afraid I would otherwise drop it in the mud, where it would have been irretrievable. My hands were fisted — since I also feared the ring might slip from my finger — my fingers all being little more than bone, I had lost so much weight. So I went with my hands in fists, in my dark cotton dress and my legs caked with mud to below the knee — and I discovered a whole group of women, similarly dressed in dark clothing — barefoot and begrimed — sitting on their haunches beneath the raised porch.

"They have gone away," I was told. "Too many birds were singing."

I understood the reference to the singing birds, because it was common knowledge that only the distant birds ever sang in the hours when the market at the fence was being conducted. These birds, then, must have been human — possibly Japanese — signalling their presence to one another. If that were the case, the marketeers were in danger and had retreated.

After about fifteen minutes of squatting beneath that barrack, our necks in cramp and our rumps in the mud — one of the women — an Australian nurse whose name was Deirdre McNab — offered to return to the fence to see if anyone was there. The bird calls had ceased and only the high-pitched voices of the faraway night birds could be heard. Some of their songs were ironically joyous — lovely — and one was like a nightingale, though no such bird exists in the equatorial world.

Five minutes later, Deirdre McNab was back.

"We're to go up one by one," she said. "The goods are very high-quality stuff tonight. There's a quota..." Then she said; "this is a plague we have. We have to be realistic. Greed cannot be tolerated; not on our side of the fence. Whatever you give these people — it will only bring your share. No more. I have to tell you this now — because your share will not be great. If any of you have come to barter with goods that are especially precious to you — last-ditch goods and the like — be warned. If you sacrifice them here tonight, you will not receive an iota more than women who have come with less. I'm sorry. Those are the facts."

Not one woman refused to abide by these rules. Whatever we had brought as payment would buy us each a dozen aspirin and ten quinine tablets. That was all.

I thought of my mother's ring — and I knew it was all she had left of my father.

And then I thought of Dorothy Busch — and of her swollen features and her knotted expression which told of her unbearable pain — of the swelling in her brain that would surely kill her if we could not decrease it; and I took my place — number eleven — in the line of fifteen women squatting in the dark.

To her credit, Deirdre McNab — having established the rules of barter — took the last place in that line.

Each woman rose in turn and went to the fence, lost from our sight entirely by the time she had gone no more than five paces. The dark is very dark in the tropics. No amount of stars will light it as they would up here in Maine. Two-minute intervals separated our journeys.

As my turn approached, the only thing I could think about was that I was going off through the dark to meet some man or woman whose face I would never see — whose only contact with me would be one hand to receive — and one to give — each hand pushed in turn between the wires.

That they would not see me seemed equally strange. But not inhuman. In straits like these — a hand is all the human being we need.

103: I must finish this tale. I am compelled.

At last my turn came.

The woman behind me pushed her finger in the small of my back, almost causing me to fall. When I stood, I discovered one leg had gone to sleep. It was a nightmare walk. A dream walk — all in slow motion through the mud.

When I got to the fence — I only had to touch it to let the person on the other side know I was there. No words. No vocal communication of any kind. The only language we had was in our fingers.

I felt a hand on my wrist. It squeezed, as if to open my palm. I understood it wanted to receive my barter. This is where my heart stopped. I had imagined the exchange would be simultaneous — my ring for their aspirin and quinine. Not so. They wanted to know what I was offering.

I withdrew the ring — it was gold and engraved with my parents' initials and the date of their marriage: *30 October 1924* — and I laid it in my palm and passed my hand beyond the wire.

The ring was removed so carefully — with a touch so light — a bird might have taken it. I then heard the unmistakable sound of someone opening their mouth and biting the ring.

I waited.

Surely they would recognize its purity in seconds.

At last, the fingers touched my palm again. I felt the weight of one glass phial — and then the weight of a second — each phial already hot from having rested in the palm of my anonymous trader. When I hesitated — not knowing whether that was the end of our barter — not knowing how many aspirin — not knowing how many quinine tablets might be in the phials — a whole hand pressed itself upon me and folded my fingers back across my palm, enclosing the phials.

I withdrew — and went away to Mother without looking back.

When I had returned, soaking wet and muddied now from head to toe, I found Mother where I had left her — crouching by my cot, but now asleep.

I woke her and gave her the phials and said to her; "done."

She counted the aspirin — *twelve* and she counted the quinine tablets — *ten*. Whoever had been beyond the fence at least had stuck to the bargain.

Mother went away without a word. She had lost her ring forever — and I'm certain she regretted it down to the depths of her being. But she was also triumphant. Now there was something concrete she could do for Dorothy Busch.

I crawled back beneath my netting, even as I was — all mud and sweat and fear — and I could not, and I did not sleep that whole night through. All I could think of was the fingers I had touched and the face I would never see. So I listened to the birds — and I waited for the sun.

104: The next morning, I was come for by one of Norimitsu's men. He came with his rifle in his hands and he prodded me with its barrel through the mosquito netting.

All the other women in the barrack watched in silence — (this was our rule) — as I was marched away, barefooted still, and still in my dark cotton "liberation" dress — down the steps — across the compound and through the gate.

I was taken all the way to the Colonel's residence with the gun in my back — and without a word.

When I reached his gate — I looked in past his gardens towards the wide, wooden steps that led up onto the porch. That other morning, a year before, he had stood there and watched me through the rain.

Colonel Norimitsu's gardens were all of sand and rock. No flowers. The sand was always meticulously raked — the rocks that had stood there for about two years were green with moss and they looked like islands, stranded in the sea.

It was raining now, as the guard behind me prodded me through the gate and along the path and up the steps.

At the door, he made me wait.

There was, in fact, no door as such — but a doorway only, with a short ceremonial cloth as cover.

The soldier bent beneath the edge of the cloth and I heard him announce my presence. Seconds later, he reappeared and nodded at me. I was to go inside.

I had not had time to prepare myself for this — or even to imagine why I had been summoned. It occurred to me, of course, with a rush of terrific fear, that it must have something to do with my journey to the fence the night before. But I could not quite make out why I had been chosen as the victim. No other women, of all the fifteen, had been taken to the Colonel. I knew who some of them were, and as I had passed their barracks, I had seen them. Also, I had seen Deirdre McNab going about her business with her usual quiet efficiency — and none that I saw gave any appearance of having been interrogated or punished.

Perhaps I was the first.

Colonel Norimitsu sat behind a plain wooden table that was barren as a solid desert. His face, beneath his shaven skull, was almost beautiful. His eyes were anything but cruel — though, equally, anything but kind. I found it impossible to read them.

He waited for a moment before he spoke — and I watched him watching me and I thought that I must present a picture equally difficult to read; my hair held wet against my head, my arms and shins the colour of mud and my dress like a costume worn in the wrong scene.

I thought it was certain I was to be punished for what I had done — and, since the law I had broken was among the laws for which the punishment was greatest, I dreaded what might be forthcoming.

Colonel Norimitsu, who was of average height for a Japanese — about five feet six or seven inches — rose behind his table.

His English was stilted and incorrect when he finally spoke, but he spoke with perfect civility — and even with feeling.

"I have," he said; "for you something that has been of your own."

I think I blinked at him.

He held out a small, folded square of paper.

For a moment, I could not retrieve it. I couldn't think what it was; certainly nothing I had written.

"Take, please," the Colonel said.

I "took."

As soon as the paper was in my hand, I knew what it contained. Though I did not open it, I knew by what I could feel of its shape that the perfectly folded packet enclosed my mother's wedding ring.

I held it — staring at Colonel Norimitsu — completely uncomprehending.

"Go now," he said. "No examinations."

He came around the table and went through beneath the curtain onto his porch.

I followed him, the packet still in my fist.

I dared not thank him. I knew he did not want that. He did not really want me even to acknowledge what he had done.

He pointed across at the compound with his chin — his hands behind his back — and he said; "you will stand there sixteen hours."

"Yes," I said — understanding. I must appear, of course, to be punished.

Then he looked down into his garden — and indicated briefly the way the rocks had been set in the wide expanse of tranquil sand — which, even in the rain, retained the swirls of his raking.

"Islands of Nippon," he said.

I looked.

Of course. The stones were perfect replicas of Shikoku — Kyushu — Hokkaido and Honshu — the four major islands of Japan.

105: I stood that day for sixteen hours in the rain. I faced his garden. And he came from time to time to watch me as he had before. I held the packet, still unfolded, in my hand. I made a list of meanings as I stood there: that it was entirely possible Norimitsu's hands themselves had dispensed the medicine through the fence; that he had recognized my mother's ring by its initials and knew it could only be returned by me — who had been his witness the morning after my father's death; that *even monsters are not always monsters*, as he would later say; that I was as old, in that moment, as I would ever be; and that my ignorance, until that moment, of the truth about human nature had been as wide as the Sea of Japan; and the Sea of Japan was sand.

106: Dorothy Busch did not survive, for all our pains. She will never be forgotten. I learned from her — because of her — that we sacrifice less often to the mysteries of wonder than we should. No one could define her character. She had simply been immensely alive. And the weight of her death was commensurate. It extended all the way to her enemies.

107: I like less and less my suspicion that since the world is always falling away toward the horizon, life is also falling away. And that we — like the ships I've been watching with their sails and wisps of smoke — tip over the edge and simply vanish. I wish I did not believe that death is nothing more than that; a vanishing. The thought seems unworthy, somehow, of a fifty-nine-year-old; though I've always believed I was lucky not to share the popular view of death as a punishment or just reward. If I could only learn to be at peace with that wonderfully simple, scientific fact of life: *we die.* Surely, *how* we die is all that matters, when it comes to that.

108: When I felt I had sufficiently regained my equilibrium to leave the beach, I rose from my dune and made my way to the boardwalk. Two stiff drinks had never been a problem in the past — since they would never, in the past I have lived, have been taken in the same day, let alone the same hour. I have only ever indulged in alcoholic beverages in the ceremonial sense. Occasionally, wine with dinner — occasionally, a sherry in the afternoon — a Manhattan in the evening. Gin had never crossed my lips, and vodka had not until my encounter with it that afternoon. I fully expected to suffer from the well-publicized hangover headache — but nothing of the kind occurred. I was, however, concerned about my pills. We are told so often never to take a pill in conjunction with alcohol. It is a rule I have always obeyed. Still, there seemed to be no deleterious effects and I presumed I had been lucky.

There were darker concerns than my health as I stepped up onto the boardwalk, preparing to make my way to the Hotel. What had become of Meg's pictures — and how could I find out? A simple theft is easy enough to challenge. You ask. I have always believed in that. But this was not a simple theft; the implications must have been understood as vividly by the thief as they were by me. I was not so concerned about approaching Meg as I was about approaching Nigel. Each might very well have a perfectly valid reason for lifting the photographs — though I could not quite make that valid reason up, on Nigel's behalf. Meg was straightforward enough. Surely, if she had taken them, the reason must be that she wanted to show them to Michael. But, if she had taken them, why not say so? All she had to do was leave a message with Robin: *I've borrowed the photographs of me.* But she hadn't done that. Nor had she scribbled any note.

What legitimate reason might Nigel have?

These were not photographs that compromised him. And, if he had somehow taken advantage of the opportunity to glance at them when he brought the manilla envelope, he would have seen there was nothing there for him to worry about. Besides which, if the fool only knew enough about snapshots, he'd have realized no commercial printer would have developed a photograph of a naked man. It should only have been the negatives Nigel would be interested in. But I couldn't trust him to know that.

It must have been Meg, I concluded. And she was showing them to Michael. At dinner-time, they would be returned and her explanation given. Or I would find them, even now, in my mailbox at the Desk.

I had started away, during all these thoughts, and begun my walk up the lawn — when I heard an aeroplane overhead and saw a number of people pointing to it.

Looking up, I could see a monoplane flying relatively low and heading seaward. It was dragging a great, long banner of the sort that advertises the opening of charity bazaars and shopping malls.

The message could not be read at the angle currently being displayed — and I turned, with everybody else, to watch as the little monoplane made its way above the bath houses and over the sand. When it got as far as the iceberg, it altered its course and began to fly in a parallel with the beach.

Now, its message was perfectly clear.

BERGS GO BETTER WITH COKE!

I turned and made my way past the staring others — and I didn't stop until I had reached the lobby.

109: The lobby was all but deserted. On one of the sofas were a young man and woman — transients, no doubt — sitting primly having an argument. She did not care for the Aurora Sands Hotel and wanted to leave. He said they had to stay because the Pine Point Inn did not cater to travellers who had no reservations and the nearest accommodation was miles away and they would have to "sneak around the road-block again."

These words intrigued me, because they implied that people were being prevented from coming through — but I got no

further with this intrigue before I was interrupted by the
sound of raised voices in the offices behind the Desk. One of
the voices I definitely recognized as belonging to Lawrence.
The other — raised a little less — belonged, I was fairly certain, to Quinn Welles.

Cathy was standing behind the Desk, her face a mask of
deafness.

"Ahem," I said — and smiled.

She came out of her frozen pose and looked at me sharply,
as if she did not at first realize who had spoken. "Yes, Miss
Van Horne?"

"I can't quite see my box from here, dear," I said — a lie.
"Have I had some mail, by any chance?"

She turned and looked.

"No, ma'am."

Just as she was about to turn away again, there was an
extraordinary shout from the office behind her — where the
door was only partially closed. The shouter was Lawrence and
I will not repeat here what he said. The gist of it — without
the unrepeatable adjectives — was that *Quinn Welles needed his
head examined if he didn't think that something strange was going
on.* Et cetera.

"Excuse me, Miss Van Horne," said Cathy, and she
stepped across to the door and pulled it closed.

By this time, the argumentative transients were frozen in
their seats, staring at the Desk as if it might explode. I smiled
at them benignly — thinking what a dreadful impression they
were being given of our wonderful old Hotel.

The door — just closed — now opened, and Ellen Welles
came out with Judy, the girl who alternated Desk duty with
Cathy.

Judy had been crying and Ellen had her arm around the
girl's shoulder. The possibilities of this scenario were end-
lessly alarming. What had Lawrence to do with this weeping
child? Why was he raising his voice and using such dreadful

language to Quinn Welles — who, after all, was his host? And why did Ellen look at me the way she did as she passed around the end of the Desk and led Judy out towards *The Dorm* through the front door?

The answers were almost immediately forthcoming.

Lawrence Pawley came out of Quinn Welles's office looking like a man who had just been fired. He was pale and he was shaking — and it was obvious, because of the expression on his face, that he had lost whatever argument had just occurred.

He came all the way around the end of the Desk and went all the way across the lobby to the front door before I was aware he knew I was there.

"I need you, Vanessa," he said. "I'll wait outside."

When he had gone, I collected my wits only enough to turn back towards Cathy and ask a quite unnecessary question. "Do you happen to know," I said; "if reservations must be made if a person intends to go dancing up at the Pine Point Inn?"

Cathy herself was still in the process of collecting her wits. "I...don't know," she said. "I..."

Quinn Welles was standing behind her.

"No, you don't, Miss Van Horne," he said. "But it's probably wisest to get there by eight."

I thanked him. Quinn is a decent young man. No doubt, the loss of his family's Hotel weighs heavily on his conscience. I think he's dealt with it openly and well, being perfectly honest about the reasons for the sale — though, naturally, he's never mentioned figures. And he's been quite straight about the fact he knows a good many of us find it hard to forgive him. We, after all, have just as much history invested here as he has. Some of us have more. But Quinn has never turned away from our displeasure; he's never tried to pretend it isn't justified. He has also never tried to pretend he didn't want the sale to take place. The weight that will be lifted from his

shoulders will be enormous. Not to have to endure the endless
fear of fire, to begin with. For years, he has had to balance
what he could afford, in terms of safety measures, against the
ever-accelerating demands of remodelling. I am proud to say
I have not been among those guests who complain, on the one
hand, that should there be a fire, "the place would go up like
a tinder box" and, on the other hand, that Quinn Welles has
"ruined the look of my dear old ceiling by putting in a
sprinkler system." These are the very same people who argue
loudest at the Desk because Quinn has had to raise the rates,
due only to installing the very safety measures that would save
their lives. Sometimes, he must think some of us are beneath
contempt.

For all these reasons, I feel rather sorry for Quinn, having
to cope with Calder's death in his last year as owner — and
now, at this particular moment, with an obstreperous guest in
the person of Lawrence Pawley.

I, of course, was dying of curiosity. What could have caused
the contretemps — and why had Judy been crying?

I waited — adjusting the contents of my carryall in an
attempt to let him know I was willing to hear his story, but all
I heard was; "Cathy, would you come into the office for a
minute?"

I looked up to see the girl follow Quinn beyond the door —
and then to watch the door close. Its closing was like a gentle
— almost insolent — slap in the face.

I could feel the transients watching me and turned towards
them, "happily" saying; "if you're here because of the
iceberg, you won't find a better view of it anywhere else along
the coast!"

Then I hastened towards the front door. But not fast enough
to miss the young woman saying to her husband; "iceberg?
What iceberg? I think these people here are all crazy!"

110: Out on the driveway, Lawrence was waiting for me in a state of barely contained fury.

It seems that, while I was indulging in twin Bloody Marys and sitting down on the sand, Lawrence had been busy making discoveries.

To begin with, he had been tinkering with the Buick while mulling over the possible fate of Lily Porter and wondering how we might rescue her, when — out of the corner of his eye — he had seen Nigel Forestead sauntering towards *The Dorm*.

Lawrence is no more a fan of Nigel's than I am and finds him doubly odious, I think, because he is a man. Men do not want other men to be like Nigel; they feel such men betray their sex by presenting — as Nigel does, in one impeccable package — all that is worst about manhood: vanity, acquisitiveness and misogyny. These are qualities most men have, but try to mask one way or another. They obscure their vanity with mock humility; they wield their acquisitiveness behind a flurry of jargon that is meant to make us all believe the market at large is their only concern — and they keep their misogyny at home by mistreating their wives, while women at large are treated to expense accounts. Nigel Forestead tramples all their efforts underfoot by wearing white suits and pressed pyjamas; dropping his stock-market gains like gold ingots on everyone's toes and by displaying his contempt for Maryanne so publicly it is only her own stupidity that saves her.

No wonder, then, that as soon as Lawrence saw Nigel making for *The Dorm*, he followed him. Anything to catch him red-handed in the conspiracy to hide Calder's body or kidnap Lily Porter.

What he ultimately discovered, I would call inconclusive. But Lawrence behaves as if he had found Nigel rocking Calder's corpse in his arms.

He followed him all the way to the laundromat. (Who but
Nigel Forestead, with his manic penchant for white, could
need the landromat more?) He then waited — as he said to me
with his boylike enthusiasm for games — "counting to a hundred by fives" before he went in after him. Alas — when he
went through the door, there sat Maryanne. She was doing the
Forestead wash — just as Petra had done the Pawley wash that
morning. But Nigel was nowhere in sight.

This could only mean one thing. He had gone — just as we
had — out through the back door into the lane and round to
the stable, where Calder's body lies hidden in its crate of ice.

Lawrence was about to follow when Maryanne stopped
him. One of the dryers wasn't functioning — and couldn't
"Doctor Pawley please help a woman in distress?"

I can hear her saying those very words; her eyes like saucers
— her body insinuating itself upon the space between herself
and Lawrence.

"No," said Lawrence. "I don't know the first thing about
machines."

He turned to the rear door.

"But you *must*," said Maryanne. "You're a *man* ... "

"I don't care what I am," said Lawrence. "I don't know
how to fix machines."

All this caused a delay of perhaps three minutes — what
with the other niceties of time-wasting chatter that Maryanne
injected. And then — just as Lawrence was well and truly free
of her and on his way to the door — the door opened and in
walked Nigel.

Thwarted — Lawrence said the wrong thing. "Been
upstairs with one of the students, have you, Forestead?"

He'd hoped — as he heard the sentence flowing from his
own lips, unbidden — that Maryanne would take it as a joke.

She didn't.

"Oh!" she said to Nigel, hurt and outraged. "You told me
you were just relieving yourself!"

At this, apparently, Nigel blushed.

And Lawrence left, without the concrete evidence he desired and had been so certain was in his grasp.

But he did not accept defeat.

Every ounce of his judgment seems (to me) to have deserted him from start to finish in this whole incident. The ending was worst of all.

Determined that Nigel was acting as the "keeper of the corpse" for whoever had put it there — "probably goes in and sees the ice hasn't melted and when he has to order more" — Lawrence was crossing the driveway — making once again for the Buick parked beside Rossiter, when, as bad luck would have it, Judy — the girl from the Desk — was coming off duty.

Lawrence leapt to his decision the instant he saw her. Hadn't she been the girl on the Desk the evening Nigel had made his phone calls to the Police? Hadn't she been the one who put the calls through for him?

Yes.

And so he had said to her; "Judy, could I have a word with you?"

And the word had been disastrous.

In short, he had tried to persuade her that it was her duty to monitor "all of Mister Forestead's calls from here on in." He explained to the poor child that Mister Forestead was up to something that "smells to high heaven and that..."

And here, he went the whole way overboard.

Lawrence would provide remuneration for whatever information concerning Mister Forestead's calls she passed on to him.

Judy, though I call her a child, is nineteen. Her subject at Mount Holyoke just happens to be political science. She is — the dear girl, and thank God — an idealist at heart. She had heard of Mister Nixon and his tapes and of Mister Mitchell and his wire-taps and she said; "I cannot do that."

I cannot do that.

In the light of Joel's refusal to break the law for Chilcott's side, and of Judy's refusal to break the law on our side, I can only stand up and cheer. The young have not got all the way into our society, yet. Or — I feel I must add, in the light of other realities — not *all* the young have got there. Certainly Nigel Forestead has.

"You must have been out of your mind," I said to Lawrence. "You must have been crazy to suggest such a thing."

He looked me in the eye and said with rather chilling logic, I fear; "You want to save Lily?"

And I said; "yes."

"Then I'm not crazy, Vanessa," said Lawrence. "I just want to bring this thing to a head."

I waited for a moment before I said; "what happened with Quinn?"

"Oh — the silly girl *told* him," he said. "Then I got a call to come over at once and explain myself."

"Well — you can hardly blame him."

"Oh?" said Lawrence. "Hasn't it occurred to you — all this cannot possibly be happening on Quinn Welles's property without his knowing something about it?"

I took a deep breath. It was true. Such a thought had not occurred to me.

"Now, because of that stupid blabbermouth, Judy — Quinn may be on to us."

"But we haven't done anything," I said.

Lawrence just looked at me; silent.

We had, of course, done something. Or rather — he had.

111: So, tonight I will go dancing.

Lawrence and Petra will take me. I used it as my olive branch and forced it on them by paying for a sitter. The children need a break from Petra, anyway. She's with them twenty-four hours a day and all they've ever seen her do is read a book. It can't be healthy. I never see them playing with other children. Never. All they do is hang around that cottage — or ride off down the drive on their bikes and disappear for hours; always, always in one another's company — never anyone else's. It must be wrong. They need the challenge of other people. I think I'll get that Margaret with the short, red hair; the athletic one, whom all the others seem to be so fond of. Though I'm very fond of Honor, I've always wished the red-haired Margaret waited on me — but she is on the other side of the dining-room. She waits on Meg and Michael; on Lena Rumplemeyer; Major-General and Mrs. Welch; the Boys. The Boys are always making fun of her and she adores it. Mad-for-laughter-Margaret. Yes — I'll arrange for her to baby-sit. Maybe she can do for Hogarth and Denise what no one else can do — and bring them back to life.

Petra will pretend she doesn't want to come dancing and there will be much bad temper. Good. She can throw another tantrum — scream: *I haven't worn a dress for months!* Wonderful! Petra's revolutionary-feminist pique! *I swore I wouldn't ever dress up again! I swore I wouldn't get my hair done! I swore I wouldn't put on make-up — wear high heels! You're forcing me into the mould! I'll kill you!* And she will love it. At least her adrenalin will. It will have somewhere to go, instead of all that hothouse seething it's been up to.

It's time for Petra and Lawrence to have the battle lines redrawn. The silence between them must be broken. Out of the closet — hauled out on hangers; one long dress and one blue blazer — a woman and a man; satin shoes and dancing pumps; necklaces and neckties. Into a social context at last — all four of them; parents and children alike.

Lawrence will love it, too; a chance to flail at something certain — something definable — instead of that enigmatic body up in the stable, floating in its ice-cubes — and the ambiguous Nigel Forestead, playing black and wearing white — and the elusive Doctor Chilcott, here and there and everywhere.

112: Some boundaries need no road-blocks; some are unthinkable to cross. Such is the boundary between the Pine Point Inn and the Aurora Sands Hotel.

Isn't it wonderful that adult people should maintain such myths as these — all the legends of prejudice that have kept the populations of these two hotels apart for so long?

I can barely count the things that go through my mind when I think how we detest the Pine Point people — how we cast aspersions on every aspect of their lives; their money and their taste — their motorcars and marriages — their cultural opaqueness and lack of intellectual interests — their softness, exemplified by their endless rows of golf carts on their nine-hole course. And their steel-lined swimming pool down by the sea.

Tonight, we will infiltrate their territory. Disguised as revellers. But we will only do it in order to bring Lily Porter home.

113: In the lobby of the ASH, Arabella and the rest of *Stonehenge* sat in their places watching over the rims of their steel-framed glasses. At the top of the stairs, I hesitated; *do I remember how to do this — make an entrance; not fall down?* I placed my fingers, already holding my bag, against my thigh and I lifted the weight of my taffeta skirts away from my toes. I thought of all the years we did this every night — Mother and I, together — coming down these stairs in dresses to the floor. But not since 1955 or '56; now thirty years ago and more.

I've only worn it once, this dress; the night of my induction into the Academy last fall. That was before the heart attacks and Mother's death. I stood a little straighter then — I guess. Straighter — taller — less afraid of my falling bosom. The dress is what Meg has called a *masochist's delight*; severe. It is cut entirely in straight lines — the neckline squared, with an inset panel of velvet across the chest; perfect for pearls. Though I still have my waist, I wear it without a belt. I like the way it moves; the weight, deceptive — heavy. I like to feel the weight of skirts against my legs. I cannot bear material that feels as if it isn't there. The taffeta — black — is shot through with threads of Prussian blue and green. My shoes are of satin; teal. I also wear my Chinese jacket, with all its silver birds and cobalt dragons.

Thinking of Arabella, just as I began my descent, I pushed the jacket open. I wanted to make the lining show to good advantage. It is rose. I knew it was smashing. I wished I was an actress. Still, I had to do the best I could — and I lifted the hem and came down into the light.

Arabella saw me and pulled her thread a little slower through the canvas. Her needle flashed — fishlike, leaping out of the sea of crepe in her lap. I wish it could leap, of its own volition, straight up into her eye.

I smiled. But I did not move in her direction.

All of the *Henge* was watching me.

"Nessa-Vanessa-Essa..." I heard. A nest of snakes.

Nigel and Maryanne were coming in, slow motion, off the

porch. Nigel's yellow shoes had grass stains on them; lime-green. I knew he hadn't seen them, yet. I prayed he wouldn't till he was standing centre stage in maximum light, the focus of every eye. Total embarrassment. It's overdue. He got, however, all the way to my vicinity without once looking down at the floor.

"You're wearing your Chinese jacket," he said — with bureaucratic certainty; the obvious is always safe.

I was silent.

"Lovely," said Maryanne — reaching with an impertinent hand to touch it. "Is it real?"

I stepped away. *Recoiled* is a better word. I recoiled.

"Are you going out, Miss Van Horne?" Nigel asked.

"Dancing," I told him.

"Lovely," said Maryanne again. "And so are we." She beamed at Nigel and hugged his arm. "And tomorrow," she said to me; "have you been invited?"

Nigel went as pale as his suit.

Invited?

114: Petra hiked her long green skirts above her knees and drove in her bare feet. I sat up front. Lawrence had to sit sideways in the back. Watching as we left, Margaret, the redhead, stood beyond the screen door of Rossiter and lifted one hand in a grave salute. Denise and Hogarth were apparently in exile — self-imposed — and nowhere to be seen. It was not an auspicious beginning to our evening.

Petra had not deigned to mention — let alone thank me for — the provision of a sitter and Lawrence said only one sentence before he fell into a moody silence behind us. His sentence was: "stop at Waldo's — for cigarettes." In the meantime, I was handed Petra's shoes in a plastic bag and told not to drop them. They rode in my lap like an unwanted pair of cats about to be drowned.

The drive, in spite of all its tensions, was one of those reminders of how deep your gratitude for being alive can be, when the night air blows in through the windows, redolent with pine and sea. I sat in a mesmerized silence, gazing with half-closed eyes at the passing woods and marshes, the darkling flights of homing birds and the poignant views of brilliant sky reflected in the calm, grey inlet beyond the road, to the right.

We passed the D.A.R. Retirement Home For Ladies on our left, its pale ascetic rooms looking bleak beyond its groves of maple trees and beech. Petra grunted her Democrat disapproval. This made me smile. Then we passed my own favourite establishment — Hilliard's Greenhouse and Nursery, with all its tubs of red geraniums and bags of sphagnum moss in the courtyard; all its messy loops of hose and all its dusty crates of mock-Grecian urns; its bundles of bamboo rakes and inviting shovels.

And then we came to Waldo's.

The Retirement Home and Hilliard's are on the sea side of the road. Waldo's is on the right and it sits about a dozen yards from the borderline between the public sector of the Neck and the private enclave of Larson's itself. At the farthest edge of Waldo's property — his sandy little parking lot — is the first of the signs that warns invaders: LARSON'S NECK IS PATROLLED BY PRIVATE POLICE FORCE.

Petra drew the Buick to a stop in front of the store and left the engine running. Lawrence uncurled himself from the back and made a great show of slamming the door as he left us. The yard was lit with a spill of light from *Waldo's Variety and Beer*, whose windows are filled with displays of Coppertone sun-tan lotion, mounded orange tennis balls and stacks of Campbell's soup cans. Above the door, a cloud of pale grey moths was courting disaster where the *Miller's High Life* sign burns red. It struck me, as I watched, how sad it was that miller moths should flock to perish at their name. The detritus of their burned-out corpses made a kind of dust on the steps. I closed my eyes and drew in the smells of motor oil and gasoline from the pumps and I let it mingle with the smells of salt-water marshes, trees, dirt roads — the very quintessence of Maine in summer. In spite of the running engine, I could hear the songs of nightjars, tree toads and frogs and the nervous chirping of crickets. Nightfall almost anywhere — but if I added the cries of tropical birds, I could have the whole of Java in my ears. And did.

I looked at Petra, wishing one of us would speak. But she was as grim as ever — mouth set hard against her teeth and her gaze uncommitted — uncommittable; a total refusal to engage in any kind of contact. I looked to my right, at Waldo's windows.

There was a sign in one of them I had not seen before.

Crudely made, perhaps in haste, the letters had an *ad hoc* look because they had been lifted from one of those self-adhesive letter sets you find in magazine offices, the kind that editors use to do a mock-up. Here, in Waldo's Variety window, the absence of an editor was all too obvious. The letters had been dispensed without any sense of balance and two of the words had been misspelled. The phrasing, too, was odd; a mix of pander and command:

VISITORS TO LARSON'S NECK!
ANYONE WISHING TO VIEW
THE HARPER MUSEUM
WILL HAVE TO RETURN IN TWO WEEKS TIME AS
THE BUILDING HOUSING THEODORE HARPER'S
STUDIO IS CLOSED FOR RENAVATIONS UNTIL
ON SATURDAY THE 3RD OF AUGUST
WE ARE SORRY FOR THE INCONVENIENCE

SIGNED
Wm. Billings,
Chief-of-Police

ABSOLUTELY NO ADMITTANCE

Why, I thought, should the Chief-of-Police put his name to such an announcement? Surely, it would suffice to have the museum's director do so. On the other hand, having seen this particular Chief-of-Police in action on the beach, I can well believe there is nothing on Larson's Neck he does not himself decree. He gives the appearance — Wm. Billings — both in style and manner, of a petty dictator. The Neck, no doubt is his personal Haiti.

115: When Lawrence returned to the car — the pockets of his blazer disfigured by lumpy packs of cigarettes — he broke the silence by saying that Mister Waldo had told him something more than a little disturbing.

"He was handing over my change and he obviously saw I was all dressed up and he said *going dancing?* and when I said *yes*, he made a face and said *got your passport with you?* And when I laughed and said *no, Pine Point is still America*, he looked at me, deadly serious, and said *you think I'm kidding?*

And when I said *of course I do,* he said *I'm not. It's harder to get up onto the Neck this weekend than it was to get into the U.S. Compound in Saigon back in 1975. I know, 'cause I was there. Hotel's about as far as you can go without being stopped. Stopped?* I said. And he said *cold.*"

Petra released the brake. We lurched forward past the first of the LARSON'S NECK PATROLLED BY PRIVATE POLICE FORCE signs and I found myself clutching the bag of shoes as if it was suddenly contraband.

Stopped cold. Surely that could not be right. I realized Mister Waldo had meant we could get to the Pine Point Inn without a problem — but a person does want occasionally to visit friends in the Larson's enclave. Mercedes, for instance. And no matter what was going on at the Neck, nothing could warrant the prevention of citizens using a public road. And Saigon? That was crazy.

"Do you really think Calder Maddox's death has caused all this fuss and all these precautions?" I asked. "I find it quite impossible to believe."

"Believe it," said Lawrence. "Our friend was a much bigger gun than any of us likes to think. I'm absolutely certain Chilcott or one of his people must have killed Calder Maddox and they're moving heaven and earth to cover it up."

"But surely," I said; "they can't be so inept. I mean, if they wanted Calder dead — for whatever reason — then all they had to do was arrange to let him die on an operating table. After all, Chilcott is one of the country's leading physicians. And you, of all people, Lawrence, must be aware that anything can happen inside a hospital."

"Right," said Petra. The first word she'd spoken.

"Especially to someone old as Calder was," I said. "*Phht!* he has a heart attack. *Phht!* he expires under the anaesthetic. What could be easier?"

"Lots could be easier," said Lawrence. "Letting him die of natural causes, for one thing. But the most important thing about this murder is timing, Nessa. That's what this is about. Timing, not technique."

116: The Pine Point Inn is lit with amber lights and its driveways and parking lots are bordered with wooden posts and garlands of heavy chains — the chains painted white. Valet parking provides a handsome young man wearing a scarlet jacket. I stood on the bottom step with Petra's shoes in their plastic bag. She dropped her skirts and came around the front of the car barefooted. I closed my eyes against the embarrassment of it all; the dreadful state of the car and the way that Petra walks, head down and shoulders hunched; the endless lengths of Lawrence, disgruntled and muttering, unfolding from the back seat and the way he spoke to the lad: *don't bang the fenders* — as if it mattered.

Petra started up the steps and I had to remind her she wasn't fully dressed. She put her shoes on, standing in the middle of the entrance, and handed me the plastic bag as though it was mine to deal with.

Not having anywhere to put it — (I was not about to slip it into my pocket-book) — I rolled it into a ball and kept it in the palm of my hand. In the meantime, Lawrence followed Petra into the lobby and the wide screen door swung out towards me and almost struck me in the face. By the time I got inside, I was not in the best of moods.

The lobby of the Pine Point Inn has a kind of magazine elegance of which I heartily disapprove; much red leather and oak veneer. A fire was burning in a grossly oversized fireplace. A table for twelve could have been set on the hearth, and the fire itself made no more sense than a furnace in Jakarta. This, to our right.

On our left, the reception area — marble counters and glassy offices. Straight in front of us, stairwells and hallways. The sound of music came from a distance, muffled by walls and muted by corridors. There were eight or nine people in

the lobby, some of them in evening dress — others in mufti.
When someone laughed, it was almost shocking. No one had
laughed at the ASH for days.

None of this was quite the way I had expected it to be. At
worst, I had thought we might find a convention of thugs; at
best, a gathering of sober-suited politicians surrounded by
their bodyguards. This much proved to be true; the
bodyguards were there.

Anyone with half an eye on the television news can pick
these bodyguards out of a crowd in five seconds. The President, his Cabinet and anyone else of the slightest consequence
is surrounded by them in every circumstance. They all wear
the same dishevelled suit and have the same squinting eyes.
Their jackets are always unbuttoned and their shoes look immense. They never, never smile. They are the moths around
the lights of power and they appear to court not danger, as the
moths at Waldo's do, but a challenge to their watchfulness.
They wear the expressions of aggressive boys in school-yards,
daring their playmates to attack them from behind. For all
that I dislike them, I do admit they must have God's worst job
in these days of terror, when they know that any second they
may die.

There were three of these men that night in the lobby of the
Pine Point Inn, but their presence was not explained or
clarified by the presence of any recognizable target for
violence. They were simply — watchfully — there. Standing
under their gaze, I dreaded to think what eminence might
suddenly emerge from the lifts or come down the stairs. Doctor Chilcott alone could not by any stretch — not even of his
own imagination — warrant so many watchdogs.

For the briefest moment, their animal wariness was turned
on us as we entered the lobby. This was their purview and we
were strangers. One of them nudged another — making no
secret of what he did — and the other nodded. We had been

"recognized" — whatever that may mean. It may have meant we were known by name — it may only have meant we were aliens standing in the landscape. I had to consciously prevent myself from nodding my acknowledgement of their attentions. Something childish in me wanted to make a face and say: *boo!*

As Lawrence adjusted his tie, I noted with chagrin that some industrious member of the staff had mounted a display of ICEBERG MEMORABILIA on the bulletin board. I don't know why this irked me, but it did. Perhaps because I had thought of the iceberg as being the exclusive property of the Aurora Sands Hotel — a marvel upon which only we at the ASH were allowed to gaze. Of course, I should have known better. We had already lost our exclusive rights to the makers of Coca-Cola. Still, I cannot rid myself entirely of a niggling resentment that *our* iceberg — that *my* iceberg — (I was the first, after all!) — had been commandeered by the Pine Point Recreations Officer and pinned to his bulletin board along with advertisements for Waterways Wonderland and Scarborough Downs Racetrack.

As we left the lobby and headed for Nash's Pump Room, I paused just long enough to get a closer view of this ICEBERG MEMORABILIA. The photographs pinned to the board showed various angles of the berg, including views that could only have been snapped from our part of the beach. These had the same views of Surrey Island as mine did. They also showed a few of the guests at the ASH, including — lo and behold — myself! An unpleasant surprise. Most of these photos were bad, by reason of lack of focus and general technique. Children's pictures, no doubt. Many of them were Polaroids. Pinned up beside them was a card — hand printed — soliciting more: COME ONE — COME ALL! — it said. All the pictures were to be entered in a contest. *Professional judges will award three prizes! First prize — a Minolta camera.*

Not at all bad, if you think about it; worth up to six hundred dollars. Well. I pondered. No. I am not the contestant type. I dismissed it from my mind.

117: Nash's Pump Room is a lopsided mix of Regency elegance and Rampart Street decay. The decay, I should add, is no more real than the overlay of elegance. They are both very much in league with the magazine charm of the lobby.

"There's a man over there in make-up," said Petra.

"Men have been wearing make-up for five whole years," said Lawrence. "Haven't you noticed?"

Petra waved her hand. Of course she hadn't noticed. When was she ever out of a book long enough to notice anything real?

"I'll have a Manhattan, please," I told the waiter when he arrived. I removed my Chinese jacket, exposing my pearls and velvet. Lawrence gave me a strange little look and ordered a double vodka for himself.

"I'll have a Marguerita," said Petra. "Two bits of lime on the side."

Our table was on the rise above the dance floor. It gave us a good view of the whole room — including the smoke. Nigel Forestead, shining in his whites, was visible directly opposite beyond the dancing. Maryanne was not in evidence. Some other woman was, however, and Nigel was talking to her, looking up from his place while the woman stood beside him.

She was tall and darkly tanned and I guessed at once she had to be the mysterious occupant of Halfway House. It was the way she touched herself that gave her away. Her fingers seldom strayed from her neckline — the neckline cut extremely low but, somehow, not unbecoming. She was immensely and genuinely attractive; nothing slovenly or cheap about her appearance, despite the cut of her gown. She wore no make-up and her abundant honey-coloured hair was displayed unfettered; shoulder length. It would have been a shame to hide it. She carried herself with the confidence of a *ballerina assoluta* — straight up through the back and across the shoulders.

Nigel, I noted, was nervous — perhaps because Maryanne might suddenly return and force an introduction he was not prepared to give. His eyes made forays into other corners of the room, whereas this other woman's eyes were steadfast and politely fixed on him. I decided then and there to call her the *Honey Girl* — because of her hair.

Presently, our drinks arrived and when the waiter had cleared the view, I saw that Nigel was being approached on another front. He looked up, startled — briefly giving the appearance of someone trapped.

The man who now arrived at the Forestead table was unmistakably the Pine Point Recreations Director. He was golden, young and offensively pleasant. He wore white trousers and a red blazer, the lapel of which was crested with a button I knew by instinct must have read: *Hello! I'm Jiminy Cricket!*

Nigel still did not rise from his chair. He accepted *Hello-I'm-Jiminy*'s hand and could not get rid of it. He gestured unsuccessfully up at the *Honey Girl*, who smiled and nodded and had the good sense to back away. *Jiminy* crowded in to her place, with his back firmly set in her direction and his hand firmly glued to Nigel's. The *Honey Girl* departed and *Jiminy* sat down.

At last, Nigel retrieved his hand and a relatively short conversation ensued. The only animation occurred when Nigel patted his breast pocket and drew out a long, white envelope.

Jiminy accepted the envelope; glanced inside and fingered the contents. After this, he got to his feet and, mouthing an effusive *thanks*, he strode away athletically, shouldering aside whoever got in his way.

By this time, Nigel Forestead had shifted his attention to the drink before him and — as he lifted his glass to his lips — he saw me watching him.

I saluted him by raising my Manhattan.

He did not return the gesture.

118: Now, I regretted I had not pursued the matter of the missing photographs with Meg. My qualms — that a person does not ask someone else if they have "taken" something — had been purely social. As if Meg Riches would have cared! And yet, I had been completely convinced the delinquent prints must be with her and not with Nigel. Now, it was perfectly obvious the photographs had just walked out of the Pump Room with the Recreations Director of the Pine Point Inn. My instinct was to follow them — and, in fact, I was about to rise and do so, when Lena Rumplemeyer and the Boys arrived. And Caroline, Lena's telephone-shouting friend.

Lena makes no bones about her presence. She led the way like a major-domo, brushing the traffic out of her path with the tip of her cigarette-holder — which, in fact, has never known a cigarette but only the hand-rolled black cheroots that Lena favours. She made directly for the table next to ours, at which an athletic young man was seated alone.

"My, my, my!" said Lena; "What a very large table! And where might the rest of your party be, young man?"

"Uhm..." the young man said. His eyes darted around the room as if in search of someone — anyone who might come to his rescue.

"Well?" said Lena.

"The rest of my party isn't here yet," the young man finally said. "But..."

"And when do you expect them?"

"Any minute, ma'am. Nine o'clock."

"Nine!" Lena roared. "But it is not yet eight!"

The young man hesitated. This was fatal.

"Shall I call the management?" said Lena. Smiling.

"Management? No." The young man began to stammer "No, no, no. I'll..."

"Thank you," said Lena — and moved at once to sit at the young man's table before he'd even had a chance to finish his drink. Once established, Lena completely ignored him and began to direct her seating arrangements around his still present body.

"Ivan there... Caroline there... and Peter..." each name waved above a chair from the end of her cheroot. "Good evening, Vanessa." This without a glance in my direction.

I said; "Good evening, Lena." And waited. But neither was my glance focused on her. I had just caught my first good look at the mysterious Caroline and could not have stopped staring if I had tried.

I cannot record this woman's other name, because she was not introduced to me. If older women can be anorexic — she was anorexic. She was also over six feet tall and her face was the face of an addled child. I could not imagine where Lena Rumplemeyer had found her. Backstage, surely, in a theatre. Her make-up was theatrical and out of date. Two red dots of rouge had been applied high up — (too high) — on her cheeks. Her mouth had been drawn and redrawn with lipstick one can only describe as having the colour of dried blood. She also wore a wig that did not fit her skull and dentures that did not fit her mouth. The wig was too big — the teeth, too small. Her fingers were covered with rings of indescribable antiquity and design — and I heard her talking about one of them as having belonged to Lucrezia Borgia.

"It's a poison ring," she said. "You see...?" And she demonstrated how it had been designed to tip the poison sideways through a filigree of silver into the victim's goblet. Evidently, the rings were absolutely valid. She was not, in other words, a charlatan — but a mere and absolute eccentric.

Peter Moore was subdued; he arranged his dangling, empty sleeve in such a way that it gave the appearance of his missing arm. The cuff was in the pocket of his blazer — the blazer muted and crestless — with an elegant maroon silk handkerchief tipped in its pocket, matching the ascot tied at his neck. As he accepted a light from Ivan for his cigarette, I noted how fine his fingernails were, manicured and square-cut. All these touches must be Ivan's doing; the perfect fall of the ascot — the perfect tip of the pocket-handkerchief — the perfect shape of the fingernails — though Ivan never fussed with Peter, once they were on public view. As they arrived, I was pleased to see that Peter was not yet noticeably drunk.

But their arrival had definitely thwarted my desire to follow my photographs out into the lobby. For that, I would have to wait.

Though Lawrence and I both knew that we were really there to search out Lily Porter — we also knew we had to establish the appearance of being nothing more than casual visitors from along the beach; just another table of snobs come up to slum with the rich.

119: Finally, Lawrence danced with Petra. Or perhaps I should say that Petra finally danced with Lawrence. The main thing is, they danced with one another. I watched them as a parent might have watched — much as Arabella Barrie keeps her parental eye on me.

Lawrence's parents have never crossed my path. He never mentions them. The only thing we know is that they are not yet deceased. Communications arrive from time to time in Lydia's mailbox. As for Lydia herself — my aunt and Petra's mother — she seems to have cast her children adrift. Her only reaction, should one of them appear on her horizon, is mild confusion: *what are you doing here?* After which she will almost apologetically add the word *dear.* Lawrence and Petra — in other words — are just as certainly "orphaned" as I am. So I watch as more than surrogate parent. I watch as the parent they have never had.

When I saw that Nigel Forestead had taken — of all people — Maryanne to the dance floor, I realized the moment had come for me to make my move. I took my Chinese jacket with me. Somehow, I felt I needed the extra weight.

120: It was not that I didn't want Lawrence's help in finding Lily — but only that I didn't want it yet. A dignified, older woman stands a much greater chance of intruding into the heart of enemy territory than a dishevelled, angry man who cannot conceal his belligerence. Given my years in prison, I know a good deal more about the subversive uses of charm than Lawrence will ever know.

I rose, and in passing Lena's table, I said I was going for a breath of air. *A breath of air* can take as long as it likes, whereas a visit to the ladies' room is curtailed by the natural brevity of necessities.

At last, I was acting alone. I had not enjoyed the role at all in Lawrence's argumentative company. His insistence that my suspicions are baseless and his, well founded — that my ideas are shallow and his, profound — can only be borne for so long. I also liked less and less his reasons for playing the game of sleuth. I had been disturbed, as we stood in the stable with Calder's corpse, by the tone of his voice as he discussed his dislike of Chilcott. And I had received the discomfiting sensation that, if Chilcott were caught before we had located Lily, Lawrence might have been happy to retire from the ''case'' without discovering her whereabouts. It had all become too personal to him; a project in pursuit of his own gratification.

Yes; it is definitely best to work alone.

121: I went directly to the front desk. Nervous of the men in suits — though not even certain they would still be there — I didn't want to show my nervousness by scanning the lobby before I entered. But, given the likelihood of their continued presence, I wanted them to know I wasn't any of their business. What better way to prove that than to walk right past them, not even turning a hair? If I sensed they were staring, I would turn on them — and smile.

At the Desk, there was one of those cool young men you can be certain has won all the prizes at one of those schools where they turn out efficient, inhuman management personnel. He wore a Director's coat and a grey cravat, the combination of which on a twenty-year-old stuffed shirt is insufferable. What does it mean, when you find yourself criticizing someone for having clean fingernails?

"Yes?" (Not looking at me; studiously poring over the figures on a sheet of paper in one of his smooth, clean hands.)

"Yes *what?*" I said. I simply couldn't resist it.

He blinked.

"I beg your pardon?" he said.

"And well you should," I told him.

"May I help you, madam?"

Good. A victory.

"I'm trying to locate a certain Mrs. Porter," I said; "and I understand she may be a guest here."

"Mrs Porter?" he said. "One moment."

He turned away and consulted a computer. Cards, of course, would have been a hundred times faster and more efficient — though, perhaps, their accumulated dust might have dirtied his fingernails.

I watched the screen as best I could.

"We have a Mr and Mrs Peter Porter," the young man said.

"No," I told him. "My friend would be alone. She's a widow. Mrs Franklin Porter."

He rattled over the keys again.

"No," he said. "We do have a Mrs Franklin — but no Mrs Franklin Porter."

"Ah, well," I said. "I have another friend whom I'm certain is staying here. Doctor Thaddeus Chilcott."

"Oh, yes. Doctor Chilcott is definitely a guest. But..." He suddenly looked uncertain; shifty.

"But...?" I gave him a sickening smile of ingratiation. "Don't tell me Tad is in hiding again!"

This worked.

The young man's expression actually changed from pained condescension to pained obsequiousness.

"I'm afraid you've hit the nail right on the head, madam. Doctor Chilcott is with a rather large party and they have..."

"...taken over one whole floor of your charming hotel?"

"Precisely."

"How typical. They must be driving you mad — and I suppose you're turning other guests away in droves."

"On the contrary, madam. This weekend has been booked solid for quite some time."

"Ah. Then, perhaps, that explains why my friend Mrs Porter isn't here. She had only been able to tell me she *hoped* for a reservation."

"Would you care to give me your name, madam? I would be happy to contact Doctor Chilcott and inform him of your presence."

"Oh, no. That would ruin everything," I said. "My being here, you see, is meant to be a complete surprise." And then I played my ace. "The thing is," I said — and I leaned in close to the Desk; "my *invitation* was delayed. I only just received it yesterday. I have come straight up from..."

Where should I have come from?

I watched the young man's face to see if it would confirm what I suspected.

"Washington," I said.

Bingo.

The young man smiled — evidence there really is a conspiracy of parasites.

"They're on the third floor," he said.

122: On my way towards the elevators, I noticed — out of the corner of my eye — that one of the men in suits was still very much in place. He was standing over by the door that led to the outer porch, not looking in my direction. I also noted that, for all the young man's protestations at the Desk regarding the lack of empty rooms — the lobby was otherwise abandoned.

I took the elevator only to the second floor. I didn't relish the thought of going to the third and getting off — cold — in the midst of an armed camp. I rode alone. When the doors opened, I was presented with a long, red corridor whose single occupant was a chambermaid pushing a cart. The cart was loaded with Kleenex boxes and hand-towels and, as it turned out, cellophane bags of chocolate mints of the kind they leave, in some hotels, on your pillow every night.

I could see two exit signs — one of them half-way along the hall and the other at the farthest end. The main staircase rose — and continued to the floor above — directly beside the elevator shafts. I preferred the fire stairs, I'm afraid, for the rather foolish reason that they seemed more appropriate to someone engaged in subterfuge.

I struck out along the corridor — looking, in my Chinese coat and taffeta skirt, just like any other guest returning to her room on a Saturday night. I passed the little chambermaid with a pleasant *hello* just as she was knocking on the door of Room 215.

"Who is it?" I heard — but the voice was muffled.

"Chambermaid, Mrs Maddox. I've come to turn down your bed."

By the time she had uttered the infamous name, I was six doors down the hall.

I dropped my pocket-book and waited.

Room 215 was opened and the chambermaid went in.

The door remained ajar.

I could hear the voice of "Katherine Anne Porter" clear as a Southern belle.

"You may also turn down the bed in Mrs Franklin's room," it said. "She is particularly partial to those minty confections of yours, and if you could find it in your heart to dispose of more than one, I'm sure she would be eternally grateful. And I . . . " (I could hear the smile) "would take it as a personal favour."

"Yes, ma'am."

"I believe you will find poor Mrs Franklin is not in her room this minute. She has been, I'm afraid, just a little bit unwell. But I happen to know she will be returnin' within the next half-hour."

"Yes, ma'am. Will that be all?"

"Yes. And I thank you."

I could see the chambermaid's elbow jutting into the hallway through the open door. Fearful that Mrs Maddox would step into view and possibly spot me, I turned away and fished in my pocket-book, by now retrieved.

But Mrs Maddox did not appear — and the chambermaid returned to her cart and came on one room down the hall towards me — presumably the room of Mrs Franklin. I heard Mrs Maddox say *good-night* and I heard the genteel, Lily-like click of her door. It made me think that Calder must have trained all his women to close a door this way. With his batlike hearing, he must have detested noise.

Without hesitation — my plan already forming — I stepped back, smiling, in the direction of the chambermaid. She had the house key in her hand and was fitting it to Mrs Franklin's lock when I approached her.

"Do let me come in with you," I said. "I'm one of Mrs Franklin's closest friends and I want to leave a little gift on her pillow — along with that mint you're about to deliver."

Innocence is all too vulnerable to charm. Dangerously so, if the truth be known. I learned that long ago.

This foolish girl — thank heaven — was a true believer of every word she heard. I was ushered into the darkened room — and even before the lights went on, the perfume in the air informed me I was back in Lily Porter's domain.

I stood in the shadows completing my "gift" while the chambermaid turned down Lily's bed and set out a half-dozen little round chocolates wrapped in green foil — six Lily hearts — on her pillow. When she was finished, I crossed the room and set my "gift" amongst them.

It was nothing more than my card. But on it, I had written: *I have finished your book. Please phone.*

The chambermaid let me into the corridor before her, turned out the lights and closed the door of room 217. Next door, in 215, I heard the voice of Mrs Maddox. She was placing an order for "one more bottle of Perrier Champagne."

123: As I came to the fire-stairs, I prepared to go through cautiously — lifting my skirts and clutching my pocket-book rather like someone returning from a secret assignation. This, I suppose, was precisely what I was doing.

I was elated — practically shouting with the excitement of my discovery: that Lily Porter was still alive; apparently unharmed and on these premises. *Mrs Franklin* indeed!

The fire stairs were made of cement. A cold iron rail was the only support on the open side. I went up very slowly — leaning in towards the wall.

I didn't really know what I expected to find on the third floor. Answers was all I could think of. Half-way up, I stopped and wondered if what I was doing was crazy. After all, I had found Lily. At least, I had found where she was.

But I had begun this journey — and I knew I had to finish it. And so — I gathered a little more of my skirts in my hand and went on climbing.

Reaching the third floor, I rearranged my jacket — and gave a tiny cough to clear my throat as I stood before the door.

"Yes?" a voice said.

I turned — and there they were.

Two of Chilcott's men in suits.

They were seated on the steps leading upward to the attic. One of them wore his jacket open. His shoulder holster was plainly visible.

"Can we help you?" this man said.

124: They wanted no explanations — no excuses — no apologies. All they wanted was me.

They were neither harsh, nor rude, nor insolent. They treated me without respect but, equally, without discourtesy. One of them opened the door, while the other said; "through there."

Once through, we stood in a corridor almost — but not exactly — the same as the one below. The feeling here was different. Gone was the muted sedation of the quiet rooms and the empty hall with its little maid and its cart. Here, nearly all the doors stood open and voices could be heard. Men and women made their way from place to place with brisk efficiency. The atmosphere was one of concentration; work.

Aside from the fact that I had no notion of what was to be done with me, I began to receive the eerie impression that I was somehow invisible. No one looked at me; no one spoke to me; no one looked or spoke to the men who drove me forward.

By saying they drove me forward — all I mean is that they impelled me forward — one before me, one behind — each in motion. We made our way in this fashion along the corridor towards the elevators — until, with a fool's sense of relief, I thought they were simply going to send me back downstairs to the lobby. Perhaps they would scold me; "you really shouldn't have come up here, ma'am. See you don't do it again. Good-night."

No such luck.

They conducted me two-thirds of the way along the row of doors until we came to one that was not only closed, but locked.

The man in front drew a key-ring from his trouser pocket — applied it and threw the door wide.

"There you go," he said.

As if he were showing me something I had asked to see.

I went inside, perforce — the other man crowding after me.

It was a plain, unadorned hotel room; nothing more and nothing less. There was a maple bed, a dresser and a table. Chairs — a television set and a tiny writing desk. I noticed, however, there wasn't any telephone.

"Yes?" I said. "And what am I to do in here?"

"Wait," said the man whose revolver I had seen.

"And may I ask what I'm waiting for?"

"No," he said. And then he added; "ma'am."

The other man was still in the corridor. The man with the revolver moved away from me towards him.

I began to panic. I knew by the way he was walking he was going to leave me there alone and more than likely he would lock me in.

At the door, he turned back and said; "all I need to know is your name, ma'am."

I thought about it.

Why pretend? They only had to open my pocket-book to find a dozen ways of proving my identity. If only I hadn't been so foolish as to leave my card on Lily's bed, they would not have had any way of connecting me to her.

Still, I was — I am who I am. And so, I told them.

I waited for them to respond, as if my name might set off an alarm. But it did nothing of the kind. It barely seemed to register.

"Thank you," said one of them — and then they both were gone.

The door closed.

I sat down hard on the bed.

I was holding my pocket-book. I sat very straight. I watched the door. I could hear my watch.

I wept without a sound.

125: It felt and it did not feel like prison.

I knew the windows were behind me and, beyond the windows, the many-gabled roofs of the Inn. A child might have thought of escape — but I knew better.

If I listened very carefully, I could hear the sea. I couldn't imagine why it sounded so far away until I saw the drapes were drawn — and the windows, no doubt, closed. The room had the feel of being in a vacuum. Out in the corridor, I could sense the movement of people — but I couldn't honestly say I heard them. It all reminded me dreadfully of a book I'd read in school in which almost once in every chapter the phrase "hermetically sealed" occurred. The book began with a grave being opened — and the casket had been *hermetically sealed* — and then the novel told the story of the woman's life — the woman whose body had lain in the grave. And the rooms she had lived and died in had all been *hermetically sealed* and the carriage she had ridden in was *hermetically sealed* and the clothing she had worn made her feel as if her soul had been *hermetically sealed* inside her flesh — and the religion and the politics and the morals of the society in which she had moved had all been *hermetically sealed*; so that nothing she had wanted had been possible for her; everything was either shut out or locked in; forbidden — beyond her means or beyond her reach. It was really the perfect story of what it meant to be a prisoner — and the book was *La Dame aux Camélias*.

I couldn't get it out of my mind. It was ridiculous. There I sat — waiting for heaven knows what to happen to me, wearing my Chinese brocade jacket, all dressed up for a party, knowing that someone had been murdered and having been "arrested" under crazy circumstances, shut in a sound-proof hotel room and immobilized with apprehension — but all I could think of was a woman called Marguerite Gautier, who, shortly before she died, told the world the only thing she had ever really wanted was *to be left alone*!

I started to laugh.

I felt entirely liberated.

I stood up. I looked at the walls and I wondered if they were filled with whirring tape machines and cameras. A civilized, accoutred room with bath and television makes an extremely sinister cell.

I decided it was not my fate to stay there. I would leave.

As I heard these words go through my mind, I was somewhat alarmed at my audacity. Leave, would I? That would be interesting.

And it was.

126: I went to the door.

I looked at my watch. One way and another, twenty minutes had passed since I had watched the door close. There was every possibility that one of the men who had delivered me there would be standing in the corridor waiting for me to emerge.

As I put my hand on the knob, I willed the knob to turn. I said: *they did not lock this door.*

And they had not.

Well.

I took an extremely deep breath and I turned out the light. This made me feel proprietary and proper — as if I was simply leaving "my" room to go about my business.

I pulled the door wide open — saw that no one was there and went out into the hall.

I looked both ways along the corridor. Neither of my men in suits was in evidence. I started walking towards the elevators.

Almost at once, I heard the unmistakable sound of an elevator rising up the shaft. This I did not dare face. My captors might be riding back to claim me.

Immediately, I turned and walked the other way — pushed by the whirring of the cables. The elevator arrived. Its doors began to open. I stepped inside the nearest room.

"Hello," a woman said. "Is there something you need?"

I had walked into what appeared to be an office. It was not an office, of course, but a hotel room got up to behave as one. The bed was covered with open boxes and briefcases and the remains of two or three days' worth of newspapers. The tables had all been put into service as coffee-centres and sandwich dispensers and the desk had been moved centre stage and surrounded by chairs.

The woman who greeted me was pleasant, young and not the least bit threatening. She was, however, tired and obviously overworked. Her hair was tied back the way a woman only does when she has not had time to wash it. Her mascara had smudged — and she apparently hadn't looked in a mirror for hours, or she would have corrected it.

"Yes?" she had said, "is there something you need?"

I noted — while I was fumbling for a smile and the correct response — that the woman had an identity card attached to

her blouse, and I quickly threw back the left lapel of my jacket
in order to hide the fact that I was without one.

"Yes," I said. "I was looking for . . ."

"He's in a meeting," she said. "They all are."

"Oh," I said.

She must have assumed I wanted whoever belonged in that
room.

"You're perfectly welcome to wait, if you want. They
shouldn't be long. It has to do with the big day tomorrow and
whether or not they should bring in more security."

I looked as knowledgeable as possible and said; "I do hope
not. There are so many people about already a person can
hardly move."

I was getting worried. The woman had said a little more
than she might have intended — presumably because she
assumed I belonged there. Now, I could see it just beginning
to dawn on her that she might not have seen me before — or
that I still hadn't stated my business.

"I'm going to walk up and down the hall," I said. "I've
been sitting down for hours. I need the exercise. Thank you
for your trouble." And I left. Boldly.

This time, I knew I could not remain indecisive, no matter
what occurred. I would go to the elevators and I would ring
the bell; wait; get on and descend.

And this is what I did, more or less. But in passing back in
that direction, my timing coincided with the break-up of what
I assumed was the meeting the young woman had mentioned.

As I made my way along the double bank of doors, one of
them on my left was opened just before I reached it. No one
came out, but the door remained ajar, and as I got closer, I
could see that someone's hand was holding it in place.

About a dozen voices reached me from the interior. The
man whose hand was on the door was standing — angled away
from me — speaking to another man inside the room. The
smell of smoke and whisky — not always an unpleasant smell,

depending on where you encounter it — drifted out into the corridor and the tone of the voices that accompanied it was convivial — though serious. It was the sort of talk engaged in by people who know one another extremely well, and who have just spent time decision-making; the sort of talk I usually experience when I've been involved with an awards jury over a long, intense week — or with a committee deciding the fate of a public gardens or a famous park.

I dared not pass without affirming who was there — yet I dared not affirm it too blatantly. So I merely slowed my pace, maintaining my pose as the woman waiting with a petition; the hostess who had come to claim her guest.

What I saw — the presences I was able to verify with my single, long-extended "glance" as I "marched" past — was astonishing. And yet it did not shock or surprise me. Instead, it allowed my suspicions to subside and take on the role of confirmations.

What I saw was a congregation of public figures — four of whom, at least, were instantly recognizable: the Secretary of Defense, Mister Roseberg; the Secretary of Health, Mister Skelton; the Secretary of the Interior, Mister Briggs — and the head of the CIA, Mister Maltby. Others — of the twelve or so who were mingling in the debris of their meeting — the pushed-aside chairs, the empty glasses, the sheafs of paper, the sweaters thrown across shoulders — were vaguely familiar, but not definitively so.

I suppose, though I had no intention of doing so, and no real awareness of it, I must have stopped — if only for a fraction of a second. But it was long enough for Thomas Briggs to look up and see me. He was the only one, of all the men in that room, with whom I had ever come in contact. But his eyes passed over me as if he had never seen me before, though he did look back, briefly, as if he thought he *should* have seen me before.

Then I was gone.

127: The elevators appeared to be in use on every floor but this. They kept rising up to the second floor and then descending to the lobby again, without coming all the way to the third floor, in spite of my finger on the button.

Then it dawned on me that only one elevator of the three gave service to this floor and that the button for that car had to be turned with a key.

Now — what to do?

Wait. Be calm. At some point, someone will come up — and you can go down.

And so I waited.

As I did so, I wondered what could possibly have happened to my men in suits — until I realized they were only messengers; delivery boys. They brought the undesirables up — they left them in the hermetically sealed quarantine room — and, having informed some other official the undesirable was waiting to be interrogated, the men in suits returned to their stations. It had been my good fortune — all too obviously — that whoever had been informed of my presence had failed to find the time to come and deal with me. So far.

The elevator — at last — arrived. A waiter bringing trays of Clubhouse sandwiches and bottles of beer on a three-tiered cart struggled out of the cage. I played the helpful and patient bystander, holding open the doors. As soon as he was gone I got inside and pressed the button for the lobby.

Free — at last. I felt like one whose whole experience of life is a series of major and minor incarcerations and releases. This release was particularly welcome.

128: When the elevator door slid open I was greeted with the sight of Mercedes Mannheim — wearing dark glasses — standing impatiently waiting for me to get off.

She appeared to be taken completely aback. She removed the dark glasses and almost dropped them. Apparently, she was a little more than merely surprised to see me. Her mouth fell open and she took a great, harsh breath before she was able to speak.

"I thought you were dead!" she said. I stood with one hand on the elevator door, holding it open. "Everyone said you were dead, Vanessa! I don't believe this — that I'm seeing you!" Tears had sprung to Mercedes' eyes. Clearly, she really had thought the worst. She opened her arms.

The elevator door was pressing hard against my hand as I stepped forward into the lobby's light. My old friend's features were at war — trying not to register the full emotion she so obviously felt.

"Oh," she said. And "oh" again.

We embraced. She wept.

The elevator door swept shut behind me.

"Damn," I heard her mutter against my shoulder. And then; "oh well. Better a lost elevator than a dead Vanessa Van Horne."

Mercedes and I stood apart and began to laugh.

"It was my mother who died," I said.

"Well — that explains it," said Mercy. "After I'd heard that *you* were dead, I wrote a great long letter to Rose Adella but never had an answer."

I told her very briefly about my heart attacks — how long I had been in hospital — the length of time it had taken to recover. Mercedes was appalled; almost excessively sympathetic.

"You and I are much too young to die," she said. "Now, let me see you." She pushed me away — and looked me up and down. "You're tired," she said. "You don't appear to be taking advantage of your holiday."

"It's been a little difficult," I said; "to settle in."

I looked at her as she had looked at me.

Mercy's physical appearance is always the same. Regular face-lifts have kept her looking thirty-five for years. She still retains the unique panache of a renegade from another age; the "wayward woman" who never lost her poise and whose personal sense of physical style and political commitment has made household names of unknown couturiers and social causes alike. The capricious girl who used to run away from President Hoover and Mister Vanderbilt might change her loyalties, but never her manner. She retains the same patrician carriage, the same quick laugh, the same hard voice with its perfect edge. On the other hand, her face has now undergone so much tightening, she has no choice but to *enunciate*. She speaks without a trace of visible movement and her eyes give the somewhat bizarre impression of having been sewn wide open. She has been left, effectively, with little but a *Reader's Digest* of expressions: severely abridged. But none of this affects her personality. I still adore her; still — as always — remain in awe of her, admire and respect her. All that money and energy so wisely spent and so creatively invested. For one thing, when Mercy dies and the Nation inherits the Mannheim Art Collection, we shall all be very rich, indeed.

"Now listen," she said — and she returned the dark glasses

to their place on her nose; "I've got to go upstairs and see my pal. He's been in a meeting and he's expecting me. But you and I are having lunch tomorrow; *no argument.*" She was fishing in her clutch bag and having some trouble finding what she wanted. As she did this, I noticed that an identity card — the same kind as the one I had seen on the woman upstairs — was pinned to the gold cloth of the bag, on its off side.

Mannheim, Mercedes, I read. *Visitor. Maltby.*

Oh.

This meant that her pal was Donald Maltby, the head of the CIA.

I tried to keep the sense of panic this produced in me from showing in my eyes as she looked up, triumphant, beaming at me because she had found what she was looking for in her bag.

"Keys," she said; "are the death of us! I swear they're cursed with magic and can disappear at will." She inserted the key in the elevator lock and pressed the button.

"I trust you heard me," she said. "Lunch, Vanessa. I say no more. You will be there; *Ramsgate* at noon tomorrow."

"Yes," I said. "I will be there."

"There is so much to discuss," she added — beginning to make herself ready for the arrival of the elevator, which was already humming and whirring in its descent. "*Much,*" she said again.

And then; "you been up to see some pal of yours?" she asked.

The elevator arrived — and the door opened.

"Yes," I said.

Mercedes smiled. "Pals in high places, eh?" She was grinning — as best she could, given the restrictions of her latest lift. "It never hurts," she added. "A person never knows when she's going to need a lot of help."

She was inside, now — and the doors were closing over her.
"Noon!" she called out. "Noon, and no excuses!"
"Yes. No excuses. Noon."

She was gone. But her presence had given me hope. In fact
— no pun intended — she had given me the lift I needed most.
I shed ten years.

129: When Mercedes had asked if I had been up to see my
"pal," I had answered *yes*. What I had meant was that I had
gone to find Lily Porter. But there was another "pal," in
league with Mercy's Donald Maltby.

I mean the infamous Secretary of the Interior, Thomas
Briggs. I had seen him for that one brief moment beyond the
open door. We met long before he first disgraced his Department and our Government. The matter over which we were so
impersonally brought together — four years ago, at least —
had to do with the National Parks. Even at the time, the invitation had baffled me. I can only surmise that I was chosen
as one of the hundred delegates to Tom Briggs's conference
because it came at a time when my name had achieved some
brief, contemporary prominence. This was in 1980 or '81,
and that prominence must have had to do with my then recent
contribution to Central Park.

My involvement with the Department of the Interior
proves, I think, something of the stupefying way in which
Thomas Briggs and his advisers put their schemes together.
It can only be that the word *Park* — as in *Central* — was
linked, in their hopelessly amateur minds, to *Park* — as in
National. The fact that my contribution to Central Park had
been the design of its Japanese Gardens apparently prompted
them to think of me as a natural candidate for a conference on
Wilderness Heritage. Whereas, the merest glance at my *cur-
riculum vitae* and the briefest scan of my honours would have
informed any sensible person how totally inappropriate this

was. Appointing me as a delegate to their Wilderness Conference was tantamount to appointing Tennessee Williams as a delegate to a conference on transportation. *Well — didn't he write something about a streetcar?*

On the other hand, I suppose that Thomas Briggs and Co. cannot be blamed entirely — since around that time our President was busy informing the Nation *acid rain is not the result of coal-burning industries, but of the trees of the forest giving off poisons.*

I cringe.

I cringe now. I cringed then.

But that is not the point. The point is, given the facts before us, what can the Secretary of the Interior be doing up here — in Maine — in conjunction with the Secretaries of Health and Defense and the head of the CIA? And why — apparently in similar conjunction — is the President's physician, Thaddeus Chilcott, here? What is their collective concern with Calder Maddox?

It would make me feel a good deal better if I could honestly believe such a mix of power brokers had been assembled on the same wild premise that I and my fellow delegates were assembled back in 1980 or '81. But I cannot — (who could?) believe that. No. This has all the signs of something dreadful and deliberate and sinister. And I mean to protect myself from its consequences. Do or die.

130: The Pump Room was now a mass of noise and smoke. In my absence, others had arrived and every table was now filled. The dance floor thronged with couples and I noted only that the *Honey Girl* was currently being partnered by a large, athletic black man.

Negroes are rare on Larson's Neck. Not even kitchen help is coloured. I assumed this man was one of the ubiquitous men in suits. He certainly wore the requisite garb and bore the

requisite weight. He was immense. I thought of Mercedes —
even now upstairs with her pal, Donald Maltby. It was she
who had broken the colour bar, here on the Neck. And she
had paid the usual price of being suspected of having ques-
tionable — unmentionable — tastes. But that was all. There
hadn't been a revolution.

Now, I watched amused and sad as the *Honey Girl* endured
the same dark whispers and unvoiced accusations. Nothing
changes. Nothing will.

When I reached our table, Petra was sitting back in her
chair and glaring at everything through slitted eyes. Lawrence
was nowhere in sight. His drink had turned to ice-water and
Petra had lined up three empty Marguerita glasses. I
wondered if the limes had turned her sour. She barely looked
in my direction as I sat down. Yet, I had been away for a full
hour and more.

"Where's Lawrence?" I asked.

"Looking for you," said Petra.

"What a pity. I must just have missed him. He wasn't in the
lobby. Did he say where he intended to look?"

"He may have gone outside. I'm not really sure."

I watched her openly — certain she would not look back. I
wished she could be less unhappy. It seems — whatever the
sadness is — to be a permanent, self-induced state of mind.
The waiter came and she ordered another Marguerita. I
ordered another Manhattan — just to keep her company. Also
to recover my lost energies.

When the waiter had gone, I said; "is there anything you
want to talk about, Petra — get off your chest?"

She looked at me as if I had asked her for money; surprised
and insulted. She didn't answer. She merely turned away.

"Has it ever occurred to you that other people are
unhappy, too?" I said. I was thinking of Lily — Meg and
Michael. Me.

"Of course it has."

"Then stop behaving as if you couldn't bear to share it with the rest of us. It's not your private property, you know."

"What isn't?"

"Unhappiness!" I said. And, apparently shouted. Several people, including Lena Rumplemeyer, turned to look at us.

"Why don't you dance with someone?" said Petra. "Isn't that why you brought us here?"

"I brought you here so that *you* could have a good time," I said.

"Liar," said Petra — but without emotion. "You brought us here so you could spy on Doctor Chilcott."

I'm sure I went pale. Not because she had called me a liar — and not because she was right, or partly right — but because she had spoken the Doctor's name.

"You mustn't mention him," I said. I didn't want to endanger Lily — but I couldn't say that. "I don't think he wants it known he's here."

"Are you protecting him?" Petra almost laughed.

"Of course not," I said. "I'm only saying that, if you mention his name, then you're drawing attention to the fact we know..." I stopped short of saying *what* we know.

"I really am fed up with all of this," said Petra. "Really and truly and totally FED UP!" she made a gesture under her chin with the back of her hand and drew her chair in closer to the table.

The waiter came and deposited our drinks.

I gave him a lovely smile and thanked him.

Petra jammed a piece of lime in her mouth and sucked on it. "If someone's committed a murder around here, why don't you go to the God-damned Police and get it over with?"

Thank heaven she didn't say this out loud. She said it, more or less, to the lime as she removed it from her lips.

I prayed that Lawrence would return. If Petra went on like

this, she might bring the whole world crashing down on all of us, let alone on Lily.

I tried to talk about something else.

"Don't you think Lena looks wonderful?"

Petra's loud and angry response included yet another word I will not repeat.

Lena turned and raised an imperious eyebrow. I shook my head and tried to wave her off. "Sorry," I mouthed. "She's drunk."

"I am not drunk!" said Petra.

And then it happened.

"Yes, you are," said Peter Moore. He leaned over towards us from his place beside the silent, incredible Caroline. "You are very, very drunk, indeed, young lady," he said.

Peter was now so drunk himself, he must have forgotten he couldn't balance himself without his hand and he began to slide towards the floor. It was like a dreadful, slapstick scene in a film. As he fell, he remained in his seated position, taking the chair down with him. Worse — Lena Rumplemeyer, seeing what was happening, had taken hold of his empty sleeve and now — as Peter collapsed in a heap at Petra's feet — there was the sound of rending blue blazer and there sat Lena Rumplemeyer, holding the severed sleeve in her hands like a grotesque *memento mori* of Peter's missing arm.

I swear the entire Pump Room fell silent.

"How shall we get him up?" said Caroline, speaking at last in a cracked voice. "He's wedged in tight between the tables. Help!"

"Don't yell!" I snapped. "There are plenty of perfectly capable people standing by — " which, indeed, there were; though not a single one of them had made a move in Peter Moore's direction.

Finally, Ivan came around from the other side of their table and attempted to kneel down beside his friend. He could not, however, get anywhere near him.

"Perhaps," he said; "if Mrs Pawley could rise?"

But Petra said; "no." And sat there.

"Oh, you really are a stupid cow!" said Ivan and — rising to his full height, he pulled at Petra's shoulder. "Get up!" he commanded.

Now our table was completely surrounded by gawking people, some of them still in the embrace of the dance they had abandoned to come and witness our misfortune. Somewhere in the distance the music bleated on.

Instantly mistaking the situation, Caroline now stepped forward, apparently convinced that Petra was attacking Ivan Mills. Her way of coming to his defence was to strike Petra on the back with her pocket-book. "Stop that!" she said. Her addled, childlike face was pinched with consternation.

I was frozen with embarrassment.

"Here now! Here now! What's going on?" said a voice from the back of the crowd.

The black man pushed himself forward.

"Is this some kind of war, or what?" he demanded.

He took a handful each of Caroline and Ivan and pulled them away from Petra. "Leave off! Leave off, I say!" he said.

"Oh, this is terrible," said Lena. "Terrible! What shall we do?"

"Leave off, I say!" said the black man. "Everybody stand aside."

Gladly, I thought. *I could melt into the floor.*

People fell back and cleared a space so the black man could get to Petra and pull her to her feet. She was smiling. I could have killed her.

"Who knows this man?" the black man asked, looking down between the tables at Peter Moore.

"I do," said Ivan. "I was attempting to reach him when you barged in." He glared at the black man. "Do you mind?" he said.

"Be my guest," the black man replied and he waved Ivan forward. And then; *"my!"* he said, as Ivan passed him; "you surely are a tall one."

"Yes," said Ivan. "And you surely are a black one."

We waited.

The black man was silent five — maybe six — long seconds. Then he laughed.

I think he must have forgotten, during those dangerous seconds, who he was, and where he was and what he was doing there.

Then he remembered.

I doubt that Ivan will ever be aware of why he was spared.

131: He knelt down between the tables and spoke to his friend. "Peter?" he said. "Are you all right?"

The black man shook his head. "Mister Peter is sound asleep," he told us. "That's what his problem is. Just tired, that's all."

Slowly, the people began to drift away.

I sat down. Petra sat down — having pulled her chair around the table to the other side. Lena sat down and carefully folded Peter's sleeve. Then she lit a cheroot with shaking fingers. Caroline — bereft of all expression — sat. Ivan did not. He stood above us and — impelled to speak — he said; "I suppose you think I'm ashamed of him."

"No," we muttered. "No. Sit down."

"He's had an appalling life," said Ivan. "You people don't understand. You never have."

"Yes, we have," we said. "We do understand. Sit down."

"I will not sit down!" said Ivan. "Peter has been through the wars ten times," he said. "He was dropped into France again and again and again…"

"Sit down…"

"And every time he came back, they'd done something worse to hurt him than the time before. He won ten medals. Ten! They broke his arms and legs, his fingers and his toes — but none of you would understand that."

"Sit."

It was unbearable. We loved him. Why did he think we didn't? He was perspiring. But he stopped speaking. He looked at us — one by one — and then he said; "I'm sorry." And he smiled.

And then he sat down.

Lena called for the waiter.

132: Somehow, they got Peter Moore away — but that was after we had left the Pump Room. From a distance, we saw him being walked through the parking lot by Ivan and Caroline.

Lawrence arrived, subdued and sober — not even smoking a cigarette — ten or fifteen minutes after the commotion had died down. I looked at him carefully before I spoke. In spite of the fact that I had much to tell him, I could see he was in no shape to hear it. I didn't want to force his hand. He seemed to be trying to contain himself.

"Are you all right?" I said.

"I will be in a minute. Yes."

"Would you like a drink? You can finish mine."

"Thanks. I will."

He polished off my Manhattan in a single gulp.

"Where the hell have you been?" said Petra — petulant.

"I'll tell you when we get outside," said Lawrence.

"Tell me now, God damn it! I'm sick unto death of all this carry-on!"

Lawrence looked at his wife as if he had never seen her before; as if she was an ugly stranger disrupting the peace. "I think we had better go," he said.

"You people," Petra muttered — really talking only to herself; "with your bloody plots and your bodies on ice.

Lawrence stood up and I followed suit.

We said good-night to no one. We merely nodded as we passed Lena's table and Lena nodded back. I'm sure she understood.

"You and your bloody dead men in deck-chairs," said Petra as we passed the dancers and threaded our way through hordes of other tables. "I'll give you dead men in deck-chairs! Wait'll you read the end of *Death In Venice!*"

We finally achieved the narrow hallway leading to the lobby. Alas for Petra, there was no one there.

Suddenly, Lawrence grabbed her wrist and pulled her up short and raged into her face. His language was just as crude as hers had been. I have never seen him so angry. His words were violent as slaps.

Petra hung back against the wall, more than justifiably terrified, her hand held up against her cheek.

In spite of the fact that I'd wanted to throttle her myself, I did feel dreadfully sorry for her. She was only drunk, after all, and the drink had forced her frustration into the open. Lawrence, I fear, is obtuse about his wife's real problems. He seems to honestly believe she's brought them all on herself — that he has nothing to do with them. I now suspect the violence I witnessed is not unique.

Nonetheless, however harsh his methods, he did have to make her stop. She was putting us all in jeopardy.

"Are you going to shut up?" he said into her face. "Are you?"

She turned away and nodded. Of course, she did not now dare to speak.

"All right," Lawrence said; "you walk in front of us. And if you say one word, I'll break your wrist."

Again, Petra nodded.

The garish light in the hallway; the alcoholic violence; the smell of toilets and disinfectant; the fading sound of the raucous music; the dishevelled, incongruous look of Lawrence and Petra in their evening clothes — all made me feel that I was in a living nightmare.

And then it got worse.

133: In the lobby, Maryanne Forestead was sitting by herself — lost and forlorn in a large, red chair.

"Hello," she said, with that hideous, off-putting brightness of hers that makes you think of all the *ingénues* you've ever hated. "Are you leaving now?"

"That's right," said Lawrence. Terse.

"I wish I could leave," said Maryanne. "But no such luck."

"Where's Nigel?" I asked — dreading the answer. I presumed that he was off somewhere with the *Honey Girl*. But this was not the answer Maryanne delivered at all.

"He's upstairs," she said. "Up with important people. Don't ask me who or why; I don't know anything. But all of a sudden — even though we're on vacation — Nigel is off on Government business." She raised her eyes at the ceiling. "While I get to sit down here and twaddle my thumbs."

Twiddle, you twit!

Obviously, I knew who Maryanne's "important people" were. But not why Nigel Forestead might be with them — until I remembered the passage of the long, white envelope from Nigel's jacket pocket into the hands of the Recreations Director.

I turned around and looked at the bulletin board.

Iceberg Memorabilia. Photographs.

But mine were not amongst them. Mine were upstairs — being deciphered by Donald Maltby and that trio of Secretaries — Skelton, Briggs and Roseberg; Health — Interior — Defense.

134: On the drive home, the heat was oppressive and the night was heavy. I wished for a summer storm to clear the air though I wondered, as I made this wish, if storms are always good at that. Witness the storm between Lawrence and Petra.

The road was thick with darkness; the trees pressed close; no moon — and the stars could only be seen by leaning out the window, something I was not inclined to do. I found myself afraid of what might reach for me or strike. Passing Waldo's, the *Miller's High Life* sign had been turned off and the windows were filled with the ghosts of tennis balls and Campbell's Soup and Coppertone, lit only by the faintest glow from a single bulb at the back of the store. No one spoke in the Buick. Lawrence's ban on speech had been extended to us all. For his part, Lawrence drove with the kind of pensiveness I always associate with journeys that have taken hours. He seemed to be entirely in another world, while the motorcar we rode in pulled us through the dark.

I wanted him to tell me what had happened, but assumed he had good reason — probably Petra — not to. The road was lined on either side with animal eyes which stared in frozen terror as we passed. The smell of skunk was heavy in the air.

At last, the Hotel drive appeared, with its pale, antique sign and its dangerous corners. We wound our way beneath the spruce and maple trees as if we'd come a thousand miles to get there.

The parking paddock, behind its white fence, was filled; and very few bedroom lights were burning beyond the leaves in a scattered pattern of random windows. It seemed that we were this night's wayward children, sneaking home past curfew.

At Rossiter, the red-haired Margaret came to the screen and yawned in our faces.

"All is well," she said — and smiled.

"No, it's not," said Lawrence, bluntly. "Mrs Pawley will need your help."

I thought he was being excessively cruel. After all, the girl might take away the erroneous impression Petra was a confirmed and hopeless drunk — and such an impression might then spread from end to end of the ASH.

"Wait outside," Lawrence told me. "I'll come right back."

He disappeared inside with Petra and the girl, and I was left standing on the grass. When he returned, he carried a glass of Scotch and had finally lit a cigarette. We walked through the dew towards the tennis courts and sat on one of the benches there, the Hotel rising up behind us — the boy night-watchman padding — with Henry James in his pocket — barefoot along the porches.

It should have been the setting for another kind of scene; and it would have been in any other time. But now, the moon was risen — quartered in the sky — and it shone on hapless people, an iceberg and a doomed hotel.

135: "Well," I said. "What happened?"

"I was nearly killed," said Lawrence.

He said it plainly; simply, evenly — without emotion. Then he took a large dose of Scotch and heaved a sigh.

"It's bad," he said. "Much worse, I fear, than we thought. They're up to something desperate up there." He nodded at the Neck. "It turns my stomach. Do you realize who is in that building?"

"I think so," I said. I reeled off my list of names.

Lawrence whistled. His own list was shorter than mine. It consisted, in fact, of a single name — Donald Maltby, the head of the CIA.

"Where did you go?" I asked him. "What do you mean you were nearly killed?"

He told me he'd gone out into the parking lots, thinking he might discover something by looking at the cars and their licence plates. He did discover what he described as a veritable armada of Government limos and Secret Service backups,

most of them souped-up Cadillacs, ten or twelve years old. He
said that all these cars were parked at the rear of the Pine Point
Inn, out of sight from the public road. He was walking there,
trying to look casual — taking note of the D.C. licence plates
— when a new car arrived and Maltby of the CIA got out with
two of his agents. Lawrence remained unseen as he watched
them head for the Inn's back entrance, but as soon as they
were gone, he made the mistake of stepping forward into the
light.

"Hey you!" a voice called.

"And, of course," Lawrence told me; "I ran."

But he didn't run far.

Before he had reached the safety of the forward parking lot,
another voice called out; "stop right where you are! You're
under arrest!"

"I couldn't believe my ears. I was terrified, of course, and
confused. *Arrest* — for walking in a parking lot? It seemed so
crazy." Lawrence took another drink from his glass and went
on. "Besides, I didn't fancy being arrested, given the nature
of my work. A doctor doesn't go far when he has a record."

So — he bent out of sight and began to run again, ducklike,
between the cars. It was then that a shot was fired.

"Good Lord!"

"Indeed," said Lawrence. "I was so scared, Nessa, that I
wet my pants. I hardly need to tell you, I've never had anyone
fire at me before. I wasn't in Viet Nam — I don't live in New
York City — I don't live in Chicago and I don't live in Detroit.
Stamford is not quite murder-city. Anyway — I kept on running, if you can call it that. Don't ask how — but I managed
to elude them."

There were two of "them," apparently, and they pursued
him into the Inn.

"Once inside, I had the advantage," Lawrence said. "They

had to put their guns away in there and behave like perfect guests. They lost their momentum, just as I gained mine. I got through a door and hid in a public toilet.''

I nodded, but said nothing. I was wondering where I might have been on my own odyssey while Lawrence had reached the WC in his.

"I'm very grateful to be here," he said. "I might have ended up with Calder in the freezer."

Then I told him my own adventure.

He was dubious about my having left the card on Lily's pillow with the chocolate mints. "It might be Mrs Maddox who finds it," he said. But he realized that, like his own, my efforts had been desperate and had required the taking of extraordinary chances.

Then he said something that, at first, surprised me — though now, in retrospect, I find it doesn't.

"I think we should cool it, Vanessa," he said.

"Cool it?"

"Yes," he said. "Lower our profile — wait and see what happens."

I sat there beside him and pulled the facings of my Chinese jacket tighter across my chest. I felt as if I could use a bit of Camille's hermetic sealing; weak, a little — abandoned, a lot.

"You mean we should not pursue this any longer?" I asked.

"I mean, we should wait and see to what degree *we're* being pursued," he said.

That single gunshot had certainly done its work; just as Lawrence's own attack on Petra had done its work. Both were producing silence.

I thought of protesting; of reminding him how far we had come and how close we were to an answer. I also thought of insisting that he stay in the game at least until we had rescued Lily. But when I looked at him — white and bony and dishevelled in the moonlight — I realized how right my earlier suspicions had been that Lawrence had no feeling for Lily Porter — or Lily Porter's plight. He was giving up because whatever it was he did want out of this, he didn't want it enough to go on taking chances; to remain where he'd found himself so suddenly — on the firing line.

His gate stood open, but he would not go through.

136: I sit here, now at my window.

3:00 A.M. — and all is not well.

I remember a phrase I learned in prison: *only the brave can achieve the certainties. The faint heart fails. His will falls short of his grasp.*

I pray for Lily. Hard. I pray for me.

I feel, all at once, a kinship with the iceberg. I, too, am cold. I, too, am stranded. I, too, am nine-tenths hidden. And now, I, too, must become a *stabilized renegade.*

I peered out through the screens. I could see the iceberg out in the bay.

I raised my hand.

Be well.

137: Mercedes had not said anything more than *lunch — noon — no excuses.*

Here was yet one more perfect summer day. Round about six-thirty, taking advantage of the morning fog, I left the ASH with all my camera equipment, just as if Vanessa Van Horne were taking off on one of her usual forays. Knowing I was to lunch at *Ramsgate*, I wanted to look the best I could. In my canvas carryall, I had packed a wrinkle-free pale blue dress — some stockings, shoes and a slip. Also lipstick, comb and brush.

Due to some admittedly bizarre sense of precaution, I found myself wishing I had my passport. Ridiculous as it may well seem, I have to agree with Mister Waldo that Larson's Neck appears less and less to be in America and more and more in some alien place I have not — and cannot come to terms with.

To travel in, I wore my navy cotton shorts, a plain white polo shirt and my cotton hat. I hung my tennis shoes by their laces from my shoulders. Bare feet in the sand give me such a sense of confidence. As I walked along the beach towards the Neck, I feasted on bananas and granola bars. Oddly, I was happy. Action was setting me free.

My destination was the Larson Enclave — and the means by which I hoped to reach it was the old, forbidden path that we had used as children; across the sands and between the rocks in the incoming tide and around the point to a place where the trees came almost down to the water. Meg used to take me this way to visit Mercedes — whose house stands high on the rocks above the trees. We used to go in our rubber shoes and bathing suits — running and laughing all the way. Funny old ladies would lean down over the parapets of their properties above the tide at Larson's and shake their voices at us; ''no little girls! No little girls!'' We loved to disobey — and thwart them. Too much privacy had turned them into witches.

This morning, passing Halfway House, I looked for signs of the *Honey Girl* — but only saw her two-piece bathing suit and a great beige towel that hung from the railings. I had missed her morning swim — and missed, in the other sense, the sight of her presence. I envied her beyond reason. I don't know why.

The beach, so far as I could tell in the fog, was empty of people — even of joggers. Certainly, of Nigel. Birds abounded — and the looming, oppressive shape of the iceberg was further, it seemed, from shore than yesterday. I thought of it melting, lonely, out beyond the warmth of the inner bay; a monster and misunderstood — misread and misinterpreted — dismissed as a mere phenomenon — consigned to the curiosity of science; an outcast.

It took me half an hour precisely to reach the other end. A record.

138: The tide was further in than I might have preferred, but I had a destination and no other way to reach it. This meant sloughing through water up to my thighs. I thought a great deal about heart attacks as I made my way across the sands amongst the sea anemones and kelp — with the tide rushing in against me.

In the early 1950s, a Nature Trail had been established through the woods above the sea. I meant to use this trail as my ultimate path to *Ramsgate*, the Mannheim cottage. ("Cottage," in the Larson enclave, has more or less the same connotation as "cottage" at Newport. A ridiculous, fanciful word that has no more validity than "house" would have as a euphemism for "castle.")

I surprised myself with my agility on the rocks as I clambered up above the tide and in amongst the trees. Some skills, I guess you never lose, however distant in time their inception may be.

The woods of Larson's Neck are pure, unleavened Maine. The smell of them — the sight of them — the sound of their birds and the wind in their branches is lethal to resistance. My centre melts in their presence. The Nature Trail, in the early hours of morning, is shady — probed with fingers of horizontal light — all the green light filtered through the fog. It is cool, but entirely pleasant; cold enough to discourage mosquitoes. I stood there, looking up the cliff towards the thickest part of the wood, and recovered my breath and prayed: *not now. Don't let the pain come now.*

The veery — a thrush — is one of my favourite birds. Its haunting call was sounding as I started up the path. One distinctive aspect of the veery's song is that you always seem to hear its echo, rather than its voice. It is always just a little further into the trees, just a little further into the woods than the listener can ever achieve. It beckons you on, but you never reach the source.

I followed it, now, towards the top.

Wherever water runs — whether from pools or springs — the makers of the path have laid down duckboard so you can pass without sinking into the mire. These duckboards vary in length from ten to twenty feet. On occasion, the boards are muddy and slippery — vaguely treacherous. Anyone using the path must cross them slowly.

I was doing just this over one of the greater lengths when I caught the first intimation I was not alone.

As always in the woods, our atavistic sensibilities come off *hold*. Whatever it is in cities that stifles them loses its power in the woods and wilderness. We regain the use of that part of our nervous system that reacts to crackling twigs and shuffled leaves.

I don't really know what it was I heard; but something audible stopped me in my tracks. A whisper up the hill, perhaps?

Just as you do in the presence of wild animals, I began to move again in a calm, slow fashion — as if I was browsing in the lower branches of the trees. *Go about your business slowly; never attempt eye contact. Hum; make noise; but do not sing a song.* It was Meg who taught me all these things — just as she

taught me how to swim and how to go long distances — and
how to lose my fear of being a woman — back in the days
when I was still a child.

Now, my stomach was beginning to contract and burn. My
attempts at nonchalance were valiant, perhaps, but they were
killing me inside. Nevertheless, I went on climbing the hill
which soon began to level off and thicken with trees and
undergrowth. I was now completely certain I was being
watched and had even glimpsed the briefest of movements off
to my right.

Then I heard something else: a stone — thrown — landing
— rolling through the leaves. That on my lefthand side.

I could not pretend this hadn't happened. I would only appear to be foolishly obtuse if I ignored it. An honest trespasser
would have run; but I had decided not to be a trespasser. I had
decided to be a resident.

I stopped and looked up the hill and shaded my eyes.

"Is some blind idiot throwing stones?" I asked.

There was no reply

There was, however, another definite movement. Someone stepped once, twice, three, four times through the
undergrowth.

"A friend of mine was fired on by one of you people the
other day," I said — a very nice mix of truth and fiction. "I've
a good mind to speak to your superiors about this."

Nothing.

"I've just been down to the water," I said. "That's all. I
know I'm not supposed to do that — but, heavens to Betsy, I
am a guest here and I do have rights!"

This worked.

A man and a woman — both of them carrying those funny
little firearms that look like lethal metal coat-hangers — came
out of hiding and the woman said; "which house are you
from?"

"*Ramsgate*," I answered.

"Come with me," the woman said. "I'll take you up."

So. I had delivered myself — perhaps my life — into Mercy's hands. I prayed to God and Saint Teresa she would have me.

139: When we got to Mercy's drive, the two stone rams that guard her gates were wet with dew — and, because so much of Larson's Neck is treed, their years in the shade had left them pleasantly covered with moss. As rams go, these were relatively benign — one of them recumbent, and the other staring over its shoulder off to one side. Neither directly confronted the potential invader. There was a subtlety here that Mercy's manipulative father had intended: *abandon wariness, all ye who enter here.* And most of his enemies had.

The iron gates themselves, with their double Ms, were standing open and the long, thin drive gave a view of the Mannheim cottage — grey stone foundation; grey shingled walls; grey leaded windows; many gables; many chimneys, only one of which was smoking in the morning's clear, cool air. The smell of burning cedar logs was evident, but not pervasive.

My guardians — loosely dangling their coat-hanger weapons from the ends of their healthy, muscled arms — had remained as silent as foreigners. This was just as it had been the night before at the Pine Point Inn. We walked as though our purpose were merely to reach our destination. I felt unlike their prisoner, though I knew, of course, I was — and I would be until the three of us stood before Mercedes.

I was praying silently that Mercy rose at an early hour —
and would not be in need of rousing. Rising from sleep to be
confronted by a crisis before a person's dreams have faded can
make a person cantankerous. And this I did not need.

We got to the end of the tree-lined drive where it widened
into a narrow courtyard — only sufficiently sizable to ac-
commodate the arrival and departure of two or three motorcars at once. The garages stood to one side — doors firmly
shut. There was not a sign of vehicles. Nor of staff. The smoke
from that single chimney gave me all the hope I had.

The female agent — (neither *girl* nor *woman* seemed
appropriate to a figure so deliberately armed and male) —
stepped to the door and pulled on the chain that rang
the bell.

The silence that followed this was tense and disheartening.
Please, I begged the saints, *be home.*

The other agent — the real male — stood behind me and I
heard him cough. Turning, I saw him give a nod towards the
trees. There was no one there — that I could see.

Footsteps rang against the stones of the vestibule beyond the
door — and when the door was opened, we were greeted by
the sight of a uniformed Filipino woman whose dark, impressive eyes inspired immediate confidence. The only problem was — she had never laid those eyes on me before. I did
not know her name. What I did know was that as a "house
guest" here, I would be expected to greet her.

"Is it a problem?" she asked in wonderfully accented
English. And then — to me; *"buenos días, señorita."*

I stood — mouth open — luckily remembering that open
mouths make perfect smiles; or can.

"Imelda...?" This was Mercedes, calling out from the
shadows beyond the vestibule. "I heard the bell."

Imelda stood aside.

We entered.

Mercedes emerged into a spill of early sunlight — the first to reach through the windows — and looked at me as if relieved to see me. She was wearing a Valentino housecoat; grey, of course.

"You're late," she said. "I'm half-way through my breakfast and the scrambled eggs will be cold by the time you get to them."

"I'm sorry," I said. "I got involved with the shore birds."

Imelda closed the door and passed us, making her way to the kitchen.

I started to unload my camera bag and carryall on a chair in the hall. My throat was beginning to close; my mouth was dry and I could hear my heart.

Behind my back — so resolutely turned — Mercedes was saying; "I do appreciate your concern, but I have to tell you, I can barely tolerate any more of this."

I quickly glanced in a nearby mirror, thinking she might have been addressing me, but she was not. She was speaking to my escorts.

"If behaviour of this kind continues on your part — *if there is one more incident* — I warn you now, I will speak to Mister Maltby. I urge you to remember, I am not just another distant face, so far as Mister Maltby is concerned. He knows me well; so please vacate these premises."

"Yes, madam."

Both agents went to the door. I turned to watch them go. I must say, I was impressed with the fact they did not give an inch in terms of their demeanour. They were neither sheepish nor repentant. They maintained their perfect pseudo-military bearing and made their exit without a word of apology.

When the door had closed I looked at Mercedes.

"Come with me," she said. "Of course, I lied. The scrambled eggs are in the chafing dish and scalding hot."

140: Her explanation was simple — and she gave it as we sat over breakfast in the sunlit morning room.

She had seen me coming from her bedroom windows just as she was about to make her way downstairs. "I thank God for timing," she said. "If I had glanced from those windows a moment earlier, I would have missed you. The other two I recognized at once as the troublemakers who have plagued my section of the woods for the last two days. No one — not even Donald — had the grace to inform me they had been stationed there and they almost shot me the first time I stumbled on them. I suppose you barely escaped with your life." She imposed a smile on all these words — but she meant every one of them.

I told her what had happened.

"Yes," she said. "They challenge everyone who makes a move on that hill. There are more of them back there..." she gestured over her shoulder at the garden and the woods that come to its edge. "We are virtually under siege."

"What in heaven's name does it mean?" I asked. I told her that a friend of mine had been fired at in the Pine Point parking lot the night before. I did not, however, explain what had happened to me on the upper floors of the Inn. I wanted Mercedes' explanations first.

I waited.

Mercedes had lapsed into an uncommon silence; troubled by what she was going to say next and working out a way of saying it.

Before she spoke again, she finished her eggs and pushed her plate aside. She reached for a Waterford box of Sobranies. As soon as she lifted the lid, I could smell them; Paris, Vienna, Venice... the more exotic the cigarette, the less I object to it.

"All right," Mercedes said; "attend and do not interrupt."

"Before you begin, may I ask one question?"

"One question. Yes."

"Is your pal Maltby courting you — or can it be that you are courting him?"

Mercedes gave a short laugh. "You think I have gone over?"

"I wondered. Yes."

She looked at me severely. Then she said; "sometimes I need something done. You understand?"

I nodded — thinking I could guess the sort of things she meant; support for a cause; some funding in danger of being swept away.

"Well," she said; "whenever I need something done, I look around and see who might need *me* ..." Now, she smiled quite broadly — I might even say, lasciviously. Her eyes lit up. "This time, I got doubly lucky, Vanessa — and I found not only someone who needs Mercedes Mannheim, but who *wants* her!" She really did laugh then — fully and completely with delight. Then she reached out and spread her palm before me. "He is sitting right there, my dear," she said. "Right *there*."

141: We poured fresh coffee. I sat and listened. Mercedes spoke. I did not interrupt. Her story was not a story at all. It was a description — all the more vivid because of the monotonic pitch of her voice. It told of what had been happening on Larson's Neck that weekend.

Just as events had begun to shake us — up the beach at the ASH on the Friday — so, on the Friday, other events had begun to shake the residents of Larson's Neck. The difference was that, for some on the Neck, those events had been well anticipated. At least in part.

Three months before — early in April — an invitation had been accepted in Washington. The invitation had been issued by Daniel and Lucy Greene, whose summer residence is among the more spectacular — if more conventional —

cottages on Larson's Neck. The recipients of the invitation had been President and Mrs Warner. Nellie Warner and Lucy Greene had gone to college together at Smith. Daniel Greene, a prominent Philadelphia banker, just as I have already said, is on the current rumour list for a Cabinet post. The visit between old friends was to be a private one and absolutely off the record.

But nothing remains off the record for long in any closed community — and so, in order not to offend their summer neighbours — in order not to risk disparagement from amongst the Neck's notorious roster of prominent GOP supporters — permission was sought and granted for: *one well-screened and discreet little party; preferably for cocktails; preferably in the open air; preferably late in the President's visit; preferably excluding the presence of one or two rebellious Republicans the President did not wish to risk confronting — and definitely excluding Mercedes Mannheim.*

(I had no need to interrupt to ask for an explanation of this particular exclusion. Mercedes and Lucy Greene have been at war with one another — not only here on the Neck, but in Philadelphia, New York and Washington — for years. Mercy, I fear, is somewhat to blame. She does tend to play the card of her name — and all it implies of aristocratic credentials — with a heavy hand when she feels she wants to score points against a particularly irritating or obnoxious enemy. As someone once said, concerning another society feud — this one in England: "it does seem a little excessive of Emerald to bring out her battleships to knock poor Sybil's rowboats out of the water!" Mercedes had used her battleships on Lucy Greene's rowboats — and Lucy Greene had never got over it.

On the other hand, there are rowboats and there are rowboats. Lucy Greene is a true colonial snob. Her New Brunswick airs and graces are merely amusing — but her Philadelphia ambitions are not. What Lucy would do for Daniel Greene's career cannot be imagined. And I do not mean the sort of cajoling, "you-play-your-part-and-I'll-play-mine" sort of bargaining Mercedes Mannheim engages in. I mean the sort of conniving the Borgias once engaged in. Total war — including the salon, the dinner table and the cocktail route.)

The *preferables* on Lucy's list, Mercedes continued smiling — went on for over half a page. When a purloined copy of this list had been shown to Mercy by an interested friend, Mercy had been forced to feign a coughing fit of some duration in order to keep herself from laughing out loud. Nevertheless, all the *preferables* had been adhered to and a list of no more than seventy-five candidates had been approved, on the assumption that anywhere between fifteen and twenty of the invitations would be refused out of necessity.

From the ASH, the original list of candidates had included such figures as the Canadian Ambassador to Washington, the American Ambassador to Ottawa, the British Consul from Boston, an ex-Governor-General of Canada and her husband, Arabella Barrie and Calder Maddox. But in Calder's case, the stipulation had been that he must not come unless he was accompanied by his "charming but cast-off wife." Here, a good deal fell into place, so far as I was concerned. It explained why Mrs Maddox had been summoned from Boston — and why Kyle had been dispatched to fetch her. But for Mercy, it was a perfect scandal.

"To think that Mister Maddox must appear before the Warners with his wife — and not his mistress — gives me hysterics! And that is why, you know. Lucy Greene would not have Lily Porter — Mister Maddox's notorious mistress! — paraded before Nellie Warner. I mean — Vanessa! *Nellie Warner?* Do you believe it?"

Yes.

Mercedes ground out her Sobranie in a small crystal ashtray and continued with her tale.

Everyone at the Greenes' had apparently thought the arrangements were well in hand when — to use Mercedes'
expression: *all hell broke loose.* The Canadians refused their invitations *en masse* — (she made it sound like a national referen-
dum) — and this so greatly offended Lucy Greene — herself,
of course, a Canadian — that she struck the American Ambassador to Ottawa off the list, as if — somehow — the lack of
Canadian goodwill could be laid entirely at his door. Mercedes
needed no prompting from me to remind her that our President and his Congress might have something to do with the
Canadians' lack of enthusiasm. I'd heard enough of it from
Meg — and Mercy had heard it all from her friend, John Ken-
neth Galbraith. But Lucy Greene had required a good deal of
prompting from her husband before she conceded the problem lay in *all those left-wing politicians up there in Ottawa who
might not like the President's policies...* The American Ambassador to Ottawa was consequently reinstated as a potential
guest — but that was Lucy Greene's sole concession to the
country of her birth.

"Until just yesterday," said Mercedes; "when, I must admit, a rather extraordinary thing occurred. The Greenes apparently received a telephone call from Don Maltby's
secretary, requesting them to issue an invitation to someone at
the Aurora Sands Hotel. Someone called Neville Forestead."

"Nigel," I said — too stunned to say anything else. I now
understood why Lucy Greene had come to the ASH with
Doctor Chilcott. And why she had sought out Arabella Barrie. It all had to do with Nigel's invitation.

"Indeed," said Mercy. "Then you know him."

"Yes."

I explained.

Mercedes laughed.

I told her it wasn't really all that amusing. "I think he's
cunning," I said. "I think he may even be dangerous."

"Oh?" Mercy's eyes made a vain attempt to narrow. Her latest face-lift — even more in the morning than at night — made them quite immune to expression. "In what way dangerous?"

"I may explain," I said. "On the other hand, I may not have to. I'm waiting for you to come to Calder Maddox."

"Oh?" said Mercy again — as if it might be her only word of inquiry. "That's interesting."

"It could be," I said. "It all depends."

Mercedes thought for a moment before she spoke again. She poured herself another cup of coffee and lit another Sobranie. I watched all this, determined not to offer a scrap of information until I knew what she knew.

Then she said; "what do you mean, you're waiting for me to come to Calder Maddox?"

I was inwardly taken aback by this. But I tried not to show it. Mercedes seemed to be saying she was unaware that Calder was dead. This proved, however, not to be the case. Not quite.

142: It seems now — in retrospect — that Mercy knew of Calder's death; but this was not apparent in what she said. I suspect she fudged her response to me because she was uncertain about the extent of what I knew, and therefore, we were playing cat and mouse with one another, each of us firmly convinced she was playing the cat.

What I said next was; "you said that Calder Maddox was on the initial list."

"That's right," said Mercy. "But then, as you surely must know, he became extremely ill."

I blinked and waited — giving her a nod that was so imperceptible I was almost unaware of it myself.

Mercy looked away and played with the handle of her coffee cup. The sleeve of her Valentino housecoat brushed

against the remainder of her scrambled eggs, but she seemed
not to notice. The coat was almost military in cut — grey with
deep blue facings — perfect morning colours. She looked
precisely as she might have imagined a Mannheim countess to
look, sitting at her breakfast table in Vienna a hundred years
ago. Perhaps cosmetic surgery projects its recipients further
into the past than they bargain for.

Neither of us spoke. The subject of Calder Maddox appeared to have been dropped. She didn't know what I knew;
I didn't know what she knew.

I reached into my pocket for my pills; not the digitalis — the
other ones. I got up and poured myself a second glass of
orange juice at the sideboard.

Mercedes watched me critically. She does not approve of
pills — having declared some time ago in my presence that she
thinks they offer an *uncreative response to human problems.*
When I turned around and saw her face, I lifted the glass of
orange juice in a toast and said to her; "you go your way, Mercy — I'll go mine." And swallowed the pill. Mercy laughed.

"Now," I said — returning to the table. "Come to the
point. What's going on."

"I *have* come to the point," she said. "I told you; the President."

"Mercy," I said — and leapt full tilt — "the Pine Point Inn
is like a second White House. You of all people are aware of
that. That's where you go to do your soliciting! But besides
your pal, Donald Maltby, and my 'pal,' Thomas Briggs —
Brian Skelton and Ira Roseberg are also in that hotel." I lifted
up my hand and counted off their parts in the Cabinet, one by
one; "the CIA — the Interior — Health — and Defense. Right
down the road, Mercy — not five hundred yards from here —
a second White House!"

"You left out State," said Mercedes, deadpan.

I stared at her.

"The Secretary of *State*?" I said. "What is it, then? Are we at war with someone?"

Mercedes slowly rolled the ash from the end of her cigarette.

"Well," she said. "That's a very good question, isn't it. And interesting."

She fell silent.

I waited. I got up and leaned on the back of my chair.

She lifted the cigarette and looked at it; black with a gold tip and the gold tip smudged with her lipstick.

"I spent two hours with Donald Maltby last night," she said. "Unfortunately, the time was spent concerning what he wants from me — not concerning what I want from him. *That* card, I still have to play. Consequently, I remain just as frightened as you are," she said. "And just as ignorant — and just as alarmed. These people everywhere with guns. That isn't — it cannot be — normal. Nobody knows, in the world at large, the President is here, for heaven's sake. But even if every terrorist who walks the face of the earth had tracked him down, they wouldn't deal with it like this. They wouldn't bring the Secretary of State, the Secretary of Defense, the Head of the CIA up here and then fill that hotel and all our gardens and hillsides with armed men — they would bring a helicopter and fly the President out of here." She stared at me. "Wouldn't they?"

"Yes," I said. "they would."

I sat down.

"Then what are they doing?" she said. "What are they doing?"

"I don't know."

She finally stubbed the cigarette, and watching the last of its smoke lift over her fingers, she spoke again as quietly and monotonically as she had when she began the whole conversation.

"There's a rumour," she said. "It's just a rumour —

nothing more. But it seems that everything was proceeding as it should — everything falling into place — all the way up to Friday. That's when the President and Nellie arrived. And then... something happened up at the Aurora Sands Hotel." She looked at me. I didn't budge.

"Yes?"

"Well. Suddenly, all the security here was doubled." She tried to laugh. "We thought it was the iceberg! You know — we said things like: *it's a Russian iceberg!* And *it's Cuba in disguise!*" She looked at me searchingly.

Still, I didn't give an inch.

"What was the rumour?" I asked. "What did they say had happened up at the Aurora Sands Hotel?"

There was only the briefest pause.

"That something terrible had happened to Calder Maddox."

"Yes?"

I waited.

"They said that something terrible had happened to him and — there was even a rumour he was dead."

She watched me just as carefully as I watched her.

When I didn't speak, she finally said; "that night, the Secretary of Health arrived from Boston."

"Yes?"

"And the next day... I don't know — some time very early Saturday morning, the others began to arrive; the Secretary of the Interior — the Secretary of Defense. And the next thing I knew, my phone was ringing and Donald Maltby was on the line."

"You haven't mentioned the Secretary of State."

"He only arrived this morning."

I got up and walked across to the windows.

There, in the garden, beyond the beds of roses and lilies, just like figures confirming a nightmare, two of the

President's bodyguards were standing. I almost wrote they were standing nonchalantly, but it wasn't nonchalance. It was insolence. They were standing, insolently fondling their weapons and looking at the house from which I watched as if it were an enemy stronghold.

Stronghold might not be the right word. But enemy is.

143: Mercedes said; "you must know something, Vanessa — or you wouldn't be here."

"True. Yes."

I turned away from the window. I didn't mention the two men.

"That rumour," I said; "the one about Calder Maddox. I've heard the same thing." And then, before Mercy could say anything, I added; "but I know one thing that isn't a rumour."

"Oh?" She sounded cautious.

"I know where Lily Porter is."

Mercedes did not quite react the way I had hoped she would. She said; "we all know that!"

My turn, now, to say; "oh?"

"She's up at the Aurora Sands Hotel."

I looked at her squarely. She could not, by any stretch of the imagination, be lying this time.

I was relieved. It meant that, whatever Mercedes knew about the death of Calder Maddox, she hadn't the slightest notion anything odd had happened to Lily.

So I told her. I told her exactly how Lily had disappeared —
and I told her she was over at the Pine Point Inn — and that
someone had registered her as Mrs Franklin.

Mercedes got up at once and went out into the hall. I followed as far as the door.

She picked up the telephone, glanced in a telephone book,
and dialled.

She asked for; "Mrs Franklin, please."

After the briefest moment, she said; "that's quite all right.
I'll try again later," and hung up.

"Well?"

"There wasn't any answer. So they said."

"How do you mean, *so they said?*"

"Surely when you telephone a guest at a hotel, you hear the
guest's telephone ringing?"

"Of course."

"I did not hear that this time. And when the operator came
back on the line, I had the very distinct impression it was not
the operator I had spoken to first. But you are quite right.
There is a Mrs Franklin registered — and if you say it's Lily,
then I believe you."

"It is," I said. "I saw her..."

I had been in Lily's room — certainly — but she had not
been there. And so, of course, to say I had seen her was a lie.

But what, now, was not a lie?

144: We were not allowed to drive to the Greenes'; the only
motorcars would be the official limousines used by those in

the President's party who were staying at the Pine Point Inn. We walked.

It was not a great distance, and under any other circumstance, it would have been a lovely walk. The road winds like a shaving from a pine tree through the enclave at Larson's Neck. It is one of the prettiest roads I know. It meanders entirely beneath a canopy of pines and maples and chestnut trees, all of immense size — all of great age. The surface of this road is macadam, and there is always the faintest smell of tar and pine cones — a very pleasant mixture of odours to me, so highly charged with the nuance of summer heat and childhood.

The great lawns stretching under and beyond the trees lead the eye to a sequence of splendid houses — most of them built in the golden age between 1880 and 1912. This was the age when America first asserted its powers of material creativity and when it spent unlimited fortunes fulfilling the wishes of its upper class. I know that class. I'm one of them — and from what I know of my own people, it was a class back then that cut its dreams from the rich, whole cloth of pure imagination. It was that age when men who dreamt of flight began to fly and other men who dreamt of horseless carriages first set out along the roads in motorcars. It was the age when men with wealth that had gone completely out of control built houses of equally crazy proportions, making the architecture up as they went along — a little of this — a lot of that — and the walls inside all covered with a motley show of European art. These houses — cottages — here on the Neck, were mostly built in the time of Presidents whose names were McKinley, Roosevelt and Taft; big men, with wide, substantial smiles. The cottages are mostly made of wood and stone and nothing in their appearance speaks more eloquently of the State of Maine than what the salt air and sea-winds have left there; a silvery, bleached patina of unique and unequalled beauty.

Curiously enough — but only of interest to me, perhaps —
the age of which I write, when the houses on Larson's Neck
were built, was also the age when America took up, both in
decor and in art, a passion for things Japanese. I can see this
passion translated still in the papers that cover these walls and
in these gardens, rocky and severe, that show off beds of iris
and peony and lily as if they had been lifted, holus-bolus,
from the island of Honshu.

145: The Greenes' is a cottage I have not admired. It was
built in the 1930s. Neither Daniel Greene nor Lucy, his wife,
have been encountered — perhaps by choice — in all the years
I have walked the road and passed their gate. I knew Lucy
once — but that was long ago — and she, to all appearances,
has quite forgotten that. This day, the house was obviously the
centre of the universe — and its drive was filled with a myriad
of motorcars, from limousines to any number of Fords and
Chevrolets, whose purpose there was plainly to mask the
house from the road.

This masking could be accomplished easily, because the
house itself lies just below the lip of a hill on the seaward,
rather than the bayward, side of the Neck. In ordinary times,
one sees the roofs and the upper storey only — but on this occasion, nothing save the roofs.

Three of us went from *Ramsgate* Cottage. We took Imelda
with us. Her presence in our company was part of a plot; a
plan to rescue Lily Porter — if we could find her — from the
Pine Point Inn. To that end, Imelda was dressed in what she
called her "Communion clothes" — a summer suit of white
linen, tailored and piped with chocolate brown. She wore it
with a simple, open-necked blouse that echoed the chocolate
brown in a milky shade. All this, plus a white straw hat with
a veil that covered only her brow and eyes. The bag, suspended from her arm, was also white — and large. Mercedes had

requested that Imelda carry — open — a parasol. And she was to wear white gloves.

We got as far as the drive, where a number of Secret Service agents, posing as guests, were mingling amongst the true guests — all of whom were being requested to present their invitations before they went on down the drive to the cottage.

Our problem was — we had no invitations.

146: Two things played into our hands; one was pure chance, the other was calculated risk.

The calculated risk involved the identity pass Mercy had already used at the Pine Point Inn. If this could get her into the company of Donald Maltby, we trusted it could get her into the company of President Warner. Maltby, after all, had authorized the card, and some — if not all — of the men on the lawn would be his. We had to take that chance.

For myself, I had to face the fact I was going to be confronted with a good many people I knew and I was especially not looking forward to the moment when I would come face to face with Arabella Barrie. Neither did I relish the prospect of rubbing elbows with Thaddeus Chilcott, who I was certain would be present — or with the dreadful Neville-Nigel-Forester-Forestead. Whatever delight I was taking in his mass of accumulating names, it was not going to get me through the moment when he drew himself up before me, clicked his heels and bowed. Nigel's unfortunately servile image of correct behaviour had altered my image forever of how the Canadian Government behaved abroad. Gone, to all appearances, were the days of Michael Riches' self-assured and unassuming pride in who and what he represented. Little wonder the rest of the Canadian contingent from the ASH had refused their invitations *en masse*. They had probably guessed that Nigel would be there.

On the other hand, we were not yet through the door. We had got, in fact, no further than the lip of the rolling lawn.

Here it was that we had the chance encounter that would —
if we played it successfully — guarantee our entrance into the
inner sanctum.

Standing up tall above the heads of the mingling guests and
his fellow agents was our black man from the night before. I
squeezed Mercy's arm and said; "we might not do better than
to head for that man there." I explained what had happened
in the contretemps between my cousin Petra and Peter Moore
— and how the black man had saved the day. "If he's kept his
sense of humour, he will not be able to turn us down."

We gathered Imelda — whose whole job it was to be seen in
our company — and Mercy fitted her identity card to the
breast of her Ribriona suit and put on all her smiles and all her
brisk efficiency. She also drew from her alligator bag a packet
— held together with an elastic band — of three square invitation cards — and handed one of them to each of us. "I happened to have a few of these left over," she said; "from a party
I gave last season for the Greek Prime Minister. For heaven's
sake, don't show the printed side — just keep them unob-
trusively in evidence."

We did so, and made our way towards the black man.

"You do this one," said Mercedes, *sotto voce*, just before we
got to him.

Immediately, I experienced something of a panic; though
I had no need. The black man spotted me coming.

"Hello, there," he said. "Your friends get home okay?"

"Yes, and thank you. In fact, I was just coming over," I
said; "to express my gratitude. Poor Mister Moore — the lad
on the floor — had a very hard time of it. We really did appreciate your help."

Imelda turned away beneath her parasol, as if to view the
other guests. The bogus invitation Mercedes had given her
was serving as a very graceful fan. I held my own "invitation"
— blank side out — against the face of my pocket-book.

I brought Mercedes forward at this point and said to her; "this is the lad I told you about, Mercedes, who saved the day last night." Then I turned to him — apologized and said I could not introduce him without his name.

"Curren, ma'am."

"Mercedes; this is Mister Curren. Mister Curren, this is Miss Mannheim."

Mercedes offered her hand, turning her left side into the sunlight. The plastic sheath of her identity card flashed efficiently. "How do you do, Mister Curren?" she said. "Miss Van Horne has told me how wonderfully quick you were to straighten things out in what could have been an extremely embarrassing situation."

"It was nothing, ma'am."

Then we hit pay dirt.

Agent Curren had no need to read Mercedes' card, apparently, to know who stood before him.

"Mister Maltby is not arrived yet, Miss Mannheim," he said. "But you'll find a lot of folks you know down there. And I hope you enjoy the party. You, too, Miss Van Horne."

"Thank you, Mister Curren," I said. "It was good to see you again."

Agent Curren turned away at that point, to deal with other guests, and we — the three of us — took a sufficient number of steps away from him in order to let out a quiet whoop of triumph.

"That," said Mercedes — collecting our invitations and placing them back in her bag, "is what you call playing your cards right, ladies. *Done*." And she snapped the bag shut.

147: Imelda was to leave us here — but only after we had established certain things before a number of witnesses — people whom we might well encounter, later, at the Pine Point

Inn. These included the facts that our party was made up of three, and that one of us carried a parasol.

Perhaps what struck me as being the most telling aspect at this point was that Imelda passed without being recognized once by those to whom she had opened the door, on so many occasions, of Mercedes' home. But, if Imelda had gone "unseen" before, we made certain she did not go unseen on Daniel and Lucy Greene's lawn. She mingled — I should say for ten minutes — before she drifted off towards the road and to her second station, in terms of our scheme for saving Lily.

Mercy and I were now free to enter the house itself — and we began that journey with Mercy removing her identity card and placing that, too, inside the alligator bag. We looked, I felt confident, rather splendid together. She wore, as I have said, a suit by Ribriona — one of the Spanish couturiers whose name had been made by Mercy's patronage — and I had changed from my own luncheon dress to one of Mercedes' simpler black affairs with a blue and silver belt that matched the shoes she had lent me — and which, thank heaven, fit.

At the door, we were greeted by an over-emboldened maid who directed us onto "the patio at the rear."

"The *patio?*" I said, as we cleared the maid's presence. "The *patio?*"

Mercedes said; "she'll learn, Vanessa. She's only been here since June. She will come to *terrace*, by and by."

To pretend that I felt no nervousness — had no qualms — and did not pause to slip a pill beneath my tongue — would be ridiculous. We had come here in order to see how far the plot involving Calder's death and Lily's disappearance might extend. But we had also come here as trespassers — myself uninvited — Mercedes as the one completely unacceptable guest; the absolutely forbidden intruder; a walking anathema in Lucy Greene's house.

This turned our entrance into the foyer and down the stairs

into a veritable commando raid. I felt as a terrorist might feel as he approaches his target. I, however, did not carry the explosives; the explosives walked beside me in a Carlos Ribriona suit.

Mercedes' presence, once we had achieved the stairs, did not go unnoticed. Not that anything was said. But we heard several intakes of breath as we staged our progress — and more than one strangled *oh*. I could not tell, because I dared not catch her eye, but I sensed that Mercedes was enjoying the raid immensely.

The receiving line was formal only insofar as there was one. It had been against the President's wishes that any excessive sense of formality be encouraged. His weekend in Maine — that had become a nightmare for us all — had started out to be a holiday for him and Nellie Warner — just as it had for the rest of us. If the murder of Calder Maddox had not taken place in our midst, some of our smiles might now be real. Might even — (though I wonder) — have been sincere. As it was, we were stood in a nerve-wracked line, awaiting our turn to make our progress, hand over hand, from Lucy Greene to Daniel Greene to Nellie Warner and thus, to the President himself.

I was to stay as close to Mercedes as I could. And I did. I hid behind her shoulder. At last, it came to be our turn. But as we stepped forward, an unprecedented incident occurred.

It so happened that, as the business of receiving her many guests had proceeded, Lucy Greene had drifted further and further away from her husband's left arm. Daniel Greene, for his part, had drifted further and further towards the First Lady. Possibly, this had occurred because it was Daniel Greene's task to introduce the strangers amongst us to Nellie Warner. However it had come about, there was a distance of at least four feet between the hostess and the host by the time Mercedes and I approached.

Mercedes — playing her radiance up to the hilt — simply

went and stood — all smiles — directly in front of Lucy
Greene.

She did not bother to wait for Lucy to speak. Nor did she
press her greetings on the astonished hostess. Instead, she
drew me forward and said; "I'm sure you've met our pre-
eminent landscape architect, haven't you, Lucy? This is
Vanessa Van Horne..."

But Lucy Greene did not even turn in my direction. Instead, the lady from Moncton, New Brunswick froze in her
place, having lost — for a second — her ability to speak. And
then — in lieu of words — she struck Mercedes, hard, in the
face.

In spite of the cocktail uproar beyond us in the garden room
that led to the *patio* — and in spite of the four-foot distance
between them — Daniel Greene turned towards his wife and
lost, in a single moment, all the benefit of hours in the sun. I
have never seen a man become so alarmingly pale so quickly.
I really did think he was going to faint. In the meantime,
throughout the length and the breadth of his whole domain,
there fell a dreadful, pin-dropping silence.

Mercedes lifted her delicate Austrian hand to her delicate,
lifted cheek and stood back only slightly from Lucy Greene.
Although the assembly at large was waiting, breathless, for
the apology that surely would — and surely must — be forthcoming, Mercedes herself was not so foolish. She knew there
would be no apology.

No one — not even Mercy — would have predicted that
Lucy Greene would react so crassly to the presence of her
arch-rival, but the motive for her reaction was not at all
baffling.

An offensive ghost might just as well have stepped before
the President's hostess. Mercedes Mannheim's absence from
this place had been as surely guaranteed as if she had been in
her grave.   Not only was there no apology, nothing was said

at all. Mercedes lowered her hand and took the necessary steps to her left in order to present herself to Daniel Greene. All I could do was follow.

Off at the end of the line, I could hear the President saying in his cheerful, charming manner; ''well, now! Mercedes Mannheim — you're a sight for sore eyes!''

And Mercedes said; ''yes, Mister President. And for sore losers.''

Credit must be given forever to Nellie Warner, who — having overheard this remark — was giggling so uncontrollably, she could not say *hello* to me.

148: I've already stated I went to the Greenes' with a certain apprehension concerning the other guests. But I now discovered there was to be another quotient to this apprehension, beyond the natural fear of tipping my hand. That I was there under false pretences was one thing; that I was there to make discoveries was another. I realized I would have to find resources I had not been aware of using since Bandung, and I would have to find them specifically in order to play what we used to call in prison the game of *nothing is happening here*. This is the game you played when you were sitting on your cot, with a radio receiver under your mattress, and a Japanese guard walked into your barrack.

The truth is, of course, if you once develop a resource, it becomes a part of your character in such a way that you are more or less unaware of it. Throughout my whole career, I have drawn on various strengths within myself, without acknowledging where they came from. Everyone does this. It is like discovering you have a tolerance for pain. The tolerance is always there, but it only shows itself when pain occurs. The analogy here is between my threshold of pain and my threshold of panic; both are high. Much higher than I had known until I was confined behind the wire at Bandung.

Consequently, my ability to play the game of *nothing is happening here* surprised me when I first discovered it. Now — at the Greenes', I discovered it again.

I'm not quite sure I like having made this discovery. But I'm absolutely certain I do not like having discovered that my own ability to play the game is nothing when compared to the ability of others.

There at the Greenes', in the presence of our President, I was exposed to the fact that the upper echelons of my society are made up of men and women whose smiles and frowns and unsweating palms are all examples of the ultimate mastery of the technique of *nothing is happening here.* I lied in prison; they lied there on Lucy's terrace. This should not, I suppose, have come as such a formidable surprise. But it did. And I suppose it did because, when all is said and done, I have always wanted to believe in the goodness of people. If not in the goodness of what people do then, at least, in the goodness of what they set out to do.

But the layers of lying — the brash and brilliant displays of it I witnessed that afternoon — came, I cannot deny it, as a pure and powerful revelation. It did so, beyond a doubt, because what I saw was not just some individual's ability to lie — but the individual's ability to lie *collectively.* And it was this collective ability that threw me. Completely.

What I'm putting forward here is the highly plausible possibility that virtually every single person collected there at the Greenes' that afternoon was aware of the fact that Calder Maddox was dead. Half — or more than half — knew *why* he was dead.

One person — and one only — proved she could not play the game; and that was Lucy Greene. Not because she so violently objected to Mercy's presence in her home, but because she could not hide that objection. Lucy Greene broke ranks — and, slapping Mercedes, she admitted that *something was very definitely happening here.*

As a result of this, Lucy Greene had destroyed all chance of Daniel Greene's receiving his promised Cabinet post. For that, at least, we might all be grateful.

149: Somebody laughed. It hardly matters who it was. But whoever it was restored the collective lie. Within four minutes — at the very most — of its having occurred, the slap was already being denied. In half an hour, it had ceased altogether ever to have taken place.

I moved off, arm in arm with Mercedes. We collected our drinks from a passing tray and wandered into the garden.

I hadn't yet seen Nigel Forestead nor Maryanne nor anyone else who had come to the Greenes' from the ASH. I did see Doctor Chilcott. He had Mrs Calder Maddox with him.

I turned my back on them and said to Mercedes; "do you know Thaddeus Chilcott?"

"Yes, of course."

"Can you see him over there behind me — up against the rhododendrons?"

"Yes."

"Do you recognize the woman with him?"

"No."

I had hoped this would be her answer.

"Do something for me, will you?"

"Tell me what it is, first. I make no promises."

"Go to Chilcott. I don't think he's seen me, yet. I'm going to head away from here, just to make certain he doesn't."

"What do I do when I get there?" Mercedes asked — smiling at someone, nodding *hello.*

"Force an introduction. Get him to introduce you to that woman."

"Why? I don't think I really want to know her — do I?"

"No. But I want to know what she calls herself."

"What do you think she calls herself? Isn't it probably his wife."

"Ask."

"All right, Nessa. If you really think it will help."

"It will. It will help to save Lily."

"How?"

"Mercy — please — before they wander off. Go — and force an introduction."

She grumbled and sighed — and left me.

150: I could hardly bear not to turn around and watch, but I made myself walk in the other direction. I found a pleasant little alcove amongst the cedars, where, on a circle of flagstones, the Greenes had placed an open-work iron table — painted white — and a pair of small white chairs. I sat down.

Within one minute, I heard a voice behind me.

"I'd recognize that back of yours, Vanessa — anywhere," it said.

Arabella Barrie.

Her timing — superb on her own behalf — was appalling on mine.

She came around the branches of the cedars, wearing a dress of excessive severity and an expression to match.

"It was my understanding you would not be here," she said. She was carrying a glass of champagne and a walking stick. On her dyed blue head she wore a dyed blue hat that perfectly matched both dress and hair. She reminded me of childhood images, still retained, of the late Queen Mary. The reticule suspended from her arm enforced the image one more step. Her corseleted figure completed it.

"Hello, Arabella. Do sit down."

"I intend to."

She did — and set her walking stick like a borderline between us on the table; *your half — my half.*

"What made you think I would not be here?" I asked —
intrigued.

"I asked for a list of those who had accepted. Your name
wasn't on it," she said, quite bluntly. "I always ask, before I
accept an invitation, who the other guests will be." She sipped
her champagne and set the glass before her. "In the old days,
of course," she said; "one never had to enquire. We were told
— as a matter of protocol."

"I remember."

"You've developed an unbecoming habit, Vanessa, of lying
through your teeth. The fact is, you remember no such thing.
I am speaking of an era in the social life of this country that
had faded even before you were born."

"Possibly," I said. I was fighting very hard not to let her
gain the upper hand she so consistently won. But it was not to
be. Some people, I guess, are born with authority — and
Arabella was one of them. She had never questioned it herself
— and, consequently, neither had anyone else. I had tried.
And failed.

"You may be right," I continued. "On the other hand,
perhaps my memory of protocol is so entwined with Mother's
adherence to it, I can't begin to separate them."

"A very good answer, Vanessa. Excellent. Clear and in-
gratiating." Arabella had now begun to loosen her gloves.
"You have always played on my affection for your mother.
It has won you many points. Not, I insist, your playing
upon that affection, but the affection itself. I have kept a
lifelong eye on you, just as Rose Adella kept her eye on
my children. We did this by mutual agreement. People
die — but traditions and standards do not; and will not,
so long as those of us who believe in them survive. Your
mother has perished. I have not." She smiled; "Nor do I
intend to. To perish, you must understand, is not to die; for
die, I will. But perish — never. Your mother — alas — despite
all her remarkable qualities, is all but entirely gone from us.

Nothing remains of her but thee and me. Of *thee* — I can only say you were very quick to have done with her. Of *me* — I will only say — I will not have done with Rose Adella till I die. Then, I fear, she will truly perish. Certainly, I see no hope for her in you."

I rebelled at this. I was adamant.

"You're wrong," I said.

Arabella was very slightly taken aback by my vehemence. But then, as only Arabella could, she turned my feelings against me.

"Your defence of your affection for Rose Adella is charming. And I have no doubt it was just — and only — that; a defence of your affection for her. But I'm afraid I don't give a hoot for the *loving* qualities of your relationship, my dear. And nor, I might add, did she. What I am speaking of is the adherence to — and the reverence for — the things she stood for."

"Such as?"

"The honour of her class. The standards by which she lived. The traditions upon which her class and her standards were based. Could anything be simpler?"

"Yes. A good deal." I tried to laugh. "But what makes you think I've turned my back on what Mother stood for?"

Arabella paused, her gloves in a neatly folded little hummock before her. She studied her rings — and reached for the stem of her champagne glass. At last, without drinking — but merely studying the bubbles rising above her fingers — she spoke.

"Lily Porter," she said.

I waited for more, but more was not forthcoming.

"Lily Porter?" I said.

"Lily Porter."

And that was the end of it; her complaint about my flagging standards. The words *Lily Porter* — apparently — said it all.

151: I looked to one side — the garden side, through the branches — and I could see Mercedes approaching.

I drained my glass of champagne in one vulgar gulp and set the empty goblet down — on my side of the cane.

Arabella Arbiter — for so I thought of her in that moment — having watched me guzzle my drink, refused to allow her disgust to rise beyond the tip of her chin — which lowered; slightly. This was disapproval of the highest order. Less is very definitely more when it comes to gesture, in Arabella's case. A lifted eyebrow is merely an indication of rebuke. But the shifting of a fingertip — the touching of a pearl — may indicate a death sentence.

In spite of the fact she found us sitting together, I had to trust that Mercy would understand Arabella was not an ally.

I need not have worried.

"Here comes that dreadful Mannheim woman," said Arabella — rising, preparing to leave the moment she saw her.

Mercedes came from beyond the branches into our alcove.

"Mrs Barrie, how are you?" she said. "How very pleasant to see you."

"Thank you," said Arabella, pulling on her gloves and reaching for her cane. "I trust you will forgive me, Mercedes. I really must go.

"Of course."

Arabella left her unfinished champagne and now she nodded at it and said; "if you really are so very thirsty, Vanessa — you may as well have that too. I shall find another glass — less flat."

And was gone.

After a moment, I turned to Mercedes. "Well?" I asked.

She sat down — drew a cigarette case from her pocket-book and lit a Sobranie.

"She was introduced as Mrs Calder Maddox," she said.

I was sorry to hear this. I had wanted her not to be, I guess, in order to implicate Chilcott in the murder.

"Furthermore," Mercedes went on; "when I asked her how her husband was, she told me that — so far as she knew — he was *well, but overworked.* I expressed congenial surprise that such an appreciated and admired public figure should find it necessary to work any longer at such an august age." Mercedes was smiling as she repeated this; "and she said: *oh, he does not need to work, Miss Mannheim. It is just — they keep pressin' him back into service!*"

Mercedes' imitation of the Charleston drawl was somewhat overstated.

I said; "and so?"

"And so she went on to tell me how she had come all the way from Boston to be with her dear Calder — at this reception for the President — but when she got to the Aurora Sands Hotel, she discovered her husband had been called away."

"Not dead," I said; *"but merely gone away…"*

"I beg your pardon?"

"It's just an expression. What else? Anything from Chilcott?"

"Mrs Maddox said: *I am here with Thaddeus Chilcott out of the goodness of his heart. Having recognized my disappointment I might not meet my President — and knowin' I had come the whole way from Boston, he took pity on me an' here I am on his arm!*"

"But Chilcott," I insisted. "What was his response?"

Mercy drew the remains of Arabella's flat champagne towards her, spilling some of it along the way. She took a long, reflective pull at her Sobranie. I think she was replaying the scene in her mind and making sure she had it right.

"All the time Mrs Maddox was talking," she finally said; "he was staring into space. You know how people listen to radios? Looking into space and making a picture of what they're hearing? It was like that. He was making a picture of what she was saying. And…"

The spilled champagne had begun to run down through the open-work design of the iron table top, making an audible pool between our feet on the flagstones. It sounded like rain — the first in weeks.

"Yes?" I said. "Yes?"

"It's hard to describe," Mercedes answered. "Put it this way; say she's an actress and she's on the radio. And say he wrote the script and he's mouthing the words along with her as she speaks, until..." She took a puff on her Sobranie and said; "...she forgot her lines. You see?"

I thought I did. I nodded.

"And when he realized that Mrs Maddox had forgotten her lines, he said them for her. But he only said them because they contained an important element of the plot he's written. I mean — he wouldn't have said them if she'd just been meant to go maundering on about how *devastated* she was. What he said was the only thing she'd left out that was vital."

"*What?*"

"That Calder Maddox, having gone away, was very definitely coming back and that she was waiting at the Pine Point Inn for his return."

"And did he say when that return would be?"

"Of course not," said Mercedes.

Of course not.

152: It was time for us to go. Mercedes and I had our own plot in hand and must now fulfil the next stage. The first stage had been our arrival; three women, one of whom did not come into the party, but who had very definitely been seen. She had worn a white suit and carried a parasol. That would be remembered, by anyone, we hoped, who might see three such women later.

Stage two had entailed our presence at the party and our visibility there. Until the incident of the slap, we had thought it would be necessary to mingle more; but the slap had registered Mercy's presence and, more than likely, the presence of her companion — the white-haired woman in the simple black dress. Thaddeus Chilcott would certainly remember his evasive conversation with Mercedes — and Arabella her audience with me. So it was done; we had definitely been there and now we could leave and proceed with stage three.

Stage three was to be our invasion of the Pine Point Inn; the kidnapping of Lily Porter.

153: For obvious reasons, we avoided Daniel and Lucy Greene as we made our exit.

It did not turn out to be necessary to avoid the President. He, with Nellie, had retired — and was avoiding everyone.

We could not, on the other hand, avoid the white suit, himself, nor his yellow-dressed wife. Nigel Forestead and Maryanne might just as well have been lying in wait for us — perfectly plotting their moves to coincide with our departure.

Seeing them watching us — seeing them monitoring our route to the exit — I veered from my original intention of avoiding all Foresteads at all costs — and made directly for them — beaming my widest beam.

"There you are," I said, as we got within ten feet, calling it out above the heads of those who stood between us. Nigel and Maryanne were standing right at the edge of the first stone step that led from the terrace to the lawn.

Still beaming, I stood before them and said; "I want you to meet a friend; Mercedes Mannheim."

I could see it pass through Nigel's eyes; the panoply — entire — of all that *Mannheim* stood for; the wealth — the influence beyond imagining — one of America's greatest art collections — Mercedes' name in the index of a dozen biographies — the photographs in magazines — the outrageous but oh-so-well-publicized causes she had supported and the headlines that had followed. There it all was in Nigel's face, as he almost lost his balance stepping down towards us.

"Oh, yes!" he said. "Oh, yes. And how do you do?"

And I said; "Mercy, these are the Foresters; Neville and Mary Jane…"

Mercedes nodded at Nigel's extended hand — his already cringing neck.

And then we left.

This was the kind of revenge that people dream of; perfect in every nuance — even to the voice that floated after our departing backs, and the words it spoke as Maryanne said to Nigel; "what did she say that woman's name was?"

154: The road between the Pine Point Inn and the Daniel Greene cottage has more than its fair share of turns. The actual distance is not too great, but the switchbacks make it seem so.

On our way, Mercedes remarked that once the President and Mrs Warner had made their initial foray into the assemblage of guests beneath the awnings on the terrace and down across the lawn, they had seemed — very quickly — to disappear.

"Did Nellie Warner speak to you?" I said — knowing how often they had met.

"Of course not," said Mercy. "Nellie must now divest herself of me just as surely as she must divest herself of Lucy Greene."

"I guess that's why they disappeared so fast," I said.

"Oh — I think not," said Mercy. "You may not have taken this in, Vanessa, but there was a noticeable lack of Cabinet members on view to match the number of limousines parked out front."

It was true. Not one of Pine Point's congregation of Secretaries had showed his face on the lawn that afternoon. Yet, all their transport stood at the door.

"They were there, of course," said Mercy. "Or some of them were."

"Oh?"

"Yes. I saw them."

We had reached that part of the road where a dignified plaque proclaims: STUDIO OF THEODORE ROBERT HARPER — AMERICAN PAINTER, 1836 - 1910.

Harper is an artist I have long revered. For one thing, he shared with Whistler, his great contemporary, a love of things Japanese. His women in red are just as renowned as Whistler's women in white, and his use of Japanese ornamentation has given his paintings an eerie, almost shocking ambivalence; like Japanese theatre, delicate and violent all at once.

There was not a single indication Harper's studio — now a museum — was undergoing any kind of renovation. Another lie. Though perhaps, if one were to take Police Chief Wm. Billings's spelling to heart, there might well be — hidden somewhere on the Neck — a MUSEAM, also dedicated to T.R. Harper, the roof of which is leaking even now.

These distractions had caused me to miss the full implication of what Mercedes had said.

"Saw them?" I asked. "Where?"

"Off to one side as we entered the cottage. They were seated in the library. One was using the telephone. Roseberg, I think. I didn't see them all — my view was very brief. Someone opened the door and entered the room. But before he closed the door behind him, I definitely saw not only Roseberg, but Skelton and Frye as well. Defense and Health and State."

"But not Thomas Briggs and not Donald Maltby."

"That's right."

"Wouldn't you know it?" I said. "When we get to that hotel, the only Cabinet members we know — the ones who know us — are going to be waiting there to pounce."

155: It was now not more than five o'clock; an advantageous hour — the hour of hot baths and gin. Those who do not yet recline in their tubs are impatient to do so. Those who do are effectively immobilized.

Consequently, given the added fact that most, if not all, the President's men were spread out over the grounds and through the rooms of Daniel Greene's cottage, there was every chance — if we stood any chance at all — that we just might get away with what we had in mind. Lily, if we found her, was not going to leave like a paying guest — with bellhops and luggage in tow and stops at the Desk to give thanks and pay bills. She was going to go out secretly and probably against her will.

Of course, we hadn't found her yet. We only had my witness to prove she was there at all — and even I was beginning to doubt that seeing was believing. The Lily things I'd seen and smelled in that room upstairs — and the fact that a Mrs Franklin was registered — were beginning to take on the colours of a trap. The thought of this — of someone using Lily remnants and Lily insignia in order to draw us into the open — made me uneasy. It could mean Lily was dead.

The dreamlike image of Jimmy Hoffa, floating wherever he floats or lying under whatever highway has been paved above his bones — and the absolute image of Calder Maddox, suspended in his casket of ice — returned to haunt me.

As Mercedes and I stepped over the low-slung chains that mark the boundaries of the Pine Point parking lot, I saw Imelda sitting on the porch behind the screens.

To be sure, there was still much evidence that men of power were in residence. The parking lot contained a number of their cars with their blatant licence plates; the shaded places along the boulevards between the hotel buildings and its swimming pool and tennis courts contained the shadows of at least three men who could not afford, because of weaponry, to lounge in their shirt sleeves. And another man stood as if made of wood at the top of the steps.

Imelda had placed herself entirely in the shade. Her tinted stockings, white gloves and her veil were sufficient to hide the tone of her peanut-coloured skin — but her Spanish Filipino features were not so easily overcome. I thought: *what a pity her beauty is.* If only she had been plain, she might not then have been in such danger of attracting attention.

Half-way across the parking lot, Mercedes muttered: *are you ready?* I said: *yes.* But I did not — could not — mean it. I would never be ready for subterfuge.

We stepped in unison towards the portico; just as at the Greenes' — two smart women, arm in arm. We also began to chatter as if we had actually been impressed by the august company we'd just been keeping. *He said* and *she said* and *I said* and *you said*: rather like a song.

It worked.

The man at the top of the steps was so unmoved by our presence, he actually started coming down as we went up. All we got from him was a lukewarm: *ladies...* as he passed behind us into the parking lot we had just deserted.

Turning to our right, we went through the screen door onto

the porch where Imelda sat in her wicker chair, hard up
against the shingles. A trio, made up of two men and one
woman, sat in chairs beyond her, drinking something cherry
red from highball glasses.

"Lily!" said Mercedes. "So there you are!"

Imelda turned in our direction, smiling the pure white,
maddening smile of one who has never brushed her teeth with
anything but salt.

"Mercedes!" she cried — too loud, and using the Spanish
pronunciation of *Mer-ke-des*.

Admittedly, the gentlemen looked up and the woman who
was seated with them had to redirect their attention. But it
couldn't have mattered less. We were already marching back
along the porch towards the entrance to the lobby; laughing,
all three of us, and speaking our formal dialogue in the stilted
tones of three Eliza Doolittles out for a stroll: *gin was mother's
milk to her* and *them she lived with would have killed her for a
hat-pin — let alone a hat.*

156: The lobby was more daunting.

To begin with, the priggish young man in his Director's
coat was back at his station behind the Desk. He was making
life unbearable there for a clerk who had apparently done
nothing more amiss than mislay a piece of paper. I thought, as
I witnessed this, of Lawrence and the unfortunate Judy. Suddenly, our two hotels had become remarkably and disappoint-
ingly alike.

There was also the size of the lobby to contend with.
Though it had not seemed quite so large last night, this afternoon we found ourselves stranded in what seemed to be a
public arena the size of the Colosseum.

"Elevators — elevators..." Mercedes muttered, urging us
in that direction.

"No," I said. And I was adamant. In elevators you can be trapped with perfect strangers who turn out to be the very strangers you want to avoid. "We will walk," I said.

Imelda said nothing. She kept her head down and pretended to look for her keys in her pocket-book.

Keys in her pocket-book.

I stood immobilized.

I then informed Mercedes that a hotel room more often than not has a key to the door. And if that hotel room contains a prisoner, that door will very definitely be locked.

"Just go to the Desk and get it," said Mercedes.

She had to be crazy. "I can't do that," I said. "I had a run-in with that young man last night and he would be bound to recognize me."

"All right," said Mercedes. "I will do it."

She started briskly towards the Desk, where the bad-tempered concierge was still browbeating the clerk. I took Imelda by the arm and led her over to the foot of the staircase.

"Turn your back on the Desk," I said. "Remember, you are Lily Porter."

"Why, if I am truly Lily Porter, do I not go over and take a key — my own — from the man?"

"Because," I said — and dried completely. I could think of no good reason. When I recovered, I said; "you are feeling faint and your friend has gone to collect it for you."

"I do not know *to feel faint*."

"Falling down," I said.

At once, Imelda began to fall to the floor. I stopped her just in time and said; "no — no! You needn't lie down. Just take a good hold of my arm and look as if you would *like* to lie down."

She did this rather well.

As we stood there, Imelda clutching my arm with both hands and gazing with evident longing at the carpet, I chanced to find myself staring at the bulletin board. There, amongst so many garish others, was the photograph in which I appeared. In spite of our present situation, I was determined to remove my image from this public place.

I led Imelda closer to the board — but she did not, at first, understand how I could move her if she was *feeling to fall down*. I explained that she really felt exceptionally well and was merely pretending to be ill.

"I do not like pretending to be ill," she said. "It makes me dizzy."

Behind us I could hear Mercedes firmly raising her voice. I prayed she wouldn't overstep the mark and tip our hand.

Before me, I could see the iceberg rising out of the bay and the knots of people staring at it, me among them. There was Sybil Metsley, giving off *Titanic* emanations. There was Lily Porter, hand on the back of her head to hold her hat — with its streaming silks — in place. There was Meg in her bathing suit — and Kyle, the chauffeur in his uniform — and, down by the water's edge, the Boys. And there was Calder Maddox — living — alive in his towels and his yellow bathrobe — waiting to die; to be killed.

I became so lost in the people there, I forgot for a moment what I wanted to do with them — which was remove them and destroy them. Because I was one of them. I began to extract the pins that held the picture in place and dumped them, with the photograph, into my pocket-book.

"Done," said Mercedes — who had come up behind us, quite unheard.

My heart leapt — but when I turned, I saw she was holding up the key to room 217.

"He wasn't going to give this to me, of course. But I threatened him with Donald Maltby. That works every time. Let's go."

We proceeded up the stairs — where, once we got to the

landing, Imelda effected a miraculous recovery, let go my arm
and stood up straight.

"Am I Lily Porter still?"

"Yes," said Mercedes. "And you will be Lily Porter until
we find Lily Porter."

157: The upper hallway was much as I had expected. The
sound of pouring baths could be heard beyond the doors.
There was also the sound of singing and of television sets. The
scent of *Bain du Soleil* and of Nivea Cream and Noxema
permeated the air, co-mingled with the smell of sea-damp
carpets and wilted flowers.

A woman of gigantic size came thumping along towards us,
dressed in a long white terry-cloth robe and swinging a
flowered bathing cap. She smiled and nodded vigorously and
swung her bathing cap at us — spinning off drops of
chlorinated water. Pool water. She was the only person we encountered on our way to Lily's room.

My fear that Lily would not be there was equal to my fear
she would be. Both scenarios provided problems.

We came to the room — number 215 — in which I had heard
Mrs Maddox. Now, of course, there was no sound coming from
it — and then we reached the door of number 217. While Imelda and Mercedes stood back surveying the corridor in either
direction, I stepped forward, key in hand, and knocked.

"Lily?"

There was a fearful silence.

"Lily?" A trifle louder.

Still — the silence.

I knocked again; sharply.

"Lily."

Not a sound.

"Go on," said Mercedes. "Quickly. I can hear the elevator.
Turn the key."

Turn the key? I could barely get the key into the lock.

"Do!" hissed Mercedes. *"Hurry!"*

At last, I had the key in place and turned it.

The door drifted open.

The room was in semi-darkness, all the curtains pulled across the windows — but not the drapes — and all the windows shut. Not a single lamp was lit.

Still, there was light enough to see that someone was in the bed — and, once I'd moved a little closer, there was light enough to see that it was Lily.

158: "Is she alive?" Mercedes asked — still whispering.

Imelda shut the door and shot the bolt.

I could smell, within the mustiness, the undeniable scent of Opium, Lily's perfume.

Imelda hung back, but Mercedes and I went over and stood beside the bed.

"I can't hear breathing," Mercedes said. "Turn on a lamp."

Imelda lit a discreet and distant lamp on one of the bureaus.

"Open a window," said Mercedes.

Imelda crossed to the windows and pulled one set of curtains and let in light — then air. The sound of the window rising was like a rocket taking off.

"Oh, do be quiet," Mercedes said.

"Yes, ma'am."

Imelda was herself again — the servant. She was already removing the hat and veil, beginning to take off the gloves.

"Are you any good at this?" said Mercedes. "I'm sorry, but it really is the only time I'm a coward." She backed away. "I cannot bear to touch the dead."

Looking down at Lily, with her unnatural, discoloured complexion, her pinched expression and her hands clutching pieces of Kleenex tight as the reins of a runaway horse in her fists — it was all too familiar to me.

I sat down beside her and loosened the fingers around the wads of tissue. The wads had been soaking wet — most likely with perspiration — but they had dried like balls of hardened papier mâché.

I got fresh Kleenex from the box beside the bed and asked Imelda to bring me some toilet water — any toilet water from the vanity. She brought me a bottle of *Royale Lyme — for gentlemen and ladies of discretion.* I tipped some onto the Kleenex and wiped Lily's brow with it. The smell was pungent — almost 100% proof.

I leaned down close to see what I could hear — but all I could hear was my own heart.

Mercedes said; "neck pulse. Neck pulse."

I felt for the neck pulse.

Yes. It was there. But faint.

I turned and nodded.

"Praise be to God," said Mercedes.

And Imelda crossed herself.

I poured more *Royale Lyme* on a second piece of Kleenex and held it under Lily's nose. I thought the pungency, the alcohol, would waken her.

It did.

"Oh!" she said. "Don't!"

I sat back and looked at her.

Her hair showed clearly where the dye was growing out. It was also clear, the way her hair was lying, that Lily was going bald. The most remarkable thing about her appearance was that she had no eyebrows. Or else her eyebrows were so pale that, without the aid of a pencil, they barely seemed to exist. She looked as old as my mother; but I surmised that part of this aging process had taken place the last few days; the way a person who is very ill can age in a matter of hours. There was not a trace of her beauty anywhere in her appearance.

"Hello," I said. "It's Vanessa."

The expression in her eyes was more than disconcerting. It was absolutely apparent she did not know who I was.

I looked at Mercedes.

"I think they must have drugged her to the eyeballs."

"Well," said Mercedes. "Not any more."

159: Dressing her in the clothes that Imelda had worn on our walk to the Greenes' and consequently through the public rooms of the Pine Point Inn was worse than having to dress a corpse. Neither her arms nor her legs would co-operate.

"What in the name of God do you think they've used to put her in this state?" Mercedes asked, as she struggled with Lily's stockings.

"At a guess," I said; "I'd say it was *Maddonix*." I pulled up her sleeve to demonstrate. "You see? They shot it into her with a needle."

"But, why?"

"*Maddonix* to put you to sleep — *Maddonite* to wake you — and *Maddoxin* to calm you in between," I said. "Unquote. They were Calder's drugs of choice. So why not use them on Lily Porter?"

"But — *why*?" Mercedes said again. "Why?"

"I cannot even begin to guess," I said. "But I suppose we're going to find out."

Over in a corner of the room, Imelda — already wearing the plain blue uniform she had taken from her bag — was putting

on her other shoe. She would precede us out of the hotel, using all the back doors she could find, and make her way to the
Mannheim cottage.

"How on earth," said Mercedes; "are we going to get Lily
downstairs? And how can we possibly take her through the
lobby, Nessa? It's madness."

"It is madness to go any other way," I told her. I explained
what had happened when I had tried to use the service stairs
the previous night, though I did not explain that I had been
arrested.

"But we're sending Imelda that way. Won't they stop her?"

"All Imelda has to say is that she's staff. In that uniform,
they'll believe her."

Mercedes shot me a look of scorn.

I understood, and said; "she doesn't have to worry. The only men she's apt to see aren't going to know they don't hire
coloured people at the Pine Point Inn."

At once, Imelda said; "I am not coloured."

Mercedes laughed. "Yes, you are," she said. "As long as
you're in this building!"

160: Lily sat on the bed. She was dressed in Imelda's white
linen suit; the milk chocolate blouse; the white straw hat with
the veil. She also wore Imelda's open-toed shoes. The effect of
this was unnerving. As a costume, it suited Lily as badly as if
we had dressed her as Clare Booth Luce. There was not a
single flowing line — nor a single touch of colour. White so ill
became her that she really did look dead.

I hitched my skirt and knelt before her, taking both her
hands in mine.

"Lily," I said; "you don't have to stay here any more."

She looked at me placidly. Who I might be, she could not
tell. Worse — it did not seem to interest her that she was being
offered her freedom.

"Mercedes and I are your friends, dear. Your *real* friends — and we're going to get you out of here. All right?"

Lily smiled. She looked sideways at Imelda.

"Who's that," she slurred.

"That's another friend, dear. She's going to help you, too. Come on. You're going to stand up now."

Still holding her hands, I got to my feet and began to pull her up with me.

"Can't," she said.

"Damn well will," said Mercedes.

"Can't."

"Must," said Mercedes.

We pulled her forward onto her feet. The weight of her was alarming — like a recalcitrant feather; light — but uncontrollable.

"Walk."

"Won't."

"Walk!"

"Can't."

We edged her forward. She moved her feet like someone trying to roller-skate.

Then she stopped. She had seen herself in a full-length mirror and she was squinting — peering — trying to make herself out.

"Who — " she said; " — that?"

"You," said Mercedes.

Imelda opened the door and scouted the corridor.

"Yes," she said. "No one."

"All right," Mercedes said. "Go."

"Goodbye," Imelda said.

"Goodbye."

She slipped around the door and was gone.

In the meantime, Lily had been standing unsteadily between us, held in place with our arms around her waist. She

Timothy Findley

now looked over her shoulder and surveyed the room, with its
drawn curtains, its dark corners and its unmade bed.

"Hell here," she said.

"Yes," I said. "that's why we're leaving."

She turned back then and stared at me.

"You are Va..." she said.

"That's right," I said. "And this is..."

"Meg."

I shut my mouth tight.

Mercedes didn't utter a word. I think we both only had one
thought. By saying *Meg* — Lily had filled out our childhood
quartet.

We took Lily over to the door.

"Please," she said, half turning back towards the room;
"things. Bureau."

"She wants her stuff," I said.

"All right," said Mercedes. "But for heaven's sake, hurry."

I ran back to the bureau and, thank heaven, found one of
Lily's Miami beach bags in the second drawer. I threw all her
perfumes, all her powders, all her watches, bracelets, scarves
and blouses into it — but couldn't save any more than that.

In the meantime, I heard her speaking her pidgin English
to Mercedes; "you. Trouble. In."

"What did she say?" I asked.

"She said I'm trouble. But that's hardly news."

"No, she didn't. She said trouble. In."

"That's right," said Lily. "Trouble. In."

"Ah," said Mercedes. "Well. That's hardly news either.
Now — do come on."

"No," said Lily. "Not come on without corder."

"Corder?" I asked.

"Pillow. Corder."

I went back and reached under the pillows. There indeed
was a *corder*. A Sony. I put it in my pocket.

Lily smiled.

"Music," she said. "Mine."

161: The corridor was deserted.

"Can't we take her in the elevator?" Mercedes asked.

"No," I said. "We will get trapped in there with one of them. I swear it. Trust me."

It took us a good five minutes to manoeuvre Lily all the way to the end of the hall, walking her as one might walk a victim of paralysis. When we made the turn to lead her to the stairs, she complained that we must; "Stop. Please stop." But we dared not stop for fear she would fall asleep.

Somehow, we made it to the landing and just as we were about to descend the next flight of steps, the figure of Mister Curren — the black man — came bounding up towards us.

I was certain his intention was to stop us — but all he said was; "You ladies require some help?"

"Yes," said Mercedes.

"No," I said — too quickly — cutting Mercedes off before she could extend her invitation further.

"Thank you Mister Curren," I said. "It's good of you to offer, but really, we're quite all right."

"Suit yourself," he said. But he did not go away. Instead, he smiled and went on chatting, as if he might keep us there all evening. "You enjoy the party? Meet the President?"

"Yes," we said, "yes."

Lily had begun to rummage in her bag and I was nervous she might produce, all at once, some memento of her incarceration and drop it at his feet. I was also afraid she might look up and recognize him as one of her jailers. On the other hand — he could not have been her jailer. He seemed not to recognize her at all, except as the woman in white who had stood with us on Lucy's lawn. Besides which — he didn't have a jailer's eyes. A killer's, perhaps, but not a jailer's.

At last, he took his leave and, as we descended step by careful step towards the lobby, I found myself almost feeling sorry for Mister Curren. After all, he had stood before his boss's prisoner and let her pass.

I say I almost felt sorry for him — until I remembered how he made his living and, then, I didn't feel sorry for him at all.

162: We were now in the parking lot.

The sun had sunk to a level that struck us squarely in the face. We turned away, blinded.

Coming directly towards us was Doctor Chilcott — still arm in arm with Mrs Maddox. They looked exceedingly grim. I was certain they had seen us, until I realized the sun was in their eyes — blinding them as it had blinded us.

"Quick," I said. "The parasol."

Mercedes was carrying it, dangling from her free arm.

"Up, up," I said. "Put it up."

She struggled. And failed.

I grabbed it from her, letting my half of Lily go. Lily immediately leaned against Mercedes. Both of them nearly fell over.

Like a parachute that opens at the very last minute, I just got the parasol raised in time. I thrust it — like a shield — before our faces and we passed by, nothing more than three sets of anonymous legs and feet.

163: Once on the road behind the hotel, Mercedes said; "Three ladies out for a Sunday walk," she said. "How charming."

As we walked — like snails, I must add — Mercedes said; "my only fear is that Donald Maltby will turn up at my door."

"I thought you weren't afraid of him."

"I wasn't. But harbouring a fugitive rather changes things. Wouldn't you agree?"

"I don't know," I said. "For some strange reason, I'm less and less afraid — now that we have Lily out of there."

At this moment, we heard the sound of a motorcar approaching.

Since it was coming from the direction of the Greenes', we thought we were in for the worst.

"I think I'll carry a gun from now on," Mercedes said as we waited, frozen in the path of the oncoming car. When it finally appeared, she burst out laughing. "It's all right. It's just Imelda with the Daimler."

Imelda stopped the motorcar and opened the door. "You require a taxi?" she said.

164: Once ensconced in the back seat, with all her belongings piled up beside her, Lily looked at Mercedes. In fact, she stared at her very hard. Having settled me in her addled brain, she had still not settled Mercy.

Finally; "you're in trouble," she said.

Mercedes smiled. "She's at it again. But at least her grammar's improved."

"It's true," said Lily. "You in trouble."

Mercedes refused to believe her. She simply waved her hand and scoffed. But I did not. I was certain Lily meant it. Otherwise, why did she harp on it?

However, I wasn't certain she meant that Mercedes Mannheim was in trouble. I wasn't certain of this, because I didn't really think she had fixed Mercy yet, as being Mercedes. What I did believe — because I knew about the fixations people develop when they are heavily drugged — was that *someone* was in trouble. And — for whatever reason — Lily believed that someone was Meg.

165: At *Ramsgate* we moved Lily into the guest-room furthest from the front of the house. That way, if anyone came —

whether Maltby or Chilcott or whoever — there would be little danger of Lily Porter wandering into their presence.

"She'll sleep all night now," said Mercedes.

"Yes."

We were walking back along the corridor towards the drawing-room.

"What do you intend to do?" Mercedes asked.

"Go back to the Aurora Sands, of course."

"And leave me alone with Lily? What do I do with her, Vanessa? I'm an old, busy woman."

I said; "tomorrow, I will come back. I promise. By tomorrow, I'm certain there will be more answers."

Mercedes really didn't want to baby-sit a zombie. I knew that. But she would have to.

I made a bargain with her. I said; "I've been lying to you, Mercy. But only because I had to. Now — I will tell you the truth."

We had reached the drawing-room. Mercy was pouring herself some brandy.

"Do I want to hear the truth?" she asked.

"Yes," I said. And I went across to where she stood and poured myself a brandy — larger than hers.

"But you don't drink," she said.

"I do now."

We settled into chairs.

"All right," Mercedes said. "Go ahead. Tell me."

"Calder Maddox is dead."

"Oh," she said, obviously disappointed. "That."

"You knew?"

"No," she said; "but I had a hunch."

She turned away from me and then, having debated with herself for about fifteen seconds, she turned back.

"Now I will tell you something" she said; "only a guess — but an educated guess. And it goes like this."

She took a deep breath.

"I suppose you can't have been fool enough to think it was chance that half the President's Cabinet turned up here this weekend?"

I shook my head.

Mercedes continued; "so suddenly — so urgently — so out of the blue?"

"I didn't realize," I said; "they hadn't been expected."

"Health; Defense; the Interior; State; the CIA," said Mercedes. "That's a pretty hefty group."

"Yes." I felt my insides begin to turn, partly because of the brandy and mostly because it was my turn, now, not to want to hear the truth.

"Calder Maddox," said Mercedes; "had contacts with each of those government departments." She waited; "Did you know that? Were you aware of that?"

"No."

"Well," she said. "You're aware of it now."

"But he's dead."

"That's right. He's dead. *He's* dead — and no one's supposed to know it. It's a secret. Yes? And all those Secretaries are here — the ones he did business with — and that's another secret. One and one makes two. Think about it. Don't speak. Don't try to answer any of this, now. Go home to your hotel and think about it there."

I nodded. I was numb.

"The thing is," Mercedes said; "I can't drive you back. I can't even send you back in the car. I think we can't be seen together right now. When you come here tomorrow, you will have to walk again."

"Yes," I said. "All right."

I finished my brandy and left the drawing-room without another word. Mercedes just sat and I could hear her fingernails tapping on her glass as I went away.

166: When I had packed my crushable dress, my shoes and the lingerie I'd brought to wear to Mercy's lunch — and when I had looked in to see that Lily was genuinely, peacefully at rest, I made my way back down the route by which I had arrived — slowly along the drive beneath the trees and past the rams, over the road and through the woods, with the evening birds in song and the light behind me all the way.

This time, the Maltby Shock Troops — as I had come to think of them — paid little heed. After all, I was just an aging — probably eccentric — woman wearing walking shorts and canvas shoes and carrying over her back a camera bag filled with clothes. In her pocket — safely protected from sand and lint — was a tiny audio cassette in a pale grey envelope. The envelope bore the Mannheim crest — embossed — and the address: *Ramsgate — Larson's Neck — Sutter's Hill — Maine — 04076.*

One of the uniformed women even had the audacity to wave at me as I passed — thinking, perhaps, we were sisters under the skin. But hers is a sisterhood for which I have no use — other than as a source of wonder that women should do what men have always done so well, and without the need for equivocation.

I had no real notion what it was that was in my pocket. Its being there was gratuitous. I had simply done what Lily had requested. But, once I got to *Ramsgate*, and I was in the guest-room assigned to me for changing my clothes, I had placed the pocket Sony on the dresser and turned it on without a thought of what I might hear. Music was what I suppose I expected, since "music" had been Lily's word for it. But what I got was a human voice.

It was a voice I didn't recognize at first — male, middle-aged and flat. But it had been recorded with impeccable fidelity and infinite professional care — so that, even though I heard it on the tiny machine provided, I fairly quickly came to realize the voice was that of Thaddeus Chilcott. In the background I heard what I thought at first to be the accidentally recorded sound of a ticking clock. But as I listened further, I understood the presence of the clock — with its remorseless and mesmerizing rhythm — was quite deliberate.

Unfortunately, I had to shut the tape recorder off before I'd heard much more than just enough to intrigue and puzzle me. This abortive audition came about because Imelda was approaching along the hall with a fresh cup of tea.

"I thought you might like this," she said, putting the tea on a bedside table; "now the trouble is over."

As she left the room, I couldn't help wondering what she meant by "over."

Maybe it will not be over ever. There. I want to draw lines around events as if events were like the gardens I design: where I see every nuance before it exists. Sometimes I even see them through the eyes of one whose work is done and who walks away from a gate just closed — the garden real and aromatic behind her — all its stones in place and its iris bending to seek the moisture of a pool where, if a stone were thrown, the whole ecology of imagination would suddenly flower with perfect shapes and textures. I don't want ever to have reality be this real again. I want to shut myself away, with nothing but the gardens in my mind.

167: On my walk down the twilit beach, I saw no more than half a dozen others on the sands. Two of these were sombre children with their parents. Another was a stone-picker, turning over pebbles one by one and the last was the *Honey Girl* of Halfway House.

She was sitting on her veranda with a glass in one hand and a pair of binoculars in the other. She had put on a white cotton shirt in place of her usual halter top; and the soles of her feet, propped up on her railing, seemed strangely, almost alarmingly pale. Her honey hair hung loose and dishevelled — but pleasantly so.

As I passed, she gazed at me without a trace of chagrin that I was so clearly staring at her. She smiled — and nodded — and said; "our iceberg is pink this evening."

I looked to my right and saw it was so.

"I think I prefer it when it's green," she said.

"Green? I have never seen it green."

She pushed her hair back, showing all her face and giving a conspiratorial smile, she said; "you will one day. You just have to be there in the moment."

She sat back, then — declaring by her posture and the lifting of her binoculars that our exchange of words was over.

"Good-evening," I said. But she did not reply.

When I came to that part of the beach exclusively within the purview of the ASH, there was not a soul in sight. I was now completely alone — and I went to my private dune and smoothed its sand and sat down facing the iceberg.

The tide was well advanced on its outward ride and the whole beach below me shimmered wet and hard and smooth as a sheet of gleaming brass. The reflection of the iceberg stood up straight as a mirage — though it was upside down and tilted slightly towards me.

All that kept me company were a number of shorebirds — knots and ruddy turnstones and flocks of sanderlings all racing back and forth from the water's edge. I unslung the camera bag and set it beside me, rummaging for Lily's tape recorder — praying its batteries would hold until I had heard enough of the recording to judge what it really might be. Removing the tape, I carefully folded and smoothed Mercedes' envelope and put it back in my pocket. Then I inserted the cassette, struck the appropriate button and waited.

168: What I heard at first was merely the continuation of what I had begun to listen to in Mercedes' house.

It appeared to be instructions; not as to a cohort — not as to an underling — but more as to a potential convert to some religion.

For instance, quite early on, Doctor Chilcott's voice — so disturbingly without inflection — was saying: *you do not need to be concerned with what you know . . .* And it said this several times. After which there would be a mechanical *click*, as if the machine had shut itself off — but it hadn't. The click was just a tick point; a sort of cue: *Step one; you do not need to be concerned with what you know.* Then, three seconds after the *click*, the voice said: *what you think you know and what you think you remember are now to be forgotten.* This, too, repeated many times and then another *click*.

Now the voice said: *what you have known till now is a lie and what you remember is false.*

Click.

What you have known till now is a lie and what you remember is false.

Click.

The iceberg faded through pink towards maroon.

The clock on the tape went on ticking.

What I will tell you now is true.

What I will tell you now is true.

What you will now recall is factual.

What you will now recall is factual.

Whatever you resist, you resist because you resist the truth.

Whatever you resist, you resist because you resist the truth.

Each of these statements repeated and repeated and repeated. *Click. Click. Click.*

I was now completely alarmed. I feared I might succumb to these messages myself, if I did not resist with every ounce of conscious effort I could muster. Yet, the tone of the voice was flat — and the message, banal.

For a moment, I turned the machine off and told myself — aloud — the next thing the voice would tell me would surely be: *peace is war* and *war is peace* and *two and two make five*. Surely I had stumbled somehow on a tape of *1984*. Lily's music was just the voice of Big Brother.

I had hoped I would laugh when I told myself this. But I did not laugh. And I did not smile. And I did not move.

I could not.

At last — I took a deep breath and pressed the button.

Your desire for the truth is absolute.

Your desire for the truth is absolute.

Your acceptance of the truth is absolute.

Your acceptance of the truth is absolute.

These truths are absolute.

These truths are absolute.

Your memories of the death of Calder Maddox are…

I turned the machine off and waited.

I counted to ten and turned the machine back on.

I heard the word:

Wrong.
Your memories of the death of Calder Maddox are wrong.
Click.

I was breathing so hard, I might have run the mile. Not because of what the voice had just said, but because of who was saying it: Chilcott.

The tape, like any book of propaganda, had begun with instructions of the kind directed to all potential converts. But suddenly — now — it had switched to the particular; to Calder Maddox and his death; and to how that death was perceived by a single listener: Lily Porter. This tape, I suddenly realized — the whole of it — had been created for her alone.

Calder Maddox died of natural causes; it said.

Your conversation on the beach had nothing to do with the death of Calder Maddox.

Marguerite Riches had nothing to do with the death of Calder Maddox.

Marguerite Riches did not kill Calder Maddox.

Nobody killed Calder Maddox.

169: Ten minutes later, I sat entirely stilled.

I could not see. I could not hear. I could not think.

After a quarter of an hour, as the sun's light made its final foray over the iceberg, I switched the machine back on and lowered the volume to a whisper.

The tide had turned.

Boom!

I held the tiny box to my ear. The voice now seemed to come from so far away, it was as if I heard a voice from Mars.

Tell no one the lie that Calder Maddox was murdered.

Tell no one the lie that Marguerite Riches spoke to you before Calder Maddox died.

Honour the truths I have told you.

*No matter what you hear; no matter what you read; no matter
what you would prefer to believe; you will believe what I have told
you.*

This case is closed.

170: Once I had bathed and dressed, I went downstairs and
sat in the dining-room above my plate of lobster Newburg and
did not eat and could not get my mind off Meg.

I looked across the crowded tables and watched her peeling
a pear for Michael and slicing it into long, thin strips.

What possible reason could the voice have had for connecting Meg to Calder's death; and for trying to convince Lily
Porter the connection — whatever the connection was supposed to be — did not exist? It was crazy.

Meg kill Calder? How, out of all the given suspects, could
the voice have chosen her?

Surely I would have made a more plausible killer than Meg.
At least my disdain for Calder had been visible.

Except...

The photographs.

Nigel stole them — I have to presume — and had them passed to Doctor Chilcott — I also have to presume. All Chilcott
had to do was examine the figures and note Meg's presence
among them.

And the presence, too, of a dozen others.

What had they done — the makers of this tape with its in-
sane innuendoes? Put on blindfolds and stuck their pins at

random into my pictures? And if their pins had landed on the iceberg? What then? A tape for Labrador?

171: When Judy came from the Desk and said I was wanted on the telephone, I supposed it would be Lawrence wondering where I had been. But I was wrong. It was Mercedes; being enigmatic.

"I've been told," she said; "the moon will be spectacular tonight."

"That's nice," I said. "Who told you that?"

"A friend. And the same friend says the very best view of the moon in these parts can be had from the beach. Did you know that?"

"It's best from my window, so far as I'm concerned, Mercedes." I was being distracted from our conversation by the presence at the Desk of one of the men in suits from the Pine Point Inn. He was asking Judy questions.

"Oh, but you should really try the beach," Mercedes said. "Wonderful, according to my friend. Round about midnight. I just thought I'd let you know — given your proclivity for all the natural wonders. Do try to see it — I think it really will be worth your while. Good-night, dear."

"Good-night..." I started to say; but she was already gone.

I hung up, but I did not leave the telephone booth. I watched the Secret Service agent badgering Judy — and Judy politely holding her ground. I thanked heaven for Quinn Welles. He'd told her she didn't have to answer any questions about the guests — or listen in on any phone calls. Now, it was paying off. The agent had obviously come to make enquiries about the whereabouts of Lily Porter. But Judy just kept shaking her head. I cheered.

172: I was afraid to leave my room, even knowing I could lock the door behind me. It now contained not only my remaining photographs, but Lily's cassette and the recorder — and, of course, this book.

I dressed with great care; feeling the early effects of what might turn out to be a cold. I wore my woollen slacks and the thickest sweater I owned — a hand-knitted grey from the Orkneys. I also put on a woollen hat I bought long ago on one of my infrequent trips to Canada.

Then I sat down and waited. It was only nine-thirty when I started preparing myself. By eleven I was perspiring — and removed the sweater. It was all very irritating — being dragged out into the dark to look at the moon and not knowing why.

In one of my favourite Japanese classics — *The Pillow Book of Sei Shonagon* — the ladies of the court often did such things as make long journeys to see the moon from a special vantage point — or to hear the cuckoo sing. But that was simply to see the moon and hear the cuckoo sing; not for some ulterior motive.

I make, here and now, a resolution that after this night is past — whenever I am looking at the moon, I will be thinking of the moon. And if I should ever be lucky enough to hear the cuckoo sing again, I will open every pore of my being to its song. Ulterior motives be damned.

At last, it was eleven-thirty, and carrying all my jeopardized possessions with me — including my pills and my pocket-book — I went down the back stairs feeling like a thief.

Indeed, the moon was a glorious sight. Now fully quartered, she was tipped on her side directly above the iceberg in the bay.

I walked on the grass, aware that dozens of eyes were doubtless watching me from various lighted and unlighted windows on the seaward side of the ASH. It reminded me of the last night Calder Maddox had sat up wrapped in his blankets, counting all the stars.

The bath houses gleamed on my right as I passed. The

ghostly towels and bathing suits that were hung in the yard all
looked like people left behind to gossip in the dark. When I
hit the sand, a great cool wave of air rose up to greet me — the
tide now having risen almost halfway up the beach. I no
longer regretted the sweater, though the air was still and balmy
enough.

Way off before me, the lights of Halfway House were ablaze
— and I thought how odd it was of that independent, seemingly quite unflappable girl to feel the need to surround
herself with light in every room. Still, the facts must be admitted; she did live there entirely alone in what — at night — was
a kind of wasteland, and every passing figure must seem to be
a menace.

Not I, however. I passed by quite benign, not even staring
in her windows; though the temptation, I confess, was great.
What did she do in there so utterly alone? Did she entertain
the black man in his official suit? Or Nigel Forestead?

Hah!

I breached the darkness that came so suddenly and so completely after her lights had been put behind me. But I could
see no sign of Mercedes.

I kept on walking; cautiously.

Then I heard someone cough. Behind me.

Just keep walking; I told myself. *You've been in far worse
situations than this. At Bandung, up against the fence, dealing in
contraband — not even able to see the faces of those who took what
you had to trade. And always, the danger of a prison guard making
a sudden appearance — the way they could be right on top of you
out of total silence. All those little men who seemed so huge in the
dark: informers — enemies — killers. Yes; you have been in far
worse situations than this.*

The cough came again — masculine — heavy — this time,
downwind of me, closer to the water's edge.

I waited — not breathing.

I counted, thinking: *any minute, whoever it is will have to pass the moon path on the water and I will see his silhouette.* I hunkered down, praying my knees wouldn't crack.

From this vantage point, I caught a perfect view of him — perhaps five seconds' worth; enough to recognize that it was David Brodie, my alcoholic neighbour. The poor man. He lives, like the *Honey Girl*, an absolutely solitary life, but his was lived in the midst of almost two hundred guests who surrounded him at the ASH. He spends most nights afraid of the light and turning out the bulbs. I wondered if tonight he had it in his crazy mind to try the moon.

If only he would whistle — or sing — or talk to himself. It would have been so much easier to keep track of him. But he was gone, now, utterly — into the dark — and it was quite impossible to know if he was a dozen paces further off — or a mile.

I moved up closer to the dunes in the hopes that David Brodie would stick to the shore, and continued my search for Mercedes. But when, after five more minutes — which seemed an hour — I had still not located her, I had the chilling thought perhaps this was all an elaborate trap; that Mercedes had been forced to make the phone call and I was to be kidnapped — just as Lily had been. I did not at all relish the thought of someone taking my arm and marching me up to the Pine Point Inn, where I would be drugged and brainwashed with massive doses of *Maddonix* and magnetic tape.

"Vanessa?"

Mercedes' voice — so sudden — was so calm it made me want to hit her, à la Lucy Greene.

"We're over here," she said.

We?

The word gave me pause. Perhaps she was warning me to go away. Nothing had been said on the phone about another person.

But I could not resist. If this was a trap, it was a trap. I called back, barely above a whisper; ''where?''

''Turn right and come straight ahead. I can see you against the water.''

When I reached her, she was standing just at the lip of a dune.

''Was that man with you?'' she asked.

I told her, no — but I knew who he was. I said we must be careful. Within the next fifteen minutes or so, David Brodie would probably be coming back.

''Come up,'' said Mercedes. ''Lily is here.''

173:   I let Mercedes help me up over the edge of the dune and we both went down into the hollow.

The sand was so dry and pale, it was almost powdered glass. It reflected a good deal of moonlight and we could see each other remarkably well. As soon as we hit the lowest part of the dune, the sound of the surf immediately vanished. The effect was like sitting in a vacuum; just another place with prisoners.

Lily still looked quite unlike herself — too dishevelled — too undone. Her hair seemed windblown, although there was not, as they say in Maine: *a lick of wind*. She was seated on the sand with her knees drawn up — her legs bare — her feet shoeless. A pair of high-heeled shoes was beside her, perfectly arranged side by side, toes pointing down into the pit of the dune. There was also a filled string bag and the raffia carryall I had packed for her at the Inn.

''Hello, Lily,'' I said.

''Hello,'' she said back — her voice still dead.

''Are you coming to the ASH with me tonight?'' I asked. They both said: *yes* in unison.

''She is,'' said Mercedes.

''I am,'' said Lily.

''I can help you carry your things,'' I said. I felt as if I was

talking to a child. Little Lily Cotton. I half expected that —
when she stood up — her dress would be pink, with a wide
blue sash.

Lily was not paying what I would call full attention either to
us or to the darkness around her. She might have been sitting
in the sunlight. She took up a handful of sand and let it trickle
through her fingers.

I took Mercedes aside and said, *sotto voce*; ''couldn't you
have taken her home in the car?''

''I told you; no.''

''You could have sent her home in a cab.''

''Vanessa; this is a war. Sometimes, the prisoners have to
walk home.''

I said; ''I know that.''

''Well then, behave as if you knew it.''

I gritted my teeth and said; ''what sort of shape is she in,
now?''

''A little better. As you pointed out, she's been so heavily
drugged she can barely speak. But there's a curious thing —
which I recall from one of my sojourns in the clinic,'' said
Mercedes — meaning, I suppose, the clinic where she has her
face-lifts done, ''namely, that people excessively drugged cannot lie down and sleep. Or else — like Lily this evening — they
do lie down and sleep and you think they'll stay there forever,
when — suddenly — they're wide awake and standing in your
living-room asking where they are.''

''What happened when you told her?''

''She said: *oh*. As if it did not particularly surprise her but
then she said, right out of the blue: *have you got my music?*
What do you think that means? She thinks she's a concert
pianist?''

I blushed. Of course, I knew exactly what it meant — but
what I said to Mercedes was; ''I haven't the foggiest.'' Then
I said; ''has she recognized you, yet?''

"She hasn't called me by name, but she seems to accept the fact that I'm someone she knows."

"Oh, Lord," I sighed. "and now she's coming back to the Hotel and what in the name of heaven am I going to tell people? For one thing — how can I explain that someone in the Government did this to her?"

"Tell them she's drunk. They'll believe that, won't they?"

"Not of Lily Porter. No."

"Shock. It's grief at the death of Calder and she's taken too many Valium..."

"Oh, I just don't know," I said.

"Vanessa. Take hold of yourself." Mercedes' voice was hard. She was wearing a stylish suede coat — again with a vaguely military cut — and it gave her the look of a little general. "Stop making this more difficult than it is."

Her lighter flared in the dark.

"That man will see us," I said.

"Let him." Mercedes was very angry. "Do you want me to go on helping you?" she asked.

"Of course," I said. "Though I'm not quite sure what there is to do."

"If you're not quite sure — you're crazy. There are a million things to do. One of them is to discover who exactly did this to her." She gestured at Lily with her Sobranie.

"Thaddeus Chilcott," I said.

"You really do hate him, don't you."

"What makes you say that?"

"The way you say his name."

"All right, I hate him. I think he's repugnant; cold as a snake — and very, very dangerous."

Mercedes stared at me through the smoke. In the moonlight, she looked like a girl. Completely. Eighteen. Nineteen. Twenty — not a minute more. It was absolutely spooky. There we were — three of us who had been children together. Lily the youngest — Mercedes the eldest — me in the middle. And there was Lily spilling sand on her shins like a kid of ten and Mercedes looking like a young Valkyrie. Me — I looked like their mother. Even their grandmother.

"You don't like him, either," I said.

"Not liking a person isn't hating him," she said. "Don't forget what he's done, Vanessa. Don't forget who he is. He saved the President's life."

"I haven't forgotten who he is — believe me. And I'm telling you, he did this to Lily. What we have to find out is why."

"She won't say why. She just keeps saying she was sick."

"I *was* sick," said Lily.

We both looked over at her — having been unaware she was paying any attention to what we were saying. Then she said to me; "have you got my music?"

"No," I said. "I haven't Lily. I'm sorry."

"There — you see?" said Mercedes. "the music again. They put her round the bend."

"Has she eaten?" I asked.

"Imelda forced some consommé into her and, I think, a lettuce-and-tomato sandwich."

"Did you search her belongings?"

"Are you crazy, Vanessa?"

"Did you look in her pocket-book?"

"You must really . . . "

"Did you look in her pocket-book?"

"Yes."

"And?"

"Everything I can imagine should be there was there."

"Pills?"

"No."

"Oh . . . !" I swore. If Lily had been given as much *Maddonix* as we thought, she would have to have more. Absolute withdrawal too suddenly could kill her. But then I calmed down and said; "never mind. Surely I can get some from Lawrence."

"Who is Lawrence."

"Lawrence Pawley. Last night. The tall one with the Adam's apple. He's married to my cousin Petra. You know him. You just don't remember. He's a doctor."

"Oh, yes. Well — if he's a doctor... you're lucky. A doctor in the family."

I didn't feel lucky. I wasn't about to put my heart in Lawrence's hands. I might have, once — but not any more.

"Did she say anything else I should know?" I asked.

"No," said Mercedes. "Just: *where is my music* and *I've been sick* and *Calder Maddox is dead.*"

I thought about it.

"Where those her actual words, Mercedes?"

"Which?"

"Calder Maddox is dead."

"Yes."

"You don't find that odd?"

"Odd?" She asked; "no. Why?"

"If Meg had to tell you that Michael had died — what do you imagine she'd say?"

"She'd say: *Mike is dead.*"

"Not: *Michael Riches is dead?*"

"You've got to be joking."

"No. I don't have to be joking. *Calder Maddox is dead.* Unquote."

"It is odd, isn't it."

Not if Mercedes had known what I know — not if she had listened, as I had, to Lily's "music." It was all *Calder Maddox* in there.

And it worried me.

If Lily had learned to call the man she loved only by his whole name — because of having listened to her "music" —

then the rest of the music, too, might be set in place inside her brain.

174: Before we left the dune, I asked Mercedes if anything had happened at Larson's Neck that night.

She told me it had been almost alarmingly quiet. The Greenes' party — meant to have been such a great success and the finishing touch to Daniel's bid for a Cabinet post — had been ruined by what Mercedes called: *the slap heard round the world.* This, of itself, had cast a pall on Larson's. Lily's disappearance could also be felt, she said.

Though no one knew precisely what had gone wrong, it was evident that a crisis had arisen within the President's coterie. And the police were everywhere. Wm. Billings had been round and round and round the enclave with his squad cars, tracing and retracing the pattern of the streets. Obviously, someone was looking for someone.

"Did they come to you?"

"Wm. Billings did; a privilege he always reserves for himself; me and about five others. He imagines that standing on my doorstep talking to Imelda is hobnobbing with the high and the mighty. Naturally, Imelda didn't let him come in. She's extremely good at that."

I told her about the Secret Service man I'd recognized from the Pine Point Inn coming into our lobby while I was on the phone with her — how nothing had come of it.

"Good," she said. "I make no promises, but I'm going to walk in on Donald Maltby tomorrow. I'm just going to walk in. I've devised a scheme for making him talk — and I can't believe it won't work."

"Oh?"

Mercedes relished her moment — took a final drag — and threw the cigarette down beneath her boot.

"I'm going to tell him I know that Calder is dead," she

said. "And if he asks me what in the world ever gave me such a crazy idea, I'm going to say: *Lily Porter*."

I said I thought that was awfully dangerous. But Mercedes said; "I'm glad you agree it's dangerous. I was afraid you'd think it was silly."

175: Mercedes and I helped Lily to her feet and told her it was time to go.

"Oh, good," she said.

"Goodbye, dear," said Mercedes — and kissed her on the forehead.

"Goodbye," said Lily.

"Well," said Mercy, when she turned to me; "I guess it's still the same old story, Nessa. You go your way — I'll go mine!" She kissed me. "Goodbye. Take care."

She disappeared into the dark — but I could see the star-and-moonlight shining on her hair as she clambered out of our dune and marched along its crest towards the Neck.

Lily said; "she was very nice to me, that woman. Gave me soup and a sandwich."

"Good," I said. "I'm glad, Lily."

We made our own way out of the dune, carrying Lily's bags and shoes.

After a moment, as we walked along the beach towards Halfway House, I said to her; "you've had a very bad time. I'm sorry."

"Yes," she said. "I have."

We went on. I thought: *I have to have answers, but I don't know the questions* — and I was just in the process of trying to formulate one of them when Lily spoke.

"I feel sick," she said.

We stopped.

We were just beyond the light-spill of Halfway House — and I could now hear music floating out through the open windows.

"It's all right," I said. "Are you going to throw up?"

"Yes."

She really was exactly like a child. She became quite frightened and could not figure out how to put her shoes and her bag on the ground. It was as if she thought she was obliged to go on holding onto them while she was sick.

I took them away from her as gently as I could and led her back towards the dunes. We got about half-way there and she was violently ill. I had not seen anyone be so ill for years. It frightened me.

When it was over, I led her all the way down to the sea and we used our handkerchiefs to clean her face and wipe her hands.

She was sniffling, still, and shaking. I put my arm around her and said; "do you want to sit down a while?"

"Oh, yes," she said. "If we could."

You might have thought I'd passed her a million-dollar bill, she was so remarkably grateful. Just to stop. Just to sit down.

I sat her on a log and I left her there and went back to fetch our things. When I returned, she was sitting with her arms around herself. I gave her my sweater.

"People should not be kind," she said.

I said; "I think they should be."

She said; "I mean to me."

And I waited.

"I've done something bad," she said. "I think. I'm not really sure — but I think I've done something bad."

"Like what?" I tried not to sound too eager — but interested.

"Oh, Vanessa, I've been so sick."

"I know," I said; "but that's not bad. Not a bad thing to have done."

I was glad to hear her use my name so freely — without any pause before it or struggle for it, as there had been earlier. She still sounded childlike — but not quite so lost.

"I mean, up there at the other hotel. I was sick up there. I..." she wept a little and then went on. "I only know — I was there — and I was ill. I had a headache. Dreadful headache. The worst I've ever had. And — there was a doctor. Do you know his name?"

I took a chance. "Yes. His name is Chilcott."

"That's right. Doctor Chilcott. Curly hair — going bald. Wears a waistcoat... And I threw up."

More tears. More sniffling.

"Yes?" I said.

"I threw up over and over and over again — and I felt — have you ever had a convulsion?"

"No."

"I think I may have had a convulsion. I was very, very, very sick. They put me in this room and — people came and looked at me. I don't know who they were. They came and stood in the room and looked at me and said: *what time?* and *where?* and *her colour is bad*... And then I slept, I think. And when I got the sleeping over with, the doctor was there again... what's his name?"

"Chilcott."

"He kept saying: *I'm just going to give you this* — and putting things in my arm and — I don't know. But finally — it may have been then, it may have been later — he came in and sat down right on the bed and he said: *we've found out what was wrong with you.* And he told me I had been poisoned..."

As Lily continued to talk, I pushed myself forward, hunching there in the dark, believing every word — because every word made such perfect — such terrible sense. But all the time she was leading me towards the truth, I was leading myself there, too — coming towards it from another direction; seeing Meg in my photographs — watching Meg's face through the magnifying glass — wondering why she had looked like that and then knowing.

It had been in the sun-tan cream — that bilious ochre mess that Calder himself had invented. In the pictures, just as in Lily's narrative, Meg had handed the cream to Lily, telling her she'd seen her drop it — knowing by its name and colour it had to be Calder's. *Here* — she had said; *take it. He'd be furious if he thought you'd lost it, Lily.*

"And I was so grateful," said Lily to me in the dark. "I really was so grateful, because he has — he had such a dreadful temper. And you shouldn't lose anything or make a mistake. So I took it and I rubbed it all over his legs and his arms — and — it killed him."

The silence that followed this was part of her speech. She didn't weep any more. She didn't falter. She didn't describe how she'd wiped it off her own hands. She just said: *and it killed him* and went quiet.

Finally she said; "so when Doctor I-can't-remember-his-name asked me — that's what I told him. I told him Marguerite Mackey had given me the tube of cream."

I was stunned.

I wanted her to repeat it — I had to make her.

"Tell me again," I said. "Tell me who gave you the tube of cream."

She looked at me. I could just see her eyes in the moonlight.

"Marguerite Mackey," she said.

Mackey was Meg's maiden name. Lily must have called her that because she had gone back through the *Maddonix* all the way to her childhood.

And Doctor Chilcott would have wondered who this Marguerite Mackey was.

And Nigel Forestead would have told him.

So it was they — not Lily Porter — who had come to the name of Marguerite Riches. Yes.

It didn't matter that she had said Marguerite Mackey. What mattered was, she knew the identity of Calder's murderer.

With all their drugs and all their tapes, they hadn't managed to wipe that out.

176: Then Lily stood up.
"I'm going to my room now. Sleep."
So — I took her back to the ASH. And the end of this story.

177: It is dawn, now. Just.
Lily came back last night. Mercedes brought her into the dunes and I brought her here. She's asleep in her room and I think has achieved some kind of peace. Confession does that — so I have witnessed.

But there is peace that is not peace. And honesty that does not pay — in kind.

That morning at the end of August, forty years ago — we all sat, hand in hand, on our beds and our bunks — some of us in dresses — the nuns in their habits — others in dead men's trousers and shirts and we waited and waited — no one stirring — all of us wringing wet with perspiration and tension — many, many, many of us ill.

The great trees stood up before us, out beyond the clearing where my father had died — and the sky turned white — then yellow — then blue. Great flotillas — sheets and sheets of silent fruit bats returned to their resting places deep in the rain forest, high in the branches. They always come home mute when they have fed.

But the parrots, the egrets and the storks and all the other

morning birds were anything but silent — and the sound of
them, in the human silence, was deafening. It made you want
to close your eyes — but you couldn't. You couldn't because
the road was there and because you had waited all those years
to see it emptied of its Japanese.

And the gate stood open.

And no one went through.

And Moira held my left hand — and Mother held my right.

And we waited.

Finally — they came.

Australians. In hats that said: *Australia*. And they stood as
far away from us at the edge of the trees as we were far away
from them in our barracks — a world away — and all the
blinds and shutters lifted so that all the eyes could see.

And then, I think it was Juliet Roberts who stood up first
and got down off the steps and started to walk across the compound and towards the gate.

I wanted to — but I couldn't go with her. I had to wait for
Moira.

Mother got up and said; "we can go now. Come."

And I stood up — but Moira did not.

Her pregnancy had begun to show. And she knew — and I
knew — and Mother knew what everyone would think; what
everyone would say.

But I said: *we are taking your baby to Singapore. All three of
us. Together. But we . . .* I said . . . *can't get her there without you.*

She stood up after that. But still reluctantly.

And then we all went down the steps and we all made our
way — so slowly, but together — across the dirt of the compound. And we passed my gardens — all of them — the dead
tree branches — the stones — the sand that Colonel Norimitsu
had dumped there when I was ill, so that when I got better, I
could have a garden just like his — and we went out through

the gate and I left my life — and I left my gardens there forever.

And we came out into this world — where Moira is dead. And her baby. And Colonel Norimitsu. And my mother. And Calder Maddox. We came out into the world where the Bomb had not fallen just on Hiroshima and Nagasaki — but on all of us. Forever.

Well.

I cannot say. I cannot say; not yet, what other deaths will follow.

178: This morning, two things happened rather early.

The first was the sound of garbage trucks. Not two, as usual, but three or four. They always come to the other side of the Hotel and I cannot — nor do I want to — see them. But always, I can hear them.

Three, I should say, must have been there this morning — and they made such a racket everyone complained. Even the staff in the dining-room complained. Both Joel and Honor told me they had been awakened by the whole lane shaking out behind *The Dorm.*

"That never happens, ever," said Honor. "Never so many trucks."

But it did today.

The second thing that happened this morning was Lawrence.

I had just come down the stairs into the lobby, having

checked that Lily was still in her room, when the screen door flew open and Lawrence practically ran me down.

"Vanessa!"

"Yes?"

"Come here."

His hand was on my wrist and he was drawing me back towards the front door.

"I beg your pardon," I said. "But I don't like being held like that."

I drew my arm away and took a step back. I was outwardly calm — but inwardly, I was shaken. Lawrence's eyes had the look of someone bent on doing damage.

"You must come with me," he said.

"Must I?"

"*Yes.*"

He stood his ground, and I have to say, I did admire the way he attempted to bring himself under control.

"Wait one moment," I said, and I went across to the Desk where — thank the Lord — trustworthy Judy was on duty.

I handed her a medium-sized manilla envelope — sealed — and I said; "I want that put in the safe, dear. Now — while I'm watching, if you don't mind."

Luckily, Lawrence's temper, and the energy it charged, had forced him out through the door — I think so he could breathe. Consequently, he did not witness my deposit in the vault.

"Thank you," I said to Judy, once she had shut the door and spun the ratchet. "I shall probably want it back by noon."

"Okay, Miss V.H. See you later."

"Indeed," I said — already going.

"Have a nice day!" she called after me.

Her one detestable habit.

179: Lawrence took me out to walk in the parking paddock — the only place he was reasonably certain we would not be heard.

His language was deplorable. I have no notion whatsoever what it is that drives him to it.

Once he had got a dozen of the worst words out of his system, I told him to stop.

"If you want to tell me something," I said; "stop putting all those barriers up in its way. Speak. But in English."

He leaned against the hood of someone's already battered motorcar and put his face in his hands. I waited what seemed an intolerable time. Finally, he took his hands away and set them down like two red bricks on his knees.

"He's gone," he said.

"Who?" I said.

"Maddox, of course."

I slumped back, myself, against someone's Rabbit — probably Elsie's.

"So we have no proof any more," said Lawrence. "Not a whit."

I studied my fingers — one by one.

I already knew what I would not tell him. But I did not dare withhold it all. I hoped that — if I told him something — however slight — he might be satisfied. But I had to stop before I came to Meg.

"Well," I said; "you lose some — you win some. Calder may have flown — but Lily Porter has returned."

This barely interested him. Lily never really had fired his imagination. But I pressed a little further. Her return was all I had to keep him at bay.

"She's had quite a ride," I said. "I think the lads at the other end of the Neck had hoped to pin their dirty work on her. But she — " I used the word carefully; "escaped."

This did catch his interest.

"Just who is up there?" he asked. "I mean — I know about Chilcott and that lot. But I wasn't shot at just because of them. So — who is really up there?"

I looked off towards the dining-room, thinking in my heart of hearts of Meg going in there just about then and wheeling Michael's chair along past all the guests; the Boys and Lena Rumplemeyer; Sybil Metsley and Natty Baumann; the Major-General and Arabella Barrie...

"The President," I said.

Lawrence looked absolutely blank. I was certain he had misunderstood.

"Of the United States," I added.

180: At noon, I took Meg out for a walk along the cliffs that rise past Sutter's Rock.

It is not a place we often walk, since every year a little more is eroded by the sea. It used to all be public property — and that's the other reason we rarely use it now. In the last ten years, the county has taken to selling it off to private owners and there are now at least six monstrous houses — all with monstrous windows facing the sea, affording grotesque opportunities for spying on trespassers.

Meg wouldn't leave Michael, at first. It would mean too long away from him — an hour or more — and what if he needed her?

But I had thought of that. I had already taken the liberty of speaking to Baby Frazier and she was only too happy to stay with him. More cigarettes — a few more drinks. The comfort of being needed.

We set out with my carryall and hers; mine with photographs and cameras; sketch pads and pencils; binoculars and bird-guide — just as if it were any excursion. Meg brought wine and plastic glasses in hers — and sun-tan cream for her sensitive nose — and two or three extra packs of du Mauriers and matches — as if she feared we would founder and be lost for days in the wilderness at our doorstep.

I did not, of course, make any mention of the medium-sized manilla envelope that was also jammed into my carryall. I wanted to wait for that.

There is a windblown promontory jutting out over the deepest cut in the shore. The drop is about one hundred feet and truly spectacular. The rocks below are black — and always flecked with foam — and the booming sound of the waves being driven deep into the cavern beyond is almost symphonic.

We got there just about noon-plus-half — and we sat on the grass and kicked off our shoes and I let Meg drink two glasses of wine before I began.

"I've brought along something I want to play for you," I said. "Only on this tiny machine, I'm afraid. But it's all I have. You should be able to hear — even in this wind. The sound isn't that important. It's what's being said."

"Is there music?" said Meg. "I warn you — there are certain kinds of music I abhor."

"Some have called this music," I said. "Though I do not. I call it what it is — I hope — a kind of fairy-tale or fable."

Meg looked quizzical — but then she smiled.

"You remember what old Mrs Gunnison used to say to us when we were dreadful children telling those dreadful jokes? *You're a caution!* — she used to say. Well, Nessa — you are still a proper caution, my dear — if you really have brought me out here to listen to a fairy-tale.''

"Are you ready?''

"Sure.''

"Just promise one thing.''

"Fine — but only one,'' said Meg.

"Don't speak until it's over.''

"Okay. If you say so.''

"I say so.''

"Do you mind if I smoke?''

She had wanted me to give my usual answer to this, which I'd done since the late 1940s: *I don't care if you burn.* But I couldn't say that any more. So I pretended I had not heard her.

181: The tape took ten minutes to play through once — without all its repeats.

I sat with my arms around my knees and watched the sea. Meg lay stretched on her side — and half-way through the tape, when her name first appeared, she lay down flat on her back for a moment and then she sat up briskly and opened the second bottle of wine.

When the first run-through was over and I had switched the machine off — there was a very brief pause before she held out the bottle and silently filled my glass.

We still didn't speak.

She sighed. She stood up. She went to the edge and threw a cigarette down — still alight — and then she came back and sat down and looked at me and said, without emotion; "Where did you get that? Who from?''

"I'm not going to tell you," I said. "Surely you can understand why.''

She didn't answer.

Then she said; "am I done for?''

"What do you think?"

"I think I'm done for. But — I mustn't be done for until — not until Mike is dead." She sighed again. "Do you think you can make — whoever this person is — hold off for a couple of weeks? Michael will be dead by then. That's a kind of promise, Nessa. Two weeks."

I said I had no power to hold it off — until I knew more about it.

"More? *What* more?" she said. "I killed him. That's about as *more* as you can get."

"No, it isn't," I said. "I want the *more* that tells about why you did it."

"Oh."

This neither pleased nor displeased her. It simply surprised her.

She poured another glass of wine for herself and sat up straight in the grass — with her back like a ramrod and her legs spread apart and the glass of wine and her cigarette packs piled up between them, down in the folds of her tailored skirt. She was wearing, again, another of Michael's shirts. It looked so neat and bright. Pure white. She also wore his regimental tie; blue — with a wide green stripe.

"All right," she said. "It goes like this."

182: *Meg said:*

For reasons that are now so far behind us I cannot begin to recall them for you, Michael had a breakdown. Due, I guess, to those wonderful euphemisms — *exhaustion* and *stress.* Anyway, it couldn't matter less why he had it. He had it. This is not the story of Michael's life — it's the story of Michael's death — and his death began in 1978 in the *Makin Memorial Institute* in Montreal. The thing is, the *Makin Memorial* was built in the 1870s. One of those gothic horrors Charles Addams draws. You only got to go through its front door after you'd walked up one hundred steps, the ice from which was never removed in winter. It had a tower — this awful edifice — and I see that tower to this day every time I close my eyes.

So — Michael had his breakdown and someone — I don't know who — suggested the *Makin Memorial*. There was a doctor there — the wonder of all the psychiatric world; and his name was Allan Potter; Doctor Allan Potter.

Allan Potter had a flaw. And the flaw went undetected, because he'd had so many successes and so much praise; they couldn't afford to take him to task for one little flaw. And the flaw was ambition. Ambition of the unbridled kind. Potter had so many theories — so many projects — experimental treatments up his sleeve, he simply didn't know where to turn for the money to finance them.

But others, hearing of his ambition — hearing of the monies he required — decided to couple their own ambitions to his. And, to that end, the villain of this piece — one of the first of a long string of villains — enters. This is the CIA.

No — don't interrupt. I don't want any sympathy in this — and none of your cluck-cluck-clucking. The CIA is what it is. It's there.

The only thing is — it's there in *your* country — not in mine. At least, it should not be in mine. But it is. And it was, because it had found — in the person of Allan Potter and in the patients at the *Makin Memorial Institute* in far off Montreal, Canada — the perfect medium and the perfect subjects for various experiments the CIA was eager to have conducted. Absolutely secret, mind you. And absolutely illegal.

What — you will want to know — experiments?

Brainwashing, my dear. That sort of thing.

The idea was — you take a troubled person — and you wipe that troubled person's slate — his mind — completely clear of all it knows. You wipe it clear of trouble and whatever else the mind bears witness to. Then, once you have this barren slate

— this barren, emptied mind — you fill it up again — with what you will; with lies — with false events and with heinous interpretations of life that have nothing to do with the person who once possessed the troubled mind — which, at least, was a mind of his own. Good things — mind you — were the intention of these experiments; *pleasant* lies and *happy* false events and *positive* heinous interpretations of life.

But how. That has to be your question. How.

Well — I will tell you how.

With drugs and chemicals and with electro-shock and sensory deprivation and with what was known — in the language of that devastating place — as *psychic driving*.

What drugs! Name any drug you can think of — from LSD to amphetamines to massive doses of every tranquillizer known to man and maniac.

Electro-shock? You betcha! Sixteen — seventeen — eighteen times a week.

Sensory deprivation?

What about being put to sleep for fifteen — sixteen — twenty — days at a time.

And *psychic driving?*

Well — we have here sleep and drugs and little tapes of the kind you just played to me. *Big Brother tapes* — all for the good of the soul-destroyed and mind-obliterated. You take the clean slate and you write whatever you want on it — by endless repetition during sleep.

Finally, we come — if you can take in any more of this — to the experiment that put the capper on Michael. A program in which such massive doses of a certain drug were introduced into his system that by the time they were through with him, he no longer knew what his legs were for — or his fingers — or his tongue — or his eyes — or his ears — or — name it!

It wasn't that he couldn't *physically* walk or hold a pen or speak a word or see a sky; it was just that he didn't know which of his physical parts had been created for these purposes. And thus — the man you see.

What then has all of this — or any of this — to do with Calder Maddox?

Everything.

Sixty percent of the chemicals and drugs which were given to Michael Riches — and dozens and dozens of other Canadians — were manufactured by Calder Maddox Laboratories. And in their *Makin Memorial* manifestation, *every one of them was used while still in its experimental stages.* Every bloody one. But the drug which put an end to Mike was *Maddoxin*: to calm the nerves. In its liquid form — abandoned now, since Michael.

There's more. But I won't go on. Two more things, however, you must be made aware of — or you will one day wake up and say: *but... but...*

One is: *why did you allow such things?* Why did Michael allow such things to be done to him?

Put it this way.

No one was told what was being done to them.

And secondly — *why didn't I, Marguerite, sail up the hundred steps and batter on the doors until my husband was released?*

Put it this way.

Every time I made overtures to go and see Michael, I was told — in the nicest possible way — that my presence would *disorient* the patient. Not *disturb* — and not *upset* — but *disorient*. And who, if she loves a man, would want to jeopardize his chances of recovery by *disorienting* him.

When they gave him back to me, at last, I got him in a wheelchair; with apologies. For all their valiant efforts, they had not been able to save him.

What a God-damned pity.

Eh?

183: Her first attempts at recompense were through the courts. These failed.

She then — with a number of other victims and relatives of victims of the *Makin Memorial* experiments — had approached the Canadian Government to intervene on their behalf between the CIA and the American Government.

This, too, failed.

Next — the same group attempted to sue the CIA — but the CIA denied any involvement — having already destroyed all evidence pointing in its direction.

This failed.

Finally — the American Government.

When this failed, most went home and said: *we tried* — in which they took some solace, at least — for it was true. They had tried.

But Meg was not through.

To her chagrin — and she admits this, in her current frame of mind — Doctor Allan Potter died of natural causes — an honest heart attack.

But there was still Calder Maddox.

And Meg said; *if I had been able to do it with an axe, I might have had more satisfaction. But at least he died of his own experiments.*

184: When she was finished, she smiled at me and said; ''while I sit in my cell, I hope you will come and visit me.''

And I said; ''you aren't going to sit in any cell.''

And I stood up and took the tape and threw it down into the sea.

At long last, then, she wept.

185: Mercedes telephoned again that evening.

"Meet me," she said; "at the foot of the drive. I shall be in the Daimler. Eight o'clock sharp."

"Eight o'clock is when I dine," I said.

"Eight o'clock sharp," she repeated. "Foot of the drive."

186: At the foot of the drive, I stepped into the Daimler and was driven away by Mercedes herself — to what she proclaimed was her favourite place in all the world — the Quaker graveyard.

She did not descend from the car, at first, but remained — windows up — until she had told me the burden of her initial discoveries.

"It seems," she said; "at some point in the last two days, our friends at Pine Point discovered — by dint of painstaking research and raking over many coals — that Maddox had been murdered by the victim of what Donald Maltby called, in my presence: *some inconsequential experiment of Calder's that took place many, many years ago.* I asked, of course, what they intended to do with this information. Would this person be put on trial? He hemmed and hawed and tried to avoid the answer — but I prevailed. Blackmail is truly wonderful, when you are desperate.

"At any rate, he did explain the furor that had taken place these past few days; the panic arrivals of all those Secretaries, et cetera. It seems — and who can doubt it — that Calder Maddox had a great many contracts in the works — each of some importance — and each with a different department of government — all those departments represented here this weekend; the Interior — the CIA — State — Health — and — more importantly, I gathered, with Defense.

"Donald has his own way of telling such things. There is always that wonderful edge of condescension; the implicit words: *you do understand*, while he's working both sides of heaven and hell to keep you from understanding. At the same time, he can be quite charming — though it doesn't work with me — that charm. Still, I find it useful, sometimes, to *pretend* it works — *is* working. I pretend it might even get him the *ultimate*." She looked at me. "Not sex, Vanessa. Ye gods, no. But me — the name — the money. That's what Donald Maltby and Co. would like. Fat chance."

She rocked with laughter at her own audacity.

"Now, let us walk," she said. And we abandoned the car to wander among the gravestones — all so simply presented: all the Catherine Marys, all the Charity Graces and the Alberts and the Obadiahs of 1785 and 1863 and 1912.

Mercedes said; "you see — our friends at the Neck — you should pardon the expression *friends*..." she said to one of the Quaker markers; "our friends at the Neck had a deeply disturbing problem. Once it had been determined by Thaddeus Chilcott that Calder had not in any way died of natural causes — but that a deadly, paralyzing chemical had been infused into his system by means of a sun-cream — they had this problem of wondering which of their various programs with Calder Maddox might have provided the motive for his murder. Every experiment has its victims, you see — and some of these victims want revenge. So...

"Was it the experiments being conducted on behalf of the Department of Health? Or of the Interior? Defense? The CIA?

"What they had to know, you see, was which of these

experiments had just been put in jeopardy? Who must they find and *stop* before more damage could be inflicted on our National Security.

"But, as things worked out, they discovered through the auspices — don't ask me how — of your friend Neville that the experiment provoking the murder had just been that 'inconsequential' experiment that had taken place some years ago in Montreal, Canada.

"As a result of this discovery — they have decided to opt for what they intend to call a death by natural causes. Perhaps a heart attack or a stroke. This way, they will save themselves the embarrassment of a public trial — since all such public trials invariably lead to a great deal more being revealed than should be revealed." She waited for a moment. "Wonderful, isn't it?" she said. "Their concept of risk has nothing to do with the people they kill and maim with their experiments. It only has to do with who finds out the killing and maiming are going on."

Mercedes had stopped at the foot of a family plot and she read off the names on the stone:

> *Amos Ivey and Lavinia his wife*
> *born and died in the arms*
> *of Jesus*
> *and their sons forever*
> *through time*
> *Enoch — Isaiah*
> *Jesse*
> *and*
> *Adam*
> *all perished in the*
> *great plague of cholera*
> *June/August 1847*
> *God is Love*

Mercedes simply stood and studied the stone as a casual
tourist might — remarking on the pleasant, Biblical names
and the sadness of this family's tragedy.

But then she said; "just think. If Calder Maddox had been
alive and doing his life-work then, in 1847, not one member
of the Ivey family need have perished."

I didn't have to think about it long.

"I suspect they might have preferred to die as they did," I
said.

"Could be you're right," said Mercy. "At least they went
together."

187: When Mercy got me back to the ASH, it was late and I
was tired. I went in alone. The lobby was only dimly lit. From
the dark, I heard the all too familiar voice; "Good evening,
Vanessa."

"Good evening, Arabella."

She was seated over in her corner, all alone.

"Please," she said; "I have waited for you. Be seated."

She indicated my mother's place — the very pillow where
Rose Adella had sat as one of *Stonehenge.* It was a place I had
never sat before.

Arabella leaned forward, the imperfect light a perfect com-
plement to every bone of her face and every wave in her hair.

"Are you done with it at last?" she said.

Her hands and feet did nothing. They were simply there.

"I don't understand you, Arabella."

"Must I be plain? You do disappoint me."

"I'm sorry."

She shifted from buttock to buttock and settled on her right — very slightly tilted away from me.

"Perhaps I have spoken too much of disappointment, lately."

"Yes," I said. "You have."

She smiled.

"That I do like," she said; "your quickness."

I was silent.

"I must now," she said, "reveal the reason for waiting here on your behalf."

"On my behalf?"

"Yes."

She took a deep breath.

"Since the death of Calder Maddox on the beach, I have witnessed — through these last, apparently endless days — a certain consistency of activity on your part. Namely, that everywhere a Calder rumour went, Vanessa was sure to follow."

I nodded.

"I shall not presume to give a précis of events, Vanessa, since it is all too clear you could best me in many details and many incidents. However, I must say this — I have watched you growing old these last few days, and we do not grow old so suddenly without good reason."

"I am soon to be sixty, Arabella."

"Pah!" she said. "Do you think I mean *age*?"

I shook my head. A lie.

"I mean that you are burdened. Yes?"

I said nothing. I made no gesture. I left my hands where they were.

"It was a proper way for him to die," she said, all at once. "A violent death is the least attractive. But he had lived a

violent unattractive life — especially in the eyes of those who
were truly aware of who he was and what he did.'' She waited
just a fraction of a second. ''I believe you were aware, or
rather, you have now become aware of who he was and what
he did.''

I looked down. *Yes.*

''How sad it would be, don't you think,'' she went on; ''if
this just and proper death were to be marred by a meaningless
injunction, at this point, of *justice.* Of course, by justice — I
mean: *the Law as she is writ. . .* '' There was a long silence here
and then; ''it would serve no good purpose to seek and find
his killer. Surely some have suffered quite enough.''

She knew.

I nodded.

I should have been astounded. In fact, I was not. It was not
unlike the moment when I stood in the rain that morning my
father died — was killed — and I saw Colonel Norimitsu staring back at me; each of us knowing what the other knew; each
of us recognizing *the Law as she is writ* and each of us obeying
it, while each of us regretted it.

I wanted there to be some way for me to look directly into
Arabella's face. I wanted there to be some way for her to look
at me. I wanted each of us to see the other — right then —
precisely the way we were in that moment of recognition. But
I knew it could not be. A part of the gulf between us would
always remain. A kind of tact.

Arabella stood up.

''It is late,'' she said. ''We have said enough.''

I stood up, too.

She was watching me from chosen shadows.

''There is something here I would like you to have,
Vanessa.''

I saw her reach behind the cushions.

''I finished it this evening.''

She held out a slim, soft package wrapped in plain white tissue paper.

"This is for your birthday," she said. "But I want you to have it now."

I took it from her hand.

"Please. Open it."

I did.

It was a piece of needlepoint.

"A pillow cover," Arabella said. "Or you may frame it."

I thanked her.

It showed a single Japanese iris — rising from a stone.

188: I slept all night: the first time in days. I dreamt of truths — I think: of Meg, in the dark, with a flashlight — searching for something on the beach — and later, of her fighting with a child who had found what she could not: a tube of lethal sun-cream. And this morning, when I woke, it was early — as it had been long ago when I was young. Or do I only mean when I was younger.

The lawns beyond the windows were covered with birds; with great black crows and fat white gulls, the gulls with various tips of black and grey: herring gulls, black-backs, kittiwakes and ring-billed gulls. In the pre-sun mist — not quite a fog — they gather there on the grass most mornings — clacking their bills and screeching at one another. I crept from my bed and crossed to the window just to see them.

As I went into the bathroom to draw my bath, I heard someone down below me, singing in the kitchen. The same joyful voice as before — the same sad song.

Some say a heart is just like a wheel,
When you bend it — you can't mend it.
And my love for you is like a sinking ship
And my heart is on that ship out in mid-ocean.

I wondered if Lily — down one floor and over three windows — could hear it. I hoped so.

The thought of her is distressing.

Thank heaven I have destroyed that other "music" — her tape. It is hard to know, since Meg's explanation of how such tapes were used, precisely what effect the voice and its messages may have had on Lily Porter. It is also hard to know what effect I want it to have had. Meg has said that some of the patients at the *Makin Memorial Institute* were subjected to bouts of eighteen and twenty days of drug-induced sleep. And, while they were sleeping, they were exposed to tapes that might have told them anything one human mind can devise in order to destroy another. It therefore gave me hope that Lily's short exposure might have failed to wipe out her mind and replace it with another. She had, after all, been able to recall my name and she seemed to know who I was, in terms of my relation to her. But she hadn't known Mercedes — and she had seemed to believe that what she'd heard, in her sleep, had truly been music and not voices. And yet, she had still not accused Meg: still had not pointed at her.

I must be wary; and watchful. I must find some way to monitor what Lily says. It is only she, besides myself and Arabella, who can put the word *Meg* alongside Calder's death and turn what Arabella called a just and proper death back into murder.

That must not happen. Must not — and will not happen. This means, of course, that — if I have to — I will prevent it. I dare not imagine how.

I will wait to take my cue from Lily. If Lily Porter moves in Meg's direction — I will have to move in hers.

Surely it goes beyond the limits of irony that Lily Porter gave me this book in which I write — and that its very first words concern the "queer things people do..."

189: Hearing a great deal of noise and excitement, I went down onto the beach this morning around about eleven.

It seems that one of the lobster boats had been exploring the waters close to the iceberg and a crew member had seen a dark and alarming shape below the surface.

The darkness of this shape had only been due to the shadows that enfolded it, for when a diver had gone down to investigate, he had come back up and said: *it's a human body.*

We all stood waiting on the shore; myself and all the others — even Meg with Michael in his chair. And Lily, in her blowing sleeves and scarves, and Peter Moore and Ivan, Natty Baumann and Boots the dog and Nigel in his bee-leg bathing trunks and Maryanne in her bikini and Sybil Metsley, alone and muttering, as usual.

I knew, of course, who it would be — though why I write *of course* with so much confidence, I cannot really tell. It may just be that she was so like Moira, with her honey hair — and Moira had been so like her, with her desperate apartness and her appalling loneliness. And the way she eyed the distance out beyond the gate.

Yes. It was the *Honey Girl.*

They've blamed it on the iceberg and they've called it an accidental drowning. The bastards. They don't see anything that's real.

190: It ends like this, for now.

At last, they have admitted Calder's death and printed his obituary.

It tells us that he *died of natural causes — a heart attack — on the beach of the Aurora Sands Hotel in Maine, near Sutter's Hill... et cetera.* It also says that *his wife was with him... et cetera*; and it lists his many accomplishments, et cetera, on behalf of the Nation.

Stories all over the front page — up and down the country — east and west. The wonder and glory of Calder Maddox.

This explains why they kept his corpse on ice — so Lawrence says. They had to wait until they knew what had brought the ''heart attack'' on — and what they would, consequently, have to do about it.

I feel, I admit, somewhat — though not completely — sorry that Lawrence remains in the dark — and will have to remain so.

On the other hand — if the truth should rise to the surface of Lily's mind and I am forced to move against her — then Lawrence will no doubt presume it was she who did it — that she killed Calder, I mean. Though I suppose that, too, will depend on what is written in her obituary.

And, over time, in mine.

I admit I have joined my enemies. I admit that I am prepared to do what they have done: even to use their weapons. I do not admit that this is wrong. I would ask whoever questions this to tell me what is right.

I think of the four of us — down in the photograph — down in the library, even now — Meg and Mercedes and Lily and me. I think of who we were and what we wanted. And I think of who we are and what we got. I think of this Hotel, its being where we met, and I think its rise and fall have been our rise and fall; the lot of us together. Someone sold us out — but only when we ceased to pay attention.

Yes. It is time the icebergs came.

And they are here.

And so I pull the shade.

And the shade is green.